Chasing the Dead

by

Tom Towslee

CHASING THE DEAD Copyright ©2018 Tom Towslee
ISBN# 978-1-943789-99-3

Published by Taylor and Seale Publishing, LLC
3408 South Atlantic Avenue
Unit 139
Daytona Beach Shores, FL 32118

Cover design and layout by WhiteRabbitGraphix.com

Publisher's Note: This is a work of fiction. Names, characters, places, and incidents are a product of the author's imagination or used fictitiously. Locales and public names are sometimes used fictitiously for atmospheric purposes. With the exception of public figures or specific historical references, any resemblance to actual people, living or dead, or to businesses, companies, events, institutions, or locales is completely coincidental. Any historical personages or actual events depicted are completely fictionalized and used only for inspiration. Any opinions expressed are completely those of fictionalized characters and not a reflection of the views of public figures, author, or publisher.

Taylor and Seale
Daytona Beach Shores, Florida

To

Jerry Baron

Chasing the Dead

Tom Towslee

Prologue

The man in the trunk of the car wouldn't stop banging around. He kept kicking the inside of the wheel well or hitting his head against the trunk lid. In between were yells muffled by duct tape.

"Should have hit him harder," the driver muttered to himself, then wondered why he just hadn't shot the bastard and saved all this trouble. But what fun would that be. He hadn't driven across the country just to put a bullet in the guy's brain. He had other plans. More complicated, but also more rewarding.

The driver hit the high beams so as not to miss the turnoff he'd found the day before after hours of driving around in the north Georgia wilderness. He'd marked the turnoff with a stick and a bicycle reflector he'd purchased at a hardware store in Marietta two days earlier, along with the tape and a can of kerosene. At another store he picked up a flashlight and wire cutters. He got the latex gloves and plastic booties at a drug store before heading north. He'd used the wire cutters to get a ten-foot length of barbed wire off a fence around a cow pasture. Everything was neatly arranged on a blue plastic tarp covering the floor of the back seat.

The driver checked the odometer. The turnoff he wanted was two-tenths of a mile ahead on the left. The road in front of him was a straight stretch of narrow asphalt leading into the Chattahoochee National Forest near the border of Georgia and Tennessee. A dirt embankment marked the right side of the road. Oaks, pine trees, and a dry drainage ditch marked the left. A full moon backlit the trees, casting spike-like shadows on the dark gray roadway. The road was too narrow for even a white stripe down middle, making it more like a golf course cart path.

The digital clock on the dashboard of the copper-colored Cadillac said 2:07 a.m. The driver smiled. Plenty of time.

When the headlights caught the reflector, the driver slowed, and checked the mirror for any headlights behind him. Nothing. Not at this hour and not out here in hell and gone. He slowed almost to a stop, turned left, and eased the car over a narrow, plank bridge across a scum-covered ditch. Safely on the other side, he let the car coast over the rutted dirt road, careful not to scrape the undercarriage. This was no place for car trouble.

The clearing was five hundred yards into a stand of trees and brush. When he got there, he turned the car around, and reached under the seat. He pulled out the .45 caliber Glock G41, checked to make sure the safety was on, screwed on the silencer, and got out.

With the car stopped, the man in the trunk started banging even more. The muffled yells turned to muffled screams that sounded something like "get me the hell out of here." The driver popped the trunk, grabbed the man by the collar, and punched him in the back of the head as hard as he could. The body went limp. The kicking and screaming stopped.

The driver walked around the passenger side of the car, opened the door and began to undress. He neatly folded his white suit and white turtle neck, laying them carefully on the white leather of the front passenger seat. He took off his white shoes and white socks and set them on the floor mat. He thought about taking the large ring out of his pierced eyebrow but decided to leave it in. No reason to take it out. This wasn't going to take long.

After putting on the latex gloves and the booties, he took the things from the floor of the back seat. Spreading out the plastic tarp, he carefully laid out each item in the order he would need them, including the pistol. Then he grabbed the man, dragged him through the dirt to a small pine tree that was about 15 feet tall and just over a foot in diameter. Using the barbed wire, he tied the man's arms and legs around the tree then stood back to wait.

The driver looked out into the trees. He could smell the moss, the rotting leaves, and sounds of critters moving through the thin underbrush. Not all forests were alike. This one had different kinds of trees, ones he'd never seen before. Not like Oregon where everything was pretty much some kind of evergreen. He didn't know much about trees, certainly not their names. He just knew that, in the fall, the leaves fell off some, but not others.

It was a warm night, so being naked didn't bother him. Running his hand over his closely shaved head, the driver stared at the man hugging the tree. He was in his late sixties, a full head of gray hair, with a mean face and a wiry build. He wore jeans, T-shirt, a Carhartt jacket, and worn-out Nikes. He had dirty fingernails and callused hands. Mechanic, the driver thought. Maybe a backhoe operator. Not that it mattered. He could be an accountant or a lawyer but things were still going to turn out the same.

It hadn't taken the driver long to find him, if he didn't count the three-day drive from Oregon to Georgia. The guy was listed in the phonebook, which made things pretty easy. Once he found the man's house and followed him to a bar in Marietta, it was just a matter of waiting for the right time.

It came three hours earlier, in a dark parking lot. A quick shot to the head with a sock full of quarters, wrap him up in duct tape, toss him in the trunk, and here they were.

When the man came to, he looked at the driver standing, naked, ten feet in front him, the Glock dangling from his right hand. "Jesus fucking Christ," he yelled, followed by a scream as the barbed wire dug into his wrists and ankles. "Fuck. Untie me, goddamn it. What are you doing? Who are you, some kind of pervert?"

The driver picked up the flashlight, squatted down so they were face to face, and shined the light in the man's face.

"Are you scared, Charlie Boggs? I would be."

"Untie me, goddamn it."

"You are Charlie Boggs, right?" the driver said, smiling. "That's what your driver's license says. By the way, I took the two hundred bucks in your wallet just to cover expenses. Besides, you won't be needing it."

"Fuck you. You have no right to—"

The driver shot him in the left kneecap.

Charlie Boggs screamed again, only louder. His eyes rolled back into his head as he slumped forward, face against the tree trunk and vomited into the bark.

"Do you know why I'm here, Charlie Boggs?"

The man screamed again. "I don't know and I don't care. You can't do this." His voice trailed off. He banged his forehead against the tree and struggled hopelessly against the barbed wire. Blood from his wrists dripped on his legs. More blood from his destroyed knee pooled in the dry dirt. He vomited again, this time on to his shirt sleeve.

"You made someone very angry, and now it's time to pay. That's why I'm here. This is just a job. Don't take it personally."

"I'll pay you. Whatever they're paying you, I'll pay you more." Boggs was begging, the anger gone, replaced by fear and confusion.

"No, you won't. Besides, it doesn't work that way."

"Who sent you? Tell me. We can talk. Work this out. Jesus. My leg."

"You mean you don't know? Really? Think about it, Charlie. Who would send a complete stranger to drag you out here into the middle of fucking nowhere, tie you to a tree, and almost blow your leg off?"

The driver leaned closer until his face was inches from Boggs's. "Any names come to mind?"

Boggs started to cry. It began with a whimper and turned quickly to chest-heaving sobs. "No. No. No one would do this. I haven't hurt anybody. I promise. Please." He was losing blood. His words beginning to slur, his face getting pale.

"You're sure?" The driver moved closer, pressing the barrel of the gun into Boggs's forehead. "Think real hard."

"Yes. Yes. I'm sure. Don't kill me, please. There must be some kind of mistake." Then he stopped. His eyes grew big. "Wait." Charlie Boggs shook his head as if trying to keep from passing out. He stared at the driver, his mouth opening and closing like a fish. "It can't be. Tell me it's not. Jesus, tell me it can't be."

The driver smiled and stood up. "Bingo," he said, then walked to the car and put the pistol back under the seat. He walked back to get the can of kerosene off the tarp.

Boggs seemed to know immediately what was in the can. All he could say was "Oh God. Oh God," as the driver poured half the kerosene over Boggs's head. Boggs sputtered and screamed at the same time. "No. I can explain. It wasn't what you think. Oh God! No! You can't do this."

Done talking, the driver walked back to the Cadillac and got dressed. Checking his look in the car's side view mirror, he went back for the can of kerosene.

Boggs could barely talk. His whispers were more of the same begging and whimpering. He didn't even raise his head as the driver threw the tarp at the base of the tree then poured the rest of the kerosene in a trail on the ground back to the driver's side of the car. He threw the empty can into the woods and got behind the wheel. Charlie Boggs started screaming again, this time at the top of lungs, most of it incomprehensible except the word "please" over and over again.

The driver started the car, struck a match, and dropped it out the window. The path of burning kerosene streaked back across the clearing. As he drove away, he looked in the rear-view mirror in time to see Charlie Boggs burst into a ball of flames.

The driver stopped at a turnout two miles up the road to throw the wire cutters, gloves, booties, and duct tape into a drainage ditch filled with scum-colored water. He took the stolen Georgia plates off the car, sailed them into the woods, and put the Oregon plates back. It was a little after 2:45 a.m., three hours earlier in Portland. He got the cellphone out of the center console and dialed. A man answered on the second ring.

"It's done," the driver said.

"Problems?"

"No."

The man at the other end of the phone didn't answer. "Your reward is waiting in New Orleans. I'll text you the number and the address. Everything is taken care of, including the money. It's in your account. Enjoy yourself. Just don't hurt any of the girls. The owner is a friend of mine. Oh, and thanks."

The driver put the phone away, dug the vial of cocaine out of his suit pocket, and snorted the powder off the back of his hand. He pulled the choke chain with the silver skull and cross bones out of the glove box and hung it around the rearview mirror. Eight hours to New Orleans. Should be about right. He pulled the Cadillac back onto the road and disappeared into the Georgia night.

Chapter 1

John. The world's most common name. John Smith. John Doe. John Q. Public. Dear John. Juan in Mexico and Spain. Ian in Great Britain. Giovanni in Italy. The name of four American presidents and 23 popes, if you include the two John Pauls. The name whores give their clients and homeowners give their bathrooms.

Standard. As in basic, normal, typical. The name of newspapers in Great Britain, Zimbabwe, and Montana. Standard time. Standard fare. A word that inspires neither greatness nor pity—only shallow feelings of something ordinary.

That would be him, he thought. John Standard.

Or at least the old him.

Just a guy trying to knock out a living writing declarative sentences with enough facts, figures, and quotes to satisfy low-paid editors at obscure websites and interest readers who confuse opinions with facts. Someone who used to get up in the morning to have coffee with his wife and drive into the city to a designated parking spot out of the rain. On weekends, it was a barbecue with the neighbors or season tickets to Trail Blazers basketball or University of Oregon football (Go Ducks).

Then it all changed.

No, change is too easy a word. More like meltdown, disintegration, total self-destruction, the lifestyle equivalent of genetic realignment. A descent to the bottom in the fraction of the time it took to get to the top.

Standard's job at a Portland, Oregon, daily newspaper was gone along with his wife, the Blazers and Duck tickets (Gone Ducks), and the house. That left him in a three-room apartment, with a view of an air shaft and on a first name basis with mice, centipedes, and sugar ants. His new best friend was a former circus midget turned website designer. His girlfriend was a receptionist who once did lap dances in a strip club on SE Foster Road. He wrote on a five-year-old laptop by the light of a 65-watt bulb, and cruised Costco for lunches of free samples of freeze-dried burritos served by women wearing hairnets.

As bad as it sounded, Standard had persisted in pounding out a life that had achieved a certain comfortable rhythm and simplicity to it. A few bucks here and there from a wire service in need of a stringer, a magazine looking for a fanciful freelance travel piece, a website looking for fake news, or a company wanting to use editorial pages to defend itself against allegations of rat turds in its all-natural granola.

And then she showed up.

Just thinking about it made the whole thing sound like something a drunk would mutter to a bartender at closing time. Some poor schmuck with a sad, trite tale about a woman who screws up his life so bad he feels compelled to seek solace from an uncaring barkeep in a cross-town bar that catered to pathetic losers.

It sounded that way because it was true.

It started on a January day when the outside temperature hovered near freezing, turning the incessant winter rain into anemic flurries of sparse snowflakes that disappeared against the window. For Oregonians who didn't ski or fish for steelhead, it was a day to hunker down and wait out the last two months of soggy winter, all the time hoping the rivers didn't flood.

Standard had wasted half a day struggling to turn a rainy weekend in a yurt in a state park into an airline magazine article that would appeal to passengers on a flight to Hawaii. Fortunately, the building's furnace seemed to be having a better day, which meant the temperature in the apartment hovered around 70 degrees instead of the usual 50. There was no in-between.

He greeted the knock on the door with dread, expecting anything from a process server to a Jehovah's Witness. Not even close.

She was a stunning blonde with a small but mesmerizing gap between her front teeth, an intriguing flaw that added to her beauty and mystery. Revealed with a tight smile, the imperfection stood out in plain sight, proudly proclaiming: "This is what's wrong with me. What's wrong with you?"

Plenty, Standard thought, but he didn't like sharing his life with strangers.

The tight smile disappeared and, just for a moment, it looked like she was going to apologize for bothering him. Instead, she remained rigid and elegant in her black cashmere coat, matching hat, and fur-lined boots. Standard got the impression that, if he touched her, she would either scream and run away or shatter into a million pieces.

Finally, she looked past him into the dingy apartment then glanced in both directions up and down the hallway. He held back the urge to reassure her that the cockroaches, homeless winos, and other vermin didn't come out much during the day.

"Are you sure you're in the right place?"

"I am, if you're John Standard."

She flashed frosty blue eyes. Sapphires on a white sand beach. She was tall, just half a head less than Standard's six feet. He guessed her age at late twenties and her background as privileged. That meant Standard had ten years on her and might have once shared a similar lifestyle, probably in Dunthorpe, the West Hills, or maybe the same leafy southeast Portland neighborhood where he'd once lived.

A knit cap dotted with raindrops covered the tops of her ears. She pulled it off to reveal a jumble of shoulder-length hair made limp and unruly by the weather. When she shook her head, large hoop earrings winked from behind the wheat-colored strands. The cold outside had

3

colored her cheeks a red made more vivid by her pale skin. Her face had a sallow look, like a fashion model with no back teeth and a week-long case of the flu. Her thin lips were a faded pink.

"Would you like to come in?"

She didn't move.

Standard made it a practice of never apologizing for the apartment's condition. Most people didn't understand the effort that went into finding tattered furniture, unframed movie posters, and threadbare rugs good enough to go with the dingy yellow wallpaper. Then there was always that difficult search for cement blocks and boards to make bookshelves. It wasn't like Drexel Heritage carried this stuff.

"Perhaps you'd be more comfortable somewhere else. There's a wine bar on the corner. You'll have to buy."

The offer hung in the air for a moment before the thin smile returned to provide another glimpse of the hypnotizing gap in her teeth. "No, this is fine."

Standard took a step back. She walked in and glanced at the furniture, carefully assessing each tattered piece before settling onto the orange, crushed-velvet couch. Standard pulled a chair over from the desk. They sat facing each other, locked in an awkward silence. She glanced around the room some more, her eyes wandering over to the computer, the battered office chair, the cluttered desk, and the ancient portable television on top of the cheap veneer dresser. If she had a verdict on him or the surroundings, she kept it to herself.

She unbuttoned her coat but left it on. Underneath was more black—a knit business suit that looked a size too big and hid her figure the way a sheet hides a chair in a closed-up house.

"I assume you're here for a reason?" Standard said.

"I'm sorry. I don't mean to be rude. My name is Allison Shafer, but I like to be called Allie." Her voice had a hint of a long-neglected southern drawl. Something far southeast, he thought. Alabama,

Mississippi, or Georgia. She looked at him to make sure he'd signed on to the use of her desired nickname.

"As in McGraw?"

"No." She spelled it slowly enough that Standard felt he should be taking notes. She settled back into the couch, apparently no longer afraid that it would bite back. The steam radiator in the corner let out a slow, patient hiss. "I'm going to do something, and I want you to help me with it."

Standard stared at her. He didn't get much walk-in business, and certainly not from someone who looked or dressed like Allie Shafer.

"And what would *it* be?" he asked.

She pulled off her leather gloves, one finger at a time, to reveal a diamond tennis bracelet and graceful fingers with no rings. Her nails were professionally manicured, not the kind done at home on Sunday night while watching *60 Minutes.*

"Before I tell you, I need your absolute guarantee that, if you don't want to do what I ask, then you'll not tell anyone else that I was here or what we talked about." She paused long enough to check for a reaction. Standard gave her nothing to check. "If you don't agree to that, then I'm afraid our business is concluded."

Standard's first inclination was the same as with all ultimatums he'd in received his life: thank her for stopping by and show her to the door. But he didn't. Maybe it was the possibility of making a buck. More likely it was Allie Shafer, herself, and that damn gap in her teeth that kept calling to him. Maybe it was just that she was beautiful.

"First, let's make it clear what I do. You did come here looking for a writer?"

"I'm in the right place, but you are a hard man to find. Have you considered a listing in the Yellow Pages? Facebook? Maybe a website? Twitter?" His answer was an icy stare. "I wanted to find you because I remember reading your articles when you worked for the newspaper, and I've seen your stories in that local tabloid, *Inside Oregon* I think it's called. I need someone who can write with passion and clarity, someone who can make people understand complicated things. I think you're that person."

She was peeing on his leg. He couldn't wait to find out why. "How did you find me?"

"I called the newspaper where you used to work. I got somebody who knows you. He told me where you were."

"He?"

"I didn't catch his name."

"He probably didn't give it to you. I'm not exactly remembered there with any great fondness."

"I wouldn't know about that," she said. "Anyway, I'm here."

"And why would that be, exactly?"

"Do you agree to my conditions, to not say anything if you don't want to do what I ask?"

"Does it pay?"

"I would think so, but that depends on you."

"Okay then. Let's hear it."

"There's one more thing we need to get straight first. I don't want my life turned into a circus, with lots of helicopters and television cameras or those anchor people with all that hairspray and false sincerity."

She wrinkled her nose to register her disgust. The move was cute. It made Standard that much more eager to hear what she had to say and see what made her think it was worthy of all the press attention. Time to play along.

"I know," he said. "I hate that, too. Especially that hairspray thing."

"I don't know what I'd do if word of this got out and reporters were hanging around outside my house. Do you know what that would be like, to have something personal become utterly public?" He nodded yes. "You do? Are you sure?"

"Pretty sure."

She shrugged and twisted her gloves. Her eyes took another lap around the apartment then stopped, apparently finding solace in the cheap *The Maltese Falcon* movie poster on the wall next to the desk. Standard waited, playing Humphrey Bogart to her Mary Astor.

"What I want are things done on my terms, so that the world will understand why people in my position do what they do. I think you'll respect that. At least I hope you will."

"So, what are we talking about here?" he said, trying not to sound impatient.

"I'm going to kill myself, and I want you to write about it."

Chapter 2

Back in the days when he had a six-figure household income and could go to poker night with more than paperclips and bottle caps, Standard would occasionally find himself as the third hand in a game of high-low. Looking at his cards, he'd get a pinching feeling in his balls. It was a message to fold, which, of course, he ignored and ended up the odd man out while the other two split the pot.

A woman with champagne style showing up in his beer-bottle world produced that same pinching feeling. Everything about her screamed stay away, don't get involved. Standard eventually learned to pay attention to his instincts, fold his hand, and get a cold beer. This, however, was different. There was money on the table and he was a threadbare freelancer with maxed-out credit cards. With little to lose, he decided to hang in there and see one more card.

"I'm sorry if I shocked you," she said. "I didn't mean for it to come out that way, bluntly, I mean."

Standard need to know more. "You'd better start from the beginning."

She nodded then spoke slowly and deliberately, carefully choosing her words as if they were evening dresses at Saks, the constant twisting and untwisting of her gloves the only outward sign of nerves.

"I came to you, Mr. Standard, because I'm dying." She paused, bit her lip, and stared down at her gloves. "Two months ago, I was diagnosed with an advanced case of ovarian cancer. Rather than endure chemotherapy or radiation treatments, I've decided to make use of Oregon's physician-assisted suicide law and end my life. I'd like you to chronicle my last few days and write about it after I'm ... gone."

"I'm sorry," Standard said. It was an inadequate acknowledgment of her condition. He needed a cigarette, but sat still, afraid to light up in front of someone dying of cancer.

Anyone who'd covered the news in Oregon in the last twenty years knew about the Death with Dignity Act. The law permitted capable adults with terminal illnesses to request life-ending drugs from their physicians, who were held harmless for prescribing them. The law went into effect after withstanding court challenges by conservatives and fundamental religious groups intent on running other people's lives. Since then, one or two terminally ill patients had gone public with their stories, but none of them looked or acted like Allie Shafer.

Standard ran through the mental list of magazines and other media outlets willing to pay good money for a heart-wrenching account of the last days of a beautiful young woman. The law had been around in Oregon long enough that it wasn't big news anymore. Also, none of the dire consequences predicted by opposition groups ever happened. As a result, the law stayed on the books unchanged and people used it. End of story. Still other states were considering it, and there had been very little written about the victims, particularly before they died. The story, if he decided to do it, held the promise of enough money for rent and groceries.

"A simple business deal, then. In exchange for waiting until after your death, I get exclusive rights to publish your story."

"I want you to publish it wherever you feel it's appropriate. I'm an accountant, Mr. Standard. I know nothing about your world. It really won't matter to me where the story appears or how much money you make selling it. My only requirement is that nothing be published until I'm ... until after."

"Then why do it?"

"As I said, I want people to see why someone in my position would do this. If everyone understands that it's a personal choice, not one forced on me by laws or convention, then maybe they'll gain a greater appreciation of the importance of living and dying on your own terms."

"Pretty noble."

"This isn't about nobility," she shot back. "This is about people's rights under the law."

Standard stared at her for a few moments before getting up and walking around the room. The cigarettes were on the desk next to the computer. They called out, but he left them there.

"You'll have to forgive me. It's not often that stories walk in the door, let alone one like this."

"I understand. Coming here isn't easy. None of this has been easy." Her eyes glistened again with tears.

"No doubt."

"If you know anything about physician-assisted suicide, then you'll see that I'm the perfect candidate," she said. "The evidence gathered so far shows that those who have used the law were single and they had a high school education or more. I'm all of those things."

"Statistics also show that most of them were quite a bit older than you, late sixties, if I remember right."

"Those same statistics show that most of those who took advantage of the law were white and had cancer. That makes me the rule, not the exception."

She sounded indignant, turning her head away to look out the window behind the desk. The weather had decided on sleet as a compromise between rain and snow. Icy drops exploded against the glass, like bugs against a car windshield. Rain with guts.

Standard sat back down and leaned forward, forearms resting on his knees. He could smell her perfume. There were little anchor designs on the buttons of her dress. No signs of cat or dog hair. Nothing. She was single and didn't even own a pet, at least not one with hair.

"Do you have any family?" he asked.

She avoided his stare. Looked at her gloves again and shook her head "no."

Standard took a deep breath. "Where are you in this process?"

"I've made the first oral request. The deadline for the second oral request is tomorrow. I have an appointment with the doctor at ten in the morning. I plan to give it then. After that, I'll give the doctor the written request."

"So you don't have much time left?" The law could only be used by those with less than six months to live, as if such things could be predicted with that much precision.

She nodded then turned her face toward the window. She seemed to want to look anywhere but at him.

"You know you can rescind the request at any time?"

"My mind is made up. I've seen what cancer treatment can do to people. I'm not a fighter. I can't live that way."

That pinching feeling came back. *Tell her no. Walk away right now. Go back to writing insurance company newsletters and op-ed pieces for corporate polluters.* There were other freelancers at work in the city. He could give her half a dozen names, including a woman who might have a better understanding of Allie Shafer's condition. At least one of them might not share his deep-seated discomfort with mortality. Let them have the money that could be made off her misery. Let them pay the rent and buy groceries by pimping her story to any magazine or cable show with a fat checkbook.

Instead, he ignored his instincts.

"I'll do it," he said. "I assume we need to get started right away."

Chapter 3

Encased in the tanning bed, Benny Orlando looked like a six-inch hot dog in a foot-long bun.

"How much longer?" Standard said, yelling to be heard over the machine's deep hum.

Benny stuck a tiny hand out from between the two halves of the bed and held up three fingers. Standard left to get a beer and poke around in Benny's refrigerator for something to eat. When he got back, the machine was off, the lid up. Dracula had awakened. Benny's miniature body was burned brownish-red.

"That thing isn't good for you," Standard said.

"It's all right if you're careful. Besides, I got a great deal on it from this tanning salon that went bank-o after one of the employees got caught videotaping the female customers. It's a pretty funny story. He was showing the pictures at this party. One of the women he'd taped was this other guy's sister. Things got ugly. The DA indicted the guy the same day he walked out of the hospital with a broken nose and two fewer teeth."

Benny was a little over four feet tall, with a head a bit too big for his pudgy body. He was once Baby Benny, a clown who worked his way up to Ringling Bros. and Barnum & Bailey before ending up with a small circus that toured the Southeast. After years of chasing other clowns around the big top and substituting in the freak show as the wild man from Borneo, he had retired five years earlier after his aunt died and left him the apartment building in which Standard had been living for the last eight months.

Benny quickly sold the building to a development company, with the provision that he would stay as resident landlord, rent-free, as long as the building was there, which probably wouldn't be that much longer. He used the money from the sale to start a successful business designing and maintaining Internet websites for circuses, theme parks and, lately, Indian casinos.

Benny did most of his work late at night, hunched over one of the computer keyboards, with calliope music blaring in the background. His office was a back bedroom, with tinfoil over the windows to keep out the light. Sword swallowers, snake charmers, bearded ladies, hermaphrodites, and the world's strongest man stared down at him from the posters that covered the walls.

Standard's friendship with Benny started the day he agreed to rent him an apartment after being turned down at two other places. His unexpected act of kindness helped forge a friendship that gave Standard access to Benny's formidable computer skills.

On those frequent nights when sleep seemed like something left behind in a past life, Standard would come down to Benny's apartment to drink straight shots of cheap bourbon and watch him work. His tiny hands would fly around the keyboard, his eyes seldom leaving the screen. It was reminiscent of a mad scientist from some '60s-era horror movie. Sometimes Standard would come and go, fortified with enough booze to promise a few hours of sleep, without Benny ever knowing he'd been there.

Two weeks earlier, a local Indian tribe hired Benny to build what the tribal chief insisted on calling "the mother of all websites."

"Not only do these Indians pay well," Benny said when he got the job, "but I get comped for everything if I want to go to their casino and gamble for a few days, which I don't. Not a bad concept, though, when you think about it. Pay someone a lot of money to do a job and then get it back at the crap tables by giving them the chance to stay in a suite for nothing."

Benny's apartment was on the second floor, right above the front entrance to the building and four floors below Standard's. His office was really two adjoining bedrooms with the wall knocked out to make one long room. The tanning bed fit right in with Benny's three computers, a couple of printers, a router, and other pieces of unrecognizable high-tech equipment. Discarded laptops, desktops, keyboards, and CPUs filled the shelves at the far end of the room.

Benny crawled out of the tanning bed, slipped on a robe then hopped toad-like onto an office chair. "You going to make the rent this month?"

"I've been offered a couple of new jobs," Standard said, sitting down on a stool next to the door. "One of them is with a newsletter for this conservative fundamentalist Christian outfit that's set up shop out in Gresham. They want a profile of Jesus."

"How conservative?" Benny asked.

"Very. I swear they get out of the shower to pee. I don't think I'll take the job."

"What's the problem? It's not like there's a lack of material."

"I don't feel worthy." Standard set his half-empty bottle of beer on the floor and put a cheap lighter to a cigarette.

"Try a new angle," Benny said.

"Like what?"

"I don't know. Say Jesus was gay. He never married. The Apostles were all guys, you know. Wasn't Mary Magdalene a hooker? Hookers love gay guys."

Standard waved him off. "I'm sure they'd love that. Besides, I ran across something more interesting." He described Allie Shafer, her condition, and the possibilities for selling the story of her death. Talking about it made him feel crass and mercenary.

"Beautiful woman. Physician-assisted suicide," Benny said. "Sounds like you could make a buck or two off that."

"That's what it's all about, isn't it? Making a few bucks off of someone's misery and misfortune. Is this a great profession or what?"

One of Benny's computers beeped. Another e-mail message had come in from his network of circus freaks, computer nerds, and petty criminals. Benny ignored it.

"Don't you want to see what that is?" Standard said. "Maybe Betty the Bearded Lady wants some advice about opening that electrolysis shop."

"Don't be a smart-ass," Benny said, giving the robe's lapels an indignant tug. "So, how much do you think the story's worth?"

"Hard to tell. Eldon Mock at *Inside Oregon* will pay his usual fee, maybe more. I could rejigger the story a couple of times. Find a few more places to sell it. I think the Hemlock Society has a magazine of some kind, but I doubt it pays much."

"Just don't take it out in trade," Benny said, jumping off the chair. "Hang on for a few minutes. I'll get dressed and we'll go find something to eat. My treat."

A half-hour later they were in a small tavern, two blocks away on SW Jefferson, munching on bacon burgers and sharing a pitcher of beer. There used to be a porno theater next door. Sometimes, late at night when no one was playing the video poker machines, moans of pleasure could be heard coming through the wall. They talked football and politics. Benny did most of the talking, holding forth on the evils of instant replay in the NFL, the lingering effects of terrorist paranoia, and America's fascination with guns.

"Terrorists and guns are old news," Standard said. "Finding them by spying on millions of Americans is the new news.

"What happened to the banks, Wall Street, and CEO salaries?"

"So yesterday."

Benny raised his beer in mock acknowledgment of a new reality.

They were sitting across from each other. Benny's face looked dark, thanks to the tanning machine and the New York Yankees'

15

baseball cap he wore everywhere he went. Two women in their twenties came in and took the booth across from them. Benny waved at one of them. She had frizzy, red hair, pale skin, Buddy Holly glasses, and a pierced eyebrow.

"Didn't you date her?"

"About six months ago for a couple of weeks." He had to use two hands to pick up his beer glass. Even with the telephone books the bartender put on his side of the booth, Benny still had to stand on the seat to drink. "She probably doesn't remember me."

Standard stifled a laugh. "Yeah. Probably not, given all the eligible midgets in town."

Rain splattered against the windows. A streetlight back-lit the occasional pedestrian, casting shadows that walked across the tables and chairs inside the bar. When they finished eating, the bartender cleared the table except for the half pitcher of beer. Benny filled both their glasses.

"I thought you had a thing about death," Benny said. "Didn't you tell me once that you don't like talking or thinking about it and that you always tried to avoid writing about drive-by shootings, traffic accidents, and suicides?"

Benny was right. Death was not a subject Standard could write about with any confidence, which made the decision to accept Allie Shafer's offer that much more mysterious. His parents were killed in a plane crash years earlier. He hadn't seen that much of them before that. Their disapproval of his decision to be a reporter, instead of a lawyer, had lingered a lot longer than it should have. Then his brother died of AIDS five years earlier in Miami, but he'd been years older and they were never close.

High school in Salem, Oregon, led to a scholarship in journalism at a small Midwest college. After graduation, it was an internship at the *Chicago Tribune* followed by reporting jobs at daily newspapers in Des Moines and Minneapolis. The job in Portland came delivered on a platter by a college classmate who'd risen to editor. Reporting came naturally, and he always seemed to be in the right place at the right time with the right questions.

In other words, Standard bobbed through life until a freak accident chewed him up and spit him out. In a split second he'd gone from gold to goat on a dark night on a rural road. His career died along with two small girls he'd run down after dozing off behind the wheel.

The accident changed him. Fatalism replaced optimism, in large part because he became a victim of his own profession. The two girls who died were Hispanic. The local sheriff hinted to a television reporter that Standard had been drinking. He hadn't, but it didn't matter. Blood was in the water. Suddenly, he became the story. "Drunken Yuppie Mows Down Helpless Children."

Standard's open and well-chronicled dislike for the superficiality of television news made the story payback time for the city's four TV stations. The hunter had become the hunted. He awoke each morning to cameras outside his house. That was enough to send Christine, his wife, scurrying back to her parents in Arizona, and his editors to the publisher, demanding that he be fired.

Christine found a new husband, and the newspaper found a new reporter. Standard ended up with a stack of legal bills, no place to live, and a suitcase full of dirty clothes.

"Anyone in my place would have a thing about death," Standard told Benny, "but Allie Shafer's story is intriguing and, as usual, I need the money."

"And she's a babe."

"A dying babe."

Benny shrugged. A devilish look crossed his face. "Since when did you care?"

"Don't be an asshole. Remember Valerie."

"Oh, yeah. Where do things stand with you and the lovely Valerie

Michaels?"

"The usual."

"Usual with you two means you're together, apart, about to get back together, or about to be apart."

"Apart. She's in Cabo San Lucas with some of the girls she used to work with at that club."

"A covey of lap dancers loose in Mexico." Benny gazed at the ceiling. "Let me ponder that one for a minute."

"Former lap dancer."

"Whatever."

Standard didn't like talking about Valerie Michaels. Their on-again-off-again relationship was too complicated. It didn't make sense to anybody but them. All he knew was that she loved him, but he wasn't sure why.

After Benny paid for the dinner, they walked back to the apartment building. Standard moved slowly, hands stuffed deep into jacket pockets. It was after nine o'clock. The temperature hovered just above freezing, but at least the rain had stopped. Benny bounced along, working up a sweat despite the cold, trying to stay even with Standard's long strides.

"So, when do you write this story?" Benny said. He was starting to pant. His bandy legs moved three strides to Standard's one.

"I can't write anything until she's dead."

"How does that work?"

"I do all the research and interviews ahead of time, probably write most of it. The deal is I can't sell it until she's gone."

"I don't know." Benny shook his head. They were back at the apartment building, standing in the foyer waiting for the elevator. "If I were you, I'd reconsider that Jesus thing. At least he's already dead."

Chapter 4

Reuters called the next morning about a Japanese container ship that had pulled loose from its anchor during the night and run aground on the southern Oregon Coast. The bureau chief in San Francisco said it was hard on a sandy beach, next to a bird sanctuary, and leaking oil like an old Ford.

"It's empty except for thousands of gallons of bunker oil," the bureau chief said. "It's an environmental disaster in the making. Can you get down there? We don't want to miss this. AP is all over it, and we're hearing that the networks are on the way. We need someone there. Now."

"Usual fees?"

"Of course, and then some."

Standard thought about turning it down. Allie Shafer's story had caught enough of his imagination that even a stranded ship about to foul Oregon's precious beaches seemed insignificant. Then there was the money. It was always about the money.

"Byline?"

"Absolutely."

"I'll leave right away. You sending a shooter?

"He'll meet you there. Name's Grady."

A half-hour later, Standard was in his ten-year-old Jeep Grand Cherokee headed south on Interstate 5. At 9 a.m., and just north of Eugene, he called Benny from the car. The recorder was on. He left a message about what happened and not to expect him for a few days.

Allie Shafer would be waiting for a call. The feeling that he was abandoning her nagged at him on the drive through the Coast Range.

He called about noon from Reedsport, a small town a half-hour north of the stranded ship. No answer. He tried not to think about what that might mean.

The grounded ship quickly became major news. Apparently, it had been anchored off the mouth of Coos Bay when, in the middle of the night, a storm came up and the anchor pulled loose. The vessel ran aground before the crew could pick up enough speed. The radio reports on the drive down left the impression that the ship's captain probably hadn't made the dean's list at seafaring school.

Reuters had arranged for a room at the local Red Lion. When he checked in, the clerk handed him a message to meet Grady, the photographer, at the Coast Guard Air Station in North Bend. Standard threw his bags in the room, got directions from the hotel clerk, and jumped back in the car.

Fifteen minutes later, he was standing in a cavernous airplane hangar with thirty other reporters and a bank of television cameras. The hangar was electric. Questions echoed off the steel-beamed ceiling. Cameras flashed. Television lights brought the temperature up twenty degrees. Near the back of the hangar, Coast Guardsmen stood around their bright orange helicopters, laughing as a spokesman from the ship owner's insurance company described some vague plan to get the ship off the beach without damaging the environment.

Fat chance, Standard thought, but dutifully scribbled notes and shouted a couple of questions. The answers came back defensive.

"You the stringer from Portland?"

The question came from a ruddy-faced Irishman with a cigarette in the corner of his mouth. The Nikons hung around his neck like shrunken heads. He wore baggy pants and worn out Nikes. A safari vest, filled with lenses, filters and other photography gizmos and whiz-bangs, hid a faded polo shirt.

"Yeah. John Standard. You must be Grady."

"That's me," he said in a deep brogue. "I got pretty much

everything I need. You?"

Standard glanced over at the crowd of reporters still asking the same questions and getting the same answers. "Yeah, I'm good." On the way out the door, Grady suggested he call in some quotes to the Reuters bureau in San Francisco.

"Good stuff," the desk man said. "Call back in an hour whether you got anything new or not."

Standard hung up, then tried Allie's number again. She answered on the first ring. He told her where he was.

"I'm watching it on television," she said. "You're actually there. How amazing!"

"It may be a few days before we can talk."

"I think I can hang on 'til then."

The odd lightness in her voice made him feel like he was more concerned about her than she was about herself.

He hung up and went back inside, where a Coast Guard officer was trying to explain why no media would be allowed anywhere near the grounded ship for the next twenty-four hours. It wasn't going over well.

Grady and Standard had no other choice but to set up shop on a ridge across the bay, amid the satellite trucks and blondes doing live stand-ups for television stations from Seattle, Portland, San Francisco, and Los Angeles. It was the best they could do.

The ridge wasn't far away from the Coast Guard station, so they left the car and walked. From a crowded vantage point, the mist-shrouded, black and red ship looked like a toppled skyscraper. Standard leaned against the fender of a satellite truck while Grady stood nearby, chatting up a young female reporter from Portland. Just before dark they were summoned back to the hangar to hear more reasons why the ship couldn't be pulled off the beach.

"There's no fookin' way they're getting that fookin' boat off that fookin' beach," Grady predicted after the press briefing. He stomped off, mumbling something about getting a ride on one of the Coast Guard choppers.

The drama went on for two more days. Standard salted his stories with quotes from pissed off commercial crabbers, inconsolable oystermen, and outraged bird lovers. Politicians showed up to cast worried glances at the beached ship then left after promising to introduce legislation that would prevent this from ever happening again. He filed his stories on a laptop Grady brought with him from San Francisco.

Standard thought he should be loving every minute. A good story, good pay, good equipment. Instead, Allie Shafer kept buzzing around inside his head. He tried to stay focused on the grounded ship and the paychecks that came with it. She and her story would have to wait. Still, a dying woman seemed suddenly more important than a threatened beach. Thinking about it made him impatient to get back to Portland.

In the down time between news conferences and deadlines, he used the laptop and the glacial Internet connection at the motel to mine the Web for information about assisted suicide. It didn't take long to figure out that the battle lines were sharply drawn with no middle ground. He used the notes he took to frame questions for Allie Shafer when the time came.

Late at night, he and Grady smoked cigarettes, drank Early Times, and exchanged war stories. Grady had been to Iraq, Kosovo, and Afghanistan. It would be back to Iraq next or South Korea.

"They're lovin' your stuff in San Francisco." Grady poured each of them another drink. "They got fookin' jobs down there, you know? Everybody's bailing thinking bloggers are going to kill the news biz. Ain't gonna happen. Those wankers will never get out of their mother's basement. It's a great life if you don't want a fookin' girlfriend, wife, or kids, and your parents are dead."

Standard promised to look into it. Who could resist an offer like that?

He called Allie two more times, telling her the latest about the grounded ship and asking how she felt. She said she was fine but sounded depressed. The lightness in her voice during their earlier conversation was gone.

The next afternoon, the ship had finally been hooked up to a giant tug that had come down from Seattle. The Coast Guard said the ship would be gone with the next high tide.

It didn't happen.

About five in the afternoon on the fifth day, the towline that connected the ship and the tug snapped in a high wind. The steel cable bullwhipped back toward shore, killing a man who had volunteered to clean tar balls off the beach with a garden rake. He was an unemployed mill worker wearing bright yellow rain gear and ear buds. The pack of bored reporters went ballistic. Grady had caught the man's death with a telephoto lens and an auto-drive.

That night in the motel room, Standard scanned the pictures. They showed the man's body exploding into a half dozen parts, as if it was an action figure. The faster he flipped through the pictures, the faster the pieces flew around the beach. The next day the dead man's wife told the NBC affiliate that her husband had been laid off a year earlier from a local saw mill and was "just starting to get his life back in one piece." Grady thought that was the funniest thing he'd ever heard.

That night Standard called Allie Shafer again. She answered on the second ring.

"Are you sure you want to do this?" he said. "Die, I mean."

"I think you mean are *you* sure you want write about it."

"Death is not my favorite subject."

"Mine either, but at least you have a choice."

They talked for an hour without mentioning her cancer or her

23

impending suicide. He told her about the ship, the dead man, and how he wanted it to be over. She told him about books she'd read and how hard it was to go to work each day and not tell anybody about what she was about to do.

Somewhere in the middle of the conversation something changed. A beached ship and a chance to be real reporter again seemed suddenly insignificant. He wanted to get back to Portland. To her.

"When will you be back?" she said.

"As soon as I can."

"Will you come see me right away?"

"Do I need to hurry? Is there something wrong?

"No. No. I feel okay. I'm looking forward to talking to you about this. You're the only one who knows, other than the two doctors."

He searched her voice for a hint of something more than just wanting him to tell the world about why she killed herself. "Of course. You're sure there's no need to hurry?"

"We have time."

Two days later, the ship was finally pulled off the beach and towed out to sea. The Navy used it for target practice for a few hours before a nuclear submarine, with nothing better to do, mercifully put a torpedo mid ship, sinking both the ship and the story. The drama was over in two minutes. The container ship disappeared below the whitecaps, to lay forgotten in five thousand feet of water.

Standard got back to Portland at midnight with a stack of clips and enough money in stringer fees from Reuters to cover the rent, pay some bills, and buy a couple of dinners at one of the city's eclectic food carts. Maybe that Ethiopian-Korean fusion place near Portland State.

He was on a roll. "Keep it going," he told himself.

Chapter 5

Allie Shafer lived in a secluded neighborhood a couple of blocks off SW Barnes Road, near St. Vincent's Medical Center. Standard pulled into the driveway and sat in the car for a few seconds, struggling with the discomfort about what she was going to do and his desire to see her. The question kept coming: Why am I doing this? Was it really the money or was it her? Was it something else? Did she remind him of the life he once had? Was he just plain crazy?

A neatly trimmed boxwood hedge lined both sides of the path to the front door. She answered before the doorbell's echo faded.

"Welcome back," she said. "How was the battle?"

"The Navy one, container ship zero."

"Any casualties?"

"Four snowy plovers and a guy with a rake."

"How awful."

The inside of the low-slung, two-story house was dark and warm. The highly polished baby grand piano sat in the corner of the small living room. Thick carpet absorbed the usual house noises. A jazz station whispered from an unseen stereo system. Walnut bookcases, filled with hard-backed bestsellers, short story anthologies, and biographies, lined an entire wall of the great room. No television set, just expensive couches and hardwood coffee tables arranged for talking rather than watching. Standard imagined couples sipping expensive wine while casually discussing month-long forays to Tuscany. The kitchen had granite countertops and a gas stove. Copper pots and pans hung from a rack over a massive butcher's block. The small dining room consisted of a large glass-top table with six high-backed chairs. Several dozen bottles of Barolo, from different Italian wineries, filled the wine rack in a carpeted alcove off the kitchen.

"Let's go outside," Allie said.

A cobalt blue sky had replaced the rain clouds that marred their first meeting. The sun hung low in the south, giving off light but no heat. The early afternoon temperature hit the low fifties, a kind of false spring that nature periodically used to torture sun-starved Oregonians before bringing on another three or more months of rain. They sat on the wooden deck under bare-limbed oak trees. Wind pushed gray leaves around the yard and up against an aging wooden fence.

"I had you pegged for Dunthorpe or the West Hills," Standard said.

"Not me. I'm just a little girl from Georgia. Money and prestige make me feel like I'm putting on airs."

"It shouldn't."

"I'll take that as a compliment."

"You should."

"I will, thanks," Allie said. "So, where should we start?"

She wore running shoes, heavy cotton sweat pants, and a bulky sweatshirt over a turtleneck. The green sweatshirt had a large University of Oregon logo on the front. The small logo on the collar of the turtleneck said, "Ventana Canyon."

They faced each other across the top of a round wooden picnic table, with a hole in the middle to hold the colorful umbrella that would come out during the summer. The heatless sun and bare trees made it feel like visitor's day at a women's prison.

"Let's just talk for a while," Standard said and put a small, portable tape recorder on the table and turned it on. "Give you a chance to get comfortable with the idea of the tape recorder and of me."

She looked the same as before: no makeup, pale skin, splotches of red on her cheeks and nose, brilliant blue eyes. Only her hair was different. She had pulled it back into a tight ponytail. The gold hoop earrings had been replaced with large diamond studs that glittered prism-like in the harsh sunlight. She was the best looking terminally ill woman he'd ever met. Also the first.

"This is a little odd," she said. "Maybe some wine would help." She disappeared inside, returning a few minutes later with one of the Barolos from the rack in the dining room and two large wineglasses. "This should do it." She poured healthy portions for each of them. "After all, it's after five o'clock somewhere, isn't it?"

She swirled the wine in her glass, sniffed it then took a sip, giving it a silent nod of approval. "I hope you like this wine. It's one of my favorites. You can also smoke if you like, Mr. Standard. It doesn't bother me as long as we're outside. Besides, cigarettes had nothing to do with my condition."

Standard smiled and took a sip of wine but left the pack of cigarettes in the pocket of his leather bomber jacket.

"You can call me John."

"John it is."

They sealed the deal with more sips of wine.

"You know your wine," he said. "This is good."

"As they say, life is too short for bad wine."

It took a moment for what she had just said to sink in. He cut her off before she could say anything. "Tell me about yourself."

"You mean just the normal stuff? Height, weight, age. Things like that?"

"If you like."

For the next quarter hour, she talked about what little she remembered of Georgia and then growing up in Kalispell, Montana; about a mother who never married her father and who died drunk in a traffic accident at age forty; about no brothers, sisters, aunts, uncles, or grandparents; about putting herself through college by waiting tables in the winter and fighting forest fires in the summer; about becoming a certified public accountant and the chief financial officer for a small Portland-based corporation that owned several restaurants.

While the tape recorder did the listening, Standard concentrated on the way she talked and acted. With Allie Shafer just a few weeks away from death, he needed to gain a better understanding of what that knowledge could do to someone. The preconceived notion was that she'd be either sad or angry at the prospect of having to take her own life at age thirty. She seemed to have none of that. Her voice was strong, emotions in check, hands steady around the fragile stem of the crystal wine glass. The attempts at humor were self-deprecating and laced with irony. Allie Shafer seemed ready to meet her fate with the faith and conviction of an Arab terrorist.

"I was pretty happy with where I was in my life and where I was going," she said. "It hadn't been easy, but all the hard work was starting to pay off."

"No husband? Children?"

She shook her head but showed no regret. "That was on my list, but not anywhere near the top."

When Allie grew more comfortable with him and with the tape recorder, he pulled out a reporter's notebook and a pen. "My memory's not what it used to be."

She rested her chin in one hand and watched with amusement as he fumbled to find a clean page. "Do you like what you do?" Her smile offered another glimpse of the hypnotic gap in her front teeth.

"Most of the time. Freelance writing takes some getting used to. Finding things to write about is easy. Finding someone to pay for it is a different story."

"Is this going to be a story that's easy to sell?"

"I'm not sure yet."

She accepted the answer with a knowing nod. "I told you about me. Are you going to tell me something about you?"

Questions like that invariably led to why he lost his job at the

28

newspaper and everything that happened before that and after. But there was something about Allie Shafer that made him want to tell her all about it. Still, he fought back the urge. Whatever he'd been through seemed inconsequential compared to what was happening to her. He had only fucked up his life. Allie Shafer was losing hers. He might get lucky and someday recover something that had been lost. Not her.

"Let's talk about me later. Tell me about the last few weeks."

She swirled the wine in her glass. "It happened pretty fast, really. The company I work for started offering health insurance to employees. I was required to take a physical as a condition of coverage. That's when I found out."

"No symptoms prior to that?"

"Some pains in my stomach and indigestion, but nothing serious, at least I didn't think so."

"Ovarian cancer is unusual in women your age."

A thin smile of admiration crept across her face. "You've been doing your homework."

"Am I right?"

"Yes, but I've never been pregnant or had children. That increases the odds. Also, this was my very first physical. I just turned thirty. It didn't seem like I needed one. We're all supposed to be invincible at this age, right? That's why we do things now that we don't do when we're fifty. Anyway, I guess I should have had a physical a long time ago, because if you don't detect this kind of cancer early, there's not much anyone can do."

"So you blame yourself?"

"Not really, but I guess there's a lesson here about it never being too early to prepare for the worst."

"That must have been a difficult time, the day they told you." Standard immediately regretted the hackneyed question. Still, she didn't miss a beat.

29

"It was very weird. I know that most people with terminal illnesses go through this process of denial, anger, bargaining, depression, and acceptance. I really didn't feel any of those things. I was just disappointed that this was all the life I would get to have, that I would never get to know how everything was going to turn out." She poured more wine for both of them. "I always wanted to live on an island in the South Pacific. Not one of those fancy ones with big hotels, but a sort of quaint little island with palm trees, white sand, blue water. Some place where *my* accent is foreign. The kind you see on calendars or in *National Geographic.* You know, grass shacks and coconut bras." She laughed at her own joke. "Places like that must exist somewhere, don't you think?"

She looked away for a few seconds to let her eyes well up then return to normal. "It's almost like I knew this was going to happen. Looking back, I can see things in my life that should have told me what was coming."

"Such as?"

"You know, events. Being born illegitimate. My mother being killed just before I graduated from high school. Not having any other family. It's like some force in the universe decided that the Shafer family was an unsuccessful experiment, so let's get rid of the last one and move on to other things. Like the dinosaurs."

"Would that force in the universe be God?"

"I'm not sure, but maybe I'll find out."

"I take it, then, that you're not a religious person."

She gave a shy smile. "I'm quickly becoming one."

They talked for another hour. The conversation rambled between the past and the present. The future never came up. When it got late, they moved inside, out of the cold that came with the early sunset. Standard sat on one of the facing couches drinking wine. Allie bustled around the kitchen, putting together a plate of cheese, crackers, and fruit.

"Tell me about your job," he said when she brought in the food and sat down, her knees up and stocking feet on the coffee table.

"I was a low-level accountant at a big firm downtown. One of my accounts was a guy with a small restaurant. Over time, the business grew to be pretty good-sized and I kept the account because I was doing a good job with it and the owner liked me. Eventually, he offered me a full-time position with his company, the title of chief financial officer, a nice salary, and a small percentage of the gross. That was five years ago. I took it and it's paid off well. I bought this house and a car. Upgraded my wardrobe." She nibbled at a piece of Tillamook cheddar. "I really don't want to drag them into this, though. This is about me, not them. Is that okay with you?"

"You're not going to give me free rein on this story, are you?"

She gave her head a slow, determined shake. There was no room for compromise.

After another hour of mostly more small talk, Standard finally yielded to questions about his past, but gave her the short, clinical version that didn't come cluttered with bad memories about dead Hispanic girls, divorce, and being fired. The urge to tell her more was hard to fight back.

Before leaving, she showed him the written request for the life-ending drugs. They were standing in the kitchen, leaning against the counter. Standard wanted to go but kept finding reasons to stay.

"I need two witnesses," she said. "I have one already. A nurse at the doctor's office. Would you be the second?"

He hesitated. "I still haven't made my mind up about this. I don't know if I agree with what you're doing or not."

"If this creates a moral dilemma for you, then I can find someone else."

"Of course it creates a moral dilemma. If this doesn't, then what will? If we can't struggle over the moral implications of taking one's own life to avoid the indignities of dying, then why bother debating anything? Why bother arguing about abortion, racism, science versus religion, war versus peace, faith versus reason?"

Allie stared at him for a few seconds. A smile came slowly across her face. "Or plastic versus paper?"

They both burst out laughing at the same time.

"I was right in coming to you," she said. "My only regret is that I'll never get a chance to read what you're going to write."

She moved closer. Her hand went to his shoulder, fingers on his neck. When she kissed him, her lips stayed too long on his cheek before brushing against his ear as she pulled away.

"Please," she said.

Standard nodded and signed the paper.

Chapter 6

Two nights later, he saw her for the last time.

His emotions had been slapping him around for the entire forty-eight hours. Nothing could get her out of his head. He wanted her. He wanted a woman who was dying of cancer and was going to kill herself because of it. A woman who wanted him to chronicle her death so other terminally ill women could feel better about what lay ahead. He felt like an asshole.

"My house, tonight. In an hour," she said when she called late on a rainy afternoon. "I have something to show you."

He arrived with what he thought was a good bottle of California cabernet. She smiled, set it on the kitchen counter next to the electric can opener, and got another bottle of the Barolo from the wine rack.

"I'm fixing you dinner and then we have to talk," she said as she opened the wine.

"You've changed your mind? You're going to seek treatment?"

She laughed at the hopefulness in his voice. "No, but I'll explain later. Let's eat first."

Dinner was rack of lamb, red potatoes roasted in butter and rosemary, and a salad dressed with walnut oil and vinegar. They ate at the dining room table set for two. Soft lights from the chandelier gave the room a mellow glow. Over espresso and Amaretto, the conversation turned to everything except the inevitable. Standard did more listening than talking, letting her lead the way to wherever the evening was going.

"Why do I feel that you have something on your mind?" he asked, finally.

They were still at the dining room table. Lamb bones littered his plate. Allie had done more drinking than eating. She had cut her food into little pieces and hid them under the salad.

"Okay. I guess now is as good a time as any." She got up from the table, went into the bedroom, and came back with a small piece of paper. "I went to the doctor today. She gave me the prescription."

When she held out the pink piece of paper, Standard grabbed it. The squiggly lines that passed for the doctor's handwriting spelled out a witch's brew of barbiturates. He recognized one of the drugs, Tuinal. The others sounded even more ominous. It seemed so abstract and, in a very real way, nonchalant. Just scribble a few words on a piece of paper, hand them over, and, voila, death without punishment or recrimination. He looked at Allie. She was staring over the rim of her coffee cup.

"This is what we're celebrating?" he said. "Kind of creepy, Allie."

She ignored him, "I'm afraid the pills won't work." There was edge to her voice, like someone with an expensive new car and buyer's remorse.

"I don't know much about prescription drugs, but this looks pretty lethal to me," he said.

"But what if something goes wrong? Most of the others died within thirty minutes of taking the drugs, but one lingered for nearly twelve hours. Twelve hours! Can you imagine? I don't want that to happen."

He handed the prescription back to her. Offering advice on the correct way to take a deadly dose of barbiturates was out of his league. "What did the doctor say?"

Allie held the prescription in her hand, reading the scrawled words as if they were secret runes unlocking age-old mysteries. "She said this would accomplish everything and to call her right after I take them."

"Then what?"

"She'll come here to the house later. Declare me dead and take care of the arrangements."

"You mean she doesn't even come here to be with you? You'll be alone?" Allie nodded. "That doesn't make sense."

"You're not the one with cancer."

Standard conceded the point with silence. With as much patience as he could muster, he said the whole thing made the doctor sound like a cleaning service that was going to stop by and pick up a soiled arm chair while she was at work. "What do you do? Leave the key under the mat?"

"I want it this way, John. I don't want anybody here, anybody to talk me out of it or give me reasons to live when I know I won't."

"I'm sorry. It just sounds too clinical, too clean."

"That's just me talking." Allie was still staring at the piece of paper. "The doctor was much more professional and understanding. This is not a Kevorkian thing. There's no machine for someone else to operate. It's best this way."

He stared into the glass of Amaretto but didn't feel like drinking anymore. "You sure you want to do this?" How many times had he asked her that?

Her smile showed more sympathy for his plight than for her own. "We've been all through this, John. I know you don't like the whole idea but understand that it's the right thing for me. I'm not asking for your approval, only your compassion."

"Let's talk about something else for a while."

He started clearing the table, but she said to leave the dishes for later.

"What about your story?" she said. "The one you'll write about me. Do we need to talk some more? You can interview me again. We'll do it in the living room."

"I've got plenty for my story."

When she went into the kitchen for more coffee Standard got up

35

from the table, wandered around the living room then started rummaging around in her CD collection. Miles Davis, Etta James, Alicia Keys. Too downbeat. There was also some Pink Floyd, but the night was weird enough already. He forgot about the music and sat down on the couch, leaned back to stare at the ceiling.

Allie came with a cup of coffee in one hand and more Amaretto in the other. She slumped down next to him, her weight gently against his shoulder. She looked into her snifter as if it were a crystal ball through which she could see more of the future she'd already selected for herself.

"I need to ask you something," she said.

"Anything."

"Do you have a fearless heart?"

He saw what was coming like a train in the night. "Why would I need one?"

"Because I'd like you to do one more thing before I go away."

Whatever was left of Standard's precious detachment was about to be shattered into a million pieces. "Are you sure?"

"That prescription I have also kills regrets," she said.

At least for you, he thought.

They came together slowly at first, testing, exploring, finding what worked and what didn't. Instinctively, with soft moans and gentle nudges, each learned what the other wanted. He watched Allie's face and body as she moved when he ran his hand across her breasts and down her stomach. It was as if she wanted to take as much as she could of him to the grave. Desperation, impatience, despair, triumph, and in the end, contentment in waves that left Standard wanting more of something that would soon be gone forever.

It started in the bedroom on satin sheets, moved to the couch in the front room, the counter in the kitchen, and the tiled shower in the bathroom. It ended in frenzy on the glass-topped dining room table amid the lamb bones, potatoes, and half-eaten salad. Plates and glasses broke against walls and windows when she swept the table clean with her arm. Spilled red wine felt sticky against his back. It dripped over the edges of the table onto the chair seats and carpet leaving spots like telltale drops of blood at a murder scene.

Their images mirrored back at them from the windows. The candlelight reflected off the ceiling and created a halo around her head. Dressed only in shadows, she held him inside her, eyes closed, smiling. She slowly rocked back and forth, softly whispering encouragement until she came. The strength of the shudders that rippled through her body left both of them in stunned amazement. The silence louder and more profound than anything either of them could have said.

For Standard, it was like a key fitting into a lock and freeing the other half of his soul. Something different and powerful. Magical, even. There were moments when he felt completely lost in another world, where he was allowed to stay just long enough to appreciate its beauty, but short enough to leave a craving for more.

What started out as a feeling that sex with her was, at best, an act of charity ended much differently. At worst, he was taking advantage of an emotionally vulnerable woman about to do something few could ever imagine. It was all he could do to keep from whispering promises that could never be kept.

Her body showed no signs of disease or of the paleness that haunted her face during their interviews. Instead, she seemed to grow stronger, more confident, as they learned together what felt best. In the end, sitting in the warm water of her bathtub, her back against his chest, the smell of her hair filling his head. Death seemed like the last thing in the world.

Standard left a little before six the next morning. A skiff of snow had fallen during the night. It clung to the dwarf evergreens near the driveway and covered the cracked asphalt on the narrow street in front of Allie's house. Lights were on in the house next door. A car idled in the driveway across the street, blue exhaust pumping out onto the ground, the defroster gradually melting the thin crystals of ice on the windshield.

If he'd learned anything the previous night, it was how much passion had seeped out of his own life and how badly he wanted it back again, if for no other reason than shelter from the storm. Allie Shafer probably wanted no more than to get laid one more time before dying. Still, something about them together terrified him.

During the night Allie had awakened him with a whisper. "Oh God, John, tell me this isn't happening."

At the time, he thought she was talking about her cancer and the decision she'd made to end her life. Suddenly, standing in the driveway, the cold wrapping itself around him, he wasn't so sure. Maybe, just maybe, she was talking about him, about them. Maybe it was the two of them she hadn't bargained for.

He sucked the cold into his lungs. *Leave now*, the voice in his head screamed. *Walk away. Get in the car and drive. Don't look back. Forget the car. Run if you have to*. She was determined to die. They could have more time together, more nights. In the end, though, it wouldn't make any difference. She'd still be gone. *Get out of here. Now!*

He got in the Jeep. After a night out in the cold, the aged battery was barely able to turn over the engine. It caught on the third try. He slipped it into four-wheel drive.

Drive faster. Don't look back.

Still, he waited to back out of the driveway to take one more look at the front door. Would it open? Would she come out and ask him not to go?

Now, damn it. Get the fuck out of here.

He stepped on the gas then slowed to look again at the front door. Drove away again then backed up and waited. Stepped on the gas again, easier this time. The Jeep moved slowly. The voice screamed in his head until he tromped on the gas. The tires whined in the ice.

Within minutes he was sliding through the icy darkness down Burnside into downtown Portland, wondering if he would ever see her again. Wondering if he wanted to. Knowing that he had to.

Chapter 7

Standard spent the morning hanging around Benny's apartment, drinking bourbon-laced coffee and eating dry cereal out of the box.

"What the hell's wrong with you?" Benny said.

When Standard didn't answer, Benny eyed him for a few seconds from across the room. He was sitting in an overstuffed chair, the morning paper looking like a bed sheet in his tiny hands.

"You didn't? Please, tell me you didn't." When Standard didn't answer, Benny wadded up the paper and tossed it on the floor. "What a chump! Now you're probably in love or some fool thing and she's going to . . ."

Standard was out the door before Benny said any more. This was not the time to be lectured by a midget who learned about sex from a trapeze artist. Back in the apartment, he snatched up the phone and dialed. Nothing. Again. More aggravating rings. She didn't even have her recorder on. Attempts to start work on the article about Allie turned into a staring contest with the computer. He called a third time. Still no answer. Finally, he drove to her house. No one was home. After an hour waiting in the car in the driveway, he drove back to the apartment, paced up and down. Dialed her number a few hundred more times and even made one more trip to her house.

Pissed off at himself, Standard decided to get out of the apartment, do something that might take his mind off Allie Shafer and what she was going to do or had already done. He had an early dinner in China Town then a movie at the Fox Tower. It didn't work. He got up twice to go out to the lobby to call yet again. Still no answer.

It was after eleven that night when Helen Badden, Allie's doctor, called. Standard was sitting in the dark, smoking cigarettes. He knew what the call was about before picking up the phone. Still, he listened to the doctor's clinical voice. Allie was dead. She'd been found lying face up on the king-size bed with Miles Davis' "Kind of Blue" on the stereo.

He sat on the tattered sofa, dumbly listening to the doctor describe the scene as if it were a painting she'd seen in an art gallery. What she didn't describe, he could imagine on his own: the glass that contained the milkshake-like mixture of deadly barbiturates sat empty on the nightstand. Next to it, the expensive bottle of champagne Allie had bought weeks before just for the occasion. She'd even showed it to him that first day at her house. Allie was wearing a short, red satin nightgown, cut low across her chest and slit deeply up both sides. She kept it draped over the chair in her bedroom. She never put it on for him because he never gave her the chance. There were candles burning on the oak dresser, the flickering light dancing off the mirror onto the expensive fabric wallpaper. The curtains were open so Allie could see out the picture windows into the secluded backyard, with the giant Douglas firs and oak trees stripped bare by winter winds. Patches of snow that had fallen that morning perched atop soggy clumps of grass in the shaded areas next to the house.

Standard started feeling sick as soon as he hung up the phone. He crawled into the shower, turned the water to hot, and sat on the floor of the small tiled stall, sucking in the damp, steamy air that filled the bathroom.

What had her last moments been like? He wanted to think that she lay there, peaceful and angelic, drifting off to sleep in a billowy haze of barbiturates. The drugs would first take away her anxiety then her life. The shallow gasps of air from weakening lungs were like passengers leaving a sinking ocean liner. One breath followed another until the ship was empty.

But there were other images. Dark, disturbing pictures that made

41

him squeeze his eyes shut and dig fingernails into wrinkled palms. He saw her arms flying up in front of her face in feeble attempts to fight off the inevitable. An over-matched boxer, maybe, cringing against the ropes, waiting for the bell that never comes. Her expression never changing, blank eyes focused somewhere no one would ever know about. Blood caked in a mouth that never closed. How long did she last? Hours? Minutes?

Standard vomited into the drain.

Each day afterward, the dueling images of how Allie Shafer died battled for supremacy, until eight months later when a Baptist minister from northeast Portland showed up to tell Standard that the whole thing could be a lie and that Allie Shafer might still be alive.

Chapter 8

Even before Allie Shafer, Standard had come to expect that anyone who visited his office—slash—apartment brought bad news. Most times, the news didn't start out bad. It just turned out that way. Allie Shafer was special for who she was, not for what she did. At least that's how he came to view things since her death.

So when the Reverend Elijah Folsom arrived unexpectedly on a sunny Tuesday afternoon in late September, Standard's shields automatically went up.

It was a little after two when Folsom's head appeared in the office door. The reverend's massive body was encased in a burgundy, three-piece suit, with horizontal stripes that resembled latitude lines on a globe that had grown hands and feet.

"Afternoon, John," he said after knocking on the door and coming into the cramped office before Standard could get out of his chair. When he smiled, the bright light from the window reflected off a gold incisor that gave off a pixie-like twinkle. Small, wire-rimmed glasses sat low on a nose that spread across a mocha-colored face. "You're a hard man to find," he said in that basso voice that had both scared and inspired a generation of northeast Portland churchgoers.

Standard pushed the chair away from the desk and started to get up. "Reverend Folsom! Elijah!" He was both surprised by the visit and immediately cautious about the reasons behind it.

"Stay right there," Folsom said, "I need a place to plop these tired, old bones. Five flights of stairs and at my age. Just my luck that you'd live in a building with a broken elevator."

"I'm sorry. It was working just a couple of days ago. You should have called first. I would have come over to the church, or we could have met somewhere for lunch or coffee."

"It isn't like I can look you up in the Yellow Pages under freelance reporter, or whatever you're calling yourself these days. As it is, you wouldn't believe the strings I had to pull just to get your address."

Folsom moved heavily across the room toward the chair in front of the desk. Standard reached out. They shook hands, Standard's all but lost in Folsom's.

For the last fifteen years, Elijah Folsom had been the glue that held together Portland's small, but influential, African-American community. His stature, nearly six-and-a-half feet tall and well over three hundred pounds, and booming voice matched the role he played in making sure the city's power structure didn't forget the northeast corner of the city or that it was home to a substantial share of Oregon's minority citizens. Seldom did a Sunday go by that the Reverend Folsom didn't stand at the pulpit of his Baptist church, demanding equal rights for blacks, Asians, and everyone else of color. By the following morning, his stinging words were usually echoing through city hall and rattling the crystal in the mayor's office.

Standard had met Folsom eight years earlier in front of the burned-out shell of his beloved church. The seventy-five-year-old structure was a smoldering pile of ashes, bricks, and broken glass. The only thing standing was the brick steeple, with its charred bell hanging from scorched timbers. A half-dozen of Folsom's most devoted parishioners sadly poked through the rubble while the cinders hissed under a cold November rain. The conventional wisdom was that the church had been the victim of a white racist copying a string of similar fires that had destroyed black churches across the South. It eventually turned out that the blaze had been intentionally set by a black teenager trying to earn street cred with a local gang.

Standard was still working at the newspaper then. For a few days, the church fire was a hell of a story that offered a rare glimpse into

Oregon's suspect attitudes toward minorities. It wasn't a particularly flattering story, especially for the limousine liberals who lived in Portland's numerous white enclaves where they discussed the sad state of race relations in the United States while sipping Willamette Valley pinot.

After a vigorous fundraising campaign that had Folsom popping in at every corporate headquarters in the metropolitan area, the church was quickly rebuilt. A year after the fire, the sound of raucous Sunday morning gospel music once again echoed off the surrounding buildings.

Standard went to the first service in the new church. The polished pews and vaulted ceiling were as close as the builder could get to the original design. Along with the mayor, a couple of city council members, and a handful of local legislators facing re-election, he was one of the few white faces in the congregation. Folsom had been in fine form that day. His indignation over racism and black-on-black crime was muted, but not his praise for those with pockets deep enough to pay for the restoration of his beloved church.

Between what Standard wrote and what Folsom preached, they forged a mutual respect for each other. Folsom was one of the few people to express in writing his disappointment and anger after Standard was fired from the paper. It was a gesture Standard always planned to acknowledge but had yet to write a thank you note or drop by for Sunday services.

"I'm sorry about being so hard to find, Reverend, but now that you're here, it's good to see you."

Folsom settled into the folding chair on the other side of the desk, letting out a grateful sigh of relief to be off his feet. "Elusive, reclusive, and exclusive. That's the way you've always been, John. God made you that way. So, I'd be the last one to complain."

"And nothing has changed," Standard said, sitting back down. "What's it been? A couple of years? You're looking . . . dapper."

45

"Three years in November, and don't be making fun of my suit. Sister Clara made it for me. Lovely woman. I'll be having supper at her house later today, and I'd sorely hate to disappoint her by not wearing it." He brushed some lint off the lapels. "Although, it's not exactly something I would have bought for myself, you understand."

"I wouldn't blame you if you did."

"Nice of you to say so. I'll pass your kind words on to Sister Clara."

They exchanged updates on each other for several minutes until Standard said, "It's not often I get a man of the cloth in my office."

Folsom's massive head rotated to the left then around to the right before dark eyes peered over the top of his small glasses. "Looks like it isn't often you get *anybody* in here with a cloth." He chortled at his own joke. "Nevertheless, this place makes your old office down at the newspaper look like The Ritz."

"Behold the difference between a self-employed freelancer and a slave to a corporate media giant. What is lost in style and income is made up in peace of mind."

"Amen. Amen."

Folsom pulled a starched handkerchief from his breast pocket, ran it around his face a couple of times before refolding it and carefully putting it back into the breast pocket of his suit. The three points posed perfectly against the burgundy material. "You miss working for the newspaper?"

"Only when I look at my bank account. By the way, I never thanked you for the note you sent after I was let go. It was a tough time. Your words helped."

"I meant every word of it. I even wrote a letter to the editor, but they never printed it. When I called to ask why, the publisher said it was a personnel matter or something to that effect. Anyway, I know what it's like to be mistreated by the press. I remember one time when I was in Mobile . . . well, never mind about that now. Besides, I've probably told you that story, anyway."

Standard fired up a cigarette and waited for the preacher to get to the point of his visit. Folsom got the hint.

"You probably already figured this out, but I came for a reason," he said. "Those stories you did after the fire at the church turned around some attitudes in this city, at least for a while. I can't say they stayed that way, but race relations here are better than in most places this size. The thing is, you did a great service to the African-American community, and I'd like to return the favor. You being in the freelance business and all, I figure you could use a chance to make a little money."

"Amen," Standard said, trying to look enthusiastic while secretly praying that Folsom wasn't going to ask for help with the church newsletter.

Folsom fired back an enormous grin and wiggled his butt tighter into the chair, his large hands resting on his stomach. The diamond pinky ring looked lost amid sausage-like fingers. "I also figure I could give you a chance to save your sorry ass."

They both stopped smiling at the same time. As the room got a few degrees cooler, Folsom's face turned a couple of shades darker.

"Let me explain," Folsom said. He cleared his throat.

"Please," Standard said.

"A few months back, you wrote some articles about a Miss Allison Shafer."

It was the first time Standard had heard anyone mention Allie's name in more than five months. He was almost to the point where the night they'd spent together had taken on a dream-like quality. Left alone, he could begin to wonder if it ever really happened. Suddenly, Elijah Folsom had dragged everything back to square one. Once again, bad news had walked in the door, this time wearing a burgundy suit.

"That's the woman who ended her life using that physician-assisted suicide law the voters passed a few years back," Folsom said. "I believe you also did some television interviews—CNN or one of those cable things."

"I remember."

"I don't doubt it. It's not something one could easily forget, I'm sure. I don't support the law, myself, but I can see where some people would find comfort in taking matters into their own hands. Well, it's come to my attention that Miss Allie Shafer may not be dead after all."

Standard didn't move. His eyes stayed locked on a point in space somewhere between the Reverend Folsom and the top of the desk. The room got smaller, the air thicker. Standard had to remember to breathe.

Folsom looked around the room again. "You got anything to drink? A soda would be most appreciated."

Standard got up and walked trance-like into the kitchen. A can of diet pop hid in the refrigerator, behind a head of lettuce that was starting to turn black around the edges. There was a reasonably clean glass in the sink and some ice in the freezer. As the cubes rattle into the glass, Standard stared out the window into the air shaft for a few minutes before walking back to the office on rubbery legs.

"Diet. That's good," Folsom said. "I'm diabetic, you know, or maybe you don't. Anyway, where was I? Oh yes, Allison Shafer. One of my wealthy and influential parishioners had a rather . . . close relationship with Miss Shafer. He was devastated by her death and by its circumstances. I was personally touched by his sorrow. I've known this man for a number of years, so I can attest to the fact that he is not prone to showing his emotions. His reaction to Miss Shafer's death showed me a side of him I hadn't seen. I spent several hours counseling him. We even prayed together, which was also a revelation, at least for him. Going to church is one thing. Praying is another. Anyway, he came to see me after last Sunday's services to tell me that he'd recently acquired some evidence that appears to indicate that Miss Shafer is alive and well."

"Who is this person?"

"I'll get to that in a minute." Folsom chugged half the soda then refilled the glass from the can. "I don't know what this evidence is, but needless to say the man is confused, frustrated, angry, and mighty interested in bringing her back into his personal fold, if you know what I mean."

When his cell phone rang, Standard quickly hit DECLINE. "Keep going, Reverend."

"He feels Miss Shafer's death was a hoax. The problem for you, John, is that his anger is directed at those he feels were involved in this hoax. One of those, of course, is Miss Shafer herself. You would be one of the others."

Folsom let the statement sink in. Standard fought back the urge to defend himself. He needed to know more.

"Why me?"

"You were the chronicler of her last days. It's only natural that you'd be among those he'd like to talk to. The others on the list would be the two doctors who prescribed the drugs that were intended to end her life."

"I was one of the two witnesses to her sanity prior to her death. I signed a form."

"I'm not sure he knows that, but if he does then it would add to his already growing suspicion of your role in all of this."

Folsom finished the soda. He placed the glass and the empty can on the desk. Standard crushed out one cigarette and lit another.

"You're convinced this evidence is legitimate."

"Doesn't make any difference what I think. He thinks it is, and that's all that really matters."

"Something tells me there's more." Standard suddenly realized that he'd been holding his breath again.

"The reason this person came to me last Sunday was to seek counseling and advice," Folsom said. "When he mentioned your name, I was taken by surprise. I assured him of your good character and took it upon myself to volunteer to discuss the issue with you and perhaps work out an arrangement that might serve both your needs. That's why I made the effort to find you and to walk up five flights of stairs."

Folsom sighed deeply, took out the handkerchief again, and ran it across his face.

"I appreciate that."

"My pleasure, but I should tell you that this man is no one to trifle with. I did a little freelancing of my own and described you as someone who wouldn't take kindly to being bamboozled by anyone or participating in any kind of a hoax. That is the truth, as I see it, so it wasn't like I violated God's word or anything. Anyway, I figured that perhaps the two of you could reach a mutually beneficial . . . partnership."

"Partnership? I don't do partnerships."

Folsom held up one of his huge hands. "Now, hold on there and hear me out. Maybe partnership overstates the case. We're not talking a legal arrangement here. What I'm proposing is one less formal in nature. I believe it would involve finding Miss Shafer."

"What if I'm not interested in a partnership to find her?"

Folsom picked up the glass. He sucked a couple ice cubes into his mouth then spit them back in the glass to rattle around like dice. "Then I believe you're going to have a difficult situation on your hands. As I said, this man is wealthy, influential, and angry. My guess is he'll do whatever it takes to find Miss Shafer and punish those who assisted her so-called death, if you know what I mean."

"Assuming the evidence he has is proof she's alive?"

"Absolutely. My point is that proving the validity of that evidence may be just as important to you as it is to him. You catch my drift?"

Standard leaned forward, elbows on the desk, cigarette smoldering in the ashtray. He wanted to get as close to Folsom as possible to make sure he understood what the reverend was suggesting. "In other words, this man thinks that the articles I wrote and the interviews I did about Allie's death were part of the hoax. He thinks Allie, the doctors, and I engaged in some kind of conspiracy to fake her death?" Folsom nodded slowly. "Now this man wants to take out his anger and frustration on the co-conspirators, except Allie, of course."

Folsom produced the handkerchief a third time. He ran it around his face then folded it into a neat square that he held clenched between his hands. "Perceptive as always, John. Although I'm not totally convinced that Miss Shafer is immune from his wrath. My guess is that his feelings provide her with a certain amount of protection. However, his anger can be mighty."

"And I can assume that this man is not prone to idle threats and that my life, such as it is, is in danger?"

Folsom's eyes became slits above his round cheeks. "That would be an excellent assumption, unless, of course, the two of you can work out an arrangement to either find Miss Shafer or prove she's really dead. If she is dead, then my guess is that his wrath would focus on those who sent him this so-called evidence."

"I see. And what would be my motive for joining in this conspiracy?"

Folsom shrugged his huge shoulders. "That's something you're going to have to discuss with him."

All Standard could do was fall back into the chair, amazed by how life could go from bad to worse with so little effort. "It sounds like this man must be quite a challenge to you, from a religious aspect."

"I do what I can," Folsom said. "I don't condone violence, but the struggle between the material and the spiritual has been a long and arduous one. I don't claim to have any greater success in officiating that conflict than any other man of God."

Standard looked at his computer screen. The first few paragraphs of an article for *Sunset* magazine on bed and breakfast inns in Central Oregon taunted him from the monitor. He glanced longingly at the delete button.

"I appreciate your intervening on my behalf, Elijah. For what it's worth, I find it hard to believe she's alive. If there's a hoax here, it's got to be this evidence, whatever it is."

"I believe that's a very distinct possibility and one the two of you should discuss, although I can't admit to having as much knowledge of Miss Shafer's circumstances as you do. Nevertheless, the questions created by the possibility that's she's still among the living is why I suggested that the two of you get together and work out an arrangement to find out the truth. If she is alive, then it's in your interest to find her. If she's not, then you have an equal interest in finding out who's playing this dangerous game."

Standard suddenly got that pinching feeling in his balls again, odd man out in a high-stakes game of high-low poker. "So, who is it, Elijah?"

Folsom paused like someone about to deliver bad news to a loved one. "It's Moses Blue. He owns The Blue Café. The blues club in the Pearl District."

"What's the connection between Blue and Shafer, other than good friends?"

"Miss Shafer was employed by Moses Blue. She was his accountant, among other things."

"Other things? Define other things."

"According to Moses, they were lovers."

Chapter 9

In the weeks after learning of Allie Shafer's death, Standard did little more than sleepwalk from one day to the next. Nights were spent staring at the cracked paint on the ceiling over his bed or drinking beer with Benny. They watched enough old movies to reach the conclusion that Warner Oland made a better Charlie Chan than Peter Toler. The bottom came when he found himself sitting with Benny at eight o'clock on a Saturday night, watching the start of Alien Abduction Week on The Learning Channel.

"Why would aliens travel halfway across the universe to snatch an insurance salesman from Pensacola?" Benny asked.

Standard got up and left.

The days were a succession of walks around town, with stops in corner bars that reeked of stale beer and burnt popcorn. Guidance came from staring into gallon jars of pigs' feet and pickled eggs that sat on bars next to the beer taps. If there was anything to be proud of, it was that he didn't even try to share his story with the bartenders. Looking back on the time with Allie Shafer was like an out-of-body experience. Detached somehow from actual events, he could see himself interviewing her, eventually being seduced by her, making love with her, and, finally, trying desperately to find her before she killed herself. When it was over, he had nothing left but to beat himself up for having failed to stop her.

It was around that time that Reuters called again. An obscure Native American tribe on the Washington state coast had decided to revive its ancient whale-hunting tradition despite the protests of Greenpeace and other save-the-whale groups. Apparently, the tribe had traced its economic and health problems to the lack of blubber in its members' diet. Standard reluctantly took the assignment for no other reason than a change of scenery. He spent several days standing on a rain-soaked jetty, waiting for the tribe to kill a small female gray whale and drag it up on the beach. News helicopters hovered overhead so the entire world could get a bird's eye view of the kill that involved a token harpoon tossed from a wooden canoe before the speed boats moved in to mercifully shoot the beast in the brain with a high-powered rifle. In the end, it turned out to be a tragic parody of an ancient tradition.

The only consolation for Standard was a paycheck and a chance to get his mind off Allie Shafer.

Standard headed back to Portland, saddened by the grotesque spectacle but relieved that his life wasn't so desperate that it required paddling around the ocean poking sharp sticks into dumb animals.

Grady, the photographer, called the day after Standard returned home to say Reuters liked the whaling stories and was ready to offer him a job in San Francisco.

"It'll be fookin' great working together again," Grady said. "Things are heating' up everywhere. The Middle East. Africa. Ukraine."

If ever there was a time to toss it in and head off to the jungles or the deserts with a crazed Irish news photographer that was it. Still, Standard said no. He would have said the same thing to a limo full of Victoria's Secret models. It would have meant doing something other than feeling sorry for himself.

"Tell them thanks for thinking of me, but I like my current boss. If they ever need a stringer again have them call me."

"You're making a big mistake," Grady said, "but you got to do what you got to do. I'm sure we'll hook up again someday. Good luck."

Bored with the city, Standard had taken long drives to the coast or along the endless miles of two-lane highways between distant towns in Eastern Oregon. The bars were the same, only the music different.

Garth Brooks instead of Dave Matthews. If he slept at all on those trips, it was an hour or so in the back seat parked in a roadside rest area or campground. Tired of the bars, he went to the movies, mostly doleful films with characters who lives were worse than his.

Before long, Standard became convinced that Allie Shafer's death was symbolic of what life had become. All he wanted was to earn a few bucks selling a compelling story. What he got was some money and a deep, empty feeling inside. Eventually, he began to hate the memory of that night together as much as everything else he saw, touched, heard, tasted, and smelled.

In late spring, he started to snap out of it. She was gone, her ashes spread over the Pacific Ocean from a small plane piloted by a funeral director who specialized in dumping people's remains out the window of his two-seater as it glided over wind-swept whitecaps. At least that's what her doctor said. Determined and driven by the need to generate some sort of income, Standard eventually worked up the energy to write the article that Allie had wanted written.

There were long, painful sessions staring into the blank, unforgiving face of the computer. The words came hard, but they came. Most of it in late-night cathartic sessions at the keyboard, with emotions made raw with the help of scotch or wine.

The finished article appeared in *Inside Oregon* in early June. Publisher Eldon Mock immediately released it to the Associated Press. For the next three days, Standard did endless interviews with local radio and television stations. The two daily newspapers in Portland, both AP clients, refused to pick up the wire service story because of their long-standing prohibition against publishing anything that appeared in *Inside Oregon*. The national media, however, had no such ban. The story hit right in the middle of an effort by conservative Republicans in Congress to enact a national ban on physician-assisted suicide. The article generated a flood of telephone calls from producers for the network morning shows, as well as MSNBC, CNN, and Fox. Standard did each interview as calmly as possible, including the sensationalized versions aired by the more generous television tabloids. He accepted requests for articles from several newspapers and magazines asking how the experience with Allie Shafer had shaped his own views on physician-assisted suicide.

The frenzy was over in less than a week. The story of Allie Shafer's cancer and the decision to take her own life, rather than endure the indignities of uncertain cures, had been fed to a hungry public and forgotten as quickly as a Chinese dinner. In the end, the income generated by the death of Allie Shafer lay somewhere in the neighborhood of twenty thousand dollars, plus an expense-paid trip to New York City. Standard had little choice but to accept the money. Still, depositing the checks left behind a feeling that he was betraying her memory. He rationalized that it was part of their agreement. Nevertheless, the whole thing felt sleazy and tawdry.

By mid-June, Standard was back in the business of writing freelance magazine articles, newsletters for small school districts, and opinion pieces that would be published under the name of an executive for some beleaguered corporation caught doing something that was more of a public relations problem than a legal one. After all, down-and-out freelance writers were cheaper than double-breasted lawyers who moved more slowly the higher their hourly rate.

Slowly, Allie Shafer had gone the way of all those who die and leave behind friends, families, and one-night stands.

By early August, he'd stopped seeing her on the other side of the street, no longer walked faster to catch up with some woman who walked the way Allie did or had the same hair color or wore the same perfume. She gradually slipped into a dark corner of his memory, only creeping out after too many drinks or too little sleep to wreak havoc inside his head. She no longer wandered around in his dreams, banging on locked doors, demanding to be let back in so soon after willingly and capably downing the drugs that the law allowed her to take.

Slowly, like a log being batted around in the surf, he worked back to the safety of the dry-sand beach that was Valerie Michaels.

Now, thanks to Elijah Folsom, not only had the once-vanquished memories of Allie Shafer returned, but they came joined at the hip with a pissed off gangster.

Chapter 10

Elijah Folsom was gone. It was just Standard at the desk, the mice in the walls, and the spiders around the light fixtures.

He thought about calling Valerie. Maybe hearing a friendly female voice would help. He picked up the phone then put it down knowing he would only get her voice mail. He tried Benny instead. No answer. He left a message on the recorder to call back. That was pretty much the entire list of friends to call.

Frustrated, Standard turned back to the computer and started searching his electronic files for the articles about Allie. A half hour later and he had nothing. All he could figure was that he'd deleted them in a subconscious effort to purge even her electronic legacy.

Angry, Standard pushed open the window to let in the afternoon breeze. A late September heat wave was making up for what had been a no-show summer. All he could think of was what if Allie really was alive, then that first meeting with her took on an entirely different light. The careful choice of words and the restrained emotions had been nothing more than an elaborate act. The absence of makeup an attempt to create the gaunt look of a cancer victim.

"No way," Standard muttered. She was an accountant from Montana, for Christ's sake, not an actor. If a hoax was being played on Moses Blue, it had to be by someone other than Allie Shafer.

Another search of the computer, in a vain attempt to find the electronic folder that contained the stories about her, produced the same result. Benny called just as Standard was about to give up on the computer files and start rummaging through the stack of paper file folders scattered across the apartment.

Instead of hello, Benny asked "You ever read any books by George Chesbro?"

Standard ignored the question. "I've got a problem."

"Does this problem have a name or are you behind in the rent again?" A beep in the background announced the electronic arrival of another e-mail coming into one of Benny's computers.

"Moses Blue."

Benny sighed into the phone. "That's not a problem. Global warming is a problem. You're in shit city. Tell me more."

"Not right now. Would you mind pulling some information together on Blue? I'll be down later to tell you the rest."

Standard went back to looking for the Allie Shafer stories and the notes from the interviews with her. He finally found both, plus a cassette tape buried under a pile of folders. He recognized the cassette immediately. It was the day on the deck under the cold winter sun.

The file with the sketchy notes smelled musty, each word a memory. The indelible way she described her emotions leading up to her decision to commit suicide. Maybe it was the calm way she went about the business of taking her own life. She was, after all, an accountant: dispassionate and obsessed with details. Looking back on that day, there was a certain element of adding up the debits and credits and deciding to file the ultimate bankruptcy.

Still, there was nothing dispassionate about their night together. Obsessive, maybe, but not dispassionate.

At one point while interviewing her, Standard had put away the pen and notebook and let the tape recorder take over. He just listened. She seemed to get lost in the need to justify her actions, to convince herself that her fate was sealed once she learned of her cancer. Maybe she was right, and she did see what was coming, that past events were harbingers of future ones.

What Allie Shafer had said about dealing with her own death

could've been nothing more than bullshit. If it was, then all she had wanted from Standard was a way of legitimizing her disappearance.

Standard ran his hands through his hair and stared up at the ceiling. He didn't believe it. She had to be dead. But the doubt was there, squirming around, refusing to go away. If Allie was dead, then he was smart. If she wasn't, he was a fool. Simple as that.

He found the tape recorder in the bottom drawer of the desk, pulled it out, set it on the blotter, and inserted the cassette. After staring at it for a few minutes, he turned it on, grimacing at the sound of his own voice, cringing at the sound of hers.

Standard: "Let me play devil's advocate for a minute. There are those who believe that life is the gift of God and only God can take it away."

Shafer: "That would be the Thomas Aquinas school of thought, which goes back to the Thirteenth Century. Did you ever read the essays by de Montaigne? He came later, the Sixteenth Century, I think. Anyway, he was the first to argue that suicide is a matter of personal choice and rational, in some cases."

Standard: "You've done your homework."

Shafer: "Of course I have. I don't discount the seriousness of this issue, both for me and for society in general. Euthanasia, which is what we're really talking about here, is Greek for 'good death.' I would be the first to acknowledge that there are those who believe that no death is good unless dictated by God. I believe in God, but I also believe that God endowed us with the intelligence to make our own decisions. I don't believe it's a sin to make use of what God has given us."

Standard: "You obviously don't buy into the argument that, by suffering yourself, you're making a conscious decision to associate yourself with the sufferings of Christ."

Shafer: "I am not anyone's savior. I see no redemption in suffering."

Standard: "There are alternatives, you know? Hospice. Pain control."

Shafer: "I have no family, and, because of my condition, I couldn't be denied coverage under the health plan that required the physical that discovered my condition in the first place, but what was the point? It wasn't like they were going to save my life. I could pay for hospice care until my money ran out, but I choose not to. In Oregon, I have that right. If I lived in some other state, then I'd have to make other choices. Pain control means painkillers. I just can't bring myself to accept a life of constant drug use."

Standard: "Radiation? Chemo? Those aren't options either?"

Shafer: "Of course they are. I could go through that, but I have an advanced case of cancer. They found this too late, so my options are limited."

Standard: "It appears you have your mind made up."

Shafer: "Are you still playing devil's advocate?"

Standard: "What do you make of the argument that allowing physician-assisted suicide sends us down the slippery slope of deciding who lives and who dies?"

Shafer: "You mean the idea that death squads of government bureaucrats are going to roam the halls of nursing homes and mental institutions, picking out those who get to live and those who get to die? Right-wing nonsense, scare tactics used by religious groups desperate to stop people from dying in a manner of their own choosing. It's nothing more than that. This measure passed because the baby-boomer generation is growing older and has lived in a society in which they were free to choose how they want to live their lives. It's only logical that the same generation would want to have the same freedom of choice in the way they want to end their lives. It doesn't mean everyone is going to use it. In fact, I believe there are very few people like me. I think the point is that people want to know the option is there in the event circumstances require its use."

Standard: "You don't think much of those who oppose physician-assisted suicide, do you?"

Shafer: "I don't think much of hypocrites. Most of those who oppose physician-assisted suicide support the death penalty. They can't have it both ways. Life is either a sacred gift or it isn't. There was this one opponent of physician-assisted suicide who was quoted in the paper saying, 'Killing sick people is bad medicine.' How glib! How can anyone be taken seriously when they turn something like this into a bumper sticker slogan? The law works. None of the bad things that opponents predicted ever came true."

Standard: "Maybe suicide isn't the right word for this."

Shafer: "There are those who prefer the term self-deliverance. Either way, it doesn't matter. I know life is precious, and we should all fight to keep it, but I know where this is going to lead. I simply want to die with my dignity intact."

Listening to her disembodied voice on the recorder made Standard more angry and humiliated. She'd been so sincere as he fed her one line after another, like softballs to Derek Jeter. Inside her head, she must have been laughing. No. He refused to believe it.

Standard threw the recorder against the wall. It burst into a half dozen pieces, the tape coming apart to spill across the floor like the intestines of a small animal. Something didn't add up. She had a house, a career, money, and her entire life in front of her. So why fake her death? Why get him involved? What happened to her money? She went through a lot of effort to find him, to convince him of the advantages of getting the front row seat on the heart-wrenching story. It didn't make sense.

There was only one answer: Moses Blue's proof must be phony.

Chapter 11

At four o'clock, Standard decided to walk downtown to meet Valerie Michaels when she got off work.

Her office was in Old Town, in the northwest corner of the city. The fifteen-block walk would give him time to think before sharing his revelations with her on the way back. It wouldn't be the first time. Talking with Valerie always made things clearer, even if it involved telling her something that would make most other women uncomfortable—or gone.

The South Park Blocks were filled with a mix of students from Portland State University and leather-and-stud street kids. Two cops strolled under the late afternoon sun rousting the homeless dozing on park benches. The leaves on the elm trees looked brittle and tired of the season. Mount St. Helens, its peak turned into a graceful dome by the volcanic eruption in 1980, glittered white to the north. In the east, the gray-and-white spire of Mt. Hood stood bright against the blue sky.

Standard headed down SW Ninth, past the Portland Art Museum and the wine bar at South Park. At SW Yamhill, he cut over to SW Park and into Nordstrom's, cruising the perfume counter for a few minutes before buying a small bottle of Valerie's favorite fragrance. The clerk at the counter asked if the gift was for a special occasion. She was a young brunette with a lot of makeup. When he said no, she smiled.

"You must be one of the good guys."

"Yeah," he muttered. "I must be."

At the Starbucks, on Broadway, he got a cup of black coffee to go, drinking it while strolling down SW Morrison past Pioneer Courthouse

Square. At the east end of the street was the Willamette River, which ran north and south through the city, dividing it roughly in half. He traded the coffee for a beer at a bar on the MAX line before heading up SW First Avenue, under the Burnside Bridge, and into Old Town. He sat on the bench in front of the restored Blagen Building. MAX trains rumbled by at irregular intervals. Street people in rags and business types in pinstripes paraded by. Ten minutes later, Valerie Michaels came out the double glass doors, looking like someone just released from prison.

When Standard met her, Valerie was working as an exotic dancer in a tittie bar on the east side of the city. He had just moved into an apartment on the other side of the airshaft from hers. She seldom pulled her drapes, so several nights a week, he'd sit in the dark smoking cigarettes and drinking cheap scotch while watching her rehearse in front of her mirror. She'd practice a new act, oblivious to his benign, half-lidded stare from across the way. As a result, he'd seen her naked no less than two dozen times before ever screwing up the courage to introduce himself. Once he did, he found someone experienced enough with life and men not to expect too much from either. They seemed a perfect match.

Standard worked hard to distance himself from what she did for a living and what they did together. It wasn't easy. The more comfortable they became with one another, the more curious Standard became about her life as a dancer. The curiosity lasted until one night when he went to the bar where she worked.

He stayed back in the shadows, hidden behind the lights, while she stripped on a raised circular stage, swinging around a brass pole and spreading her legs for tips. When she disappeared into a mirrored alcove for a lap dance with a guy who looked like he couldn't find a woman in a dress shop, Standard left and went home. He never told her he'd been there.

They lived together for a few months, and he helped her find the receptionist job. It was tough convincing her that she needed to escape the nightclub and start earning about a fourth of what she did taking off her clothes, but she finally relented. After agreeing that their relationship would survive longer living apart, she'd moved into a place of her own. It was an agreeable parting. They swapped cooking dinner for each other two nights a week and staying over if the spirit moved them.

Despite seeing every type of man imaginable, mostly from a narrow, harsh-lit dance floor, it never showed on her face, at least not so anyone could tell. She had every reason to be jaded and cynical but was outwardly unaffected. Standard, of course, knew better from the long conversations while lying in bed, trading dark, painful secrets.

Except one. Standard had never told her about Allie Shafer.

Valerie came along at a time when Standard needed things that were dependable and didn't require a lot of effort. Knowing she had a special place in Standard's life was more than enough to sustain her. In return, she had taught him that relationships were like water, eventually they found their own level, which more often than not is somewhere between triumph and tragedy.

"Hey, sailor," she said after seeing him sitting on the bench framed against a passing MAX train.

"Beware of geeks bearing gifts." He handed her the perfume.

That earned a kiss on the cheek as they walked arm-in-arm back along SW First toward downtown.

"Any special reason for the gift?" she said as she opened the perfume and took the top off to smell. They were under the Burnside Bridge near Skidmore Plaza.

"The woman at the perfume counter asked me the same thing. I just wanted to do something to make me feel better about myself."

"Something tells me there's a story here. Either you've done something very good or very bad. Either way, I love it. Thank you."

Valerie was twenty-eight. She'd let the blonde hair she had when they met go back to its natural color, a tawny brown. It hung down her back and glistened in the sun reflecting off the glass store fronts along the street. When they made love, she let it hang down like a soft curtain Standard could hide behind. There were times when it was the only place he felt truly safe.

Standard suggested a walk along the river at Tom McCall Park.

"No way," Valerie said. "I need a drink."

They headed instead up SW Washington, checking out store windows and fantasizing in front of travel agencies, before going into Pazzo's at the Vintage Plaza Hotel on Broadway. The bar was a little below street level. They got a small table in the corner, watching skirt hems and pants legs walk by outside. He drank Corona, while easing into a description of his day, including the visit with Elijah Folsom. Valerie, the perfect listener, hung on every word, especially the part about Allie Shafer.

"In the time we've known each other, you've told me everything there is to know about you," she said. "Except about her."

"I figured you'd notice."

"I figured you'd eventually tell me."

"She came to see me during one of the times we weren't together. I think it was when you went on one of those vacations of yours with some girls from that club where you used to work."

"The trip to Cabo?"

"That sounds right. You know me well enough to guess the rest."

"You mean how you like having your heart slapped around like a hockey puck?"

"By women who are no good for me."

"That would be about right." She sipped her drink, which was something called a Lemon Drop. "Did she remind you of your former life? The one with the trophy wife, the fancy house, and the season tickets to the Trail Blazers?"

"You mean the life before my best friends were a midget and an ex-stripper?"

She laughed. "That's the one."

Standard drained the Corona. "Why do you put up with me?

"Because I love you. Now order me another drink."

"How about dinner? There's some breathing room left on my credit card."

Valerie nodded eagerly. She loved eating out. Standard motioned to the waitress for two menus. He ordered a steak, rare. Valerie went for the seafood fettuccine and a bottle of Oregon chardonnay.

"I wanted to tell you about Allie Shafer," he said, finding himself more interested in the wine than the steak. "In fact, I could've used your help. You're much wiser about these things than I am. It was just that it took me a long time to find the words."

"I also read palms, tea leaves, and chicken entrails. It was part of an old act that had this kind of voodoo thing going." She stopped when he held up a hand, signaling his dislike of stories about her days as a dancer. "So what do you do now?"

"Beats me. If she's alive, and I doubt she is, this so-called evidence is with some guy I don't even want to meet."

"You'll meet him." Her face turned serious. Her plate of pasta forgotten for the time being.

"What makes you so sure?"

"You'll do it because that's what you do. You'll do whatever it takes to find out the truth. It's not because of your feelings for her, although that's probably part of it. You'd play this out if she were some old lady with dentures and a walker. It's just the way you are."

Standard was less sure about his motives but didn't feel like arguing. "The wild card is Moses Blue. I don't know much about him other than street talk about his ties to organized crime. I asked Benny to check him out, but my guess is that I'm not going to like what I find."

"Didn't this Reverend Folsom run interference for you?"

"If that's all I got, wish me luck. Moses Blue may go to church on Sunday, but it's what he does the rest of the week that concerns me."

Standard paid the bill and they walked to the MAX stop across the street from Nordstrom's.

"How about you come home with me and stay over?" she said, hooking her arm inside of his. "I'll get out one of my old costumes, maybe the candy striper or the cowgirl."

"You amaze me. After what I just told you about Allie Shafer, most women would have dumped a drink down my pants."

"Now you know why you'd be a fool to let me get away. So, are you coming home with me?"

He knew that turning down the offer would not hurt her feelings. "Tempting, but how about a rain check? I want to see what Benny came up with on Moses Blue."

"Then what?"

"Who knows?" The train arrived. "I'm going to play this one by ear. All I know right now is that I'm not going to like this, no matter how it turns out."

She kissed him on the cheek. "Do I have a reason to be concerned about you and this Moses guy?"

"Let's hope not."

The MAX train was covered with advertising for the nightly news show on one of the local television stations. The doors opened, parting the huge faces of two blow-dried anchormen who were Portland's answer to Siegfried and Roy. Valerie got on board, the door closed behind her, and the two faces reunited. As the train hissed away, she waved out the window at him. Standard walked home thinking life was not as bad as he sometimes made it out to be, which was always a sign to start being careful.

Chapter 12

When Standard knocked on Benny's door, the answer was a series of muffled bangs. It sounded like something that involved tools, which made him immediately suspicious. Benny may have the title of landlord, but he did very little in the way of real work other than write rent receipts. Anything else involved calling a handyman or threatening the complaining tenant with eviction.

Leery, Standard turned the knob and pushed. The door moved a few inches before the banging started again, this time hard enough to crack the thin veneer of the door's center panel. He shoved again and let the door swing open. The two men standing in the living room looked like a couple of Benny's offbeat friends who earned a living imitating the cast of *Fargo* at office parties.

"Who are you and where's Benny?"

One of them emitted a laugh that came out as a series of snorts. He was short, with long greasy hair and a triangular-shaped face. His close-set eyes, flat nose, full lips, and big ears reminded Standard of Mr. Potato Head.

"My name's Rico," he said in a high-pitched, geisha-like voice. Just the sound of it pissed Standard off. "This is my associate, Carp." He pointed to the man standing slightly behind him. He was twice Rico's size. A refrigerator with arms, legs, and a shaved head. His left eyebrow was pierced with a gold ring large enough to hold a napkin. He was dressed all in white—suit coat and pants, turtle neck, socks, and shoes.

"You Standard?" Carp said.

"Me Standard. You Jane?"

Rico let out a few more snorts then blew his nose with a gray-white handkerchief pulled from the breast pocket of his plaid, green sport coat. Standard decided that Rico was oily enough to have entered the apartment without opening the door. Carp could have destroyed it with a forearm.

When the banging started again, Rico snorted out a few more laughs. Carp emitted a half-lidded stare that came out of a dark face with a hawk-like nose, his jaw muscles flexing like a cat under a sheet.

Standard swung the door shut and looked behind it. Benny was hanging on a coat hook by the back of his belt. His fat little arms flayed helplessly in the air, while he continued to kick the door with the heels of his shoes. A gym sock was crammed into his mouth, the toe end hanging out like a long, dirty-white tongue. Benny's square face had turned dark purple. His angry demands for help reduced to little more than a muffled jumble of obscenities. Standard pulled out the sock then immediately regretted it.

"Get me down from here, and we'll kick the shit out of these two assholes," Benny yelled.

Benny's use of the word "we" made Standard think again about unhooking the little man from the door. Taking on two men, one the size of a Volkswagen, with a retired circus midget for a partner didn't make a lot of sense.

Not that Benny wasn't formidable in a fight. One night in a bar downtown, a drunken businessman began making jokes about Benny's size. Benny laughed off the first two. After the fourth joke, Benny hit the man so hard in the balls that even the women grimaced and crossed their legs in sympathy. But this was different.

"What's this all about?" Standard said.

"Goddamn it, Standard. Get me down from here." The unmuffled Benny was yelling even louder, his feet banging more furiously against the door.

Standard ignored him and concentrated on Carp. The big man's face was blank, his eyes small and cruel with deep wrinkles at the corners. A tough guy in an immaculate white suit. This was going to end badly. Maybe not here and now, but one day.

"Our boss would like to see you," Rico said. He hiked up his pants. They were the polyester, beltless kind favored by professional golfers in the 1960s. "Now."

"And your boss is who?"

"Moses Blue."

No surprise there, Standard thought. That Blue felt the need to send two goons and humiliate Benny in the process, however, was. Thanks to Elijah Folsom, a meeting was inevitable. Why not just call?

"Standard!" Benny was yelling again. His face flushed, arms and legs flailing.

"Your little friend didn't want to cooperate," Carp said, his voice a deep, dumb monotone.

"Yeah," Rico said. "When he started being a pain in the ass, we decided to hang around and wait for you. Hang around? Get it?" He started laughing again and poked Carp in the ribs.

Carp ignored him and said, "We need to go now."

Benny kept yelling and kicking the door. "Get me down from here, damn it."

"Just a second, Benny," Standard said.

Despite Benny's determination to gain some measure of revenge against his tormentors or die trying, it was best to keep him hanging from the door for a while longer even though Standard knew it was not going to go over well. Benny was small in stature, but not in pride. The longer he hung there like a cured ham, the crazier he'd become.

"What is he, some kind of dwarf or something?" Rico said.

"I'm a midget, you moron. Dwarfs are different," Benny yelled back. His eyes had gone dark. Spit flew in Rico's direction, but hit Standard in the face. Reluctantly, he lifted Benny off the door then set him on the floor, but kept a firm grip on the back of his shirt.

71

"There's no reason for this to get out of hand," Standard said to Rico, but with one eye on Carp. "I'll be happy to go with you. I was planning to call your boss anyway. This just makes things easier, but you need to wait outside until I get Benny calmed down. What do you say?"

Rico and Carp looked at each other. Carp gave an almost imperceptible nod of his huge head.

"Okay," Rico said, "but be outside in ten minutes, or we'll come back to get you. You wouldn't want that and neither would your little friend."

The threat made Standard wonder how tough Rico would be without the brooding Carp at his side.

A growl came out of Benny's mouth as he struggled like an angry pit bull against Standard's grip. Rico growled back, snorting out another laugh, walked past the two of them, and out the door into the hall. Carp didn't move. He glared at Standard, flexing his jaw muscles by grinding his back teeth. "Don't be stupid or I'll fuck you up."

They locked eyes for another second before Carp followed Rico out the door.

With Carp and Rico gone, Standard let go of Benny's shirt and closed the door. "I'm sorry about this, Benny."

Benny sputtered for a few more minutes. The purple drained slowly from his face, and his voice returned to normal. "Sons of bitches. Tell them I don't care where they work or who they work for. I'm not going to forget this. I have friends in this town."

Standard got a beer from the refrigerator, twisted off the cap, and handed it to Benny. "Drink this and calm down. We can talk about this later. Right now, I need the short version of what you learned about Moses Blue. I don't want to walk in there without knowing something about this guy."

Benny grabbed the beer and stomped off toward his office in the back of the apartment, shouting obscenities and vowing revenge against "those fucking morons." Standard followed him down the hall. Benny hopped into his chair, his short legs dangling over the edge, his tiny feet eighteen inches off the floor. Grabbing a rail that ran along the front edge of the long, curved desk, he pulled himself up in front of one of the screens.

While Benny ramped up his computers, Standard rattled off a fast description of Elijah Folsom's visit and Moses Blue's belief that Allie Shafer was still alive. Benny gave a sympathetic look, but stopped short of saying anything. There was nothing to say. Benny was not one to make an issue of it. Besides, he was still too pissed to care about Standard, Allie, or anyone else.

"I went back and read the article I did for *Inside Oregon*, re-read the notes I took during my interview with her, and listened to a tape recording of one of my conversations with her. She was too convincing. If Moses Blue is right, and this is a hoax, then Allie Shafer missed her calling. She should be on Broadway."

"And what does that make you?"

"The dumbest son of a bitch known to man."

"Let's hope not." Benny pulled his way down the desk a few feet to where the printer was spitting out a sheet of paper. "Here's what I got on Moses Blue. His real name is Aaron Thibeaux Hutchins. Graduated from Jefferson High School twenty years ago and got a scholarship to UC Berkeley, graduated with honors, and went to law school at Georgetown. Graduated from there but never took the bar exam. He came back to Portland and opened a soul food restaurant in Northeast. The place was a hit with the limousine liberal crowd until they found something different. Still, he made money that, along with a hefty bank loan, went into renovating a building in the Pearl District that eventually became The Blue Cafe. His title is president and CEO of Native Tongue Enterprises, which is the holding company for The Blue Cafe, the soul food place, and a half-dozen other bars and restaurants in Seattle, Spokane, and here in Portland."

"Did you pull all that off the Internet?"

"Some of it, but most came from the Portland Black Chamber of Commerce newsletter. Four years ago, Blue was the chamber's businessman of the year."

"Native Tongue Enterprises. That's where Allie worked."

"So she was more than just his accountant?" Benny said.

When Standard nodded, Benny shook his head and turned his attention back to the print out. "Blue has been linked to everything from murder to importing endangered parrots from the rain forest. The police question him every time a parking meter expires, but so far he hasn't been arrested or indicted for anything more serious than serving liquor to a minor. The Blue Cafe is a favorite hangout for some members of the Trail Blazers, which probably gives him a certain amount of immunity."

"Great."

"It gets better." Benny handed Standard the sheet of paper. "Now it looks like you get to go meet him."

Chapter 13

The white leather interior of the copper-colored Cadillac smelled of cheap after-shave with a slight tinge of kerosene. A silver skull and cross bones dangled from the rear view mirror on a thick choke chain. Music from a heavy metal radio station pumped out of the speakers in the deck behind Standard's head. Empty candy bar wrappers and soda cans littered the floor of the back seat.

Rico fidgeted in the passenger side of the front seat. Carp used only his index finger to steer the big car up SW Clay. Rico popped a Tic Tac in his mouth then shook the plastic box in his hand like a baby's rattle until Carp snatched it out of his hand and tossed it out the window into the side of a passing bus. Rico stared at his empty hand as if Carp had just performed a magic trick.

At SW 10th, they turned right and headed north. A dozen blocks later, they crossed West Burnside into the Pearl District. The eclectic area of Northwest was home to trendy cafes, high-priced condos, and art galleries. No one spoke until Carp wheeled the Caddy into a no parking zone a half block off NW Hoyt.

"In there," Rico said, pointing to a black lacquer door set in the middle of fifty feet of red brick wall. Next to the door, in neon script, the words: "The Blue Cafe."

Standard followed Carp inside, Rico bringing up the rear. The interior was a rarity for Portland—a place to have a quiet drink and intimate talk, free of echoes or rattle of dishes found in most local places. The Blue Café had black enamel tables with leather barrel-backed chairs; worn leather couches set around glass-topped tables; a low bar with chairs instead of stools; dark walls adorned with offbeat art illuminated by track lighting in the ceiling. The jazz coming from speakers hidden in the walls was just loud enough to appreciate without interfering with conversation. The black paint on the walls and ceiling gave the place a comfortable, intimate feel that made it seem smaller than it was.

The sparse midweek crowd drank wine or beer and munched on finger food. A set of drums, some speakers, and a couple of microphone stands occupied the small bandstand in the corner. A poster-size sign on an easel read:

Jazz

Saturday Nights

8 p.m. to Midnight

$10 cover

Carp led the way through the tables, toward the bar in the back. The area behind a glass partition resembled a sunken living room, with a leather couch a cut above the ones near the bandstand and the front door. The man sitting on one of the couches looked like he'd just finished a round of golf on a Saturday morning. He was in his early forties, with a square jaw, a neatly trimmed goatee, and a shaved head that reflected the glow of the dim lights like a polished mahogany tabletop. A burgundy colored polo shirt with a Bacardi logo fit perfectly on a trim torso. Dark glasses and black pants completed the carefully groomed look of a man totally at ease with himself and his place in the world.

"Mr. Standard," he said, standing up. "I'm Moses Blue. Welcome to The Blue Café." They shook hands. Blue's grip was weaker than Standard expected, like a rubber glove filled with half cooked macaroni. "Thanks for agreeing to meet with me. Please sit down." He motioned to a leather chair across from the couch and asked Standard what he'd like to drink.

"Some kind of diet cola is fine," Standard said. Blue nodded to Rico, who scurried off to the bar. Carp remained, tense and statue-like, a few feet away. "Do you mind if I call you Moses? Mr. Blue reminds me of that old song by The Fleetwoods. I always hated that song."

Blue smiled. "Of course." He took off the dark glasses to reveal a left eye that resembled a flawed marble. There was no pupil, just a blank surface the color of coffee with cream. It was hard not to stare at it.

Rico showed up with a diet cola. He set it on a brass coaster engraved with the initials MB.

"We have a mutual acquaintance who speaks very highly of you," Blue said. He was articulate, his speech smooth. Standard would've taken bets that the word "motherfucker" was not going to be part of the conversation and that he didn't refer to women as "bitches." Double or nothing that Blue didn't listen to much rap music.

"Reverend Folsom is a great man," Standard said. "I have a tremendous amount of respect for him." Blue answered by raising his glass of what looked like brandy in a silent toast to their mutual respect for Elijah Folsom. "He made it very clear to me that you and I needed to talk. I assume he told you the same thing."

"Yes he did. We talked on Sunday. He offered to find you and explain the . . . situation."

"If that was the case, then there was no reason to send Yogi and Boo Boo over to get me or to harass my friends." When Blue looked confused, Standard gave a brief rundown of what happened at Benny's apartment. Halfway into the story, Blue turned to look at Rico and Carp standing together just out of earshot. Carp had donned a pair of wrap-around dark glasses that added to his ex-con imitation, which, Standard had decided, probably wasn't an imitation at all. "All you had to do was call me. If you hadn't, I would have called you."

Blue mulled that over while swirling his brandy. "You're right. I apologize. Sometimes when we get so used to doing things a certain way, we don't consider alternatives, even ones that are easier and more obvious."

"I'll convey your apology to my friend," Standard said. They clinked glasses to seal the deal. "It seems that we also have another acquaintance, Allie Shafer, which is why we need to talk."

Blue's face went dark for a moment, then recovered. "Thank you for getting right to the point. I don't know how much Reverend Folsom told you, but my guess is that it was enough to make you understand why learning that she's still alive was upsetting, to say the least."

To both of us, Standard thought. "You mean that she *may* be alive."

"I'll accept that for the time being, but right now I'd like to hear your side of the story."

Standard took it for granted that Blue had read his stories about Allie's death. "She told me she was your accountant, but she said nothing about the personal relationship between the two of you. I learned about that from Reverend Folsom. In fact, Allie was very insistent that I not mention where she worked in any of the stories I wrote about her death or any interview I did. If you read those stories or saw those interviews, then you know I honored that request. She mentioned nothing about her personal life other than to say she was single and had no family."

"I did read the articles and I appreciate that you kept your promise to her," Blue said. "That, however is secondary. The real issue is that I have a great personal and professional reason for finding her."

Standard glanced over Blue's shoulder at the bar. A man, wearing a rust-colored polyester leisure suit over a black silk shirt, stood holding two buckets of ice and looking like he didn't know what to do with them. Glasses with thick, chrome frames covered tired eyes buried in a dark, brown face. A beret clung precariously to bushy, salt-and-pepper hair. Standard guessed his age at anywhere between sixty and eighty years. The bartender, a young blonde woman wearing a white shirt and black vest, took the buckets and poured the ice into the sink. Finished, the old man glanced up, caught Standard's eye for a moment, then disappeared into a back room. Standard turned his attention back to Blue.

"You're convinced, then, she's still alive?" he said.

Blue shrugged. "It's beginning to appear that way."

"Folsom said you have some evidence."

Blue picked up a manila envelope that had been sitting on the table and handed it to Standard. While opening it, Standard glanced at Rico and Carp still hovering nearby. Rico chatted up one of the waitresses, a black girl in a short skirt and the same white shirt and vest as the bartender. She was admiring Rico's cheap, green plaid sport coat. Carp stood nearby looking like a wooden Indian that had lost his cigar store.

Standard opened the envelope's metal clasp. Inside was an eight-by-ten, color photo of a half-dozen people sitting at a bar. They had drinks in their hands or on the counter in front of them. Five of them were men in T-shirts or tank tops, talking to each other, not paying attention to the camera. The only woman in the photo was in the middle of the group. She wore sunglasses and a large straw hat. Her tan shoulders made the spaghetti straps of her top look a brilliant white. The same was true of her tan face and white teeth, teeth with a small alluring gap in the middle that added to, rather than detracted from, her beauty.

Standard's stomach tightened.

"Recognize her?" Blue said.

Even with the hat and glasses, there was little doubt that it was Allie Shafer. Standard searched the photo for some clue as to where and when it was taken. With the clothing, tan, open-air windows, blue skies, and palm trees in the background, it clearly wasn't Oregon.

His eyes kept coming back to Allie's face. It was healthy and vibrant. Her smile real and unposed for the camera as if she didn't know the photo was being taken. Standard had seen glimpses of that smile, but only on a pale face, never against a deep tan. The man next to her was looking directly at her. They were laughing as if sharing a private joke. He fought off competing feelings of jealously, regret, and excitement. Maybe she was alive.

"Do you know when this was taken?" Standard asked.

"The date on the photo says three months ago, but that could have been when it was printed," Blue said. He handed Standard a magnifying glass. "Take a look at the calendar just over her right shoulder."

Standard took the glass and peered through it at the thatched wall in the background. The image in the top half of the calendar showed a white sand beach with a palm tree drooping over a turquoise lagoon. Something typical of calendars and jigsaw puzzles. The bottom half read June of this year.

"Photos can be faked," Standard said. "Thanks to technology and the Internet, there's no truth anymore."

"Possibly, but let's assume for the sake of argument that it's real."

"Then who do you think took this?"

"No idea. It showed up in the mail Saturday, five days ago, with no return address and a Portland postmark."

Standard laid the photo on the table. Face down. "Your first reaction was that she's alive and that her doctors and I were part of a conspiracy to fake her death. That right?"

Blue nodded. "Not an unreasonable assumption."

"I agree, but why go to Elijah Folsom?"

The black man in the leisure suit with frayed cuffs and lapels had appeared behind the bar again, this time minus the ice buckets. He headed toward the bandstand, walking stooped-shouldered on arthritic knees through the tables to the jumble of amplifiers and microphone stands. He got one foot caught for a second in the gray cords that snaked across the floor. After moving one of the mikes to the front of the small stage, he clumsily wrestled a barstool from behind the speakers. Before sitting down, he pulled a shiny steel-faced guitar from a battered case at his feet.

Blue didn't pay any attention to the old man. "I've known Reverend Folsom all my life. I went to him for guidance and advice. I've done that before. It has always helped. I went to him this time because I was very attached to Allie and he had helped me a great deal when she . . . died. I wanted the benefit of his wisdom before I started acting on my assumptions."

Standard picked up the photo again and glanced at the brown glow of Allie's face. God, he said to himself, don't make me go through this.

"Until this moment, I believed Allie Shafer was dead," Standard said, still looking at the photo. "She may still be, but this photo makes it pretty clear that she's either alive or someone has gone through a lot of trouble to make you think she is." Blue's face was expressionless. "That brings up two questions. If Allie is alive, why did she fake her death? If she's dead, why would someone want you to think she's alive?"

Blue accepted the concepts with a casual nod.

"Let's take the first one," Standard continued. "People fake their deaths to get away from something, such as wives, husbands, taxes, debts, the law, or life in general. Maybe a boyfriend. Who hasn't wanted to chuck the rain of Oregon for some carefree life in a tropical paradise? But what would Allie want to get away from so badly that she'd arrange this elaborate plan? If she wanted to live on an island somewhere, why didn't she just pack up and go? She had money and she had skills. She could live on one for a while then on the other."

"And if she's dead?" Blue asked as he settled back into the cushions of the couch, his drink cradled gently in one hand.

"Then someone thinks they can get something from you by making you believe she's alive. That's why you can't rule out the possibility that the photo is fake. You and Allie were more than just employer and employee. I didn't know anything about that when she came to me and asked me to write about her death. Now, somebody thinks that by convincing you that Allie's alive, it's going to cause you to do something. Any idea what that might be?"

While waiting for an answer, Standard reached for the diet cola, wondering how much Blue knew about Allie's last days or about the night he'd spent with her.

The man at the bandstand sat on the stool with one bony knee crossed over the other. The guitar rested on one thigh. The long fingers of his left hand caressed the strings and frets. The music came out effortlessly. It was the loose-stringed twang of the delta blues. The first dozen notes were straight from the juke joints of Clarksdale, Mississippi. Standard recognized the tune as Robert Johnson's "Come on in My Kitchen."

Blue turned to look at the stage then motioned for Rico to come over. "Tell Skinny not tonight. I want to close early." At the mention of the name Skinny, Standard turned one more time to look at the old man on the stage.

Rico walked over and whispered to the old man. His eyes went first to Blue, who was looking the other direction, then to Standard. With a slow shake of his head, he obediently put away the guitar and shuffled off the stage.

"Allie was—is—a remarkable woman," Blue said. "You met her, talked to her. I think we can agree that losing someone that remarkable could be extremely painful to anyone close to her. Allie and I were close. Draw whatever conclusions you want from that, but the exact nature of our relationship is no one's business. I have led a very privileged and successful life so far. I include having known Allie as part of that. Getting her back would mean a great deal to me."

"I find it hard to believe she's alive."

"Let's just say I'm not convinced she's dead. If she faked her death,

I don't know why. I had no knowledge of any of the problems you mentioned in your articles about her. If she really had them, I believe she would have come to me. The last time I saw her, she seemed happy and well adjusted."

"And when was that?"

"Two weeks before she died, if that's what happened. She told me she wanted some time off to visit friends in Montana. She wanted me to go along, but didn't think they were ready for an interracial couple. I agreed and she left. We talked twice on the phone. She called me and, both times, I thought she was still in Montana." Blue finished his drink. Rico magically appeared to replace it with a fresh one. "The next thing I know, I saw your article in some weekly newspaper. I thought at the time that it was odd that Allie would tell her story to a stranger, but Allie always did things for a reason. Based on what I knew of her, I had every reason to believe that she wanted to share her story with others in the same situation. What I couldn't understand was why she didn't want to share it with me."

"So you knew nothing about her cancer? About her illness being terminal?"

"Not a thing."

A waitress appeared to shuttle drinks and bar food to the tables of customers who most likely lived in the Pearl District's condos and loft apartments. Some of them would glance at Blue, looking as if they wanted to come over to say hello but didn't want to interrupt. The old guitar player was back behind the bar, this time with a load of clean glasses. The jacket of the leisure suit had been replaced with a stained apron, the beret with the white paper hat of a dishwasher.

Standard leaned forward to make sure Blue could hear. "All I can tell you right now is that, if Allie's alive then, she duped me big time. I wrote articles about her death. I went on television to talk about what happened to her. People paid me a lot of money for it. That's what she wanted me to do. That was the deal she came to me with. She didn't pay me a nickel. By taking the job, I was betting on the outcome, gambling that her story would earn me a few bucks. That's why I took it, and that's exactly what happened. End of story. No one is going to look like a bigger fool than me if she turns up among the living."

"That doesn't help me much," Blue said, "or you."

"I can see where my involvement in this looks suspicious to you, but you have my word that this photo is as big a surprise to me as it is to you."

Blue's face turned icy. His delicate features suddenly went hard around the edges. The milky eye became a white slit in a black socket. "Then prove it."

Standard's answer was a confused look. "Prove it how?"

"Find her and bring her back. Then it won't matter if you were part of it or not."

"Then my word's not good enough for you?" When Standard reached for his glass Blue's hand was around his wrist. The blood to Standard's fingers stopped like someone had turned off a faucet.

"Your word isn't worth squat," Blue hissed. He'd gone from collegial to demonic, from nightclub owner to gangster, all between the anvil-like beats of Standard's heart.

"And if I don't deliver?"

Blue's lips barely moved when he talked. "Carp once killed a man by tying him to a crab pot and dropping him in Tillamook Bay. When he pulled him up three days later, he had a dozen legal-sized crabs and a thigh bone."

Standard felt the trap closing. There had to be way out. He turned to look at Rico and Carp. "What's wrong with your boys over there? Why ask me when you have them?"

Blue didn't even look at them. His grip turned tighter on Standard's wrist. "Because this is the way I want it. You have something to prove to me. They don't. Rico is a barely functioning idiot with a big mouth and bad taste in clothes. He won't do anything stupid as long as I don't give him anything too complicated. He drives me around and fetches drinks. If I could find a basset hound to do the same thing, Rico would be living in the street."

"And Carp?"

"An animal. He'd rip your eyes out and eat them if I told him to. He doesn't know the difference between life and death, right and wrong. What's nice is that he doesn't care."

"You trust him?"

"As much as any animal." Blue let the words sink in. The confident look of a man holding all the cards rippled across his face. The grip eased. Blood started pumping back into Standard's pale fingers with a harsh tingle. "The only thing you have in common with those two is that, if you fuck up, you die," Blue said. "Same thing would happen to them. They know that, so they don't fuck up." Slowly, Blue's features melted back into those of the genial host Standard met when he walked in. "Besides, in case you couldn't figure it out, finding beautiful women is not something they would be particularly good at."

Standard looked over at Rico and Carp again. Carp flexed his jaw muscles and took off the dark glasses. He hung them from the breast pocket of his suit coat. Rico blew his nose then looked into the handkerchief. Blue had a point.

"What if I find out she's really dead?"

"Then find out who wants me to believe otherwise."

"Same deal if I don't?"

Blue smiled. The edges of his face softened a little more. His good eye brightening a bit. "Let me throw in an added incentive."

He motioned to Rico, who came over and leaned down to let Blue whisper something to him. Rico nodded and scurried off, disappearing through the door behind the bar. On the way by, he pushed the old man out of the way without so much as an "excuse me." Blue and Standard sat in silence until Rico reappeared a few seconds later with an envelope. When Blue took it, Standard wondered if Rico would get a pat on the head and a dog cookie.

"Here's fifteen-thousand dollars to help you save your own ass," Blue said. "I'm giving this to you out of respect for Reverend Folsom and his faith in your honesty. This is to finance your search. I want to make sure that you have every chance to find Allie and that you're doing it as my employee. This provides you with a certain amount of protection, in the event you need it, and me with a certain amount of loyalty from you. Besides, you're a freelance writer. Let's say I just commissioned you to do an article for me. I paid in advance. You deliver when you're done."

"Sort of puts a new twist on the idea of a deadline, doesn't it?"

Blue smiled. "That's one way to put it. Now, when you learn the truth, you can keep what's left plus another fifteen thousand."

"And I don't have to go crabbing with Carp?"

"Precisely, but with one more requirement." Standard held his breath again. "You never, never write another word about Allie Shafer, me, or anyone else involved in this. If you do, Carp or someone just like him will be the last thing you ever see."

Standard took the money with a sigh and shrug. "You got me, Moses. I don't have many choices here."

"I'm aware of that, and I respect your ability to recognize it. Now, let's seal this deal with a drink and you can start work." On cue, Rico appeared with two glasses of brandy. "To Allie," Blue said, holding up the glass. "Wherever she is."

Standard drained the brandy then thumbed the money in the envelope. It was all hundred-dollar bills. He counted out five of them, placed the bills in a neat pile on the table, and put the rest in his coat pocket. It was Blue's turn to look confused.

"That should cover any damages," Standard said, then got up and walked over to where Rico and Carp were standing. "Excuse me, Rico." Carp moved closer as if protecting Rico. "Would you mind introducing me to that girl over there?"

Standard pointed to the black waitress in the short skirt—the same one Rico had been hitting on earlier. When both men turned their heads, Standard reached out, grabbed the gold ring in Carp's eyebrow, and jerked as hard as he could. Carp grunted. A stream of blood squirted onto his white suit coat and pants.

Rico backed away. "Holy shit" was all he could say. He said it over and over again as he stared at the blood streaming down Carp's face.

Behind Standard, the people at the small tables started to twitter like a box of canaries.

Carp grabbed his face with one hand. Blood ran out between his fingers, covered the side of his face, and quickly filled his lower lip. The drops that hit his shoulders turned dark purple against the white fabric. In a motion that would've made a magician proud, a gun appeared in Carp's right hand. Standard recognized it as military-type Glock.

"Carp." Blue's voice wasn't loud or firm. It was more like that of a hunter to a well-trained dog. It stopped Carp before his arm came up. The gun stayed close to his leg and pointed at the floor.

Standard moved closer to slide the gold ring with the bloody chunk of eyebrow clinging to it into the breast pocket of Carp's suit coat. The big man didn't move or speak. He just stared. The right side of his face began to twitch as if something inside was trying to get out. If hate had a face, Standard was looking at it.

"I'll give Benny your best," Standard said, picked up the photo of Allie Shafer, and left.

Chapter 14

The art galleries were closed, but the eateries of the Pearl District were doing a respectable dinner trade for a Thursday. German sedans and American SUVs moved in a slow, thin conga line along NW Hoyt, looking for a convenient parking spot before giving up and turning the cars over to valets. The people moving along the narrow sidewalks looked prosperous and self-absorbed. They were dressed casually, which in Portland meant a liberal smattering of cargo shorts and baseball hats. The renovated warehouses and apartment buildings blocked the cool night breeze coming off the Willamette River.

Left without a ride home, Standard walked a few blocks south toward Burnside. He called Valerie near what used to be the Blitz-Weinhard Brewery, before it was torn down and rebuilt to house an upscale complex of restaurants, shops, offices, and apartments.

"Meet me in front of Voodoo Donuts on SW Third. I'll be there in thirty minutes," she said. "I just got out of the shower."

"Make it twenty and I'll get you a maple-bacon bar."

"Deal."

The six-block walk down Burnside provided enough time for Standard to smoke a couple of cigarettes and lament his situation. Cars whizzed from stoplight to stoplight, past auto dealerships, dive bars, and low-end restaurants. Every half block or so, Standard squeezed the fourteen thousand five hundred dollars in his coat pocket just to make sure it was still there.

"Allie Shafer," he muttered. "The gift that keeps on giving."

Her death had already earned him twenty thousand dollars. Proving he had been either right or wrong about what happened to her would earn what was already in his pocket and possibly fifteen thousand more—less expenses, that would hopefully be more justifiable than the five hundred he'd just dropped humiliating Carp in front of his boss.

"That's okay," he thought, "It was worth it for Benny's sake."

Voodoo Donuts was closed, but the bar next door was open. Standard sat at an outdoor table, ordered a beer, and watched the traffic and weirdoes parade by. Fifteen minutes later, Valerie pulled up in her ten-year-old Sentra.

"How can a place named Voodoo Donuts be closed at night?" he said, sliding into the passenger seat.

"Damn," Valerie said, shoving the car into first gear and roaring into traffic. "I was really looking forward to that maple-bacon bar."

Valerie's wet hair was limp under a Colorado Rockies baseball hat. Granny glasses had replaced the contacts she used during the day. She wore baggy bib overalls over a faded T-shirt from Newt's Club, one of the places where she used to work.

"I'm starved," she said as she steered the Sentra up SW Oak toward her apartment building at the upper end of northwest Portland.

"We had dinner four hours ago."

"I'm still hungry."

They hit Zupan's on West Burnside for take-out lasagna, salad, bread, and wine. When Valerie suggested fresh crab, Standard said "Let's pass," and headed for the checkout stand. When the clerk rang everything up, he pulled some of Blue's money out of his pocket.

"Nice wad," Valerie said.

"I'll explain later."

They got lucky and found a parking spot less than two blocks away from her apartment. She lived on the third floor of a six-story building just off NW Glisan near Couch Park. While they ate at the small kitchen table, he filled her in on what happened after he got back to the apartment, the meeting with Moses Blue, the money, the live-or-die offer, and the assault on Carp's eyebrow ring.

"You must have a death wish," she said.

"But I have his protection."

"Only until you find out what happened to Allie Shafer."

"Maybe longer, depending on how things turn out."

Valerie shook her head in disgust.

Finished eating, she picked up the dishes and put them in the sink. Standard watched her. It was one of those times when he couldn't take his eyes off her. She looked cute in the faded denim overalls and baseball hat. She'd kicked off her sandals. Bright pink toenails winked from under the turned-up cuffs. The more he watched Valerie, the less he wanted to find Allie Shafer, dead or alive. Too bad there was no choice in the matter.

"I need to borrow your car," he said, "or you can drive me over to my place, and I'll get the Jeep."

She tossed the keys hard enough that he had to duck rather than try to catch them. "You seem determined not to stay with me tonight. It's a good thing I'm not easily hurt."

Standard smiled. "I'll be back, but it might be late."

"You have a key."

A half dozen cars were parked on the street in front of The Blue Cafe. Carp's copper-colored Caddy was gone from the no parking zone at the front door. Three couples came out during the two times that Standard cruised by in Valerie's Sentra. It was nearly eleven o'clock. Figuring there couldn't be many people left inside, he pulled around the corner into the alley in the rear of the nightclub. The open screen door to the kitchen cast a rectangle of yellow light on a half dozen battered dumpsters. A black Jaguar XJ6 crouched in one of the two parking places. In the other was a yellow ragtop Oldsmobile with two primer fenders and Mississippi plates.

After backing the Sentra into the driveway of a loading dock, Standard turned off the engine and popped the top on a Bud Light he'd taken from Valerie's refrigerator. The next quarter hour was spent sipping beer and watching three cats fight over a napkin full of fish bones. The spitting and yowling spilled out of the dumpster onto the hood of the Oldsmobile until a large tabby with matted hair and half an ear emerged the winner. The cat was still on the hood, gnawing the spoiled victory, when the old man shuffled out of the kitchen door. He muttered an obscenity at the cat and shooed it away with his hand. He stopped to light a cigarette before opening the car's back door and placing the battered guitar case inside.

Standard slid down in the seat and watched the old man get behind the wheel. The Oldsmobile sputtered to life, died, started again, then slowly rumbled out of its parking spot. When it reached the end of the alley, Standard fired up the Sentra. By the time the Olds reached the street, he was fifty yards behind it.

The Olds headed west on NW Couch. Standard fell back a bit when it pulled onto I-405 and headed north to cross the Willamette River on the Fremont Bridge. Traffic was light, so the old car stood out like a sternwheeler at a boat show. He was two cars back when they reached the east side of the river and picked up Interstate 5 northbound.

Five minutes later, the Olds exited onto Northeast Killingsworth. It moved east at an experienced pace that hit each stoplight perfectly before heading north again into a labyrinth of residential streets. They drove past rundown single- and two-story houses with broken down porches and chewed up lawns that were mixed in among the gentrified in-fills and remodels. Those that were kept up demonstrated a pride of ownership rare in an area of the city once known more for drive-by shootings than Tupperware parties. Putting bars on the windows took priority over installing hot tubs.

The Oldsmobile's tires scraped the curb as it pulled in behind a cannibalized Monte Carlo sitting engineless on its rims in front of a small, gray-shingled house. The cement-block stairs led to a covered front porch with a roofline a few bubbles off level. Light from a large living room window illuminated a front yard of parched grass and dead shrubs. Standard drove by, turned around at the corner, and came back. The old man was just hoisting himself and his guitar up the stairs.

From a spot in front of the house two doors down, Standard watched him go inside then waited. The neighborhood was alive with the sound of stereos, televisions, and screaming babies escaping the open windows of houses on both sides of the street.

After a few minutes, the old man came back outside onto the porch. He had a pint of whiskey in one hand. In the other was the guitar, its shiny face reflecting the light from the dim street lamps. He collapsed onto a broken-down couch on the porch, took a swig off the bottle, and put the guitar across his thighs.

At the sound of the first twangy note, Standard got out of the car and walked up the street to stand in the shadows just outside the circles of light that covered the grass. The chords were pure and perfect. Mississippi, circa 1935. Standard moved across the lawn into the light near the porch.

"You're Skinny Hale, aren't you?"

The old man kept playing while a cigarette burned in an ashtray on the arm of the rain-stained, swayback couch. The bottle of cheap whiskey nestled between his feet like a pet cat.

"You followed me all the way from downtown to ask me that?" he said without looking up. His voice was deep, his face biblically old with watery brown eyes surrounded by dull gray. The blue lights from the street lamps gave his skin the shiny darkness of oiled teak. His fingers effortlessly sought out the notes to a blues song born three-quarters of a century ago in the Mississippi Delta.

"Was I that obvious?"

"Not really. I just picked you out when I got in the car. Didn't surprise me none that you was there. I think you had me figured when you saw me in the bar."

"Then maybe you know why I'm here."

Skinny Hale shrugged and picked out a few more notes on the guitar—sweet notes that spoke without words. "You know something about the blues, son?" he said. He looked up while continuing to softly play the basic chords that were the foundation of all blues music—notes that were the stock and trade of a bluesman.

"A little." Standard had taken a summer off during college to drive around the country. He made a point of going north from New Orleans to Memphis along Interstate 55 then turning west at Grenada and picking up Highway 61. Indianola, Clarksdale, Tutwiler, Cleveland. He hit them all. The trip was a rich collage of hot days and humid nights, of smoky evenings in bars and clubs, and letting the music slowly wrap itself around him. He drank warm beer and ate spicy barbecue with collard greens and cornbread. There were rail yards, factory smokestacks, and a woman's sudden laugh. There were row crops and workers with straw hats and long-handled hoes. The music was so dark it made being lonely sound like the only life worth living. There hadn't been a day since that he didn't promise himself to go back.

"I made it over to Holly Ridge to see Charley Patton's grave and to Quito to Robert Johnson's," Standard said.

"Moorhead?"

"Where the Southern crosses the Dog."

Mention of the junction of the Southern & Yazoo and Mississippi Valley railroads near the city of Moorhead, Mississippi, produced a close-lipped smile that spread across Hale's face. "I'd love nothing better than to get back there one day. It's too cold and damp up here. Down there with all that heat seems to make time move slower. That means a lot to me right now, given my age and everything. The slower time moves, maybe the more time I got—more time to figure out how to play this here guitar."

Hale played a few more notes that echoed his thoughts about steamy days and nights in the Delta.

"You play pretty well as it is," Standard said.

Hale shrugged again. "I seen 'em all, you know," he said. "Muddy Waters, John Lee Hooker, Howlin' Wolf, Charley Patton, Bukka White, T-Bone Walker. I was born just outside of Clarksdale the same day Blind Lemon Jefferson died, so I missed him. Heard his records, though. There was one hell of a bluesman. I learned to play a guitar just like this one by hanging out with my daddy and the other sharecroppers on Saturday nights in the juke joints near the corner of Issaquena Avenue and 4th Street in Clarksdale. Man, them were good times. I'd sit outside under the window of them old joints, listening to blues all night, watch the men and women dancing and getting all sweaty. The next morning we'd all go to church together and hear that gospel music shaking the tar paper off the roof."

His hands left the guitar long enough to take a drag on the cigarette and knock out a couple fingers of whiskey from the pint bottle. "When I grew up, I played with a lot of them, too. Never with the great ones, but some good ones. Big Bill Broonzy, Sonny Boy Williamson, Otis Spann, Peetie Wheatstraw."

Each name rolled slowly off his tongue wrapped in memories of late nights in sweaty juke joints playing music that belonged only to him.

"You play?" Hale asked.

"Not a lick."

Standard knew Hale from reading the liner notes on his father's collection of blues albums. Hale may have been from Mississippi, but he worked mostly in Chicago after the blues moved north in the forties and fifties. Hale's reputation didn't extend much beyond the tight-knit circle of Delta bluesman, and certainly never to the record company executives leery about the whole idea of recording black music played by black artists. Sometime in the sixties, when Jimmy Page, Eric Clapton, and other English rockers discovered the Delta blues, Hale was nowhere in sight. Standard thought he was dead, but ran across a magazine article that said he did five years in Louisiana's Angola Prison Farm on a drug charge. When he got out, no one remembered him. No one until Standard saw him busing dishes behind the counter at The Blue Café and heard Moses Blue call him Skinny.

Hale took another long pull on the bottle then held it out. Standard took it as an invitation and stepped up on the porch to sit down at the opposite end of the couch. He took the bottle and tipped it up. The whiskey tasted like kerosene. "How long have you been working for Moses Blue?" Standard asked, handing back the bottle and wondering if it was safe to light a cigarette so soon after swallowing.

"You might say all his life."

"How's that?"

"I'm his daddy."

Chapter 15

Skinny Hale started playing his own version of Bukka White's "Fixin' to Die Blues." His fingers found the chords with ease. Watching him, Standard wondered what kind of son would turn his father into a bus boy, especially a father who'd spent a lifetime on the fringes of America's only original form of music. What could be more important to a blues club than having a resident bluesman such as Skinny Hale?

"I moved out here when his momma died. He was only six at the time," Hale said. "She'd left me in Memphis a year earlier and moved out here to Portland with a guy who sold athletic equipment. You know? Jockstraps, kneepads, things like that. He left her high and dry after two months. Three years later she got shot while whorin' down along Grand Avenue." Hale played a few more notes. "Me and Aaron, that's his real name, Aaron, which was the real first name of T-Bone Walker. His last name is Hutchins. He got that from the jockstrap salesman. Me and Aaron kicked around the country for a while, but I couldn't take care of him. I brought him back here and left him with his aunt. She raised him. Whatever's good about Aaron is to her credit." He plucked a few more notes. "Whatever's bad about him is my doin'."

The front door squeaked open. A short round woman in her fifties, with crepe-soled shoes and a Denny's uniform, stepped out on the porch. "I got the graveyard shift." She had small eyes and a bat face. "There's some leftovers in the 'fridge, and don't forget to take them clothes out of the dryer, fold them, and put them away before you go to bed."

Hale gave her a smile and a wink. She waddled off across the lawn and drove away in the Oldsmobile.

"Fine woman," Hale said, watching the car disappear down the street. "Takes right good care of me. Hard worker, too, but she has a tendency to be tied a little tight when it comes to chores."

When Hale held up the bottle, Standard worked up enough courage to down another shot of whiskey and follow it with a cigarette.

"That was a hell of a stunt you pulled on Moses' bulldog tonight," Hale said. "I seen a lot of things happen in bars, men stabbed, shot, killed, and wounded. Can't say I've ever seen anything quite like that. Pulling a ring out of a man's eyebrow. That's cold, man. Really cold." Hale chuckled then stopped. "Not sure how smart it was, though. Carp's no one to screw with. My guess is you knew that and didn't give a damn. That being the case, I figure you must have some kind of death wish or something."

"So I hear, but let's just say that I stopped playing it safe after life took a couple of bad turns on me."

Hale's chuckle was a kind of low cackle. "I know that tune. Yes sir, I know it real well." He handed Standard the bottle again. It went down a bit easier.

"How much do you know about what's going on?" Standard said.

"They don't tell me much, but I see things, hear things. Moses wants you to find his woman, that blonde what worked for him then died. 'Cept she ain't dead, is she?"

"I don't know yet. What can you tell me about her?"

"Not much other than a lot of blues songs been written about women like that. Yes sir, a lot of blues songs. I was there at the club when Moses found out she was dead. Shit. All I can tell you is that it wasn't pretty."

"How long were they together?"

"Three, four years, maybe longer."

Standard knew what one night with Allie Shafer could do. A

shudder went through him that passed for a twinge of sympathy for Moses Blue. It passed fairly quickly. "What if she isn't dead?"

Hale played a few notes then put the guitar down. He looked naked without it. The cigarette smoldered between his callused fingers. "There's some women that just ain't good for some men. You know what I'm sayin'? It's like they's a drug or something. Too little ain't enough. Too much and you die. Man knows she's bad for him, but no way is he going cold turkey."

"It was that way with Moses and Allie Shafer?"

"Oh yeah. Maybe the worst I've ever seen, and that's saying a lot."

"He looked under control tonight."

"You don't know him. What you saw tonight was an act to make you fear him. My guess is he's home right now, crying into one of those high-priced bottles of hooch he likes to drink."

"That bad?"

"The worst."

"Have you seen the photo?"

Hale nodded. "I caught a glimpse of it. Turned my blood cold."

"What about Moses? What did he do when he saw it?"

"Sat and stared at it for a long time. If it'd been me, I'd have torn the place apart, but he didn't move for the longest time then he and Rico left. That's all I know about it until you showed up tonight."

They passed the whiskey bottle back and forth. When it was gone, Hale tossed the bottle over the fence into the neighbor's yard where it shattered against the foundation of the house next door.

"Damn you, Skinny Hale," a woman yelled. "Stop tossin' your whiskey bottles into my yard."

Hale chuckled again then went into the house and came back with two sixteen-ounce cans of Coors. Standard opened his and took a long swig to wash away the taste of the whiskey.

A low rider, filled with teenagers in oversized Laker jackets and stocking caps, cruised past yelling obscenities at the world. Hale's eyes followed the car as it rumbled down the street. "Did you know that most of the great bluesmen spent time in prison? Ledbelly, Son House, Bukka White. Most of it because they'd been young and stupid. Trust me. I know. Did five hard years myself in Angola. The Farm they call it." He motioned with his chin at the low rider, its taillights disappearing around the corner. "Don't seem like much changes, does it?"

"I need to know more about Allie Shafer and Moses. Will you help me?"

"Nothing I can do. I just wash dishes, tote ice, and play a little guitar when Moses lets me."

Standard wrote his telephone number on a blank page from a reporter's notebook, tore it off, and gave it to Hale. "It doesn't have to be much, but if anything comes up and you can see your way clear, I'd appreciate a call."

Hale slipped the paper in his pants pocket.

Standard got up to leave then stopped. "One more thing. How did Moses lose his eye?"

The guitar was back in Hale's hands. "I got drunk one night and hit him. We were in a hotel room in Memphis. He was about seven years old. We'd been traveling around since his mother died. Things weren't the same between us after that. No surprise there, right? Anyway, it was after that I brought him back here to be raised by his aunt." The guitar whispered a few notes. "He ain't never forgiven me. Everything he's done, fancy schools, fancy cars, fancy women, fat bank account. It was all done to rub my nose in it. He keeps me bustin' my hump in the kitchen just so I can see how successful he is and what a miserable piece of shit I am. It's his way of paying me back." More notes floated out of the guitar. "Hell of a deal, ain't it?"

"Is Moses legit?"

Hale sucked on his lower lip. "Don't know. Don't want to know. He pays me and the checks don't bounce. That answers all the questions I

99

have."

Standard suddenly wanted to leave. There was more going on between Skinny Hale and Moses Blue than he wanted or needed to know.

"I seen men like you before," Hale said. "You walk on hard nails, as we used to say down South, probably because of something that happened to you. Something bad."

"What's your point?"

"None really, just that I don't like the way this is goin'. I know Moses and I seen enough of you tonight to know that there's trouble ahead, yes sir." Standard turned to leave. "You know the story of Robert Johnson?" Hale asked before Standard was half way across the yard. His words were getting slurred. The whiskey kicking in. The notes coming out of the guitar had a harder edge.

"You mean the one about going down to the crossroads to make a deal with the devil? His soul in exchange for success?"

"That be the one," Hale said. His fingers found the notes to Johnson's "Crossroad Blues." Standard waited for the punch line. "Could be you made your own deal with the devil tonight."

Chapter 16

It took less than twenty minutes to get from Skinny Hale's porch back to Northwest Portland. After two trips around the neighborhood, Standard found a parking place five blocks from Valerie's apartment building. It was a two-cigarette walk.

With the day's events still rattling through his head, he got a beer from the refrigerator and smoked another cigarette, blowing the smoke out an open window. An hour later he turned out the lights and went into the bedroom. He undressed and climbed into the warm bed next to Valerie. She stirred when he slipped naked between the sheets, murmured something he didn't catch then went quickly back to sleep. Standard could only stare at the ceiling.

His mind kept creeping back to the interviews with Allie, sitting on her deck on that clear winter day, and over cheese and wine in her front room. He tried remembering her face as she talked about her cancer and about her lost aspirations. Had she said anything that would provide a clue about whether she was alive or dead? There must have been something, but he kept drawing a blank.

Finally giving up on sleep, Standard went to the kitchen and poured the last of the wine from dinner into a juice glass. His jacket hung on the kitchen chair, the money from Moses Blue still in the inside pocket. He took the bills out and spread them across the checkered tablecloth. He got the photo of Allie Shafer, stared at it for a second then tossed it on top of the cash. Seeing the money and the photo together seemed to sum things up.

From the beginning, Allie had been about money. It was money that made Standard accept the job of writing about her death in the first place. It was money that dragged him out the doldrums after she died. Now, more money was sending him in search of either a ghost or a hoax.

Worse was not knowing which one he wanted to find.

Skinny Hale's belief that Standard had made the same deal with the devil as Robert Johnson made sense up to a point. The difference was that at least Johnson had a choice, which was more than Standard had gotten.

Why did Moses Blue think that I could even find Allie, dead or alive? Standard wondered. What was it about reporters that made people think they were endowed with some mystical powers? The ability to write a declarative sentence had its advantages, but it certainly doesn't bestow superhuman status on anyone unless, of course, you worked in Washington, D.C., and got invited to appear on cable news shows.

After another hour of no answers, Standard was ready to start chewing on the tablecloth. Instead, he put the money back in the coat, sneaked back into the bedroom to get dressed, and slipped out the door. It was little after two in the morning.

The Sentra chugged west up Burnside along the northern perimeter of Washington Park. The car picked up speed as the road wound downhill past Mt. Calvary Cemetery, veered off to the south, and turned into Barnes Road. A quarter moon hung in the west amid stars dimmed by the ambient light of the city.

St. Vincent Hospital loomed over the cloverleaf where Barnes Road empties onto the highway to the coast. Standard parked the Sentra in the structure across from the front entrance to the hospital then walked down a flight of stairs, his footsteps echoing off the low concrete ceilings. The rear entrance opened onto a grassy area, surrounded by trees and carefully landscaped mounds covered in fresh bark dust. He walked back to the entrance road he'd come in on and followed it down to Barnes Road. To the couple of cars that whizzed by, Standard probably looked like a drunk lost in the wrong part of town.

After a three-block walk, he turned down a side street into a residential area of upscale homes with three-car garages and in-ground irrigation systems. The lawns were all mowed. Tall, perfectly trimmed hedges muted the sound of traffic from the nearby coast highway.

Houses lost their spirit after being vacant for too long. The paint seemed to fade faster and the roofs appeared to sag under the weight of being empty. The dust-streaked windows look like the sad eyes of a nursing home resident. Even the weeds grow faster, quickly covering up any signs that someone had once tended the flower beds, played on the grass, or barbecued steaks on the back deck.

Allie Shafer's house was no different.

Standard nearly walked by it in the darkness. The low-slung, two-story house sat a little below the street on a large, tree-filled lot that gave it breathing room away from the other homes in the neighborhood. The porch lights were dark, probably burned out after eight months. At least the house looked like it believed Allie Shafer was really dead.

He walked down the driveway and pulled up on the garage door. Locked. Same with the front door and the sliding glass doors around back. The last chance was the side door into the garage. The lock was strong, but the wood weak. One shoulder blow split the weather-beaten center panel. Standard reached in the shattered door to open the lock from the inside.

His breath came in short gasps as he slipped in and waited for the alarms to go off. Everything stayed silent. He looked outside to see if any lights had come on in the surrounding houses. Still nothing.

Allie's dust-covered BMW occupied one half of the garage. A dim streetlight shone through a window and illuminated the cobwebs that cascaded down across the Formica-topped workbench in front of the car. A thin film of dust covered the hammer, wrenches, and screwdriver sets that hung from the pegboard. Metal shelves on the wall next to the tools were stocked with spare rolls of paper towels, napkins, and bottled water.

Standard moved around the car and along the workbench, careful not to touch anything or disturb the dust. Next to the door that led from the garage into the laundry room, he found a flashlight recharging in a wall socket. The electricity is on, Standard thought. At least someone is paying the bills.

Since he didn't know what to look for, it didn't matter where he started, so the kitchen seemed as good a place as any. He opened the cupboard doors and the drawers under the counter. The perishable food had been removed from the cupboards. Only the indestructible was left: boxes of Rice-A-Roni, bottles of vinegar, and cans of tomato paste. The silverware, glasses, plates, and place mats were still there, but someone had at least emptied the refrigerator. He tried the stove. The gas was still working. He picked up the wall phone and got a dial tone.

Everything was covered with a gritty dust that had seeped in to cover the wine bottles and float in the air like algae on a lake. Standard could've written his name in the dust on top of the grand piano. The dining room table was bare, but the broken glass had been cleaned up. Allie could have done that herself after he left the next morning.

The blood-like spots of red wine were still visible on the chairs and carpet, rubbed to pale pink in a half-hearted attempt at total elimination. Allie could have done that as well then given up when she realized that it didn't matter if the stain came out or not—she'd be dead. It would be someone else's problem.

One look at the table and the memory of her face framed by the candlelight reflecting off the ceiling shot through his head. He quickly pushed the memory away and looked around for business cards left by realtors who might have shown the house to prospective buyers. If there was a realtor, then there was a listing agreement and somewhere to send the offers from any interested buyers. But there were no cards, at least none in plain sight.

He went upstairs, still keeping the flashlight beam low. The second floor smelled musty, as if the dank winter had taken up residence right after Allie left. Two of the rooms contained neatly made single beds and five-drawer dressers. He checked each drawer. All empty. The third room must have been Allie's office. The two-drawer file cabinet in the corner was also empty, except for two unused buff-colored legal sized file folders and some paper clips. The only thing on the computer desk was a mouse pad and the outline of where a computer monitor once sat. In the closet was a small safe, its door open. The inside was empty except for more paper clips and a handful of rubber bands. He looked through the desk that sat under the window overlooking the backyard. Again, nothing. No bank statements, credit card receipts, or utility bills.

Back downstairs, he checked the fireplace. There was no burned wood, only thin, wispy ashes that had once been paper. He poked around under the grate, looking for something that might have survived a fire. Everything was charred and unrecognizable.

Her bedroom was exactly the same. A floral bedspread covered the king-sized bed with the mahogany headboard and matching nightstands and dresser. A metal sculpture of a pine forest filled the wall over the bed. In the corner, by the windows looking out into the backyard, was an easy chair under a crane-neck lamp. Standard pulled open the dresser drawers, feeling around between the sweaters, blouses, socks, and nylons for anything that might tell him if she really was alive.

In the bottom drawer, pressed in between pairs of walking shorts and tank tops, was a black-and-white photo in a small pewter frame. The picture showed Allie in faded jeans, a heavy wool sweater, and the same knit cap as the day she came to his office. She was standing next to an older woman wearing a nylon parka, dark pants, and a stocking hat. They were standing on a beach with their backs to a gray ocean. The day looked cold and windy.

He pulled the photo out of the frame. There was nothing written on the back that offered any help as to when it was taken or where. He turned it over again to study both faces more carefully, glancing back and forth until sure that the similarity between the two women wasn't just his imagination. The resemblance wasn't so much in their faces, but in the way they stood and the shape of their bodies. The woman on the right was an older version of Allie Shafer.

Allie said she had no family and that her mother was dead, killed in a car crash when Allie was in high school. So who was this woman?

Standard put the empty frame back, slid the drawer closed, and tucked the photo into his coat pocket.

The flashlight was starting to dim as he walked back to the front room. Pieces of mail littered the floor inside the front door. He gathered them up and took them back to the bedroom. After making sure the blinds were drawn tight, he turned on the small lamp next to the bed. The mail was mostly advertising flyers from drug stores and supermarkets. It was all labeled "Occupant" or "Current Resident." Anyone with a pulse, and some without, got the same stuff and more every day.

The only exception was an envelope tattooed with two changes of address stickers. The postmark was December 10th of the previous year, six weeks before Allie's death. The return address was a post office box in Astoria, Oregon, a city at the mouth of the Columbia River, a couple of hours northwest of Portland.

Standard ripped it open. It was a Christmas card with silver snowflakes falling on a pair of happy little reindeer. The message inside was typical Hallmark. Underneath was written:

"Season's greetings. Visit me sometime. Miss you. Love, Mom."

Chapter 17

The next morning, Standard spent some of Moses Blue's money on a cab to take Valerie to work and himself back to his apartment. Valerie had been too tired from his comings and goings during the night to even ask what was going on. At breakfast, she did little more than stare into her coffee cup before sleepwalking into the bedroom to get ready for work. That was fine. Watching her stumble around the apartment was better than trying to explain meeting Skinny Hale and breaking into Allie Shafer's house. The less she knew about all that the better.

With an air kiss and a promise to call soon, Valerie got out of the cab at the corner of First and NW Davis, a half block from the Blagen Building. Standard plopped his head against the back of the seat. Sandpaper covered the inside of his eyes, and his legs twitched from lack of sleep. The cab worked its way south along Front Avenue then west toward the Park Blocks. It dropped him on the corner nearest the apartment. The ride cost thirty of what Standard was starting to think of as Blue Money.

Benny was up, but barely functioning after a night working on a casino website. He was at the kitchen counter, standing on a chrome-tube chair, staring at the Mr. Coffee. Standard joined in the silent vigil until the machine produced two cups of dark liquid.

"Check this out and tell me if it's the real thing," Standard said, handing Benny the envelope with the photo of Allie Shafer.

In the cluttered living room, Benny sat in the Lay-Z-Boy, looking like an oversized doll while Standard paced the room, gulping the coffee and hoping the caffeine would kick in quicker the faster it went down. Benny pulled the photo out of the envelope and held it up in the light. His small eyes focused on Allie Shafer's face.

"It's her, isn't it?" he said, his voice filled with equal parts sympathy and outrage.

"Yeah."

"Are you sure you want to go through with this?"

Standard remembered using the same line on Allie in trying to talk her out of killing herself. Hearing it again, even from Benny, was a reminder that he might have been played for a sucker.

"I'll explain later, but the short version is that I really don't have a hell of a lot of choice here."

"I take it Blue's got you by the short hairs."

"And then some."

Benny buried his face in the coffee cup again then came up for air. "Then finding out what happened after you left here yesterday with those two goons will probably have to wait as well, right?"

"Be a friend, Benny. I need some room."

"I just hope you defended my honor."

"I've taken care of that part. What I need you to do is tell me if that photo is real or fake."

The little man nodded. "It's your funeral," he said then hopped off the chair and waddled into the kitchen for more coffee.

Standard went upstairs to his apartment, showered, and rummaged through the closet for a clean pair of pants and a shirt that didn't smell like yesterday's vegetable soup. The tape recorder still lay in pieces on the floor. He started flipping through the cryptic notes he'd taken during the interviews with Allie. On a wine-stained page he found four words that made him think Blue might be right: Small

109

South Pacific island.

"Son of a bitch."

Slowly her words came back. "I always wanted to live on an island in the South Pacific. Not one of those fancy ones with big hotels, but a sort of quaint little island with palm trees, white sand, blue water. Places like that must exist somewhere, don't you think?"

Standard peeled off five hundred dollars in Blue Money then stashed the rest in a Tupperware container in the closest thing he had to a safe–the refrigerator. He needed to keep moving. Stopping would mean having to think about how tired he was and about the Christmas card signed "Mom" and about small islands in the middle of the ocean. His mind's picture of Allie Shafer lying dead on her bed after an overdose of barbiturates was quickly fading.

He grabbed the telephone book off the desk, flipped through the Yellow Pages, and found a listing for Doctor Helen Badden. He jotted down the number and the address, which appeared to be a medical office complex in an area of southwest Portland known as Hillsdale. He dialed the number and asked for Badden. The receptionist said she wasn't in yet, but they expected her any moment.

"Would you like to leave a message?" she asked.

"No, but thank you. I'll try later."

Standard fixed toast and a fried egg, put the two together into a sandwich, and ate while walking down the street to where the Jeep was parked. It would take fifteen minutes to drive to Badden's office, not counting a stop at Starbucks for more coffee.

If anyone knew Allie was alive, it had to be Helen Badden. After all, there was no way Allie could've faked her death without the help of her treating physician, at least no way that Standard knew of.

Standard had never met Badden face to face, only talking to her twice on the telephone. The first time was to help understand Allie's condition. The second was when she called to say Allie was dead. Both times, he thought Badden was the compassionate professional dealing in a forthright manner with a grieving friend. Looking back on it, she'd sounded evasive and too eager to hang up the phone after delivering her grim news as if it were the morning paper.

Keeping one eye on the rear view mirror, he drove south out of downtown on Barbur Boulevard. The events the previous night at The Blue Café guaranteed another visit from Carp and probably Rico, as well. The question was under what circumstances. The five hundred dollar act of revenge against Carp may have made Standard feel better, but seemed foolish in hindsight.

While Rico came off as a harmless wise ass, Carp was brooding and sinister. Maybe Standard would have been better off just kicking Rico in the balls and calling it good. It would have saved some money. But Carp's eyebrow ring had been too tempting.

Standard glanced in the rear view mirror a half dozen more times before pulling off Barbur onto the Beaverton-Hillsdale Highway. Helen Badden's practice was housed in a rabbit warren of medical offices wedged in among the strip malls not far from the Oregon Health and Science University. The other half-dozen physicians with offices in the same complex were either gynecologists or pediatricians.

At Badden's office, he walked into a waiting room filled with women in various stages of pregnancy. The clerk, sitting at a desk behind a sliding glass window, looked surprised when he asked to see Doctor Badden. Her face went blank when Standard said it was personal matter regarding one of Badden's former patients.

"The doctor isn't in yet," the clerk said. She was young with a starched-white smock and a little gold badge that read "Tami."

"I'll wait for a few minutes, if you'll let her know when she comes in that this is urgent." He took a seat between two expectant mothers, ignoring the well-read magazines on motherhood in favor of his own thoughts.

He knew that the most obvious and safest thing to do was simply go to the police, tell them everything, and ask for protection. But protection from what? Blue's threat was one man's word against another. Besides, the police had better things to do than investigate a game of hide-and-seek between a nightclub owner and his girlfriend, even if it did involve Moses Blue.

Going to the state Board of Medical Examiners or the Oregon Medical Association was an option. If two licensed physicians forged documents, and engaged in other illegal or unethical acts, to fake the death of a patient then there was a good chance that someone affiliated with the medical profession would like to know about it. Whether they would do anything was an altogether separate issue. For that to happen, though, he'd have to prove Allie was alive.

Standard sighed. He was right back where he started.

The only option was to keep everything to himself, find out if Allie was dead or alive, let events play out, and collect another fifteen thousand dollars from Moses Blue.

After a half-hour, Standard confronted the inscrutable Tami a second time. Badden still hadn't arrived. Tami looked worried. "I'm sorry. This isn't like her. I'm sure that something has come up and that she's been delayed for a good reason. I just can't imagine what it could be. She doesn't answer her cell phone or her pager."

"Rather than waiting, maybe you or someone else could help."

Tami listened with her head cocked to one side, like a dog that understood sounds but not words. Standard explained that several months earlier Doctor Badden had a patient and that there was a second doctor who worked on the case with her. "I wonder if you could tell me the name of that other doctor." Standard cocked his head to match Tami's.

"Gee. I don't think so, unless you're family."

When Standard said he was but couldn't prove it, Tami became even more adamant. She called the head nurse, a heavy-set woman who at first took Standard for a pill salesman. He explained the request a second time.

"I'm sorry," she said. "We can't give out that information unless you have some proof that you're a member of the patient's family."

"Even if the patient is dead?"

"We still can't help you."

Standard left and drove two blocks down the street to a convenience store while using his cell phone to call Benny Orlando. "Work your magic and get me the home telephone number and address of Helen Badden. She's a doctor with offices in Hillsdale. Call me back."

Standard got a cup of coffee and a newspaper from the convenience store. The phone rang before he had a chance to finish either one.

"Helen Badden lives in southeast, just off Stark, right around Laurelhurst Park," Benny said.

Standard wrote down the address and the telephone number on the front page of the newspaper while holding the phone between his ear and shoulder. "What about the photo?"

"I've been looking at it," Benny said. "Best I can tell it's the real thing. I've seen demonstrations of most of the computer software used to alter photos, and none of them did a job this good. I'll keep looking at it, though. Maybe make a few calls and have some propeller heads I know over at Portland State take a look at it. Something might come up." Benny paused. "She's alive, isn't she?"

"I think so."

The silence hung in the phone line. "This is fucked up, man."

"I know, but do me a favor. Check Equifax, TransUnion, or one of the other credit services. See if there's been any recent activity on credit cards or anything else belonging to Allison Shafer."

"That could take some time. How much do you have?"

"I'm not sure, but I'm not going to get anything else done until this is resolved."

"So you're going to be short on the rent again this month, right?"

"No, Benny. Not this time."

"Wait," Benny said as Standard was about to hang up. "We've ignored the obvious."

"Such as?"

"A death certificate. She was cremated, right? Well, the last time I looked, there are no drive-through crematoriums in Oregon. No one gets cremated without a death certificate. You can't just drop off a body and drive away with an urn full of ashes."

Benny was right. Standard had missed the easiest way to find out if Allie's death was on the level. "Can you check it out?"

"First thing. Anything else?"

"Yeah, find out how many small idyllic islands there are in the South Pacific."

"You're kidding, right?"

"Maybe not."

Standard hung up and dialed Helen Badden's number. When no one answered, he decided to drive to her house. If she wasn't there, he could always drive back and stake out her office.

The leafy enclave of Laurelhurst Park was wedged into a residential area between SE Stark and East Burnside streets. The park, with its tennis courts, lake, and paths was surrounded by large, older homes packed close together along tree-lined streets. In a couple of hours, the park benches and picnic tables would be filled with brown baggers eating lunch in the shade of giant fir trees.

Helen Badden's house was a two-story Cape Cod a block and a half west of the park. It had white siding, green shutters, and a large porch covering a swing and old-lady flowers in large clay pots. The small yard had perfect green grass and manicured flowerbeds. The driveway along the left side of the house was two concrete paths separated by a strip of grass that led under a trellis covered with vines that looked like concertina wire. The garage at the end of the drive had the same white siding and green shutters as the house.

Standard parked in the street and walked up to the front door. A half dozen knocks yielded no answer. Same with the doorbell. He peered in the front window, shading his eyes with both hands against the glass. The only movement inside was the pendulum on a large grandfather clock in a hallway leading to the back of the house.

Around the side and along the drive toward the garage were more perfectly tended flowerbeds and a picket fence that ran along the property line. Standard peeked in the windows in the garage door and saw the back end of a green Toyota 4Runner.

The backyard was more green grass, but dotted with color spots of late-blooming flowers. An herb garden along the back of the house was weed-free and covered with a generous layer of fresh bark dust. Rose bushes lined the chain-link fence along the back of the property. A mature elm tree provided shade to most of the yard.

The back door was locked, but inside he could see a kitten sleeping next to a bowl of milk in the laundry room. Beyond, through the door, a new laptop, still encased in the easily recognizable Apple box, sat on the butcher block in the middle of the country kitchen. On the counter were two bags of groceries. Limp looking celery stuck out of the top of one of the bags.

After banging on the back door a few times, Standard walked around to the front again and onto the porch. The front door was painted to match the green shutters. He fired up a cigarette and stepped back. After looking up at the second floor windows, he started banging on the door some more and glancing in the windows again. Still nothing.

It was time to leave and head back to Badden's office. He threw the burning cigarette into a flower bed and headed for the car. The world erupted while he was standing on the front lawn, looking back at the house one more time. With one deafening blast, the house seemed to bulge then freeze in place for a heartbeat before the windows exploded. Standard had just started to turn away and covered his face when the front door turned into a giant green bat and flew directly at him.

Chapter 18

Where's the light? Where's the goddamn light? Standard knew it was there, but it kept moving in the darkness like a lantern in a tree. There it was again, moving towards him then away. Now it looked like a train coming straight out of a dark tunnel. The closer it got, the more he tried to push back. The wall behind him was soft. There was no place to go. The light stopped. Suddenly it was huge. Instinctively, his eyes opened and stared straight into what had to be some kind of headlight. He closed his eyes, swung at it, and the light disappeared. A searing pain ran up his left arm into his shoulder and neck. Something metallic clattered off to the left.

"Easy, there," a voice said. "Those penlights are expensive."

The man who owned the voice looked about twelve years old, with thin blond hair parted down the middle and the happy face of an Afghan hound. He sat perched on the edge of the bed. Behind him, a curtain was pulled closed along a circular rod hanging from the ceiling. Benny Orlando stood on a chair at the end of the bed, his dark face a mask of worry. A third man, wearing a blue blazer and a starched white shirt with a striped tie, hovered in the background. He had a square-jaw and a buzz-cut. The scene was like something out of *Twin Peaks*.

"Is someone going to tell me what the hell happened?" Standard moved his eyes from one face to the next, stopping long enough to let each of them come into clear focus.

"I'm Dr. Martin," the man sitting on the bed said. "You're going to be fine, but I want to keep you here overnight just to be on the safe side. I'll check in later."

Taking a deep breath, Standard tried to think of the last thing he remembered. "I was attacked by something very large and green."

"That was Helen Badden's front door," Benny said. "The house exploded. The door apparently came straight at you. There was green paint on the elbows of your coat and the knees of your pants. Some neighbors found you. They said you were lying underneath it on the front lawn with broken glass everywhere. The paramedics said the door might have saved your life. Without it, you could have been cut to pieces."

"Where am I?"

"Providence Hospital."

Standard did the math. The hospital was about fifteen blocks from Helen Badden's house. "Anything broken?" He moved his arm again. The pain was still there, as if someone had left a scalpel stuck in his shoulder.

"Just a lot of bruises and a possible concussion," the doctor said. "That pain in your arm is probably from where the door crashed into your elbow."

Standard looked at Benny, still standing on a chair at the foot of the bed. "What time is it?"

"A little after seven at night. The police got your address from your wallet and found me. I've been here since about noon."

"Valerie?"

"Been and gone. One of the cops took her over to what's left of Badden's house to get your car, which, by the way, has a few more nicks and dents in it than you remember."

Standard's head pressed back into the pillow. Slowly, things came back, like learning to read again. Driving to Badden's house. Walking around her house. The deafening roar. The pressure in his ears. The explosion. The door. "Police?"

"Say hello to Detective Vlasic. He says the two of you know each other."

The buzz-cut in the blue blazer stepped forward next to the bed. Standard squinted to get better a look. "Vlasic? How long has it been?"

"Not that long, but it was under better circumstances. How are you feeling?"

Standard first met Detective Al Vlasic ten years earlier during a short and uneventful stint as a police reporter. Vlasic had just retired after twenty years in the Army and was new to the Portland Police Bureau. He was probably in his fifties by now and ready to retire on a second pension. What little contact Standard had with Vlasic left the impression of a straight shooter, with none of the usual cop biases toward anything that wasn't white, male, heterosexual, and the veteran of at least one overseas war. His idea of informal was brown socks instead of black.

"Fine, I guess."

"You were pretty lucky today." Standard could only nod. "The nurse is on the way to give you something to help you sleep, but before she gets here, why don't we run through what happened?"

Standard's mind went to work coming up with a plausible story that didn't involve explaining a fake suicide and a one-eyed gangster. "I was doing some work on an article about physician-assisted suicide. Doctor Badden has had at least one patient who checked herself out under the law. I was there to talk to her about it when the house blew up." Vlasic used a golf pencil to make notes in a small black book. "That's about it."

"Did you see anything unusual when you were there?"

"I remember looking in the front window then walking around back. There was a cat on the floor in the laundry room. I could see part of the kitchen. I remember some groceries and what looked like a new computer still in the box. It was when I went back to the front door that everything happened."

"Was anyone at home?"

119

"Not that I could tell. I knocked on both doors, but no one answered. I thought it was odd because there was a car in the garage and she was expecting me."

Vlasic made another note in his book. Standard searched the detective's face to see if the story was making any sense. "So, what did happen? The explosion, I mean. What caused it?"

"We're not sure exactly. Natural gas seems to be the odds-on favorite. Did you say you looked in the kitchen?"

"No. I only saw what was visible through the door on the other side of the laundry room. Why? Was someone inside?"

"Doctor Badden."

Standard gulped. "Dead?"

Vlasic gave a grim nod. "It looks like she killed herself. We found what was left of her near the gas oven. All the knobs were wide open. The blast wouldn't have done that. At least that's what the fire marshal tells us. It makes sense to me. The last time anyone saw her was the night before when she came home with an armload of groceries. There were no visitors. At least none that we know of." When Vlasic ran his hand across his buzz cut, it bristled like a new toothbrush. "We can't explain the explosion, but the house had to be full of gas, a bomb waiting to be lit. It could have been something as simple as the coffee maker coming on automatically."

"I threw a cigarette into the flower bed near the porch just before the explosion. At least I think I did."

Vlasic wrote in his notebook. "That might have done it."

"Anything in the house?"

"We're still looking through it. The chances are pretty good that this is going to go down as a suicide and natural gas explosion. We're lucky no one else was hurt. The only other damage was a couple of windows blown out on the houses next door and on the other side of the street."

"Autopsy?"

"Underway, but I'd be surprised if it turned up anything other than charred flesh and lungs full of natural gas."

"Can you let me know?"

Vlasic closed his notebook. "You got some interest in this other than your story?"

"No, but maybe there's a better story here, one about why a physician who assists the terminally ill to kill themselves with barbiturates uses a gas oven to kill herself."

"I'll leave that to you journalists. One thing we did find out, though. She was gay, not that it makes any difference."

"How?"

"Toys and literature mostly. We also found some letters from a woman named Traylor. Doctor Annette Traylor. Turns out Badden and Traylor were partners in more ways than one. They practiced medicine together at that clinic and other things at home, if you know what I mean. Anyway, the investigators called her and she came out to identify the body, not that there was much to identify." Vlasic closed his notebook and slipped it into his inside coat pocket. "You know the drill. We may need to talk to you again."

"I'm easy to find. Just look under any green door."

Vlasic left when the nurse arrived with a syringe on a tray. She was middle-aged and plump, with a colorful smock and comfortable shoes. "It's off to nuff-nuff land for you." The needle felt like it had a barb on the end. Within seconds a warm numbness spread through Standard's legs and arms. The shoulder and neck pain melted away. Better living through chemistry. Mercifully, his eyelids closed.

His last thought before the drug shut everything down was why would someone with fresh bark dust, a kitten, a new computer, and groceries still in the bag, commit suicide?

Chapter 19

The editor of Portland's irreverent weekly tabloid, *Inside Oregon,* had already dug his way through most of a bucket of steamed clams when Standard pushed open the door into the cool darkness of a dive bar on NE Sandy. He sat down and ordered a Corona from a waitress who appeared so quickly that Standard thought she'd been waiting all day just for him.

"Try the steamers," Eldon Mock said. He used a fork dripping with butter to point at the half-empty plastic container on the small table. "Best in town."

Standard was two days out of the hospital. Eating anything, let alone clams, remained low on his list of priorities. Instead, he pulled a bottle of aspirin from his coat pocket and dumped out four pills. "I'll pass." The waitress arrived with the beer to wash down the aspirin.

"Your loss," Mock said, popping another clam in his mouth.

Standard had spent the previous two days lying around the apartment. The pain pills the doctor prescribed were supposed to last a week. They were gone in a day and a half. Eldon Mock's call was all the excuse he needed to get outside. The pain in his left arm was still there, but at least the screaming had stopped each time he reached for a cigarette.

Now in his early fifties, Mock had spent his salad days as a copy editor at the *New York Post*. The job shaped both his views of those who read newspapers and those who wrote for them. He came west looking for greener pastures, but struck out. None of Oregon's daily newspapers would hire him. He blamed a western bias against people from east of the Mississippi. If the stories were true, at least two of his interviews had turned into near fistfights. Mock's revenge was to start *Inside Oregon* as Portland's first alternative weekly newspaper. His idea of journalism was to move under the surface of police departments and city agencies, cultivating whiners, malcontents, and passive-aggressives eager to rat out their bosses.

"How are you feeling?" Mock said. Another butter-drenched clam disappeared into his beard.

Standard answered with an unconvincing "okay" that seemed to satisfy the unsympathetic Mock.

"Good, because there's something I want you to look at." He wiped his pudgy hands on a napkin and pushed one of the city's daily papers across the table. "Metro Section. Page Three. News Briefs. Left hand column."

Standard put two more aspirin in his mouth and chased it with another swallow of beer before glancing at the paper, while Mock went back to work on the last remaining clams.

The article was four paragraphs about an exploding house in the Laurelhurst area and its dead occupant, Doctor Helen Badden. It didn't mention Standard, only the surrounding homes with their broken windows.

"Not much of a story, is it?" Mock said. "Television went bat shit over it. Helicopters and satellite trucks."

"I don't watch TV. Besides, it's a suicide. What did you expect? Newspapers hate suicides. Everyone but yours, anyway. If the house hadn't blown up, there wouldn't be any story."

"My point exactly. That's why I wanted to talk to you." Mock pointed at the paper with his fork, the last clam impaled on the end of it. "I checked the police log then talked to a couple of cops I know. One of them said you were there." Mock rocked back in the chair, arms across his chest.

Standard should've stayed home. This wasn't at all what he expected.

Mock got the same story as Al Vlasic. If Standard didn't want the police to know about Moses Blue, the photo, and the resurrection of Allie Shafer, then he certainly wasn't going to tell Eldon Mock. "I was working on something."

"Something that involved Allie Shafer's doctor?"

Standard hooked down a mouthful of beer. "Not really."

"Gimme a break," Mock said. "You expect me to believe that Allie Shafer's doctor offs herself at the same time you're standing in the front yard is just a coincidence?" Standard didn't answer. "Whatever, the important thing is that you were there when the house went up. With that, the story will practically write itself. A couple of interviews, some background on Allie Shafer and how she was Badden's patient, and bang, we're home with a cover story. You can throw in some stuff about waking up in the hospital. I'm thinking the headline is 'Physician Kill Thyself.' I still haven't figured out the artwork, but we'll get there."

When the waitress cleared the table, Mock ordered another bottle of microbrew. Standard drained the rest of the Corona and asked for one more. Something stronger sounded better, but now was not the time or place.

"If you want a story on Helen Badden, I'm not your man," Standard said. "I've got other things going right now."

"What do you mean? The local papers won't touch this story. They're too busy with ballot measures, public employee pensions, and other exciting shit like that. The television stations didn't do anything more than fly over the house a couple of times in their helicopters so everyone can see what an exploded house looks like from two thousand feet then went back to covering drive-bys and traffic jams." Mock never missed a chance to show contempt for his competitors. It was one of the things that Standard liked about him. "There's a hell of a story here. Doctor Helen Badden commits suicide just months after helping one of her patients do the same thing. What makes it great is that you were there when it happened. Both times."

"I told you. Find somebody else."

Mock leaned forward. "Look, John, you made a lot of money on the Allie Shafer story. Some of it was from me. So, here's your chance to make some more. At the very least, you get one of those true-life tragedies about why a successful doctor would stick her head in an oven. The public loves that shit. They eat it up just like these here clams."

"As long as I make Allie Shafer the hook."

Mock shrugged. "You're the journalist. I'm just a half-witted publisher. What do I know?" Mock watched as Standard gulped down more aspirin and beer before launching into the hard sell. "I know how you felt about Allie Shafer. Hell, you wore it on your sleeve for weeks. I didn't think you'd ever be worth a goddamn again. But there's no one in town that can do this story like you. What do you say? Doesn't this sound better than writing grants for some hick school district or ghost writing op-ed pieces for pencil-neck CEOs?"

"If I don't do this, you'll find somebody else, right?"

"Damn straight. This is an *Inside Oregon* kind of story. If my A team won't do it, I'll send in the B team."

"B for bumblers."

"Hey, you gotta go with what you have."

Standard needed time to find the truth about Allie Shafer. Having one of Eldon Mock's ham-handed staff writers poking around in Badden's death wasn't going to make things any easier, especially if he had to explain it to the publicity-shy Moses Blue. Standard needed to figure out a way to keep Mock at bay for a week or so, maybe longer. There was only one option.

"Tell you what. I'll look into it," Standard said. "If there's something there, I'll do it, but I want double the usual rate, and I'll get my own photos."

"Done. Call me when you know something, but don't make me wait. This story has legs. I want it first."

Don't hold your breath, Standard thought as he got up and walked out the door.

He got in the Jeep and headed two blocks east on Sandy before hanging a U-turn in the parking lot of a Vietnamese restaurant and going back toward downtown. Helen Badden's death had added a grim specter to what should've been a simple case of a missing person. Despite his personal feelings, it shouldn't have been all that complicated.

But now Badden was dead. It didn't matter how she died. Whether she killed herself or someone made it look that way, the stakes seemed suddenly higher, and the risk greater.

The Willamette River shimmered dark silver in the afternoon sun as Standard drove over the Burnside Bridge. Below, a tug worked its way south toward the Morrison Bridge. To the north, the center span of the Steel Bridge was up to let a ship move downstream toward the Columbia River.

Standard kept heading west on Burnside. The busy street divided Old Town and the mid-town business district. Homeless men and women sat along the north side of the street near the shelters and the bars, staring at the high rise banks and hotels on the south side. Standard loved Burnside for the way it gave the have-nots a good view of the haves, and vice versa.

The best he could tell, the list of people who had an axe to grind with Helen Badden was short. Moses Blue, or at least his organization, occupied the top spot. Revenge for helping Allie fake her death was a plausible enough motive for murder. For it to work, though, Badden obviously had to be part of Allie's plan. Even Blue's bulldogs, Carp and Rico, could've figured that out. Once they did, then maybe they did the job themselves. But why kill the people necessary to learn the truth? Hell, if Blue knew about Badden then he didn't need anyone else. He could have just beaten the truth out of her and left Standard out of it altogether to live his life thinking Allie was dead.

Allie Shafer ran a close second. If she was alive and intent on remaining hidden then she needed to eliminate the people who knew the truth about her so-called death. But if the photo was to be believed, Allie was on an island somewhere, whooping it up with a bar full of admiring men. At least she was three months earlier.

Standard supposed it was possible that Allie came back to Portland, offed Badden, and left again, but why risk it? Not only that, someone else besides Badden must have been in on the deal. There had to be a second physician to make the plan work. Based on what Vlasic said at the hospital, the second physician was probably Annette Traylor, Badden's former lover. If Traylor was alive then Allie probably wasn't finished covering her tracks.

With his head starting to hurt again, Standard reached for the bottle of aspirin.

The best thing to do was start at the top of the list, but first Standard wanted to talk to Valerie. He pulled into the parking lot of a boarded-up fast food place near NW Broadway. The lot smelled like urine and cheap perfume. The plywood on the windows was covered with graffiti and telephone numbers scrawled in pen, pencil, and lipstick. He parked and called Valerie's number. She answered on the second ring.

"How are you feeling?" she said.

"Like shit."

"I bet you're sorry you took those pain pills so fast."

"Sorry now. Not then." When she laughed Standard felt a hundred times better.

"Did you call for a reason?" She sounded busy and preoccupied.

"Just to say I love you."

"I already knew that."

"Good. I'll see you as soon as I can." He hung up and called The

Blue Cafe. It was a long shot, but worth the effort. When a woman answered, he asked for Rico.

"He's not here," she said. "You might try The Rialto. He likes to go in there and shoot pool or play video poker."

"Is Carp with him?"

"No. He's right here. You want to talk to him?"

Standard hung up.

Chapter 20

The Rialto was in midtown on SW Fourth Avenue between Washington and Alder. Standard parked in a garage across from the Scientology store and walked around the corner. The pool hall was dark and clean, with poster art on the walls, ceiling fans, and hooded lights over the dozen or so green-felt pool tables. The best song on the jukebox was Frank Sinatra's "New York, New York." The only things missing were Jackie Gleason and Paul Newman.

Rico was in the back, pecking away at a video poker machine. From the rear, his large ears resembled the open doors on a vintage MG. Standard took a seat at the bar. When the bartender abandoned the jukebox long enough to walk over and take his order, Standard asked for a stapler.

"Sure," she said, and without asking why, handed over a black office stapler from the back bar. "Would you like a drink with your stapler?"

"Maybe later," Standard said and moved to where he could see Rico then waited. When Rico stopped to feed another bill into the video poker machine, Standard walked up behind him, grabbed him by the back of the shirt, and dragged him over to one of the narrow, waist-high tables that divided the rows of pool tables.

When Rico sputtered out the first "what the fuck," Standard clamped the stapler on the little man's ear. "All right, you little weasel. You're going to answer my questions or I'm going to staple your ears to the side of your head."

"Wait. Wait," Rico whimpered. "Don't! Don't! Please! What do you want?"

Standard squeezed hard enough to plunge a staple into the top of Rico's ear. Cartilage cracked. A trickle of blood filled his ear canal. Rico yowled.

"You carrying a gun?" Standard asked said. Rico smelled like garlic and stale beer.

"No. It's in the car. Let go of my ear. I'm bleeding, goddamn it."

"Sit down and don't try anything stupid unless you want more holes in your ears."

"All right. All right."

When Standard eased up on the stapler, Rico pushed himself onto one of the stools and stuck a finger in his ear. It came out covered in blood and wax. He felt around the top of his ear, wincing when he plucked out the staple. "You're one crazy son of bitch, you know that?" Rico stared at the bloody staple before tossing it on the floor. "What do you want?"

"Ever heard of doctor named Helen Badden?"

A thought stumbled through Rico's head like a drunk down an alley. "No."

"Somebody stuck her head in a gas oven two days ago then blew her house up and almost got me with it. Something that stupid and clumsy made me think that you and Carp had something to do with it."

"No way, man! I just told you I never heard of the woman. Me and Carp were together all day that day. We were out at the track. Carp hit the trifecta for five bills. I can prove it. You got it all wrong."

Standard grabbed Rico's tie, pulled him forward, and clamped the stapler on his other ear. That produced an encore of pathetic whimpering. "Don't lie to me."

"God's truth, man. I don't know a thing about it."

Standard let go when the bartender headed their way. Rico grabbed the side of his head as more blood ran down his ear and on to his neck. It looked like melted candle wax. He produced a dingy handkerchief and dabbed at both ears.

"You done with my stapler?" the bartender said, staring at Rico's bloody ears.

"No," Standard answered, "but you can bring us a couple of drinks." Standard ordered a beer. Rico asked for a double shot of some unrecognizable brand of bourbon.

"You got some kind of anger management problem, don't you?" Rico said.

"Only when I think people are trying to kill me."

"The only person who wants to kill you is Carp. That stunt you pulled at the club the other night was like signing your own death warrant, man. Carp had to go to the fucking hospital. Carp hates hospitals. In fact, he hates everything, and you're at the top of the list. You ought to see him, man. He's got this big fucking bandage around his head now. He looks like some kind of god damn a-rab." Rico dabbed at this ear again. "Someday he'll pay you back for that. May not be soon, but it will happen, guaranteed. That son of a bitch is crazy."

The waitress showed up with the drinks. Standard gave her a ten, but kept the stapler. "Tell me about the day the photo of Allie Shafer showed up in the mail."

When Rico fidgeted, Standard tapped the stapler like a telegraph key. The message came through loud and clear.

"All right, all right. I was down at the club one morning, just hanging around talking to some of the girls, you know. I was thinking maybe I could get some easy action. Occasionally one of them will put out for the price of a few drinks and cheap dinner in China Town. There's no harm in trying. You know what I mean?"

"Get to the point."

"Okay. Okay. The boss was at the bar, going through the mail like he always does when he opens this envelope with a photo in it. It was one of those brown envelopes with the little metal clasp on the back.

131

You know the kind? He pulled the photo out and just stared at it for a long time." Rico knocked back half the shot of bourbon. "Then he gets this look. The one he always gets when he's figured something out. Kind of a frown that crosses his face real slow like. He picks up his cell phone, talks for a few minutes then tells me real calm and everything to get the car. I leave, pull the car around front, and he tells me to drive over to Cash's house. That's Harlan Cash. The boss's accountant. The one he hired after that squeeze of his killed herself. Cash is kind of a slimy guy, but the boss likes him. I think it's because of his name. Cash. Great name for an accountant, huh? Cash."

Rico paused to see if Standard was laughing. He wasn't.

"Then I take them both down to Cash's office in the US Bank Tower. They're in there for four or five hours, I guess. Gave me time to walk downtown and buy a new jacket. This one here." Rico tugged on the lapels of his plaid, green sport coat with fake gold buttons engraved with little anchors. It was the same one he wore the day he and Carp showed up at Benny's apartment.

Rico hooked down the other half of the bourbon. He started talking again while compulsively arranging the glass precisely in the middle of the paper coaster. Standard took a deep breath. Suffer fools, he thought, but kept his eyes glued to Rico's face.

"When the boss comes back, he's got Cash with him. They get in back. They're both real quiet, mad like. We take Cash home, and he says to the boss, 'I'll look into this more on Monday. We'll have a better idea after that of how much we're talking about.' The boss just nods and tells me to take him home. The only thing he says when he gets out is to pick him up in the morning for church."

Rico stared at the empty shot glass as if it was going to magically fill itself.

"So, next morning I'm back just like he said. He's real moody like he gets sometimes. Just sits in the back, staring out the window. After church, he hangs around for an hour talking to the minister, that big black guy. Folsom I think his name is. Like the prison. Anyway, he comes out and yells 'Rico' and there I am. Bam! Right at the curb with the car door open. That's the way the boss likes it. We drive to the club, where he grabs a piece of paper off one of those tablets with the little spiral wire thing down the side. You know the kind? And writes down your name. 'Wait a couple of days and then find this guy and bring him to me,' he says. Then he grabs a bottle of that really expensive cognac he likes from behind the bar and says he wants to go home."

Two men in business suits moved in on a nearby pool table. Rico watched them rack up a game of eight ball. They banged the balls around until something fell in a pocket by mistake.

"What about the accountant?" Standard said.

"What about him? He and the boss have talked on the phone a half-dozen times since then. I don't know what it's all about."

"How do you know this has anything to do with the photo?"

"I don't, but you asked and I'm telling you what happened after the photo showed up in the mail. Besides, what else would send the boss into a funk except news of that bitch?"

"You saw the photo?"

"Sure. I sneaked a look when the boss wasn't around."

"What do you know about her?"

Rico fidgeted some more. He checked his ear again. His finger came away wet with more blood. He wiped it on his pants. "Her and the boss were tight. Real tight. He had it real bad for her. Then she died. He was just starting to get better when that photo showed up."

"What's the connection between the photo and the accountant?"

"Beats me," Rico said.

Standard banged the stapler on the table. "Don't lie to me!"

Rico cringed. "I'm not. Jesus! Relax, will ya? The first thing he did after seeing the photo was call Cash. I told you that. You figure it out. I can't."

"I thought Shafer took care of Blue's books."

"She did, but she died. Remember? The boss hired Cash after the bitch was gone."

"Tell me about Blue's business."

Rico gave a disgusting laugh. "Fat chance. You can staple my balls to that pool table over there, but I ain't telling you anything about that. Believe me, I'd be doing you a favor. The less you know about Blue's business, the safer you are."

"Allie told me it was the nightclub and a few restaurants."

"Then that's what it is," Rico started to get up. "Now I'm getting out of here if you're done playing secretary with my ear."

"Shut up and sit down." Rico dropped back on the chair like he'd been shot. The two businessmen playing pool glanced at them then quickly looked away, wanting no part of what was going on. "Now let's hear it or you go another round with the stapler."

Rico sighed. "It's your fucking funeral, man. Don't say I didn't warn you."

"Spare me that shit. I want to know about Blue."

"The boss is mostly legit. The restaurants and the nightclub have done pretty well. A lot of the money he made went into stocks and stuff. Don't ask me what. I don't understand that shit."

"You said 'mostly.'"

"He keeps his fingers in a lot of different action. Protection and loan sharking, mostly, but he's backed a couple of dope deals that paid off big time. Real big time, as in seven or eight figures. The money rolls in like fog at the beach. Moses has got the touch, man. Dough just seems to find him."

"So, what's he worth?"

Rico shrugged. "Who knows, but it ain't like he takes his bottles and cans back for the dime deposit." Rico cringed again when Standard grabbed the stapler. "There's one thing I can tell, though." Rico stood up eager to be out the door. "Blue is the least of your worries. If I were you, I'd be keeping an eye out for Carp. I once saw him tie a guy to a light pole and put bullets into his knees. The guy screamed like nothing I ain't never heard before or since. At least he did until Carp set him on fire." Rico shivered. "Man, I can still see that guy's face turning black. Thing that was odd about it is that Carp liked the guy." The grin that spread across Rico's face made his ears stick out even further. "And Carp don't like you."

Chapter 21

The Oregon Health & Science University was the center gemstone in a necklace of medical facilities draped around Marquam Hill in the southwest corner of the city. The streets leading in and out of the area that had become known as Pill Hill were jammed in both directions with late afternoon traffic. Maneuvering the Jeep through the twisting turns of Sam Jackson Park Drive, Standard checked the time. He was good. Doctor Annette Traylor's office said she'd be doing rounds at the hospital until after seven.

What little Standard knew about Traylor came from either Al Vlasic or her listing in the telephone book: She had been Helen Badden's former lover and her specialty was Ob-Gyn. Everything after that was guesswork, including the likelihood that she helped Badden with Allie Shafer's suicide.

The road emerged into a maze of brick, glass, and skywalks that made up the medical complex. After squeezing the Jeep into one of the few remaining metered spaces in front of Baird Hall, he followed the signs to OHSU and got lost ten steps inside the glass and marble lobby. A quarter-hour of roaming the maze of hallways involved dodging patients in wheelchairs and staff members with photo IDs clipped to the breast pockets of their scrubs. Small groups of people, looking either sad or relieved, stood in doorways or the waiting areas near the nursing stations. In rooms illuminated with the faint glow of wall-mounted television sets, figures lay inert under bright, white sheets.

Standard tracked down Traylor by asking for her at one nurses' station after another. Everyone was cheery, polite, and of absolutely no help whatsoever. The best they could do was an offer to page her using the hospital's intercom system. He declined. No sense alerting her any more than necessary.

After stops at two more nurses' stations, Standard finally found her on the fifth floor, thanks to a harried-looking RN who pointed down the hallway without taking her eyes off a computer screen.

Standard said thanks and headed off. What he found was a tall woman with short black hair and a lab coat. "Excuse me, Doctor Traylor?" The woman ignored him, staying focused on the chart, flipping between pages, and using a gold ballpoint pen to write notes in a precise, un-doctor-like hand. After a minute or so, she closed the chart and looked at Standard like he had just popped out of one of the vaults in the basement morgue.

"I'm sorry. Did you say something?"

Her voice was deep. Standing up straight, she had two inches on Standard.

"I asked if you were Doctor Annette Traylor."

"Yes, I am. Can I help you with something?" She looked and sounded annoyed.

"My name is John Standard and, yes, I think you can help me." Standard gave her a vague story about being a freelance writer working on an article about physician-assisted suicide then asked again if she had a moment.

"I'm sorry," she said. "Some other time. I'm very busy, and that's really not my area of expertise."

Fair enough, Standard thought, and jumped to the point. "This has to do with Helen Badden and Allie Shafer."

Mission accomplished. He had her attention. She signaled her submission by raising her eyebrows and emitting a silent, "Oh."

"Come with me," she said. He followed her down the hall, watching as she looked in each room. "Here. This is empty."

They stepped into a supply room. Shelves filled with sheets, blankets, and pillows lined the walls, a bucket on wheels and a mop sat in the corner behind the door. The room smelled of disinfectant. They stood across from each other, leaning against counters with carefully labeled drawers of medical supplies.

"Tell me again who you are. Is it a policeman or a reporter?" she said. Her face was plain with no makeup. She had a pointed jaw. Heavy, dark eyebrows came together when she talked, to give her face an almost perpetual frown.

"Reporter. Freelance. I was also a friend of Allie Shafer."

Traylor took off her reading glasses, carefully folded them closed, and slipped them into the breast pocket of her smock. It was the practiced movement of a college professor about to lecture a classroom full of students.

"Are you the same reporter who wrote those stories about Allie Shafer after she died? Didn't I see you on CNN or MSNBC or one of those cable shows talking about her?" Standard nodded. "And what do you want?"

"I believe Allie Shafer is alive. I need you to tell me everything that led up to the decision to write the prescription for the barbiturates that were supposed to kill her."

Traylor hugged the chart book to her chest and stared thoughtfully down at the geometric pattern on the linoleum floor. "I can invoke doctor-patient privilege and not tell you a thing."

"You're absolutely right, and that's exactly how I'll say it: 'Traylor refused comment.' How do think that will sound on CNN?"

"Like I have something to hide, right?"

"You got it."

She took a deep breath. "Late last year Helen Badden came to me with an x-ray of a woman in the advanced stages of ovarian cancer. We reviewed the x-ray and the woman's medical charts together. Both of us reached the conclusion: Her situation was terminal."

"Is that when you signed off on Allie's request to commit suicide?"

"Not exactly. The medical community in this state falls into two camps. Those that support physician-assisted suicide and those that don't. There are very few who are ambivalent about it. I happen to support it as one more option for those with terminal illnesses, although I believe its use should be extremely rare." She ran her hand through her hair. "I've been involved in three previous such cases. In two of them I refused to go along with the patient's wishes because I believed counseling, pain management, or hospice care was more appropriate for both the patient and the family. In the other case, I prescribed the necessary drugs only to find out that the patient didn't use them, but found peace of mind in knowing they were there."

"And in the case of Allie Shafer, you went along with the request."

"I was the consulting physician. I agreed that Ms. Shafer was mentally competent and that she was not suffering from depression. I did not write the prescription. That was Helen's duty as Ms. Shafer's primary physician."

"So you didn't personally examine her?"

Traylor waited to answer. She tapped her front teeth with the end of her pen. "There was no need. Doctor Badden was one the most capable doctors in the city. I had no reason to doubt her. We spent hours going over the x-rays, the medical charts, the blood work, everything. We consulted a psychiatrist about Ms. Shafer's mental condition and spent long evenings discussing the ethics of this issue. In the end, there was no doubt in my mind that Allie Shafer was in exactly the kind of situation envisioned when the law was enacted. We even checked her driver's license to make sure she was a resident of the state."

"And that was your only contact with the case?"

"No. I was there when Helen signed the prescription and handed it to Ms. Shafer." She paused for effect. "It was a very emotional moment, and not one I care to relive anytime soon. Helen told me later that Ms. Shafer had exercised her rights under the law and passed away in January." She put the pen in the breast pocket of her smock and looked at Standard. "I take it that what you're suggesting is that Ms. Shafer didn't do that."

"What I'm suggesting is that Allie Shafer, Doctor Badden, and you engaged in a conspiracy to fake her death."

Traylor's thin smile said she was willing to tolerate at least one insult, but no more. Standard had at least four more ready and waiting.

"The only thing I know about Allie Shafer, other than she had a terminal case of cancer, was that she was involved in an abusive relationship," Traylor said. "All in all, it was a sad situation."

"Abusive relationship with whom?"

"Doctor Badden didn't tell me his name, only that he owned a nightclub of some kind. It really didn't matter. Allie Shafer was going to die in a few months regardless of who her boyfriend was or what he did to her."

Standard thought back to that one night with Allie. If she had bruises or other evidence that Blue beat her, he didn't see it. He could've overlooked it, but there wasn't much about her body that he'd missed that night. "Physical abuse? Emotional abuse?"

"Both, from what Doctor Badden told me."

"I understand that you and Doctor Badden were . . . close. Do you think she could have helped Allie fake her death in order to escape this abusive relationship? Maybe she faked the x-rays or used x-rays from some other woman and put Allie's name on them."

Annette Traylor clutched the chart book tighter and went back to staring at the tiled floor. "There were also blood work and medical charts."

"Can't they be faked as well?"

Traylor shook her head, as if unable to comprehend how anyone could gather that much phony information. "Doubtful. What Helen loved most about medicine was helping people. It was the people she

140

couldn't help that made her question her commitment. A plot to fake someone's death seems pretty far-fetched to me. Helen struggled with many of the aspects of being a physician, but not enough to violate the law or her responsibilities. Besides, faking someone's death can be a little tricky. There's a lot of paperwork involved. A death certificate, for example."

"I'm trying to track that down now," Standard said, making a mental note to touch base with Benny. "If Badden did help Allie Shafer fake her death, could she have done it without you knowing about it? Are you sure she couldn't have shown you fake x-rays, blood tests, things like that? Or simply lied to you."

Traylor mulled that over for a few seconds. "Well, I guess it's possible. As you said, I did not personally examine Ms. Shafer. Everything I knew about her condition, I learned from Helen."

Standard reached out with one foot to kick the door shut. Annette Traylor stiffened then relaxed when he leaned back against the opposite counter. To anyone who came in, they could've been two doctors discussing a difficult case.

"You and Doctor Badden were lovers," Standard said.

She looked disappointed, but not surprised. "The police must've told you that." She said it with a sigh. "We were lovers at one time, yes, but not for the last couple of years. I found it more important to be a good doctor than to be a good lesbian. Helen wanted more than that. We remained friends and had a good professional relationship."

"Did she have other partners?"

"Nothing that stuck."

"Do you believe Allie Shafer and Doctor Badden had a relationship?"

"I was only with them once. I didn't sense anything between them. Allie Shafer didn't seem to be Helen's type."

"What was Helen's type?"

Annette Traylor waited a few seconds to answer. "Let's just say something less feminine than Ms. Shafer."

"Were any of Doctor Badden's types capable of killing her?"

Traylor's eyes went blank for a moment as if she'd just stepped on a nail. "The police said she committed suicide."

"That would be the same police that told me you're gay."

Traylor made no attempt to join in Standard's cynical view of law enforcement. "I didn't meet all her friends, but the ones I did certainly weren't capable of murder. Most of them were professionals. There was a lawyer and a couple of CPAs. I think one played professional basketball or maybe it was golf. I can't remember." She paused and looked at Standard. "Can you tell me what makes you think that's what happened, murder I mean?"

It was Standard's turn to hesitate. A kitten, fresh bark dust, a new computer, and a bag of groceries hardly qualified as ironclad evidence that Helen Badden hadn't stuck her own head in the oven. "Nothing, really. Just a feeling."

"But you believe the story about Allie Shafer's suicide, don't you? You did write about it and go on television, didn't you?"

"That was then. This is now. Things change."

Outside the door, the squeaky wheels of a gurney moved down the hallway accompanied by the squawk of gum-soled shoes on antiseptic tile.

"For the record, Mr. Standard, I think you're wrong," Traylor said. "No one killed Helen. I knew her well enough to see that her life and her lifestyle troubled her. She came from the Midwest and had a Baptist upbringing. Being gay went against everything she'd been taught. I know how it ate at her, but I never thought she'd go as far as suicide." Traylor paused a moment to let her eyes go back to some distant memory of Helen Badden. "I feel bad that I did nothing about it, but I just didn't know. I just didn't know." She looked like she wanted sympathy. Standard wasn't in the mood.

Traylor checked her watch. "It's getting late and I need to finish my rounds. Am I to assume by this conversation that you're going to write something about all this?"

Standard shrugged. "At this point, I can't tell anybody anything. I believe Allie is alive, but I can't prove it, and the one person who I believe could prove it is dead."

Traylor pinched her lower lip for a second. "I'm sure you're a professional in these matters, so I shouldn't have to remind you that there are reputations at stake here. The decisions I made regarding Miss Shafer were based on the information I was given by Doctor Badden. I would do that same thing again given the same information by a fellow physician that I trusted. I had nothing to do with what happened after that. Am I making myself clear?"

"If any of this makes it into print, I'll be sure that your explanation of events is included."

Traylor nodded. "See that it is."

She left him alone in the supply room, flipping through the pages of his notebook, scribbling cryptic notes about doctors who trust each other enough to sign a patient's death warrant without so much as a cursory examination.

Chapter 22

The ringing of the telephone next to the bed became part of Standard's dream.

He was in a hospital with hallways that disappeared into the distance like converging parallel lines. A giant telephone sat just out of reach on a sheet-covered gurney. The phone kept ringing. Allie was calling, but the faster he ran to get it, the farther away the gurney moved.

Both awake and still dreaming, he picked up the phone. "Hello."

"Standard?"

"Who's this?"

"It's Al Vlasic with the Portland Police Bureau."

He waited then said, "Just a second," and put the receiver on the bed. The digital clock on the nightstand said a few minutes after four in the morning. Valerie stirred beside him and mumbled. Standard got up and went into the bathroom to splash water on his face in an attempt to wash away the dream. Talking to cops while half asleep was never a good idea.

"What's up?" he said, picking up the telephone again.

"Sorry to bother you this early, but do you know anyone named Richard Dunston?"

Standard thought for moment while searching the nightstand for a pack of cigarettes. "It doesn't ring a bell. Why?"

"Because he has a slip of paper in his wallet with your name on it."

"So ask him."

"We can't. Someone tied him to a light pole, shot him in both knees, and set him on fire."

Standard stared at the phone for a few seconds trying to figure out who Richard Dunston was.

"Where are you?" Standard asked Vlasic.

"The parking lot at Portland Meadows."

"I'll be there in thirty."

Valerie woke up while he got dressed. "What is it with you getting up and leaving in the middle of the night? When did you become a farmer?"

"It has something to do with Moses Blue and Carp." He kissed her through the cascade of jumbled hair that hid her face. She smelled like sleep. "I'll know more later. Then I need to drive over to the coast, to Astoria."

"What's in Astoria?"

"Answers, I hope."

Valerie threw back the covers. She was naked and warm. "How about a quickie for the road?"

"Tempting, but the police are waiting. Why not join me at the coast. It's Friday. We'll spend the weekend."

Valerie pulled the pillow back over her head. "Call me later. Maybe I'll be over my rejection by then."

Portland Meadows was just off Interstate 5, a couple of miles from where the freeway crossed the Columbia River into the State of Washington. The property with its mile track, huge grandstand, and vast parking lot had fallen on hard times. Gamblers had forsaken it for Indian casinos, internet sites, and the state lottery, preferring the larger payoffs for less effort than it takes to read a racing form. Lately, though, it had undergone a kind of renaissance, thanks to Portland's ever-curious hipster crowd.

At a quarter to five in the morning, the backside of the grandstand was dark, as were the malls, shops, and restaurants of the commercial development creeping in from the north. At first light, horses would start appearing on the track for their morning workouts.

The entrance to the track was across the street from a sand and gravel business. Using Vlasic's name, he got by the uniform guarding the gate. The gravel parking lot sat empty except for a few cars at the southeast corner near the main entrance to the grandstand. A flock of police cruisers sat in a semi-circle along a chain-link fence. Car headlamps and lights running off a generator were focused on the base of a wooden light pole.

Vlasic stood twenty feet away from the cars, talking to two men that Standard figured were either the owners of the track or stewards. He pulled up next to them and got out. Vlasic nodded to the two men and moved toward Standard. The detective's head was bare, but he wore a trench coat with the collar turned against the cool morning air.

"It's about time," Vlasic said. "The medical examiner and these guys who run the track want to get this cleaned up as soon as possible."

"Since when did you start taking orders?"

"Don't be a pain in the ass. We've been here since two a.m. Anyway, it's time to pack up."

Standard followed Vlasic between the patrol cars to where two technicians with clipboards and fingerprint equipment were huddled around the light pole. Vlasic told them to back away. "There's not much to look at."

Richard Dunston's body hugged the light pole like it was his last friend on Earth. On one side of the pole, his hands and feet were tied together with barbed wire. On the other side, his chest and crotch were cinched up tight against the pole. Both knees were black pools of congealed blood. The exposed end of a bone looked like a polished tooth. Huge hunks of hair-baring scalp had been torn away to reveal white bone underneath. One cheek was almost gone. More blood soaked what was left of a green plaid sport coat with the little gold buttons charred dull gray. The whole gory mess was singed a sickly black.

"Whoever killed him blew both knees off first," Vlasic said. "Lighting him on fire seems like an afterthought. Maybe it was just a way to stop the screaming."

"Motive?"

"Who knows? Drug deal gone bad. Revenge. Could be anything."

Standard looked away, sucking air that tasted like blood and burnt flesh. "Who found him?"

"The guy that cleans the parking lot. Damn near ran over him with the sweeper."

"How did you find out his name?"

Vlasic flipped through his notes. "The same way we found the slip of paper with your name and address on it. The guy's wallet survived the fire. One of the guys from the crime lab pulled it from his back pocket. Now, do you mind if I asked a few questions?"

"Sorry. Force of habit."

"Do you know this guy?"

"I only know him as Rico." Standard wanted a cigarette to take away the taste of blood and burned flesh. "I don't know his last name and I don't know him by Richard Dunston."

Vlasic pulled him back behind the cars and motioned to the others to finish up. "As soon as you're done," he told them. "Get him out of here."

They sat in Vlasic's car, drinking coffee delivered by a track employee. The sun was just coming up. Two horses with riders jogged gingerly on the track's backstretch near the rows of low-slung barns. The horses slowly picked up speed as they rounded the clubhouse turn before disappearing behind the grandstand. The jockeys stood up in the stirrups with butts raised and heads down.

"How do you know this guy?" Vlasic said.

Standard needed time. Helping Vlasic wasn't going to give it to him. He knew better than to tell Vlasic a total lie. Sooner or later, the police would figure everything out. The array of tests and other evidence-gathering devices at the hands of the police was too great to expect them to draw a blank at a crime scene as gruesome as Rico's.

"I don't, really," Standard said. "He works for a guy who offered me a job."

"And who would that be?"

Standard tried to figure out a way not to say it, but there was no choice. "Moses Blue."

Vlasic let out a soft whistle. "That ups the ante a bit."

Two technicians from the medical examiner's office pushed the gurney carrying Rico's body past the front of the car, the small wheels rattling on the irregular asphalt. They hoisted it into the back of an ambulance, closed the doors, and slowly drove away. There was no need to hurry.

"You better tell me the whole thing," Vlasic said.

"Not much to tell, really. Blue wanted to talk to me about doing some work for him. He sent Rico to pick me up at my apartment and drive me over to Blue's nightclub in the Pearl District so we could meet and talk it over. I guess that's where the slip of paper came from."

"He come alone?"

Standard answered with a quick yes.

Vlasic had his notebook out. "What kind of work?"

"We never got that far. When Rico came to pick me up, he hassled my landlord, Benny Orlando. He's the little guy you met at the hospital. When I found out about it I decided that I wasn't going to reward bad behavior."

"So, you told Blue you weren't going to work for him?"

"Yeah. Blue accepted that and we parted company. That was about it."

"Any idea what the work was all about?"

"Not really. I know that Blue has a corporation that owns The Blue

148

Cafe and some other restaurants. He probably needed someone to write a history of the place for the back of his menus or wanted new advertising copy. I've done the same kind of work before. It worked out pretty well for them. Maybe Blue heard about it from someone I'd worked for in the past. Anyway, it doesn't really matter because we never talked about the job itself."

They both lit cigarettes with his Bic. Vlasic looked around and muttered something about the track employee with the coffeepot. "That's the only time you saw this Rico?"

"At the nightclub, yeah." There was no need to tell Vlasic about The Rialto.

"What do you know about Blue?"

"Same as everyone else. Owns some restaurants. Won some kind of award a few years ago from the Chamber of Commerce."

"Ever hear anything about him being involved in organized crime, drugs, prostitution, protection?"

"You hear all kinds of things. All I know is that he looks pretty fat and sassy to me, so you've probably never been able to pin anything on him."

"It's hard to nail someone that no one wants to testify against." He nodded toward the light pole. "Now you know why."

Standard could sense what was coming next. He expected it from the time they got in the car together.

"The time of death appears to be sometime late last night or early this morning."

"And you want to know where I was?"

"Yes."

"Home in bed. You can confirm it with a woman named Valerie Michaels. I can give you her home phone and address. Sorry, it's the best I can do. Do you want to get out the handcuffs and take me in now?"

"Don't be a smartass. We've got your name connected with two deaths in three days. I don't believe in coincidences. Not when they involve dead people and reporters, especially you."

"You think there's a connection between Rico and Helen Badden?"

"Too early to tell."

"Well, if there is, it doesn't involve me."

Vlasic gave a sideways glance. "So, you're just on a losing streak. Everyone that comes in contact with you ends up dead."

"Not everyone. Just two."

Vlasic rubbed both eyes with the heels of his hands. "You're too smart to lie to me. You know we'll talk to Blue and to your landlord. If your story checks out with them, I'll let the girlfriend thing go."

Vlasic flipped his cigarette out the open car window then turned in the seat to look directly at Standard. "My guess is that there's more going on here than you're telling me. That's fine. I don't think you killed this guy, but you could help us find who did if you wanted to be a little more helpful. Either way, we'll figure it out."

If not for Allie Shafer, Standard would've told Vlasic everything, not that it was worth much at this point. At least not yet.

"This has all the makings of a good story for *Inside Oregon*," Standard said, "and a chance to make a little money. Just so you're aware, in case you see me poking around."

"No problem. Just remember you're still a person of interest in all of this, so we may need to talk to you again. It would be great if you didn't haul Eldon Mock into this to start spewing all that First Amendment crap."

"I'll do my best, but you know Eldon."

Standard got out of Vlasic's car. Walking toward the Jeep, he took one last look at the light pole. The patrol cars had left. Only two men from the crime lab remained behind to take care of the last few details before packing up their van and moving on to the next atrocity. Rico's blood was a black stain on the wood and on the ground.

The scene was easy to figure. Rico's death had been punishment for talking to Standard the previous day at The Rialto. The way Rico died was a message. The only question was who sent it. Blue likely. Carp was a possibility.

Maybe both. Standard shivered.

Chapter 23

Manning was little more than a wide spot along Highway 26 on the way to the coast. There's a gas station, a drive-in, and a grocery store that cater to the long lines of Portlanders that migrate from the city to the beach on Friday night and back again on Sunday afternoon. Standard pulled into the gas station, asked the attendant to fill the Jeep with regular then called Benny Orlando.

Benny had been out when Standard got back to the apartment building after leaving Portland Meadows. Rather than wait, he let himself into Benny's apartment to get the photo of Allie Shafer then went up to his own apartment to throw some clothes in a bag and grab a handful of Blue Money from the Tupperware container in the refrigerator. Valerie was at work, so he called her office and left a voice mail begging for a rain check on her earlier offer of a quickie and asking, again, that she meet him at the coast.

When Benny answered, Standard told him about Rico.

"Breaks my heart," Benny said. His voice was flat. "I'm sure he'll be missed."

"Forget that, will you. All I need you to do is not tell Vlasic that Carp was with Rico that day they came to get me, unless you have to. Just tell him that Rico was there. Period."

"What does Vlasic want with me?"

"Probably nothing, but he may call to check out my story. You can tell him everything else, just forget about Carp. You never saw him. You okay with that?"

"Yeah. Yeah. Carp doesn't exist, but what about Moses Blue?"

"Moses will take care of himself and me. He didn't invest fifteen thousand dollars in this deal just to have me involved in a murder investigation. Allie's the key to everything here. I'm convinced she's alive. I just need to find her. Any luck with the death certificate?"

"Depends on what you call luck."

"Talk to me, Benny."

"Here's the deal. Under Oregon law, a death certificate for each death in the state has to be filed with the county in which the death occurred or with the state prior to final disposition. In the case of the state, it's the—"

"Give me the short version."

"John, no one at the county or the state has a death certificate for anyone named Allison Shafer."

Standard let that rattle around in his head for a minute, trying to decide whether to be elated or disappointed. The answer was somewhere in between.

"Credit checks?" Standard asked.

"Nothing you wouldn't expect. There's been no activity on her credit cards because she canceled them well over a year ago. She also closed her checking account about the same time. Best I can tell, she made about ninety thousand a year and spent all of it. There were no savings accounts, money markets, IRAs, or anything like that."

"Can you keep at it?"

"No problem, but I think I already know where this is headed."

"So do I."

"And where do you think she is?"

"I don't know, but I think there's someone in Astoria who does. I'll be back when I can, but don't tell anyone where I am."

Benny agreed then asked if Standard had the .9mm Beretta. Benny had given him the sleek handgun a year earlier. Standard had meant to return it, but having it around provided a sense of security. It stayed stashed in the small compartment in the back of the Jeep. Standard had checked before leaving town to make sure it was still there. "I've

ght better of it until he knew where he was going to stay. Finally,
unable to put it off any longer, he punched in the number of The Blue
Café and asked for Moses Blue.

"I hope this call is in the way of a progress report," Blue said, his
voice all business.

"Not really. I just wanted you to know that Rico is dead. Someone
murdered him and the police will probably be by to see you. They
found my name on a piece of paper in his pocket."

"And what did you tell them about our . . . arrangement?"

Standard gave Blue the same story that Vlasic got.

"Very resourceful," Blue said. "There shouldn't be a problem."

"When I know something concrete about Allie, I'll get in touch."

"I'll look forward to it."

Standard stopped before hanging up. "Oh, by the way, I am sorry
about Rico."

"Yes," Blue said. "Me, too."

Standard drove away, feeling uncomfortable about whether all the
bases had been covered. Being less than truthful with cops was never
a good idea. Too many ways for stories to get mixed up. Still, he'd
done all he could.

154

Despite the beauty of the Coast Range, the drive through the mountains did nothing to erase the images from the race track parking lot. All Standard could think about was what Rico's last moments had been like. It didn't take much imagination for Standard to see himself in the same spot. It took even less to see Carp as Rico's killer on Blue's orders.

He had to assume that, before Rico died, he told Carp everything about their little talk at The Rialto: Helen Badden, Blue's reaction to seeing Allie's photo, Blue's business, and his ties to organized crime.

Rico died for talking. The question that dogged Standard was, what was the price for listening?

Chapter 24

Highway 26 wound west for another forty-five miles before merging with Highway 101 just south of Seaside, a resort town of fried seafood, penny arcades, and ocean-view motels. Standard fell in behind a conga line of campers and crept the last five miles into town.

At Seaside, he turned west and followed the main drag toward the ocean. At the last street that paralleled the beach, he turned south and started looking for "No Vacancy" signs. He found what he needed—a quaint, fifties-era, beachfront motel with off-street parking and free cable. The man in the office said his name was Vern.

"I own this here place," he said. "Glad you can join us."

Vern was in his sixties, with a potbelly, suspenders, plaid shirt, and a freshly shaven face ready for the weekend tourists. Standard paid him in Blue Money for two nights and got a room key attached to a plastic sand dollar. The room was large and paneled in knotty pine. Dry wood and paper waiting for a match filled the fireplace. The kitchen was a stainless steel sink, a two-burner stove, and a small refrigerator. The large picture windows, with a small deck outside, looked out over the promenade that ran along the beach the length of town. Beyond was a wide stretch of sand. The tide was out. The ocean looked miles away.

Standard threw his bag on the king-size bed with the red-and-white checkered spread. He filled the bathroom sink with cold water, stuck his face in, dried off, and called Eldon Mock.

"Where've you been?" Mock yelled into the phone. "I've been trying to find you. Do you ever answer that fucking cell phone? It's easier to get hold of the guy who mows my lawn. What the hell is that all about? Never mind. How's that story on the dead doctor coming along?"

Standard assured him everything was fine, but remained vague on when the story would be done and what it would say. He hung up before Mock started demanding the story by a certain time. He tried Valerie's work number, thinking he'd get her voice mail again. This time she answered on the first ring.

"Where are you?" she said.

"The coast. Seaside. How much groveling and begging would I have to do to get you to drive over here for the weekend? I found this great little motel. It's right on the ocean."

"You had your chance this morning."

"It has free cable."

"Good enough for me." She laughed into the phone. "I've got some comp time coming. A romantic beachfront cottage and candlelight dinner would get me out of here by noon."

"Don't forget the free cable."

"It's sounding more romantic all the time."

"Great, but take your time. I need to run up to Astoria for a while." He gave her the name of the motel and the room number. "I'll probably be back before you get here, but just in case, I'll leave the key with Vern. He's the owner."

Standard hung up, locked the door to the motel room, and got back in the Jeep for the twenty-mile drive to Astoria.

The City of Astoria sat at the intersection of the Columbia River and Youngs Bay, a few miles east of where the Columbia entered the Pacific Ocean. The Lewis and Clark Expedition spent one winter near Astoria then complained about it all the way back to St. Louis. The residents, many of them descendants of the Finns and Swedes who came there to catch fish and chop down trees, have spent one winter after another enduring the same conditions as the Corps of Discovery with barely a whimper.

Standard stopped at the Uniontown Cafe under the Columbia River Bridge that connects Oregon and Washington. The Christmas card he'd found in Allie Shafer's house was in the inside pocket of his leather jacket, along with the photo of Allie and the other woman at the beach. He stared at the picture, running a finger along Allie's face. It was getting harder and harder to remember little things about her. She was drifting away. Standard should have felt sad, but just couldn't get there.

"Do you know where this photo was taken?" he asked the waitress after ordering a tuna fish sandwich and a cup of coffee.

She looked at the photo for a moment. "It looks like it could be Fort Stevens State Park. It's west of here, out on Clatsop Spit, just past Warrenton."

"You sure?"

"No, but it's definitely Oregon. The wind is blowing and they look cold. The only thing missing is the rain."

"Anyone in that photo look familiar?" It was a long shot, but worth the effort.

"Sorry," she said and handed it back.

When the sandwich arrived, Standard gobbled it down, paid with a generous tip, and headed into downtown. The post office was in the 700 block of Commercial Street, two blocks uphill from the main drag that runs east through town. The man behind the counter wore a brightly colored vest and a Looney Tunes tie. Similar ties featuring Bugs Bunny, Elmer Fudd, and the rest of the gang were on sale at a display in the lobby. It was good to know the Postal Service was willing to branch out.

"Can you tell me who has this post office box?" Standard said, sliding the envelope that contained the Christmas card across the counter and pointing at the return address.

The clerk had a large head covered with baby-fine blond hair. His movements were the slow and deliberate kind of someone who cared more about getting things right than getting them done fast. If he ever got tired of the post office, he had great future at a Walmart. "Sorry, we can't give out that information." The clerk scratched his head. "You looking for somebody?"

"You could say that."

"You with the police or a private investigator?"

"Reporter."

The clerk's face grew dark. His pale eyebrows came together in a solid wrinkle. "What kind of reporter?"

"The kind who writes really nice things about really helpful postal clerks and really bad things about unhelpful ones."

The clerk squeezed his face into something that resembled a sock puppet. "What if you didn't write anything about me at all?"

"As disappointed as my readers would be, I think I could get away with that."

The clerk nodded and disappeared behind a partition. He came back with a three-by-five card that he laid face down on the counter. Without looking at Standard, he moved to one of the other registers to help a woman who just arrived carrying a large box.

Standard flipped over the card and wrote down the name: Eleanor Aquitaine Lee. There was also a street address. He put a twenty-dollar bill under the card and left with a quick conspiratorial nod to the clerk.

The offices of *The Daily Astorian* were four blocks away, on Exchange Street. Standard parked in a visitor's spot, got out to get a copy of that day's paper from the box in front of the building, and opened it to the editorial page. The masthead listed the editor of the Living Section as Anna Luukinen. He folded up the paper and went inside. The receptionist at the L-shaped counter in the small lobby said Luukinen was available, and picked up the telephone on her desk.

A few minutes later, a woman lumbered up to the counter. She was in her fifties, with an unruly head of light brown hair. Her face had the gray pallor of someone who worked indoors in a part of the state that had more rain than sunshine.

Every small newspaper in America, if there are any left, had its own version of Anna Luukinen. They started out as high school interns writing obituaries and anniversary announcements. Eventually, they graduated to feature stories then got hired full time as reporters and society editors. Thirty years later they were still there, acting as a resource library on local names, places, and politics for the freshly minted college graduates who cycled through thinking the job was nothing more than a brief layover on their way to *The New York Times*.

"Can I help you?" Luukinen said when she got to the counter.

As they shook hands, Standard told her he needed help with a story.

"What story?" she said.

A yellow No. 2 pencil with the eraser chewed off sat perched behind her left ear. She wore a shapeless corduroy peasant dress underneath a baggy cardigan sweater that was unraveling before his eyes.

"If I tell you, you'll scoop me," he said.

"There's no honor among thieves." She opened the swinging gate in the counter. "Let's use the conference room. It's the only place indoors they let me smoke."

Standard followed her through a maze of battleship gray desks into a glassed-off conference room in the back of the newsroom. She plopped down in a vinyl-covered Steelcase chair, pulled a cigarette case out of the pocket of her dress, and lit up a Camel straight. She threw the match on the floor and blew smoke out the side of her mouth.

"Okay," she said. "What can I help you with?"

Standard liked her immediately. She was one of those no-nonsense straight-razor-toed women that the hardscrabble life of the Oregon Coast produces the same way Southern California produces pampered blondes with great butts. He pulled out the photo and slid it across the table. "Is this Eleanor Lee?" He pointed to the woman standing next to Allie.

Luukinen picked up the photo and held it at arm's length. "Sure is."

"What can you tell me about her?"

She slid the photo back across the table. "To put it in local terms, I'd say that the buoy on her crab pot doesn't go all the way to the surface."

"Eccentric."

"That would be another term."

"Can you add anything to that?"

"Sure. She's a transplanted Georgian, who came here about ten years ago claiming to have roots back to Robert E. Lee, at least on her husband's side. That would be husband number four, best we can tell. The family connection met with a certain amount of skepticism by most people around here, but there's nothing in her style or manner to indicate she's anything other than what she claims. What pisses people off is that she refuses to shed that ridiculous southern drawl of hers. You'd think after a while she'd stop with the 'y'alls' and the 'honey lambs.'"

Luukinen took another drag off the cigarette. People moved silently by behind her, outside the conference room windows. There was a photographer with the trademark battered camera bag. The reporters were the ones with the plaid shirts and paisley ties. The editors were older, with coffee-stained white shirts and vacant faces. The tableau made Standard nostalgic. Luukinen ground out her cigarette in a dingy glass ashtray.

"She may be a bit odd for these parts, but she puts on a hell of a party. I'll give her that much. I've been to several, and I'd go again right now. Her Sunday brunches are the best. They start with pitchers of Bloody Marys and sort of take off from there. She flits around wearing hats with big, bright silk flowers, and asking people if they need more food or another drink. Each April, she watches every moment of The Masters on television. She could care less about golf, but wants to see the dogwoods and azaleas in bloom behind the greens and the Georgia pines along the fairways. On Kentucky Derby day, she takes all the phones off the hook, puts on the biggest hat she has, and sits in front of the television, sipping mint juleps while rooting for any horse bred east of the Mississippi and south of Maryland."

"Do you know anything about her family?"

"Her last husband was a doctor. He died about three years ago. Left her the house and a good chunk of change, if the rumors are to be believed. She had a daughter by a previous marriage. She died earlier this year. Cancer, I believe. Other than that, I don't know. My guess is she's alone, which might explain her eccentricity, if you want to call it that. She lives in one of the painted ladies up on Irving Street."

"Painted ladies?"

"They're old Victorian homes built in the late 1800s by ship captains and the families who owned the fish processing plants and lumber mills. Some of them became whorehouses during the 1920s, but now they've been taken over by yuppies who remodeled them into bed and breakfast places."

"Mrs. Lee operates a B and B?"

"No, but she could if she wanted. The house is big enough."

"What can you tell me about her daughter?"

"Nothing other than what I just said. She died. I never met her, and Eleanor never said much about her other than she was a successful accountant or lawyer or something like that in Portland."

"She never visited?"

"If she did, I didn't see her. I don't think they were close."

"Did Eleanor say anything about her daughter's death?"

"Not a word. I heard about it through word of mouth." The receptionist stuck her head in the door to tell Anna she had a telephone call. She told her to take a message then lit another cigarette. "Now, are you going to tell me what a bigshot flatlander like you wants with Ellie Lee?"

"Would you believe me if I told you that I was doing stories on old Southern Belles who live in remodeled cat houses?"

"Not a chance."

"Good, because that would be a lie. Unfortunately, it's the best I can do right now. Will you take an IOU if I promise to tell you everything when I find out myself?"

She thought for a moment. "No."

"Good, because I won't."

"I love an honest man."

Chapter 25

Eleanor Aquitaine Lee's house was a study in Victorian excess, looming over a residential intersection a dozen blocks up the hill from downtown.

Standard opened the gate in the picket fence, ready to be treated like Joe Gillis showing up at Norma Desmond's house. A stone pathway passed under a vine-covered trellis and up to a set of broad front steps. At the large porch, he pressed the bell next to the double front doors with windows of etched glass. The chimes inside played a tinny rendition of "Swanee."

Eleanor Lee answered, looking like a giant Good 'n Plenty. Her white-and-pink housecoat was two sizes too big and her feet encased in pink, open-backed slippers of matted-down fuzz that matched the moth-eaten feather boa that wound around her neck. Black, silky hair hanging loose down the middle of her back had a distinct streak of gray that started in the hairline above a wrinkled forehead and swept across the top of her head.

She used makeup like armor that could fend off advancing age. Pencil-thin eyebrows arched like a McDonald's sign above bright, gray eyes. Vivid red lipstick wandered outside the lines of her lips. Reading glasses hung from a beaded chain nestled in the tattered fringes of the housecoat's lapels.

Standard put her age as middle sixties, which meant the picture he'd found in Allie's house couldn't be more than a few years old.

A Springer spaniel, wearing a pair of man's underpants on its hindquarters, greeted Standard with a mixture of whimpers and barks.

"Say hello to Chablis," Eleanor Lee said. "I named her after that character in that wonderful book about Savannah, Georgia. I can't remember the exact name, something about good and evil gardening, whatever that is."

When the dog leapt at Standard, she grabbed it by the collar and held her back. The dog barked, whimpered, and wagged its tail all at the same time.

"Please forgive Chablis," Eleanor Lee said. "She's in heat. Those underpants belonged to Doctor. That's my late husband. I put them on her to keep the boy dogs from getting to her. One thing I don't need around here is a litter of puppies."

After making a half-hearted attempt to quiet the dog, she fumbled her glasses out of the folds of her robe and perched them on the end of her nose. She stared at Standard. "Now, who might you be?" The question came accompanied by a confused smile.

"My name is John Standard. I'd like to talk to you about your daughter."

Her eyes lit up for a second then turned sad. "Yes, of course. Were you a friend of Allie's?"

"Yes, and I'm also a freelance writer. Something has come up that I need to talk to you about."

She studied his face for a moment. "Oh my," she said, giving the pink boa another twist around her neck. "From the looks of you, this must be serious. Please come in."

She stepped back, pulling the dog with her. Standard walked into a front room that was a jumble of antique mirrors, sofas, chairs, and breakfronts. Cups, saucers, vases, and other collectibles occupied every flat surface in the room. Arrayed in front of the wide fireplace were three distinctly different fireplace sets.

Clothes, fresh from the dryer and neatly folded in piles of whites and coloreds, covered the brocade couch facing the fireplace. The image of Versailles embroidered on the back of the couch peeked out from between the freshly laundered blouses, slips, and towels. Heavy velour curtains were pulled tight to keep the sunlight out and, he guessed, prevent the gaudy rugs and furniture from fading. The house smelled of coffee and Lemon Pledge.

She shooed the dog into a study off the front room and closed the door. "Let's go in the family room where we can chat."

Standard followed a well-worn path, through the jungle of French provincial, American Colonial, and English Tudor, to a family room that had yet to yield to the advancing army of antiques that had conquered the rest of the house. An imitation leather couch covered with a soiled afghan occupied one side of the family room. The morning paper, entry blanks from Publishers' Clearinghouse, and magazines about antique furniture littered a scarred coffee table. The television was on with the sound off, so Standard had no idea what Gilligan was saying to the Skipper.

"I just keep that on for company," Eleanor Lee said, pointing to the television. "I hardly ever watch it, but it gets a little lonely around here. Would you like a snack? I got this marvelous smoked salmon from this new fish store that just opened. I'll just toss it with some fettuccine and a cream sauce. It'll take just a minute. We'll have wine. Y'all like wine don't you? Of course, you do. You're a reporter, right? You're supposed to drink. It's like some occupational obligation or something, isn't it?"

"Pretty much. I'll pass on the food, but thank you for offering. I'm not much of a wine drinker, but I'll take a beer if you have one."

"I think I have one of those six things with plastic rings. It might be beer. Then again, it might be root beer. There is a difference, right?"

She disappeared with a flurry into the kitchen. He heard the refrigerator open and close. There was a soft ping of crystal against crystal and the gentle humming of "Georgia on My Mind."

Standard sat down in a bentwood rocker, watching Gilligan's muted conversation with Ginger and the Professor.

"It *was* beer, but it wasn't with the plastic things. Someone must have drunk those and then I bought this for that nice Hispanic man who works on the yard." She handed him a bottle of Dos Equis then went back into the kitchen. Seconds later she was back with a glass of wine and a plate of smoked salmon.

"I guess I don't have any fettuccine. I just don't get to the store as often as I should and when I do I forget half the things I went there to buy. I make a list, but then I forget to take it with me. Anyway, I think beer and wine go well with salmon, don't you? At least that's what the darling man down at the fish store said, but if you ask me, I don't think it really matters anymore, do you? I mean, after all, who's to say? The wine and beer police? I don't think so."

She sat down on the couch. Her legs disappeared under the housecoat. "So," she said, "tell me again what you wanted to talk about?"

"Your daughter, Allie. I have reason to believe that she's still alive."

She dismissed the comment with a wave of her hand. "Oh my, no. Allie passed away last winter. I do miss her so. She was the only family I had."

"Mrs. Lee . . . "

"Call me Eleanor, please."

"Eleanor, I'm a friend of Allie's. The last thing in the world I want to do is hurt her or you, but two people are already dead and there may be more if I don't find her."

"Who's dead?" Eleanor Lee said. She looked concerned then excited about getting some juice from the outside world.

"One person you wouldn't know. The other is the doctor who helped her. Doctor Helen Badden.

"Oh, my. Doctor Badden was such a nice person. Sort of an odd woman. I think she sang in both choirs, if you know what I mean, but very pleasant."

"You met Badden?" Standard was surprised that the doctor had the compassion to come all the way to Astoria to meet Allie's mother.

Eleanor took a sip of wine then set the glass on a dog-eared copy of *Antiques Today.* "Several times. She came to see me right after Allie's death and then came back two or three times after that. She stopped coming last June. I've been meaning to call her, but never got around to it. You say she's dead? How awful."

"Let's start from the beginning. Allie died in January. Did you actually see her body?"

Lee waited to answer. "I don't think I like these questions. You just show up here, tell me Allie's not dead, and demand answers." Her voice grew indignant. "What's this all about and how did you find me anyway?"

Standard took a deep breath. She was right. He was coming on too strong. He needed to gain her confidence. "I'm sorry. I'm still trying to learn the truth, to put together everything that's happened since Allie died."

"Only you think she's not dead."

"Yes, and I think you can help me. You just may not know it."

If she was studying his face for clues that he could be trusted, she apparently found them. "You really believe she might be alive?"

"I think there's a chance she is, yes."

"All right, but I don't know how I can help you. Allie was a private person. Had been all her life."

"Her body? Did you see it?"

Her eyes squeezed shut to black out some dark vision. "No. I wanted to, but Allie insisted on being cremated immediately . . . after. Doctor Badden took care of all that and brought the ashes to me in this beautiful little urn. I have it here somewhere. It reminded me of a piece I bought years ago in a little shop just down the coast. It had little grape leaf designs around the top and bottom. Anyway, that was the first time I met her, Doctor Badden I mean. When she came with Allie's ashes, we drove out to the airport together. She waited for me while I went up in this cute little plane and spread dear Allie's ashes over the ocean. Allie loved the ocean, you know."

"Yeah, that's what I heard. Did she leave a will? Did she leave you any money at all?"

"Doctor Badden?"

Standard took a deep breath. "No, Allie."

"Yes, of course. The only thing Allie had was the house in Portland and she hadn't been there very long. Before that, she moved around a lot, apartments mostly. She gave the house to me when she first learned about her condition. Deeded it over, I think was the term she used. I just considered it a gift. She said I could do anything I wanted with it. I think she thought I would sell it and keep the money, but I just haven't had the courage to go over there and get her things, find a realtor, and all those other business things. I've never been good at business things. I suppose I should sell the house, but I just can't. The bills are sent here. Allie took care of that. They get forwarded here each month, and I just pay them. They're not that much. Gas and electric mostly. I suppose there's taxes to pay, but I don't know how that works. No one's living in the house, you know."

"Did Doctor Badden or anyone else send you or give you a death certificate?"

"Not that I recall, but I've never been very good at paperwork, especially the official kind. Allie was gone. That's all I really cared about. My world had suddenly grown so much smaller, so . . . meaningless."

Eleanor Lee's eyes went distant. There were no tears. If Allie was alive, Standard was having a hard time accepting what she'd done to her mother, especially the part about scattering the ashes. What was in that urn anyway or who? The lack of a death certificate, at least one in the name of Allison Shafer, seemed to seal the deal, at least as far as he was concerned. For Eleanor Lee, it didn't seem to matter. Either way, she had lost a daughter.

"And you said Doctor Badden came back to visit you after that?"

"She drove over on two occasions, I believe, maybe three. Anyway, we went out to dinner, once to this nice little Italian place down in Cannon Beach. I remember we talked about the house, and she gave me the name of a realtor. I have the card here somewhere." She started to get up.

"That's okay," Standard said. She sat back down. "Then she stopped coming in June, you said."

"Late June, I believe, but don't hold me to it. I'm terrible with dates. The days just seem to run together. She told me that she was going on a trip and that she would come to see me when she got back. But I never heard from her again."

"Did she say where she went on that trip?"

Eleanor Lee shook her head and reached for the wine, draining the glass. Without a word, she took the glass into the kitchen and came back with a refill.

Standard sipped the beer. He hated Dos Equis.

"Did you say she was dead?" Eleanor Lee asked. "Doctor Badden, I mean."

There was no need to confuse her anymore by explaining the exploding house. "Heart attack. Probably too much work."

Eleanor did more damage to the wine, a silent toast to the late Doctor Helen Badden. "That's what killed my husband. Too much work. He was a doctor too, you know?"

"Yes, you mentioned that," Standard needed a cigarette. "Let's go outside."

French doors off a breakfast nook led to a small stone terrace that overlooked a freshly mowed backyard. Eleanor gave a blow-by-blow tour of each plant and bush before drifting off into detailed explanations of past landscaping projects and new ones that needed to be done. When Standard asked a question about the house, she launched into an unabridged history lesson about past owners. He

170

didn't pay much attention, but it had something to do with dead sea captains and grieving widows.

He coaxed her into an ornate gazebo that sat sheltered from the wind amid ferns, rhododendrons, and a stand of towering cedar trees. They sat across from each other on the bench. The bottle of wine that Eleanor Lee had grabbed on the way out the door sat on a small table between them.

"Thank you for taking an interest in my house and yard," she said. "I know I ramble, and most people think I'm a little odd, but it's just that I don't get many visitors."

"My pleasure, but I still have some questions about Allie. Is that all right?"

She smiled. "Of course."

Standard fired up a cigarette and tried to gather his thoughts. "Did Allie ever mention a man named Moses Blue?"

Her eyes flashed, suddenly angry. She shook an index finger at him like an irate grade-school teacher. "You mean that terrible man she was seeing? I tried to warn her. Inter-racial relationships just don't work, at least not where I come from, especially when it's someone like that Blue person. Moses Blue! Now what kind of name is that anyway? Allie told me he beat her like a rented mule. He threatened to kill her if she tried to leave him. She was scared to death of him. She sat right there in that seat and told me all about it."

"When was that?"

"Summer before last. Poor thing cried her eyes out."

"Did you know that Allie was Blue's accountant?"

Eleanor thought for a moment. "Not in so many words. I just assumed she did some kind of work for him and that was how they met."

"Why didn't she leave him after he started beating her?"

"I told her that was exactly what she should do. She said I was right, but never did anything. Then they found the cancer. It didn't make much difference after that."

"Blue says she never told him about the cancer. Does that make sense to you?

"Perfectly. Like I told you, Allie was very secretive. She told me about it, but I had to promise not to tell another soul."

Standard began fitting the pieces together. Everything was starting to make sense, everything except where Allie went. "Did you believe Allie? About the beatings and the way Blue treated her?"

Eleanor looked down at the floor. The anger disappeared. When she spoke it was little more than a whisper. "I don't know. I know that sounds odd coming from a mother, but there was so much about Allie that was real and so much that wasn't."

"Such as?"

"Just things."

"Allie told me she was from Montana, that she was illegitimate, and that her alcoholic mother died in a traffic accident. Obviously you're alive, but is the rest of it true?"

"Oh, heavens, no. Why would she tell you that? We went through Yellowstone when we moved to Oregon. That was right after I left Charlie and when I changed my name to Shafer. As far as I know, that was as close as she ever got to Montana. Her father was a car mechanic in Marietta, Georgia. That's where Allie was born. Her father and I were divorced when Allie was ten years old. And, as you can see, I'm alive and well."

"Why would she make up something like that?"

Eleanor Lee shrugged and looked away. There was something she wasn't saying.

"How did Allie handle the divorce?" Standard asked.

She gave him a pleading look, like he'd asked for something precious that she didn't want to give up. "Why do you need to know about that?"

"Assuming she's alive, I'm looking for anything that might tell me where she is. Maybe there's something in her past. I admit it's a long shot. If there's something you don't want to tell me, I understand."

"No, no. It's just that the damage done to Allie occurred long before my marriage was over." Standard waited for her to explain. "Charlie, that was my first husband, was a drunk and a bully, and that's the nicest thing I can say about him. When Allie was born, he had just started serving three years in prison for beating and robbing a man he met in a bar. The man nearly died. If he hadn't been a Negro, Charlie probably would've gotten a longer sentence. Still, he came out of prison a much worse man than when he went in."

She took another sip of wine then looked out over the rooftops toward the river. The day was perfectly clear. A cargo ship moved slowly upriver toward Portland. Small boats skipped across the water, leaving wakes that looked like tails. The Pacific Ocean, beyond the mouth of the Columbia, looked blue gray and perfectly flat.

"I'd never taken Allie to the prison to see him, so she didn't know who he was." Eleanor said. "On the day he came home, Allie just looked at him and ran away. She hid under the house until I had to crawl under there and drag her out. After that, she would never look him in the face. She'd always leave the room when he came in. That went on for seven years. It was terrible. It made Charlie crazy. Not because he was being denied the love of his child, but because she was disrespecting him, treating him like he was beneath her. Least that's the way Charlie saw it, but that wasn't it at all. The poor child was just scared to death of him. For good reason, I guess." She topped off her wine glass, gulped down half of it, and topped it off again. "Then one day Charlie decided to get drunk. I mean he always drank, but sometimes he'd go on a real bender. On that day, he started drinking in the afternoon, left the house about seven that night, and came home about two in the morning."

Tears appeared in Eleanor's eyes. Standard lit a cigarette and let her go on.

"When his car pulled into the driveway that night, my blood just froze. Something made me want to get Allie and hide her, but I just lay there in bed, too frightened to move. You have no way of knowing what he could be like. All I could do was close my eyes when the screen door slammed shut, thinking he was coming to bed. Instead, he went into Allie's room." She bit her lip. It kept the tears at bay. "Our house was small, with paper-thin walls. Allie's room was next to ours. There was no sound for maybe a couple of minutes then I heard him say Allie's name. He didn't whisper or yell it. He just said in a normal voice. I heard Allie whimper sort of kitten-like. Then the sound of Charlie slapping her." She paused to choke back the emotions of what happened that night. Standard watched her, but didn't say anything.

"I stayed in bed, crying and shivering, too afraid to go to Allie, too afraid to save my own daughter." Tears covered her face, the same tears she'd probably been crying since that night. "After he hit her, Allie started crying then her sounds became muffled. I heard her say, 'No, no.' Then there was ripping noise. It was her nightgown."

Eleanor Lee reached for her wine. She drank half the glass as if it were a magic potion that would erase the memory. Standard could only look at his feet.

"You can guess the rest," she said. "After a while, everything was quiet. Then I heard Charlie's voice. It was raspy from too much liquor and too many cigarettes." She looked at Standard. "What he did to her was bad enough, but do you know what he said to her afterwards? Every time I think about it, I hate him all over again and I hate the world that created him, even after all these years."

Eleanor's mouth turned down at the corners. The memory that had bubbled to the surface made her lips quiver. "He said, 'Do you know what you are, Allie? You're just like me. You're just like me.'"

Neither one of them said anything for a long time. Standard stared at his cigarette, watching it burn down to the filter. Eleanor Lee broke the silence. "Allie and I ran away the next day. We left right after

174

Charlie went to work. I got a divorce several years later." A pleading look crossed her face. "She wasn't like him, you know, but he made her believe that she was." Her voice was a whisper. "Allie was never the same after that."

"How do you mean?"

"She never made friends. Allie was always alone and became more secretive, like I said. Whoever tried to get close to her would get pushed away. Maybe she thought they were going to treat her the way he did. I don't know. The things Charlie said to her that night shaped Allie's life in some way. I told you that there were things about Allie that were real and things that weren't. Well, it all started that night in her room."

Eleanor looked across the rooftops at the gray-green hills on the other side of the Columbia River. Fog had begun to push in off the ocean. It hung just above the water and hid the Columbia River Bridge where it reaches the Washington state side.

"It was as if Allie believed she was going to become like him no matter how hard she tried not to," Eleanor said. "What do you call it? A self-fulfilling prophecy or something like that."

Standard excused himself and went out to the Jeep to get the photo of Allie in the bar, and the one of her and Eleanor on the beach. There was no reason to hurry back. He stood on the sidewalk in front of the house, smoking a cigarette, to give Eleanor Lee a few minutes alone. He walked a half block down the street and back, wondering along the way about the connection between Allie's fake suicide and what her father did twenty years earlier to destroy the spirit of a ten-year-old girl.

When he got back, Eleanor hadn't moved. The wine in her glass was down another couple of inches. He sat down next to her and handed her the photo of the two of them on the beach. "I ran across this and thought you might like to have it."

Eleanor stared at the photo for a long time before gently sliding it into the pocket of her robe. Her mouth said thank you, but no sound came out.

"I want you to listen very closely, Eleanor. This is important. Someone sent Moses Blue a picture of Allie taken after she was supposed to have died. Now he believes she's alive, and he wants me to find her."

Eleanor sensed the seriousness of his tone. "What are you going to do?" She was whispering again, as if the entire population of Astoria was hiding behind the arborvitae. Her eyes were wide and bright.

"I don't know."

"Allie is dead. No one can find dead people."

"Let's pretend for a second that she isn't dead. Let's say she went somewhere to get away from Moses Blue. Any idea where that might be?"

Eleanor tapped her toe on the hardwood floor of the gazebo. The memory of Allie being raped by her father had been purged. Eleanor was back with him again. "I'm just drawing a blank."

She handed her the photograph. "Maybe this will help. This is the photo that Moses Blue received in the mail last Saturday." Eleanor held the photo by its edges. Her eyes narrowed. She squinted at Allie's face and at the faces of the men in the picture. "Did Allie ever go to the South Pacific, Mexico, or the Caribbean on vacation? Did she ever mention a place that might tell me where this picture was taken?"

"Oh, my, no. She told me she hated the tropics, too humid. Too much sun. I remember her very words, 'Mom, whatever you think, I will never go to the tropics.' Those were her exact words."

"When was this?"

"About a week before she died."

'Kind of an odd thing for someone about to die to say, isn't it?"

"I guess, but I think she was just making conversation. We tried to talk about things that weren't about her . . . condition."

They talked for a few more minutes, but Standard was at a dead end. Eleanor Lee had told him the truth about Allie's background but added nothing to his efforts to find her. Allie's professed dislike of the tropics was an obvious ruse created just for Eleanor. All it did was push him further along the road of being convinced Allie was alive and in the tropics. But where in the tropics?

Standard thanked Eleanor and got up to leave. She walked him back through the house and out on to the front porch. "You said Allie's father *was* a mechanic in Georgia. Is he doing something else now?"

"No, he was killed a year ago in Georgia. His sister called to tell me. Even though I was married to him for twelve years and had his child, I felt nothing. It was like a stranger had died."

"How did he die?"

"Someone tied him to a tree and lit him on fire after shooting him in the legs. A hunter found him a few days later. They never found who did it." She paused for a second. "What a terrible way to die, but he was a terrible man."

"What was Charlie's last name?"

"Boggs. Charlie Boggs."

Chapter 26

Standard took his time driving back to Seaside. Cars passed him on curves. Trucks honked and rode his bumper. He ignored it all, thoughts trapped in the events of twenty years ago.

It was easy to feel sorry for Allie Shafer and what she had suffered, but he suddenly wanted nothing to do with her or the lifetime of havoc caused by her pedophile father and oddball mother. Nor did he want anything to do with suicidal doctors or guys tied to telephone poles and set on fire.

All Standard could figure was that Allie had convinced Blue to send Carp to Georgia to kill her father. Not that he blamed her. Either that or killing Charlie Boggs was some kind of brutal present for her birthday or some perceived anniversary. He just wished that every child raped by a family member had a gangster boyfriend as a weapon of revenge.

One thing was certain: Allie Shafer's flaws ran much deeper than a small gap in her front teeth. Instead of killing some seed of self-esteem inside of Allie, her father had altered it some way that no one but Allie could understand. But to what end? What did it have to do with why Allie would fake her death and disappear?

Standard nearly missed the turnoff to Seaside, but not the liquor store conveniently located on the corner at the first stop sign. The Absolut was on the shelf against the back wall. The limes in a plastic basket next to the cash register and the tonic in the cooler.

When he got to the motel, Vern came out of the office to let

Standard know he had a visitor.

Valerie was sitting in a canvas chair on the little deck overlooking the promenade and the wide beach. The wind had died down. The sky still blue, except for a gray haze on the western horizon that would turn the sun bright red as it sank into the sea.

"How's my intrepid reporter?" Valerie asked.

"Beat." He hugged her. She'd taken a shower. Her damp hair smelled of sandalwood.

She stayed on the deck while he fixed two drinks, using ice cubes from the small refrigerator. While watching the gulls and tourists parade side-by-side along the promenade below, he filled her in on everything that had happened since leaving the hospital. She gasped at the description of Rico's body followed by a look of concern that Standard risked the same fate.

A quick recount of the visit with Anna Luukinen was greeted with disinterest, until he got to the part about Allie and her father.

"That's the saddest story I ever heard," Valerie said. "It makes you think there's something going on inside her that no one will ever understand. Not even her."

Valerie drained her drink and held out her glass. He went inside, fixed her another, and rejoined her on the balcony. The sun was down, the sky a darkening orange.

"Allie's alive, isn't she?" Valerie said.

"It's looking more and more that way all the time."

"But she's pretty fucked up."

"I'm not so sure. Allie didn't come up with the disappearance thing on the spur of the moment. This had to have taken years to plan. People just don't drop out of sight, not with the tools available today to find people. Allie's a schemer. I just don't know what the scheme is. She may be fucked up, but she's not stupid."

"Are you disillusioned by all this?"

"No. I just want this whole thing done with. Writing bed-and-breakfast reviews is starting to sound pretty good."

After one more drink, Valerie got dressed, and they walked north, up the promenade to Broadway, the main east-west street through Seaside. Tourists mixed with locals along the narrow sidewalks lined with arcades, trinket shops, clothing stores, and restaurants.

"Let's find something to eat then go back and knock out the rest of that Absolut," Valerie said, her tone playful.

"I promised you a nice dinner," he said then eyed her suspiciously. "Don't tell me you brought one of your old costumes?"

"I thought about it, but I know you don't like to be reminded of those days." She giggled and nestled against his arm. "We can figure something out, though, if you want. Maybe there's a souvenir shop somewhere along . . ."

"Nice try," he said before her imagination got too far along.

They got the last empty table at a noisy seafood restaurant a few blocks off the beach that specialized in clam chowder and all kinds of fish, each deep-fried to a golden brown. Valerie ordered the chowder, a dinner salad, and glass of merlot. Standard went for the fish and chips and a bottle of IPA.

"This is not the romantic place I promised you," he said.

"I like this place. It's more authentic than the fern bar you were probably thinking of taking me to." They toasted Oregon kitsch. "You know, not every woman in the world would drive two hours to spend the weekend with a man who's trying to find an old girlfriend."

The comment surprised him. He'd learned during their time together that Valerie Michaels had the emotional strength of ten women. She was neither jealous nor possessive. The only demand she'd ever made was that he be honest with her, regardless of the consequences. It never dawned on him that the search for Allie Shafer might appear to her to be more than just a need to get free of Moses Blue.

"I'm sorry," he said. "I didn't mean for it—"

"Don't apologize. I just know you better than most people. It's easier for me to see things in you."

Two little girls, ignored by travel-weary parents trying to eat dinner, ran screaming through the restaurant. One was holding a stuffed octopus. She shook it at the other while yelling, "Giant squid astern, sir." Valerie watched them wistfully.

They finished eating, paid the bill, and walked back toward the beach, stopping long enough to buy Valerie a sweatshirt with a picture of Haystack Rock on the front. A half block off Broadway, they found a coffee shop with little metal tables out front. She got a decaf latte. Standard stuck with straight black.

"All I ask is that you never take me for granted," she said, putting her elbow on the table and her chin in her hand.

"Why would I?"

"I know what your life used to be like. Big house, beautiful wife, season tickets to the Trail Blazers. I think sometimes you miss it and that I remind you of how much your life has changed." When he started to answer, she held up her hand. "All I wish is that, in addition to having a place in your life, I also have a place in your heart."

Standard leaned across the table and kissed her. Tears glistened in her eyes.

He marveled at the difference between Allie Shafer and Valerie Michaels. With Valerie, everything was up front, right in your face. Take it or leave it. No regrets and no apologies. She was a survivor capable of taking as much as she gave. Staying with him required nothing less. Allie was none of that, even though what little he knew about her was a lie that she had created. Eleanor Lee had talked about how secretive Allie had always been. No argument there. Standard just didn't have to put up with it.

"What are you going to do when you find her?" Valerie said.

"I don't know that I can find her. She could be anywhere right now."

"You'll find her, but are you sure you want to?"

Leave it to Valerie to cut straight to the chase. "There's a part of me that wishes I could just walk away from the whole thing. I guess I could, but it wouldn't be too hard to figure out how Moses Blue would feel about that. He's already convinced I'm part of the conspiracy to fake Allie's death. Running away would seal it for him. I'd never be rid of him."

"Give him back the money and tell him to get lost."

"It's a little late for that."

"You haven't spent it all, have you?"

"Hardly. Remember me telling you about Blue's father?" She nodded. "He thinks I made a deal with the devil. I thought he was crazy at the time. Now I'm not so sure."

"There's an element of professional pride in this, too, isn't there?" she said.

"She played me for a fool. That's a hard thing to let go."

They finished the coffee and walked back to the motel. Instead of going to the turnaround at the end of Broadway, and walking south along the promenade, they cut over a block early to approach the motel from the street side. Dim streetlights illuminated the cars and small houses along the narrow street that ran behind the beachfront motels.

"You didn't answer my question," Valerie said. They were still a block from the motel.

"Which one?"

"What you're going to do when you find her?"

"Get the proof one way or the other, give it to Blue, and collect another fifteen grand."

"That's not what I'm talking about."

"I know." Standard searched for the right words. "I only spent one night with her, but afterward it was like there was something unfinished between us. At the time, I thought it was just regret for not having done more to stop her from taking her own life. Now that I'm pretty sure she's alive, it's something more than that. I can't put my finger on it. Something about her scares me. Things that her mother told me about her seemed to paint her in a whole different light. She seemed so perfect before. Now she seems flawed, with problems that are deeper and darker than I want to deal with." He checked Valerie's face for a reaction. "I started out with two reasons for wanting to find her, for myself and for Blue. Now there's only one, Moses Blue."

"I'm glad that you can tell me things like that," she said, then paused. "I think."

They walked the next block in silence. Music poured out of the rental cottages on the street a block off the beach. More road-weary parents carried sleepy children from cars into the beachfront motels. Parked cars lined the gravel shoulders on both sides of the narrow street.

They were ten yards past the car parked across from the motel parking lot before Standard realized that he'd seen it before. It wasn't the Cadillac's copper color or white leather interior that caught his eye. It was the skull and cross bones dangling from the rear view mirror.

Chapter 27

As soon as he saw Carp's car, Standard grabbed Valerie and pulled her into the shadows of an elm tree that hung over the street.

"What is it?" she said. "What's wrong?"

"I think we have a visitor." He looked up and down the street then bent down to see if Carp was in the car. He wasn't.

"I need you to do exactly what I tell you, and everything will be all right." Her body stiffened. Her face lost its color. "Don't worry. I don't think we're in any danger." She didn't look reassured.

Moving out of the shadows and staying on the sidewalk behind the parked cars, they walked down the street until they were across from the motel parking lot. Standard stepped between two cars, looked up and down the street, then took Valerie's hand. "Let's go."

The Jeep was parked outside the door to their room. Standard unlocked the back window and reached inside. The Beretta was in the compartment next to the spare tire. Valerie stood behind him. Her body stiffened again when she saw the gun.

"What's that for?" she asked, her eyes wide. "I didn't know you had a gun. Where did you get a gun?"

"I'll explain later." He handed her the keys to the Jeep. "Take these. There's a Safeway out on the highway. You've got your cellphone, right?" She nodded. "Go there and call me here at the motel in twenty minutes."

Valerie didn't move. He'd seen that look before. Scared as she was, she had no intention of leaving. There was no time to argue.

"Okay," he said, "then wait here."

He walked around the side of the Jeep toward the door to their room. Not sure they'd locked it before going to dinner, Standard put the gun in the small of his back and checked the knob. Locked. A good sign. Carp would've needed a key to get in. No way the ever-vigilant Vern would give him one.

Standard tried to remember if they'd locked the door out onto the small deck before going out to dinner. Probably not.

Standard fished the room key out of his coat pocket. He unlocked the door with his left hand. With his right, he pulled out the Beretta and held it across his chest. One step inside, he closed the door, leaving Valerie pressed against the side of the Jeep, her hand over her mouth. He crouched and waited. Shades of gray draped the room, the ocean's distant rumble the only sound. Nothing felt out of place. He sensed no one else in the room. The bathroom was immediately to the left. He stood up, reached around the door, and turned on the light. If something was going to happen, that was the time.

Nothing. The blood thumping in his temples eased a bit.

Feeling more confident, he checked behind the shower curtain in the bathroom then moved down the narrow hall towards the beds. The closet was empty. So was the space between the beds. There was nowhere else to hide.

He started to turn on the lamp in the corner by the television, but decided to check the deck first. The door was locked. That's my Valerie, he thought. Outside, the dull roar of the ocean grew louder, the smell of salt air rich and refreshing. Below, a teenage couple strolled along the dark promenade. When the boy whispered in her ear, the girl squealed.

Standard looked north, toward Broadway, where cars circled the turnaround like targets in a shooting gallery. Glancing south, he jumped back immediately.

Carp was about fifty yards down the promenade, leaning against the cement wall, his back to the ocean. He wore a white suit, white turtleneck, and dark glasses. A bandage with a large pad over one eye covered most of Carp's shaved head, like a turban with the top cut off. He was looking north, toward their room. Waiting.

Standard moved back inside, confident that Carp hadn't seen him. He crossed the room then out the door into the parking lot. Valerie was where he left her, standing frozen against the Jeep. "Valerie, there's something I need you to do." She seemed to hear, but the words weren't getting any reaction. "Valerie?"

"Yes. Yes."

"Listen to me. There's a man outside on the promenade. His name is Carp. He works for Moses Blue. I don't think he's here to hurt us. He might just be checking up on me."

Valarie nodded. She was getting it.

"Here's what I need you to do," he said. "Go inside. Lock the doors. Wait five minutes then open the door to the deck. Turn on all the lights. Turn on the television set. Make sure the volume is turned up. Way up. Leave it that way for a minute or so, then turn it down. Do you understand?"

She slowly nodded. "You sure you know what you're doing?" The concern in her voice was more for him than herself.

"Absolutely," he said, trying his best to sound like he meant it.

He watched her go inside and waited until the door lock clicked. She was safe, for now.

Standard tucked the Beretta in the small of his back. He sprinted across the parking lot, back into the street that ran behind the beachfront motels. Like every beachfront town, Seaside had easy access to sand and surf. The closest was a half block south of the motel. It was a wide gravel path between two condominium complexes, linking the street with the promenade. He stopped and took several deep breaths, forcing his heart to slow down, his brain to think straight. In need of reassurance, he reached back and touched the Beretta. It felt good, too good. Guns were like that.

The garbage cans that filled the narrow alley smelled of spoiled fish and dirty diapers. One bin was filled with nothing but wine and liquor bottles. Standard moved slowly, careful not to bump into anything that would alert Carp. Shadows covered the area where the alley met the promenade. At the end of the alley, he pushed against the wall to get deeper into the darkness, but still see up the promenade. Carp hadn't moved. He was thirty feet away, still standing with his back to the beach.

Down the promenade, past Carp, the deck of the motel room was still dark. There were a few minutes left. He waited, watching Carp from the shadows and trying not to move too soon, relying on Valerie to take care of her end.

Lights from the condo units spilled down onto the beach, giving the sand the patchwork look of a giant chessboard. Two more couples walked down the promenade toward the center of town. Eyeing Carp, they gave him a wide, silent berth.

Five minutes must have passed by now. The longer he stood there, the more pissed he got. What the hell does Carp think he's doing? Despite what he told Valerie, Standard found it hard to believe that he was here on Blue's orders, which meant he was on his own dime. But what the hell for, he thought? Why didn't he just hang around The Blue Café, hitting on the waitresses, and let me do all the heavy lifting?

If things went right in the next few minutes, he might get some answers.

Just as Standard leaned out of the shadows to check the deck one more time, the lights came on. When the sound of the television set boomed out across the beach, Carp's head snapped to the left. Flipping his cigarette out onto the sand, he began moving up the promenade toward the motel room.

Standard stepped out from between the buildings. Now or never, he thought. He moved out of the shadows, crossing the promenade to the low cement wall that separated the walkway from the beach. He moved as quickly as he dared, keeping his eyes on Carp's broad back while hoping the big man wouldn't turn around. When he was directly behind Carp, he stuck the Beretta in the small of the big man's back.

"Does your boss know that you've broken your leash and run away?"

Carp hissed.

Chapter 28

"We're going to walk back to your car and call your boss," Standard said. "You can either explain to him why you're here or he can explain it to me."

Standard knew that, even with a gun in his back, he was too close to Carp—the big man could whirl around at any second and take Standard out with an elbow. But there was no other choice. He couldn't let anyone see the gun.

Shoving the barrel of the gun deeper into Carp's ribs, Standard grabbed the back of the big man's suit coat. He turned him around and began marching him back toward the alley between the two condos. Carp complied, but Standard knew it was only temporary.

Ten feet into the alley, Carp suddenly swung around to his right, his elbow out. Standard saw it coming. He ducked, Carp's arm missed his head by inches. On his haunches, Standard slammed the butt of the Beretta into Carp's kneecap. When the big man went down with a yell, Standard stood up, gun ready.

Carp grabbed his knee and growled. When he tried to get up, he grabbed the front edge of an open dumpster. Standard reached over, slammed the lid down on Carp's fingers, and held it there. Carp hung suspended, half up and half down, his face turning red, trying his best not to scream again.

"Damn it, Carp," Standard said. "You're making this harder than it needs to be."

He let go of the lid and watched as Carp fell onto his back.

"You've been a busy boy," Standard said, looking down at him. "Tying people to light poles or trees and lighting them on fire is sort of a signature move. You might think about trying something different. You know what they say about consistency."

Carp growled again, got up, and limped off toward the street, rubbing his fingers and cursing.

"I'm going to fuck you up, Standard," he grunted. "Just wait. Just wait."

At the Cadillac, Standard motioned Carp to sit in the driver's seat, while he slid in the back seat behind him. He pressed the gun hard against the big man's tense neck. Closer now, Standard could see the deep purple bruise that had started to creep from under the bandage down the side of Carp's face.

"Call Blue, then hand me the phone," Standard said.

When Carp didn't reach for the cellphone, Standard banged him on the side of the head with the gun. "Now or I'll start shooting holes in your dashboard."

Carp picked up the cell phone and dialed. He asked for Moses Blue then handed the phone over his shoulder.

"Why is your bulldog following me around?" Standard said, keeping the gun pointed at Carp's head. "I thought we were on the same team."

Silence at the other end of the line said Blue didn't know what Standard was talking about. "Where are you?"

"Seaside, trying to find your girlfriend."

"And Carp is there with you?"

"I've got a gun to his head. It's taking all my self-discipline not to start shooting. I'll be in a lot better mood if you tell me why he's here."

There was a long pause while Blue thought of a way to explain his truant employee. "One of his jobs is to protect my investments."

"Protect it from what? The only threat to me is this idiot Carp." The muscles in Carp's neck went even tauter.

"I suppose he just wants to make sure you're taking care of

business."

"You don't trust me?"

"I trust no one, but that's beside the point. I still think there's a chance that you're part of Allie's little game of hide-and-seek. Carp knows that."

"Then find her yourself. I'll return what's left of the money tomorrow. We can part friends."

"I'm not going to do that. The reason is sitting there with you right now. As far as I'm concerned, you can pull the trigger."

Standard held the phone against his chest. "Your boss says its fine with him if I shoot you. You okay with that?" He banged Carp on the side of the head again with the muzzle of the Beretta.

They stared at each other in the rear view mirror. Carp's face turned bright red, the one eye still visible under the bandage going stone dark and hard. Standard put the phone back to his ear.

"Listen, Moses. I'm making progress. Having Carp around is just going to muck things up."

"What kind of progress?"

"The photo you got in the mail appears to be the real thing. That means she was alive when it was taken."

"You mean someone might have killed her since then?"

"I mean just what I said. I have no way of knowing what's happened since then. Hell, she could've been run over by a bus."

"So where is she?"

"That's the next piece of the puzzle, but I'm not going to bust my hump to find it, if you don't keep Carp off my ass. I'm going to hand him the phone now. I want you tell him to come home and get back in his kennel. Deal?"

Blue pushed an angry sigh into the telephone. "Deal."

"There are a couple of more things. When you and Allie were together, did you ever beat her?"

"Who told you that?"

"Someone who heard it from Allie before her so-called death. If you did, it might explain why she disappeared."

Blue spoke in clear, measured tones. "I'll say this once and only once, so listen very carefully, Mr. Standard. If you believe that Allie disappeared because of the way I treated her, then find some other theory. That one's a dead-end. End of issue. Do you understand?"

"Whatever." Standard was unsure if Blue was telling the truth or just dishing out some line of street-wise bravado. "There's something else. Do you know anything about the murder of Allie's father? It happened last year in Georgia."

Carp's eyes flashed at Standard in the rear view mirror. His lips curled. Standard wondered if Carp was going to start drooling. He put a hand over the phone. "Nice poker face, Carp." He put the phone back to his ear.

"I hired you to find Allie Shafer," Blue said. "No more, no less. I suggest you concentrate on that task and forget about ancient history. Am I making myself clear?"

"Have it your way. Now, call off your hound."

Standard handed the phone back to Carp, who listened for a few seconds then put it away.

Standard poked the muzzle of the gun into Carp's ear. "I know what you did to Rico and to Charlie Boggs. Unless you want others to know about it, make sure I don't ever see you again." Standard's voice was as firm and hard as he could make it. "Leave me alone. Leave my friends alone. If you don't, I'm telling the cops about my conversation with Rico. How he told me about the time you blew a man's knees apart and set him on fire. I'm sure Detective Vlasic would love to hear about it. It might sound familiar to him. It might also sound familiar to the police in Georgia. Since you're not in jail, I assume they still haven't figured out who killed Allie's father."

Carp's entire body shook. His fingers tightened around the steering wheel until the knuckles turned white. Standard fired one shot through the front windshield of the car. The hole was small, surrounded by a tiny web of lines that, over time, would creep through the entire glass. The car smelled of cordite. Carp didn't even flinch.

Standard got out. The Caddy roared off even before the door shut. Gravel sprayed on the other cars along the street. Tires hit the asphalt, squealing in protest.

Standard walked down the street to the motel parking lot, stopping only long enough to put the Beretta back in the Jeep. He looked around once more then walked back out to the street to smoke a cigarette and make sure Carp was really gone. Up the street, cars were still moving up and down Broadway, the silence broken by some guy racing the engine of his four-cylinder Honda.

"Beautiful night, isn't it?" a voice behind him said.

Standard turned around. It was Vern. He had a drink in one hand and cigar in the other. "Yeah, it is."

"Everything okay with you and your wife?"

Wife. It was nice to know that someone still thought that two people sharing a motel room were married, even someone who owned a motel.

"Things are great."

"I heard the television blaring away there for a few minutes. I thought something had gone wrong."

"The remote kind of got away from us."

"That happens," he said. "Well, good night."

Vern turned away then stopped. "One more thing. There was this strange looking guy hanging around here tonight. Had a bandage on his head and wore a white suit. He looked like trouble to me. I saw him checking out the parking lot right after your wife arrived. I saw him later hanging out on the promenade. Sound like anybody you know?"

"No, it doesn't. Is he still around?"

"I haven't seen him in the last half hour. Maybe he left. Well, good night again."

You got to love that Carp, Standard thought. Wherever he went people took notice.

Standard had one more cigarette then went to see how Valerie was doing. When he opened the door to the room she was sitting on the end of one of the beds, staring at the photo of Allie Shafer. The look on her face asked if everything was all right.

"False alarm. Nothing to worry about." Standard took off his coat and headed for the bottle of Absolut on the kitchen counter, trying not to look like a man who needed a drink.

"Is this her?" Valerie said.

Standard said yes without looking at her.

"She's everything I expected. Beautiful. Sophisticated. It makes you wonder what someone like her is doing hanging out in Trader Jack's on Rarotonga."

"Rarotonga? Where the hell's that?"

"The Cook Islands. The South Pacific."

Chapter 29

The Air New Zealand 747 landed at seven in the morning. The jumbo jet looked like a bird sitting on a pie plate as it loomed over the line of single-story buildings that served as Rarotonga's airport. A stiff wind pushed around gray clouds, whipping up whitecaps on the ocean and tugging at the tops of the giant palm trees. The air felt like a warm, damp washcloth. The aroma of frangipani sailed by like a truckload of perfume.

Standard joined the hundred or so passengers who clambered off the plane. A five-piece ukulele band, in flowered shirts, white pants, and leis, greeted them inside the terminal. The music hurt his ears. It was too loud and happy that early in the morning and after a twelve-hour flight. He looked around for someplace to get a cup of coffee and have a cigarette. Seeing neither, he sucked it up and waited to get outside the terminal.

Filing up to the customs counters, the sleepy tourists shifted from one foot to the other. The line moved slowly, in keeping with the pace of life on a small island in the middle of the South Pacific. Just the kind of island that Allie Shafer had dreamed about. At least that's what Standard hoped.

Two days before, he had barely heard of Rarotonga or knew that it was one of the Cook Islands. The best he could tell from a quick Wikipedia search it was directly south of Hawaii and about as far below the equator as Honolulu is above it. At first blush it made sense that Allie would choose a place like this to live out her hotwired reality. The Cook Islands' affiliation with New Zealand meant no political strife, banking laws based on the English's love of privacy, and no language problem. Add it all up and it made for the perfect place to fade away.

It had been forty-eight hours since the motel in Seaside and Standard's justifiable suspicion about Valerie's announcement that the picture of Allie Shafer was taken in an obscure bar on some equally obscure island.

"How do you know that?" he'd said.

"I was there a few years ago. It was before I met you." Valerie was still sitting on the bed in the motel room, holding the photo of Allie Shafer. Carp was less than twenty minutes gone. "I told you about that trip."

"If you did I wasn't paying attention."

She'd given him one of those you-never-listen-to-anything-I-say looks. "I was still dancing in that club on the east side of town, the one where I was working when we met. This travel agent that came in all the time was selling cheap fares as part of a promotion to get more people to go there. He offered to get us rooms at agent's rates, which turned out to be next to nothing. I went with a couple of the other dancers. Those were the days when I used to make five hundred a night or more in tips, so I could afford it. The place is pretty undiscovered, or at least it was then. It was supposed to be like Hawaii thirty years ago. When I got there, it looked more like fifty years ago. I half expected Fletcher Christian to greet us when we got off the plane."

Standard still couldn't believe it. If he'd shown the picture to Valerie a week ago, it would have saved a lot of trouble. "Are you sure this is where you went? The bar, I mean."

"Of course, it's the best bar on the island. We spent every night there, hanging out with these New Zealanders and these old Polynesian guys who looked like Don Ho and liked to dance. We told them we were secretaries at a bank. They treated us like royalty."

"You went on a vacation to dance?"

"It wasn't *that* kind of dancing!" She pointed at the photo. "See this red can? You can't see the label, but I know its Lion Red. That's one of the beers they serve on the island. And look over here. This can is probably Cook Island Lager. It's made right there on the island."

"You're sure?"

"Absolutely. I probably sat on that same bar stool."

Standard had called Benny Orlando. "Get me the earliest flight to this place. Rarotonga, or whatever the hell it's called. And see what first class is going to cost me."

"Sounds like a long shot," Benny said.

"Not when you think about it. Everything adds up. She even told her mother that she would never go to the tropics. It makes sense that is exactly where she'd go."

"Mother?"

"Never mind that. The biggest gamble is whether Allie is still there."

Since Benny had never heard of Rarotonga either, Standard put Valerie on the phone. The two of them worked it out while he did some more damage to the Absolut, thought about Carp driving home with a busted windshield, and about Allie lounging on the beach on a remote south sea island.

It took Benny a couple of hours to find the right airline and to get a room at a place called the Edgewater Resort. By the next afternoon, Standard was on a plane from Portland to Los Angeles, to catch a Sunday night flight out of LAX to Auckland, New Zealand. The flight made one stop: Rarotonga. First class was booked up.

Standard started the flight wedged into a window seat, next to an overweight woman in her fifties who was too large for the seat and smelled like Pine Sol. Seeing the flight wasn't full, Standard excused himself in favor of a vacant aisle seat in the back of the plane. During the first eight hours in the air, he perused two LA newspapers, watched the in-flight movie, and started the George Chesbro paperback that Benny had given him when he was recuperating from the encounter with Helen Badden's front door. It wasn't hard to see why Benny liked it. The book's protagonist, Mongo, was a former circus dwarf turned criminologist.

Standard spent the final four hours fighting back the urge to start chewing on the seat cushions while wondering if the smoke detectors in the bathroom really worked and whether dismantling them was as much of a federal offense on a New Zealand plane as it was on an American one.

While waiting in line to get through customs, he glanced around the small terminal, thinking maybe he'd get lucky. Maybe Allie was already in the building, waiting to meet someone from the same flight. From the looks of things, coming to watch a plane land was a sort of national pastime on Rarotonga, like baseball in the United States.

By the time Standard got outside, it was raining, but no one seemed to notice. Coffee from the terminal's small restaurant came in Styrofoam cups. It was instant. He took two sips and dropped it in a trashcan then smoked two cigarettes while waiting in line at a Bank of New Zealand window to exchange money. A few minutes later, he piled into the back of a mini-van with a half-dozen giddy Canadians. Without having to ask, they told him they were all retired and had pooled their money to rent a house for six months on the far side of the island.

"No snow this year, eh?" They said it in unison, like a high school cheer.

Standard stared out the window and hoped it wasn't a long ride. The Canadians were starting to get on his nerves, and they weren't even out of the airport parking lot. He leaned forward over the driver's shoulder.

"I hope the Edgewater Resort is your first stop." The driver, a man in his early twenties, nodded and flashed a shy grin into the rear view mirror. He wore the local uniform: Faded T-shirt, baggy shorts, and sandals. "Not very tropical." Standard pointed to the gray sky and the raindrops splattering against the windshield.

"Storm just moved through," the driver said. "It will clear up, then rain again, and then clear up again." He shrugged like it was no big deal.

Standard settled back in the seat to watch the scenery slip by. He expected to find happy natives living in grass shacks, wearing loincloths and coconut bras. Instead, Rarotongan architecture was decidedly western, with lots of whitewash stucco, carports, and neatly trimmed lawns and hedges. Family burial plots and cargo containers used for storage occupied places of honor next to each house. Sleepy dogs lay in dirt driveways staring at passing traffic. They looked like you could hire them to show you around the island. Along the shoulder of the road, little kids in black-and-white uniforms walked to school or rode their bikes. The only things missing were drive-thru espresso places and a middle school named for Amelia Earhart. Then again, there was still a lot to see.

At the hotel, Standard was first out of the van and up to the registration desk. The reservation Benny had made was ready and waiting. The clerk's smile was full of bright white teeth. Her hair was cut shoulder length, thick and silky. He signed in, and she took an imprint of his credit card.

Five minutes later, he was in a small, clean room with linoleum floors and a ceiling fan. The balcony looked down into a courtyard filled with coconut palms, gardenia bushes, and paved pathways leading to the beach. Directly below, a half dozen scrawny chickens pecked the ground, looking for breadcrumbs tossed down from the rooms above.

On the other side of the courtyard, the sound of rattling dishes came out of the open-air restaurant with its cone-shaped thatched roof. Beyond that was a small swimming pool and a large, tiled patio lined with towel-covered beach chairs. Further out, the azure lagoon glistened in a morning sun that was just beginning to break through the rain clouds.

Leaving the sliding door open, Standard tried out the bed. Even the thin, hard mattress felt great after the plane seat. When the humidity crept into the room, he closed the door, turned up the air conditioner, and fell asleep watching the ceiling fan spin slowly overhead.

Standard woke up a little after noon to a cold room. The water that dripped from the air conditioner had pooled up in the corner near a cloth-covered armchair. He stayed still, trying to get his bearings. Allie Shafer. South Pacific. Rarotonga. Three hours later on the West Coast. Three p.m. in Portland. Valerie would still be at work, drinking coffee to keep her going until five p.m. Benny would just be waking up after pulling an all-nighter weaving magic on his bank of computers.

The stingy shower spit water like it didn't know it was on a rain-soaked tropical island. He shaved then dug around in the gym bag that doubled for a suitcase. He was the world's worst traveler, packing either too much or too little. This time it was about right, thanks to Valerie, who knew what was needed. The bag contained only shorts, T-shirts, socks, and underwear. The Nikes he'd worn on the plane trip completed the outfit. Anything else he could buy while he was here.

Armed with a handful of tourist brochures pulled from a rack in the hotel lobby after checking in, Standard wandered out toward the pool, looking for some lunch and a cold beer. The hotel's large patio sat spitting distance from the warm waters of the lagoon. Along the beachfront, tourists faced the ocean, reading Grisham paperbacks between slathering on layers of sun block. Thatch-covered cabanas that looked like giant mushrooms that had sprouted from the middle of wooden tables offered the only shade.

He sat at a table at the far end of the pool and spread out the brochures. Most of the glossy fliers hawked scuba diving trips, restaurants, lagoon cruises, and places that sold black pearls. One contained a large foldout map of the island that at least provided some idea where he was.

Rarotonga was shaped like a dented bicycle wheel. The center of the island looked like a Jurassic Park of jungle and emerald green volcanic peaks. A two-lane paved road circled the entire island, with numerous dead-end roads running either inland like spokes on the mangled wheel or out toward the ocean, to dead end at the beach. There were no roads across the island, only a footpath. By all indications, the lives of the twelve thousand residents of Rarotonga appeared to be confined to the island's outer edge. A small place, he thought, but still big enough to hide someone who didn't want to be found.

When the waiter showed up, Standard ordered a can of Lion Red, on Valerie's recommendation, and a hamburger. The morning clouds had scurried off to the east to let the scorching sun beat down on the beige patio tiles. Steam rose from the small puddles left by the rain. Standard made a mental note to buy a hat, sandals, and a tube of sun block.

"Do you know a place called Trader Jack's?" he asked when the waiter showed up with lunch.

"You bet. It's in Avarua, right at the mouth of the harbor. Good eats. Good drinks." The waiter wore a gold nametag that read "Taomia." His face was large and gentle, with Polynesian features. Straight white teeth filled a quick smile. "You can call me Tommy," he said when he noticed Standard looking at his badge. They shook hands, Standard's getting lost in the waiter's like a baseball in a catcher's mitt.

Standard guessed Tommy's age at early thirties. He had huge

arms, broad shoulders, and a tapered waist. In the United States, Tommy might have played linebacker for the 49ers. In Rarotonga, he probably played rugby, which explained his slightly bent nose, but not the perfect teeth. His ink black hair was cut short on the sides. The top was left long and pulled back into a tight ponytail, in a sort of a modified mullet. Tommy's huge hands made the beer can look like one of the complimentary shampoo bottles in Standard's hotel room.

"I'm the bartender, but I wait tables when things are slow." Tommy's English was excellent, his accent New Zealand. "You need anything, you come and see me. I know everybody on Rarotonga."

"I'll do that."

Standard ate while studying the map. There were at least thirty hotels, motels, resorts, apartments, hostels, and other places to stay on the island. That didn't count the private beachfront homes. Allie Shafer could be at any one of them, or none. He scanned the sunbaked tourists one more time. None of the bodies resembled Allie's. Finding her wasn't going to be that easy.

When Tommy returned to clear away the plates, Standard ordered another beer and asked if there were many Americans who lived on the island year round.

"Some, most of them are old. Others are honeymooners. The government only allows people to stay up to six months. After that, they have to apply to the Department of Immigration. You looking for someone?"

Standard described Allie, including the gap between her teeth. Tommy shook his massive head. "We get thousands of visitors a year. They don't all stay here. Sorry."

"I have a photo." Standard shuffled through the pile of brochures for the manila envelope that contained the photo of Allie sitting at the bar at Trader Jack's. "That's her in the middle. Her name is Allie, Allie Shafer."

Tommy stared at it for a few seconds. His eyes narrowed. He

looked at Standard then back at the photo. Standard sensed something. Tommy recognized her. He could feel it.

"I recognize a couple of the men, but not her." Tommy handed the photo back. "Are you with the police?"

"No. Just trying to find an old friend. The men in the picture, can you tell me who they are?"

"Not really. I think one of them might have been a guest here at the hotel."

"So they're not locals?"

"No," Tommy said then wished Standard luck and disappeared with the dirty dishes.

Watching Tommy walk away, Standard felt more confident than ever that he was on the right track, but he would need to talk to Tommy again.

Standard walked to the edge of the patio that overlooked the small beach. The lagoon couldn't have been more than ten feet deep. Large rocks, some as big as Volkswagens, dotted the sandy bottom. A pair of snorkelers, floating face down thirty yards off shore, looked like dead bodies. Two boys wearing baggy shorts and carrying surfboards walked in ankle deep water on the reef a couple of hundred yards off shore. They were silhouetted against the large waves that battered the outside edge of the reef.

This wasn't a snipe hunt, he thought. She was here. He could feel it. Maybe not at the hotel, but somewhere on the island. Tommy had recognized her when he looked at the photo. His face was too honest to hide his surprise.

Standard signed the bill, giving Tommy a wave of thanks as he went out to the hotel lobby. The Hertz counter, across from the reservation desk, offered cars and motor bikes for about ten bucks a day. The Hertz clerk could've been Tommy's cousin. It took fifteen minutes to fill out the paperwork and put down a deposit. The clerk pointed at a half dozen cars sitting outside on the lawn.

"One more thing," the clerk said. "You'll need to get a license. You can get one at the police headquarters in Avarua."

"How do I get there?"

The clerk gave him an odd look then slid the keys across the counter. "You drive."

Chapter 30

Getting a Rarotongan driver's license was more of a contribution to the local economy than an attempt to determine who should drive and who shouldn't. All that was required was six dollars and proof he was staying in a local hotel. Fortunately, there was no test, written or otherwise.

"If you're staying at the Edgewater then you know Taomia," the clerk at the police station said. She was large, with thick black hair and pudgy fingers. Her starched white blouse, with epaulets, looked uncomfortable in the afternoon heat and humidity. Her name badge read "Sgt. Taere."

"Tommy the bartender. I saw him just a little while ago at the hotel."

"We're cousins." She said it as if being related to a bartender at the largest resort on the island was a greater source of pride than being a cop. "His mother and my mother are sisters. We grew up on Aitutaki. My brother is still there. He's the only doctor on the island. Another cousin is a police officer."

"Aitutaki?"

"It's one of the other islands."

"There are more islands like this?"

Sgt. Taere's laugh echoed off the office walls. "There are fifteen other islands, but none of them are like Rarotonga. The others are small with very few people."

"Hotels?"

"Some yes. Some no."

Standard sighed. The job of finding Allie Shafer may have just gotten a little bigger. "Have you ever seen this woman around town?" He showed her the photo of Allie Shafer.

She studied it for a few moments. "She looks kind of familiar, but I couldn't tell you where I'd seen her or when." She slid the photo back across the counter. "That is Trader Jack's, though. Good eats. Good drinks."

"Yeah, so I've heard."

Ten minutes later, Sgt. Taere handed over a newly minted Rarotongan driver's license. Standard left to wander around in search of a pharmacy that carried sun block. Instead, he settled for a clothing store, where he bought a pair of sandals, a green safari hat with a chinstrap, cheap sunglasses, and Croakies. If he could find a T-shirt emblazoned with the local slogan of "Kia Orana," he'd look exactly like the other tourists on the island. Maybe someone would mistake him for a Canadian. It would be the perfect disguise.

The local Internet service was in a small store that doubled as a perfume counter. Sitting amid the cloying smells of sandalwood and frangipani, Standard emailed Benny that he'd arrived safely and that the search for Allie Shafer had begun in earnest. The email included a brief description of Rarotonga, adding that since there was more than one island spread over a good chunk of the South Pacific, the search might take longer than planned.

Since Cook Islanders drove on the left, for his own safety and that of others, he left the rental car where it was and walked across the street to the harbor. A half dozen small charter boats bobbed at anchor next to even smaller fishing boats with outboard motors tilted up out of the water. Using the map, he kept walking east toward the T-shirt factory in a tin-roofed building near the boat launch. Trader Jack's was around the corner. It sat overlooking the rock jetty that marked the narrow passage from the harbor into the ocean. A half dozen tourists sat on the outside deck talking and drinking cans of Cook Island Lager. One of the women recognized Standard from the plane. They exchanged waves.

Inside, he walked along the horseshoe-shaped bar to the place Allie had been sitting when the photo was taken. The calendar on the wall was the same one as in the photo, only the month read September instead of June. When he sat down, the feeling of getting closer to her grew stronger.

He ordered a Lion Red from the bartender, who looked like yet another version of Tommy. Standard showed him the picture when he returned with the beer and a glass. The bartender shrugged and said she looked sort of familiar. He tossed the photo on the bar and went back to cutting lime wedges.

Another vague confirmation that Allie was no stranger to bartenders and waiters on Rarotonga. He did his best not to get ahead of himself.

"What about these other guys? Do you know them?"

The bartender picked up the photo again. "Most of them look like tourists. Probably not here anymore, except the guy talking to your friend. His name is Marsh." The bartender gestured over his shoulder toward the harbor. "He owned one of the charter boats, but sold it a couple of months ago and moved back to Australia. Fishing has been the shits for more than a year. I think it's that El Nino thing."

"Were they friends or did they just meet here?"

"I don't remember much about your friend except that she kept pretty much to herself. She didn't come in that often, and I don't remember her being with any one person."

"When was the last time you saw her?"

He rubbed his chin. "I don't know. It's been a few months at least. I don't even remember her name, if I ever knew it."

The bartender knew her. He was right. She is here, he thought, or was.

"Any idea where she lived?" he asked.

The bartender thought for a moment. "No. I just assumed she was another tourist staying in one of the hotels and that she went home like everyone else when her vacation was over."

"Do you know Tommy? He's the bartender at The Edgewater."

"Everyone knows Tommy."

"Did Marsh know Tommy?"

"Sure. Marsh was around here for years. I think Tommy worked for him as a deck hand for a while before going to work at The Edgewater." The bartender frowned. "What's your point?"

"Nothing."

Standard took the beer outside to the deck. A charter boat, flying two tuna flags, moved into the harbor. The three men sitting on the back deck, drinking beer, looked sunburned and proud.

Tommy had lied. Standard knew it when he asked about Allie. Now, he was sure. If Tommy knew Marsh then there was a good chance he knew Allie, as well. Knowing he was getting closer made his hands sweat. After just a few hours on the island, he'd learned that there was at least one person here who wanted to protect her.

Spreading the map out on one of the tables, Standard tried figuring out how best to check each of the island's twenty hotels. There were two in town, both of them just a few blocks away. They were as good a place to start as any.

He finished the beer then walked east along Ara Tapu, the main road out of town. The two hotels sat side by side. Standard flashed the picture to clerks and bartenders at the Beachcomber and the Paradise Inn without success. On the way back, he stopped at Trader Jack's for another beer. The same bartender was there, but a crew of young waitresses had started setting the tables in the dining area off the bar. He showed each of them the photo of Allie. The responses were pretty much the same as from the bartender: "She looks familiar, but I don't know where she is."

Walking back to the rented Suzuki, Standard felt a certain sense of accomplishment. People on the island had seen her, and he'd eliminated two possible places where Allie could be living. He also figured that, on an island as small as Rarotonga, it wouldn't take long for word to spread that someone was looking for an American woman. Maybe Allie would find him. Then again, maybe she would catch the first flight off the island.

He gingerly drove home, getting familiar enough with the car and the traffic pattern to check out a couple more small hotels along the way. Again no luck.

Having enough for one day, he stopped at a road-side liquor store for a bottle of Absolut, limes, and a six pack of Lion Red. After a couple of drinks in the room, Standard went down to the hotel restaurant. It was island night. The floorshow featured locals with native drums and grass skirts. The women dancers were graceful and beautiful, with aloof smiles that promised everything and delivered nothing. The movement of their hips effortless and erotic.

Standard thought of Valerie and her days as a dancer. She'd even done a few of them on nights when they'd had too much wine. He didn't remember any island number in her act, but he might have missed it.

After checking out the buffet and not seeing anything recognizable in the steam trays, he walked down to a restaurant called the Spaghetti House near the entrance road to the hotel. It was getting dark. Clouds moved in from the west to shroud the tops of the peaks in the center of the island. The restaurant was empty. He took a table near the window that looked out on to the main road. It started to rain. Locals, with their rain jackets on backward to keep dry, buzzed by on Honda motor bikes.

Even inside the restaurant, he could hear the raw beat of the island night drums. With the images of the island girls performing back at the hotel still vivid, his thoughts drifted back to the United

States and to Valerie. He suddenly felt lonelier than at any time in his life.

Chapter 31

Standard was up by eight the next morning. Fortified by toast and another cup of undrinkable instant coffee from the hotel restaurant, he walked down to the beachfront patio to find Tommy. A waitress serving breakfast to tables full of guests said he didn't come to work until midafternoon.

He thanked her and headed for the parking lot. Firing up the Suzuki, he drove out to the main road to begin working his way around the island to check more hotels. He rolled down all the windows and drove slowly, still ill at ease with sitting on the wrong side of the car and driving on the wrong side of the road. Maybe a motor bike would have been better, then he wouldn't have to worry about where the steering wheel was located.

The open windows made the map, spread out on the passenger seat, flutter in the wind. He was prepared to pull over every mile or two to let the cars and motor bikes lined up behind him pass, while keeping one eye out for hotels or any place that sold a decent cup of coffee. He found plenty of the first. None of the second.

The first stop was a just a few minutes down the road from the hotel, the Manuia Beach Hotel. After that it was the Puaikura Reef Hotel and the Daydreamer Apartments. At each place he shoved Allie's picture under the noses of a dozen confused desk clerks, groundskeepers, and maids. No one recognized her. Most didn't even bother to apologize. They just shook their heads and went about their business. By noon, he was nearly halfway around the island without finding either Allie or a real cup of coffee. He'd visited eight hotels, a half dozen restaurants, and three roadside stores. He'd even pulled into a dive shop, thinking that Allie might try to add to her anonymity by seeking a few hours at the bottom of the ocean. A waitress in a tiny restaurant said she thought Allie looked familiar. So did a teenage boy behind the counter at a small grocery store that specialized in cold beer. Neither of them, though, knew Allie by name or where she was staying.

The next stop was Muri Beach. The map showed it as a large lagoon edged with more hotels, an abandoned half-finished condominium complex, and a couple of restaurants. It seemed a good place to eat while bracing a few more busboys and bartenders. Besides, the cold toast and bad coffee had worn off an hour earlier. All Standard could taste was the half pack of cigarettes he'd smoked since leaving the hotel.

At a sign that said Rarotonga Sailing Club, he turned in and parked the Suzuki in a sandlot next to a couple of overturned rowboats. Calling the place a club was generous at best. It was a small, two-story white building with clapboard siding and a tiled roof. A hut attached to one side rented snorkels and sailboards to lagoon-bound tourists.

Standard walked around to the front of the building facing the beach. A sign over a doorway read "restaurant," with an arrow that pointed up a narrow flight of stairs. The second-floor overlooked the lagoon.

"Welcome to Sails." The waiter, dressed in shorts and a T-shirt, showed Standard to a table near the large windows that were open to let in the breeze. The sounds of people playing on the beach percolated up from below.

The view was right out of a Chamber of Commerce brochure. Turquoise water stretched out toward four small islands covered in coconut palms and outlined in white sand beaches. Sailboarders zipped around the lagoon, propelled by the warm breeze. Like every place else on the island, the protective reef a half-mile away kept the ocean at bay.

212

After ordering a beer and the lunch special of coconut shrimp, Standard diligently pulled out the photo of Allie. He held it out when the waiter showed up with the beer. He was middle-aged with sun-bleached hair, a deeply tanned face, and an Australian accent.

"Oh yeah," he said. "She used to come in here all the time."

Standard ignored the beer and pulled the waiter down into the chair across the table. "Talk to me."

"Sure, mate," he said, trying unsuccessfully to pull his arm out of Standard's grip. "She always came in alone and left alone. Some of the local blokes might hit on her, but she'd have none of it. A few drinks, a few laughs, and she was out of here."

"Do you know where she was staying?"

"She never said, but I got the impression she was over at the Sokala Villas. That's just up the beach. Can't be sure, though. Like I said, she pretty much kept to herself. Not like the other sheilas that hang out here."

"Where are these villas?"

"I'll tell you, mate, but you got to let go of my arm."

Standard realized he had vise grip on the waiter's forearm. "Sorry."

"No worries, mate. I guess this is important to you."

"You might say that."

"Girlfriend?"

"I wish it was that simple. Now, where are these villas?"

The waiter pointed toward a place where two small Hobie Cats were pulled up on the sand. A handful of people sprawled on large wooden lounge chairs soaked up the midday sun while reading paperbacks. "Head that way and then take a left up off the beach. That's where I think she was staying, but I can't guarantee it. Like I said, she kept to herself. It's just that there's no bar at the Sokala, so most of the guests come here. It's the closest place."

"Did you happen to catch her name?"

"I think it was Karen or Katie something like that. I didn't get a last name. She probably never gave it. The manager of the Villas would know. His name's Piri. You can't miss him, snow white hair and a flowered shirt. He's probably about a hundred or so years old. Been here since Captain Cook himself came ashore. Tell him Jacko sent you."

Standard forgot the lunch, but left Jacko a tip equal to the entire bill. Walking up the beach, he tried not to look like someone on the way to a fire.

There was no sign for Sokala Villas, so he had to get directions from a leather-skinned woman with a two-piece swimsuit and one of Oprah's books. She pointed toward a narrow path leading away from the beach. "There's a little sign in the bushes about halfway up the path. You can't miss it."

Sokala Villas was Rarotonga's answer to exclusive, with only seven cottages scattered around manicured grounds. Each had its own pool and kitchen. It catered to couples and honeymooners. Children under age twelve, stay away. Gilligan's Island meets Embassy Suites. The waiter's description made it easy to find Piri. Standard spotted him pushing a cart loaded down with fresh towels. He was headed toward the three villas along the beachfront.

"Excuse me, but are you Piri?" The man stopped long enough to look Standard up and down, answer yes, and go back to pushing his cart. "Jacko at the restaurant up the beach said you might help me. My name's John Standard. I'm trying to find someone, someone who might be staying here or has stayed here."

Piri stopped again and gave a toothy Cook Islander grin. "I have work to do, but we can talk at the same time." He motioned. Standard followed.

Piri stopped in front of one of the villas, grabbed an armful of towels from the cart, and went inside. Standard hung with him, still trying to keep his eagerness in check. The thatch-roofed villa had dark pine walls under an open-beam ceiling. The beds were freshly made, the small kitchen spotless. Piri disappeared into the bathroom with the towels. When he came out, Standard had the photo of Allie ready to hand him.

"The woman in the middle of the photo," Standard said. "Is she here or has she ever been here? I'd really like to find her."

Piri looked at the photo, then at Standard. "She in some kind of trouble?"

"I'm not sure. I need to find her to know that."

"You police, FBI, CIA?"

"No. It's nothing like that. She's a friend. She disappeared several months ago. I'm worried about her. I've managed to trace her all the way to this place."

"Maybe she wants to stay disappeared."

Standard tried not to act impatient, but Piri was making it hard. "It's not that simple."

Handing back the photo, Piri moved slowly around the villa, straightening the covers on the beds and checking lamps to make sure bulbs weren't burned out. Standard stood in the middle of the room watching the old man move around.

"A flight landed a few minutes ago," Piri said. "We have guests coming this afternoon. We need to be ready for them. We pride ourselves in being discreet and private here. Your request is not a normal one."

"I wouldn't ask you to compromise your standards if it wasn't important. I just need to know that someone has actually seen her, that she's really been here on Rarotonga."

Piri stopped fussing long enough to look Standard in the face then turned away to fluff the pillows on the floral couch. "You look like an honest man. So I'll tell you she stayed here for two months. Most guests don't stay here that long. Our rates are higher than other places on the island, but we think it's worth it."

"I'm sure it is. These places are beautiful."

"I don't know where she went after that. It was my belief that her vacation was over and she was returning to the United States."

"Her name is Allie Shafer. What name did she use here?"

Piri thought for a moment. "Karen Vincent, I believe. She stayed right here in this villa."

Standard glanced around the room, trying to imagine her sleeping in the bed, sitting at the little table near the kitchen, standing naked in the living room.

Outside, a young woman in a white skirt and flowered blouse similar to Piri's shirt, led a young couple, wearing leis and carrying large suitcases, across the grass toward one of the other villas.

"Our guests are arriving," Piri said. "I must go."

"Did anyone visit her while she was here?"

The old man paused long enough to consider whether the question violated his oath of office. It apparently didn't. "A woman was here last June. She stayed in the villa next door. Karen seemed to know her from back home. They spent most of their time together. Sometimes they just walked down the beach to Sails. Other times, they went into Avarua for dinner or to drink at Trader Jack's. I know they went there, because the other woman, Miss Vincent's friend, came back with a T-shirt from there. She stayed two weeks. Miss Vincent left several days later. The woman has called here every week after that looking for her, but I haven't heard from her this week. She seemed aggravated that Miss Vincent is no longer here. She even accused me of lying to her. I think she is a very unpleasant person."

"This woman have a name?"

He ran a leathery hand through his white hair then motioned toward the door. They walked along a stone path through a grass courtyard to an office no bigger than a clothes closet. Standard leaned over the small registration desk while Piri opened a small drawer and slowly flipped through a stack of three-by-five cards.

"Here it is," he said. "Badden. Doctor Helen Badden from Portland, Oregon, USA."

Chapter 32

Rather than backtrack to the hotel, Standard kept heading around the island, hugging the centerline of the narrow road that never became wider than two lanes. He ignored the map, taking comfort in knowing that, on a round island, you sooner or later get back to where you started. In Avarua, he pulled the Suzuki into the same place he'd parked the day before.

Helen Badden could have parked in this spot, Standard thought. Maybe Allie had been with her. No, Allie probably drove. She liked to be in charge. Either way, they could have walked from here to Trader Joe's, stopping along the way to look at perfume or black pearls, maybe T-shirts or beach towels. He tried not to think about it as he spent thirty minutes wandering around town before finding the immigration office.

It was in a squat, whitewashed government building on the edge of the business district. The cement path to the front door was lined with stubby palm trees. A short flight of wooden stairs led to a broad porch. Wicker chairs flanked a screen door. Inside, the man behind the counter was dressed in white. A neatly trimmed mustache sat atop a welcoming grin.

"How can I help you?"

When Standard said he was looking for information about an American named Karen Vincent, the man seemed unsure of what to do. Things got moving when Standard invoked the name of Tommy, the bartender. The clerk gave him a conspiratorial wink then disappeared into a dark room behind the counter.

Standard waited out on the porch, sitting in one of the wicker chairs, scanning the latest edition of the *Cook Island Press*. Lingering over an article about the activities of the island's parliament, he wondered how many of the elected members were related to Tommy. Page two had a feature on the local jail. It had one prisoner, who was doing six months for riding his motorcycle across the local rugby field during a seasonal rainstorm. Standard had just gotten to the part about how inmates had to buy their own food when the clerk pushed open the door and motioned him inside. He handed Standard a computer printout.

"Our records show that Karen Vincent, a citizen of Belize, entered the Cook Islands in February of this year."

"Belize? Are you sure?"

He looked offended. "We keep very good records. She came in on a Belize passport on an Air New Zealand flight from Mexico City to Auckland."

"Is she still here?"

The clerk scanned with his finger. "No. She left five months later on June twentieth. Under Cook Island law, she could have stayed another month. More than that, however, and she would need to request permission from this office. No such request was made."

The twinge in Standard's stomach said that he had been so close, but now may have flown halfway around the world for nothing. Still, there was no giving up when he was this close. He pointed at the printout. "Does it say where she went?"

"No, but it does say that she returned three days ago from Australia. It gives her address as the Sokala Villas. That's down at Muri Beach."

Standard's hopes came back. "Can I see that?" He handed Standard the printout. He was right. The twinge eased a bit. Allie was back in the Cook Islands, just not at the Sokala Villas. Standard left after promising the clerk to say hello to Tommy.

On the way back into town, he stopped at Cook's Corner, a sort of mini mall with shops and restaurants that catered to tourists waiting at the bus stop. He ordered a beer at a place called The Roundabout, an open-air restaurant at the back of the mall, and sat at a small table covered in checkered oilcloth. He gulped down the beer and ordered a second. Tourists moved through the shops in the mid-afternoon heat. They looked as wilted as he felt. In the South Pacific, the sun rules everything: What you wear, drink, and the degree of sun block on your nose. Eventually, the incessant tropical sun wins and turns the shade into an ally against sunburn and thirst.

The beer cut through the humidity, clearing Standard's head and providing time to piece together what he'd learned, or thought he'd learned. There were still too many gaps. The only thing for sure was that this was the right place at the right time.

Leaving The Roundabout, Standard walked up the street into the center of town. The perfume shop, which doubled as the local Internet service, was closed. He hung around for a few minutes watching cars and motor bikes scurry through town. The beers should have made him sleepy, but knowing that Allie was close kept him hyped up. The wilted feeling disappeared. He liked the edge it gave. Keep moving, he told himself. This is why you're here.

The owner of the perfume shop returned. She was young, with long black hair and a bright print dress. Standard got a toothy Cook Island grin while she searched the return e-mails. Benny's response was there. She let him read it on the screen:

> I should have gone with you. Eldon Mock's been beating my door down looking for you. It's something about an article you're supposed to be doing for him. He said if he doesn't hear from you soon, that he's going to give the story to someone else. The man's a pain in the ass, but I assume you know what he's talking about. I couldn't care less.

Let me know how things are going in finding Allie Shafer. Valerie sends her love, but she's still miffed that you didn't invite her along. By the way, after dropping you off at the airport, I saw Carp sitting in a car outside the terminal. Probably just a coincidence, but I fought off the urge to slash his tires.

Best, Benny.

Carp.

Damn.

The name turned Standard's nerves up a notch or two. The last thing he wanted was to see Carp lurking in some doorway or sitting on a bench along the seawall, pretending to read a newspaper. He wouldn't do it, Standard thought. He wouldn't follow me here, not after what Moses Blue told him.

Still, Carp had followed him to Seaside. Why not follow him to the airport as well?

Standard thought back to the day he checked in for the flight to Los Angeles. There was no way for Carp to know. Only Benny and Valerie knew about Rarotonga. Blue said he would call Carp off. Maybe he did, but maybe Carp had gone rogue, working on his own, letting Standard lead him to Allie. But why?

Standard checked the street one more time. His edge got sharper. After a deep breath, he sent back a cryptic reply saying Allie was somewhere on the island but he still hadn't found her and to tell Mock to calm down. He'd get his story as soon as there was one to write. Standard signed off with instructions to tell Valerie he missed her. He didn't mention Carp. He couldn't even write the name, but that didn't get him out of Standard's mind.

Across the street. Standard sat on a bench with his back to the harbor. A stubby palm tree, with wide leaves, cast a shadow large

221

enough to provide relief from the late afternoon sun. What passed for a rush hour on a South Pacific island was under way. He smoked a cigarette and checked the cars and trucks that drove by. Get a grip! Carp was six thousand miles away, bouncing drunken day traders out of Blue's nightclub.

It was nearly six o'clock when Standard pulled the Suzuki back into the grass parking lot next to the hotel. He walked to his room, showered, and changed into another pair of shorts and a T-shirt.

The dozen or so guests on the patio around the pool were either finishing up a day in the sun or starting an evening on the town. They all had drinks while swapping stories about treks to the summit of Te Kou, the highest peak in the center of the island, or shopping for black pearl necklaces in Avarua.

At the far end of the patio, the activities director was giving a group of Canadians a demonstration of different ways to tie a pareau, which is a piece of cloth with mystical significance that could be used for everything from an evening dress to a swim suit.

Standard looked around for Tommy. Not seeing him, he asked one the waitresses. She pointed toward an area outside the backdoor to the bar. Standard found him deftly cutting the tops off coconuts with a large machete, the huge knife a toy in his hand.

Tommy flashed a friendly grin. "Did you find your friend?" He hacked the end off another coconut to create a container for the rum and vodka drinks favored by tourists.

"I'm pretty close. Why not help me out and tell me where she is?"

Tommy's only reaction was to bring the machete down a little harder on the next unlucky coconut.

"I don't know who you think I am," Standard said, "but I'm not here to hurt her."

Tommy put down the machete then began husking other coconuts using a long metal spike stuck in the ground. He impaled the coconut on the spike, using it to tear off the fibrous outer shell to get to the smooth brown nut inside. The male dancers on island night did the same thing using their teeth. After doing two or three, he broke one of the nuts open. He handed Standard a piece of the white inner meat and kept another for himself.

"When I showed you the photo yesterday, you recognized her," Standard said. "You lied to me about the man in the photo with her. His name's Marsh. You used to be a deck hand on his charter boat."

"The bartender at Trader Jack's tell you that?"

Standard nodded. "I went to the Immigration Office. The clerk told me she left the island and then came back, that she was staying at the Sokala Villas, only she's not there. I think you know where she is."

Tommy stuck the machete in a log then sat down next to it. He popped a piece of coconut in his mouth and chewed. "What kind of trouble is your friend in?"

The question confirmed to Standard that he was on the right track, and close. Very close. "The man she used to work for wants her back."

"She run away?"

"Sort of."

It was hard not to get the feeling that Tommy already knew the answers to his own questions. Asking them came across as his way of finding out how much Standard knew. Either that or Tommy was filling in the blanks in the story he'd been told by Allie.

Tommy pulled the machete out of the log. He dug a whetstone out of his pocket, spit on it, and began sharpening the long blade. The metal gleamed in the oil lamps set along the patio. "This man she used to work for, he sent you here to get her?"

"Not voluntarily. The man thinks I had something to do with her running away."

"Did you?"

"No."

"Who is this man?"

"It's a long story. Let's say that the reason she's here is to get away from him."

"Then why do you want to find her?" Tommy slid the full length of the machete along the stone.

"Because if I don't, it might be my ass as well."

Tommy put the stone way. He ran his finger along the edge of the machete blade. Standard finished chewing on the coconut, lit a cigarette, and waited.

"If you find her, will you make her go back with you?" Tommy said.

"If you know her, then you know that no one can make her do anything she doesn't want to do."

"And what happens to you?"

"I don't know exactly, but it won't be pretty."

"Did you come here alone?"

Standard thought it was an odd question, but said that he had. "Why do you ask?"

"No reason. It's just odd when Americans come to Rarotonga alone."

"She did, why can't I?"

Tommy stood up and piled the coconuts in a cardboard box. "I need to get ready for work." He picked up the box like it was a carton of eggs. "It sounds to me like you got a problem on your hands. Good luck to you, mate."

Standard watched Tommy carry the box in the back door of the bar, then went back to the patio where the other guests were lined up for dinner and grabbed a stool at the bar. The sandwich board announced that it was steak night and the evening's entertainment was music by Useless and the Crab Boys.

Tommy showed up behind the bar in time to serve Standard a Lion Red at no charge. He slid the beer across the bar with a casual nod. It was as if the conversation they'd had seconds before never happened. Standard drank half the beer then left the can on a vacant patio table. It was not a night for beer. The Absolut in the little refrigerator in his room was calling.

Drink in hand, he sat on the balcony, the music filtering up from the restaurant. Standard tried to remember if he'd ever heard a live rendition of "Theme from a Summer Place."

After two drinks, he called down to the Spaghetti House to have a pizza delivered. It arrived halfway through a fourth drink. He ate two slices then abandoned the food for more Absolut. Back out on the balcony, he watched retired couples leave the restaurant and walk arm in arm back to their rooms. Tommy came out the side door of the bar to pick up the machete and expertly decapitate a few more coconuts.

How much did Tommy know? Had Allie told him how she'd faked her death? That Karen Vincent wasn't her real name? Was Tommy around when Helen Badden arrived in June? Was he with them at Trader Jack's the night that the picture of Allie was taken? Did he take it? Did Badden?

Standard guessed that Allie had been just as secretive with Tommy as she'd been with everyone else. Someone who could keep big secrets didn't have much trouble keeping small ones. Even if Allie had told Tommy everything, there was no way for her to know that Helen Badden had hung onto the photo for three months before sending it to Moses Blue.

Maybe Allie didn't even know Badden was dead. But maybe she did. Allie had been off the island at the time Badden died. But so what? Badden's death was a suicide, or was it? Where had Allie been between the end of June and three days ago? The questions begged another Absolut.

Standard didn't go in for ukuleles and electric pianos, but the music fit easily with the breeze coming off the lagoon. Lights came on in the rooms around his. Other guests moved out on to their balconies. Standard listened to the couple above him marvel at how different Rarotonga was from Manitoba. He loved the insights of seasoned travelers.

A comfortable drowsiness brought on by the Absolut announced that Allie Shafer, Moses Blue, Tommy the Bartender, and the rest of the world could wait until tomorrow. He fell asleep on top of the bed. There were no dreams, only the dark, fathomless sleep that comes from too much alcohol and too few answers.

A pounding head and achy bladder knocked him out of bed at seven the next morning. It was on the way to the bathroom that he saw the note someone had slipped under the door during the night. Bending to pick it up, the hammer in his head went from mono to stereo.

The note, with its one word on the single sheet of hotel stationery, silenced everything.

Aitutaki.

Chapter 33

The Air Rarotonga jet was a toothpaste tube with wings, two propellers, and eight passengers crammed inside a cabin that smelled of jet fuel. Standard sat in the first row behind the cockpit, wishing the windows rolled down. The co-pilot, doing most of the flying, looked about fifteen years old in blue shorts, white knee socks, and a military shirt. The pilot, who at least looked like he'd been in the cockpit for more than a couple minutes, spent most of the hour-long flight reading the newspaper. There was no flight attendant, which meant there were no drinks. Instead of a public address system, the pilot would periodically put down his paper and provide updates on the flight by yelling over his shoulder.

Ten thousand feet below, the white-capped ocean looked like a blue sweater covered in lint. There were no boats and no land, just endless miles of open water broken by an occasional bird or low cloud. Somewhere in the distance lay the remote island of Aitutaki, and the even more remote and increasingly more distant Allie Shafer. It was beginning to feel like the closer he got to her the more she seemed to move away—and the more he wished he could head in the opposite direction.

After finding the one-word note under the door, Standard enlisted a mouthful of aspirin in the fight against a throbbing head while getting out the map of the Cook Islands. Aitutaki lay a hundred and sixty miles north of Rarotonga. He fumbled into some clothes, threw a few things in a backpack, and went to the front desk. The clerk said the next flight left in an hour. She called the airline and secured the last seat for him. The other passengers were Canadian day-trippers, most of them from The Edgewater.

The note was in his shirt pocket. No need to pull it out. It wasn't like he was going to forget what it said or recognize the handwriting. Even a broken-down reporter from Portland, Oregon, knew when he was being led somewhere and who was doing the leading. Still, Standard tried not to jump to conclusions. Aitutaki was the only door left. It could also be a dead-end or a false trail created by whoever was protecting Allie Shafer. Not that it mattered. Aitutaki was all he had.

The plane landed just as the smell of jet fuel became overwhelming. The in-flight magazine said that the Seabees had built Aitutaki's crushed coral runways during World War II. Apparently they had also built the airport's decrepit terminal with its rough-hewn wooden siding and thatched roof.

Standard fell in line with the other passengers parading through the terminal and out into the parking lot to the only local mode of transportation—a flatbed truck converted into a tour bus by adding wooden railing, bench seats, and a canvas top over the back. The contraption crept out of the parking lot, bouncing along the tracks in the sand that passed for Aitutaki's roads. The driver was four hundred pounds of jiggling flab encased in a faded T-shirt and baggy shorts. He pointed out the local spots of interest, using a public address system cobbled together from an old karaoke machine and mounted on a makeshift shelf welded to the rear of the truck's cab.

As the truck crept along, he described in a monotone voice the banana plantations, the abandoned churches, and even a group of dope-smoking men drinking moonshine in the front yard of a run-down shack. Everybody waved at them. The men waved back.

The man sitting across from Standard wore white shorts and a bright yellow golf shirt. The name Dave was etched into his belt buckle. It was only a few minutes after ten in the morning, but the humidity had already begun to stain his shirt dark with sweat. He looked like a poached egg.

The truck passed more little shacks and overgrown fields of avocado plants and banana trees. There were more men, drunk on home brew, sitting in the yards in front of more grass shacks. Dave pulled a gray handkerchief from the back pocket of his shorts and ran it around his face. "We're just here for the day, right?" he said to his wife.

Half an hour after leaving the airport, the truck squealed to a halt in the village of Arutanga. Standard climbed off along with Dave, his wife, and the other tourists. They had all the enthusiasm of a chain gang about to tar a road in southern Mississippi. The stop was to inspect the waterfront, with its dozen or so shipping containers piled along the wharf like a child's building blocks. Standard took the opportunity to smoke a cigarette, dry swallow a few more aspirin, and stand at the end of the pier, staring into the blue green water.

He had yet to see anything that even resembled the luxury accommodations Allie had on Rarotonga. That made it hard to believe that she'd come here to stay in one of the low-end hotels and cottages they'd passed since leaving the airport. If Allie Shafer was on Aitutaki then she had to be staying at some place Standard hadn't seen yet.

He found the driver sitting alone in the back of the truck, with a beer in one hand and a roll-your-own cigarette in the other. "Where's the nicest place on the island to stay?"

"The Aitutaki Lagoon Resort Hotel." The driver said it without hesitation. "We're going there now for the lagoon trip. It's part of the package. It also comes with a lagoon cruise, lunch, music, and soft drinks. It's very nice."

Standard checked the map for the thousandth time since leaving the hotel. Aitutaki was a long, narrow island with a small hook at one end. According to the map, the Aitutaki Lagoon Resort Hotel occupied a small island at the end of the hook, separated from the main island by a narrow canal.

He realized too late that the hotel was less than a mile from the airport. He could have walked there rather than endure the bone-shaking ride around the island. Now there was no choice but to climb back aboard the truck for the rest of the guided tour.

An hour later, the truck bounced into a sandy parking area near a narrow footbridge. While the other tourists milled around, wondering where to go, Standard took off across the bridge, his patience worn razor thin by the unnecessary snail-like trek around the island. Fuck the tourists. They were on vacation. He was on a mission. Either Allie Shafer was here or she wasn't. If she was, the resort looked like the kind of place she'd stay. If she wasn't, he would walk back to the airport to wait for the next plane back to Rarotonga.

The hotel was a model of rustic luxury. The restaurant, bar, and a couple of small shops peddling T-shirts and sun tan oil were housed in an open-air pavilion set in the middle of a grove of coconut palms. The grounds were landscaped with small rock gardens, each equipped with a small sign that read: "Beware of falling coconuts." A large, brightly painted flat-bottomed boat, with tables and chairs under a canvas roof, lay anchored in the shallow channel next to the hotel. The four-person crew carried food and drinks on board for the lagoon cruise that the driver had mentioned. Standard wanted no part of it.

The hotel restaurant was empty except for a waitress cleaning up what was left of the breakfast buffet. Standard grabbed the last piece of toast from a warming tray and a slice of papaya then left to look around the grounds. The place wasn't a hotel in the traditional sense. Instead, there were a couple of dozen individual bungalows placed amid a grove of palms that ran down the middle of a small spit of sand that jutted out in a large, triangle-shaped lagoon. Each bungalow was built on short stilts with a set of steep stairs to a small porch. The outer walls were made of plywood. The roofs were weather-beaten thatch.

Standard checked out each bungalow for anything that looked familiar. Beach towels hung on the porch railings to dry. Swimming suits dangled from makeshift clotheslines. Sand-encrusted flip flops sat on the steep stairs. Nothing reminded him of Allie. Not that anything would. She could be staying in any one of them. He was hoping to just run into her or at least see her sitting on one of the porches. If she were here, how would she react when she saw him? How would he react? Was she even here?

It didn't matter. Anything would work since he never really expected to get this far, anyway. But that feeling had returned—the one that said he was close to her, very close. Too close. He could feel the heat, but not see the flame. He fought back the urge to think of clever things to say when he saw her. It would only jinx his chances.

The spit ended at a point covered in white sand and surrounded by turquoise water. There was no shade. Only a relentless sun. A small cabin cruiser, with an inboard engine, was pulled up on the beach. Inside the boat, a shirtless man in his twenties tinkered with some kind of electronic device that lay in pieces on the transom. He was dark skinned with a strong upper body and shoulder-length black hair. His head snapped up when Standard walked out from between two of the bungalows and onto the beach.

Twenty yards away from the boat, a deeply tanned woman lay face down on a chaise lounge. Her arms dangled in the white sand next to an overturned can of diet cola. The straps on her black bikini top were undone. The matching bikini bottom was small and cut high on her hips. She looked asleep.

The man in the boat watched intently as Standard walked toward her. When he was a few yards away, the man jumped out and moved up the beach behind him. He carried a sawed-off baseball bat used to club hooked fish. A large knife hung from a web belt around his waist.

Standard glanced back at him then turned his attention to the woman on the chaise lounge. When was he was ten feet away, she opened her eyes and sat up. She didn't bother to tie her bikini top. Instead, she took off a baseball hat and shook out a head of long, black hair. She was young, mid to late twenties maybe

"*Puis-je vous aider?*" she said, cocking her head, a quizzical look on her face.

Standard could only stare. He had been so sure Allie Shafer was here. He'd been a fool to think he could just walk up and find her lounging on a beach in the middle of paradise. He should have guessed. Nothing about Allie Shafer was ever going to be easy.

"I'm sorry," he said, still staring at the woman. "I thought you were someone else."

When she nodded and smiled, Standard turned away, not sure she understood what he said.

The boy from the boat was still standing thirty feet away. When Standard walked toward him, the boy put his hand on the knife hanging from his belt and looked to his left at a woman standing on the front porch of the nearest bungalow.

"It's all right, Tipi," Allie Shafer said. "I've been expecting him."

Chapter 34

The small cabin cruiser reached full speed in a matter of seconds. The salty spray coming over the bow killed the humidity, making Standard feel less like a damp towel pulled from a too-hot dryer.

Allie Shafer sat across from him. She wore a pareau tied around her waist and a T-shirt over a bikini top. The battered straw hat, pushed hard down on her head, shaded her face and hid her eyes. Allie was leaning back in the padded seat, staring out the back of the boat, watching her hotel grow smaller and smaller. Her tan had a deep, permanent look. Her hair, cut boyishly short, had bleached out into a tangle of brittle corn silk. Her body seemed fitter and more slender than he remembered.

When the boat was a half-mile from shore, Tipi turned around with a silent request for directions. Allie held up her index finger then pointed toward her foot. Tipi nodded and faced forward. The boat picked up even more speed and veered southwest toward the far end of the lagoon.

"We're going to One-Foot Island," she yelled over the roar of the engine and the wind. "We can talk there."

For the rest of the trip, they did little more than exchange awkward smiles as the boat sped across the mirror-smooth lagoon. The small gap in Allie's front teeth winked at him. Unable to talk over the sound of the boat motor, Standard could only watch the small islands go by and think once again about what he'd gotten himself into. The scenery was great, but, based on what he'd learned about Allie Shafer, he was less enthused with the company. Not that he had a choice.

There should have been some sense of excitement or anticipation, maybe even accomplishment, when he'd walked out on to beach toward Allie. After all, he'd wasted weeks mourning her death then traveled halfway across the Pacific to find her. Instead, he was hit by a deep dread. He'd felt it briefly after their one night together. He felt it again, only stronger, after talking to Allie's mother. This time it was nearly overwhelming. Suddenly, the last place on Earth he wanted to be was in a small boat in a large tropical lagoon with Allie Shafer. The voice returned—the same one he'd heard the last time he saw her.

Get out. Walk away. Forget her.

It was too late. Standard was a man without eyelids, staring into the sun.

The boat slowed and eased its way down a narrow channel between two small islands. Tipi nosed it up on the soft sand of the island on the right side of the channel and turned off the motor. Allie jumped out into the knee-deep water. Standard followed. The water felt cool, the sandy bottom soft.

"Islands here are called *motus*," Allie said as they waded ashore. "The real name of this one is Tapuaetai, but everyone calls it One-Foot Island. Don't ask me why. There are at least a couple of different stories involving ancient kings who came ashore in little canoes after paddling their way from New Zealand or some place. My guess is that no one really knows for sure. There's really not much here."

The beach was narrow, the center of the island mostly coconut palms, rocks, and sand. The fallen coconuts, scattered on the ground, looked like footballs left lying around after a practice game.

Allie nodded to Tipi as a silent way of telling him everything would be fine and to stay with the boat. Tipi glared at Standard then nodded his agreement. She took Standard's hand and walked him down the narrow beach toward the far end of the island.

"Who was that woman on the beach?" Standard asked.

"Her name is Angelique something. Her father is the French

ambassador to New Zealand. She comes here to get away from embassy parties."

They were fifty yards from the boat. Standard took off his sandals. The sand felt like sugar under his feet.

"If anyone was going to find me, I knew it would be you," she said.

"Then you should have told me what you were doing and where you were going. It would have made things a lot easier."

She gave him a look that said, "Please don't."

They were about a hundred yards from the boat, near an abandoned jetty that stuck out of the shallow water, the tips of the rocks resembling the spine of a dinosaur skeleton. Allie looked as much a part of the place as the palm trees. Standard suddenly felt like the family accountant who showed up to scold a free-spending trust-fund baby.

"That was quite a line of bullshit you gave me about assisted suicide," he said. "I swallowed every word of it."

"I know and I'm sorry. You have every right to be angry, but it was part of the plan. Deviating from it was never an option."

"What plan? What the hell is this all about?"

"I'll tell you, but not yet." Her tone was a way of telling him to be patient if he ever wanted to learn everything.

Another hundred yards put them out of sight of Tipi and the boat. The lagoon's waters lapped at the beach. Palm trees hovered over the sand, as if ready to pounce on something. Tropical fish that looked like they'd escaped from an aquarium swam around the small rocks and coral a few yards off shore. Across the lagoon, other islands dotted the horizon. A quarter-mile away in the other direction, the ocean clawed at the reef. It was like they were the only two people in paradise.

"It's easy to see why you stay here," he said.

"It is beautiful, isn't it?"

They walked further up the beach to a line of palm trees that offered welcome shade from the sun and sat down.

"You better tell me why you're here," she said. "I've got a feeling that you didn't find me because you wanted to. Something else is going on."

Allie played with a hermit crab she picked up off the sand, letting it crawl around between her feet, while Standard told her nearly everything. It started with Elijah Folsom and Moses Blue, and ended with his tour around Rarotonga and the note under the door of the hotel room. She shook her head in disgust when he told her Rico was dead and went somber at the mention of her mother.

"I assume Tommy left the note after he called you last night," Standard said.

"Don't blame Tommy. He's just looking out for me. Ever since I got here, Tommy's been my self-appointed guardian angel. Don't ask me why, but he feels responsible for me for some reason. I was suspicious when I first met him, but it's just his nature to be nice to people and look out for them. Most Cook Islanders are the same way. He can be fiercely loyal when it comes to those he likes, and he's never asked for anything in return. All I know is that I'd hate to be his enemy. That's why he called me last night and told me someone was looking for me. I knew right away it was you." The crab started to scramble away. Allie grabbed it and held it in her hand. "Tommy's the one who suggested I come to Aitutaki for a while," she said.

"When?"

"When I got back from Australia. I don't know why. I asked Tommy if anything was wrong. He just said he wasn't sure, but he wanted me to be safe until he found out."

"And the guy with the boat?"

"Tipi? He's Tommy's brother. The two of them own the boat together. They make a few bucks giving visitors trips around the lagoon, visitors who want to be alone and not packed on a lagoon cruise with the other tourists."

"Nice work if you can get it."

Allie studied his face for a moment. "It's not what you think. Like I said, Cook Islanders are very friendly and perceptive. I wasn't very happy when I first got here. I felt lost and alone. Tommy seemed to recognize that and made an effort to be helpful. What he's done for me is out of the goodness of his heart."

"Does that include Tipi?"

"Jealousy. I like that in a man." She held back a laugh. "I give Tipi a little money for food and gas for the boat, but nothing more. Do you know he's twenty-five years old and never been off this island? His idea of a trip is to come down here and spend the day snorkeling and spearing fish for dinner." Allie let the crab go. She watched intently as it dragged its oversized shell up the beach to safety. "Amazing, isn't it? We think nothing about getting on a plane and flying thousands of miles in a few hours just to sit in the sun. He's never been more than five miles from where he was born and never further off the ground than the top of a coconut tree."

They sat in an awkward silence. Standard stared out at the lagoon. Allie drew circles in the sand with her finger.

"You know we have some problems to deal with," Standard said, finally.

"Such as, if you don't give Moses what he wants, you end up like Rico?"

"That's the way it works."

"Not if you don't go back." She said it without looking at him.

Standard didn't have an answer—at least not one he wanted to share with her. He had started the search convinced it was a fool's errand. Over time, all he wanted to do was find her. Now that he had, all he wanted to do was leave.

"He would send someone else. Carp maybe."

Allie shrugged. "Tommy and Tipi can handle Carp." She said it with a conviction that Standard didn't share. Allie hadn't seen Rico tied to the light pole or seen her father in the same position, if she even knew about it.

They got up, brushed off the sand, and started walking farther around the island. The breeze picked up on the windward side. The beach disappeared, replaced by smooth boulders, the size of bowling balls, set in the soft sand. The shoreline had been eaten away by tidal surges. The roots of shoreline trees lay exposed like tentacles.

"What does he want with you?" Standard asked.

"Moses?" She shrugged. "He wants me back, I guess. Isn't that what he told you?"

"He doesn't strike me as the kind of guy to get all weepy over lost love."

Allie laughed. "Not even me?" It was the laugh of someone with something to hide.

"Moses didn't hire me to find you because he's in love with you. Helen Badden didn't come to Rarotonga because you needed a doctor. And Helen Badden didn't send your photo to Moses as a memento of her trip. I've come a long way. Tell me what's going on. Tell me the real reason I'm here."

"You think Helen sent that photo?"

"Who else? It isn't like those admirers of yours down at that bar were pen pals with your old boyfriend."

"If I tell you, it will change everything, including what you think of me."

"I need to know what this is all about."

They walked another fifty yards before Allie spoke. "There isn't a single reason. There are seven million of them, and they're in banks in New Zealand and Belize."

Chapter 35

The water on the far side of island shimmered under the noon sun. Standard sat against a palm, its bark rough on his back. The shade felt better than a cold beer. Allie sat cross-legged in the sand, shadows from the palm trees dancing across her face then disappearing.

"You stole seven million dollars from Moses Blue," Standard said. It was a statement rather than a question, one he'd repeated at least four times in the last ten minutes.

"Not exactly," she said. "Remember, I was Moses' accountant for five years. It was six months after I got his account that I realized his money wasn't coming from selling ribs and slaw at those restaurants of his. After running the numbers, I figured out that he would've had to sell a plate of ribs for two hundred dollars each to bring in the kind of cash the place was generating. When I figured it out, I didn't believe it at first. But I kept looking, kept digging, until I knew the truth. Eventually I learned it was everything—prostitution, protection, money laundering, but mostly drugs."

"Learned how?"

"A lot of it came from Rico. The rest came from overhearing phone conversations and seeing the kind of people who came to see Moses. I wasn't sure who they were, but they weren't liquor distributors. I can tell you that."

"So, Moses was dealing drugs?"

Allie shook her head. "No. He's too smart and too much of a coward for that. Other people did it for him. All he did was front the money and rake in the profit. There was no risk to him. He acted like he was selling shoes or car batteries or something. I doubt the people who peddled that shit on the street even knew where the money came from or where it went. What he didn't take for himself, he laundered for someone else using the restaurants, picking off a few healthy percentage points along the way. The details really didn't matter, though, because there was no way the money was legal."

"Rico told you all this?"

"He had too much to drink one night at the club and started rattling off everything he knew about Moses. I think he was trying to impress me."

"Talking too much is what got Rico killed."

Allie nodded in agreement. "Rico was a bottom feeder, but harmless. I never understood why Moses kept him around. It wasn't like they had anything in common. I suppose it was Carp who killed him."

Standard nodded, but passed on the details. "So based on what Rico told you, you decided to steal Moses' money?"

"Not at first, but the more I got to know about his business operations, the easier it looked. I started out small at first. It was a few thousand dollars here and there, ten at the most. Pay some bills. A down payment on the house. Cash for a new car. A vacation I couldn't otherwise afford. Things like that. Gradually the amounts got larger and larger. When Moses didn't suspect anything, it made me that much bolder. He trusted me first as an accountant then as his girlfriend. Things got even easier when he turned his attention to getting the nightclub built and open."

"So it was business *and* pleasure?"

"No." Her eyes flashed. "It was *all* business."

Standard nodded. She'd made her point. "What did you do with the money?"

"I created Karen Vincent. I found her buried in a small cemetery in central Oregon. She and I were born around the same time. She died when she was eighteen months old, too young to have a Social Security number. I rented a small apartment in her name, got her a

240

Social Security number, set up a bank account, and started making direct deposits into it. Once her identity was established, I got her a birth certificate and applied for a passport in her name. The whole process took about a year. It's really not that hard, you know. There's even a book about how to change your identity and disappear. I ordered it from Amazon."

"The immigration office on Rarotonga says you're a citizen of Belize."

"Once I got Karen Vincent's passport, I used it to make a quick trip to Belize and set up a bank account there. Belize doesn't have an information exchange treaty with the United States, so it was the perfect place to go as long as I didn't make too many trips down there."

"And no one suspected? Not Moses? No one?"

She shrugged. "One time I flew to Mexico City then bought a separate ticket to Belize City and back. I thought it might cover my tracks. Once the account was set up, I'd wire money to it. I made the last transfer two days before I 'died' and then closed the savings account I had in Oregon. When I left the United States, I flew from Portland to Belize City, where I hired a local lawyer to help me become a Belize national. It wasn't that hard with that much money in the bank. I was only there a few days. Once I had the citizenship papers and the Belize passport, I took half the money out of the bank and left for the Cook Islands."

"Why half?"

"In case anything happened and one of the accounts was frozen for some reason, I had the other to fall back on. Besides, the interest rate in Belize when I was there was ten percent. The money was growing faster than I could spend it. Now, I pay cash for everything. When I need money, I just go to any ATM. Welcome to banking in the new millennium."

"There had to be some risk involved."

"Not really. Technology has made international banking pretty easy. I just opened an account in New Zealand with a few thousand dollars then had the bank withdraw it from one account and put it in the other."

Standard shook his head in amazement—not just at the ease with which she did it, but with the gall it took to pull it off. "And Moses never knew what was going on?"

Allie shook her head.

"And your death?"

Allie fiddled with a frond that had fallen out of the palm tree. She tore it into tiny threads that she wound around her finger into a two-foot length of crude twine. Standard watched her, thinking they could've been back on the deck of her house in Portland or sitting on the couch sharing a private joke in the middle of a serious discussion of the moral implications of suicide. Even in the beginning, she had been more myth than reality. It was like he could never see her all at once, only glimpses that fell short of revealing the true picture. Still, the more she kept hidden, the more he wanted to know. That was the attraction. That was what terrified him.

He tried not to think what would happen, if or when, he learned all there was to know about Allie Shafer. If he did, would she become old and gray and turn to dust right before his eyes?

"Some of what I told you was true," Allie said. "I did go in for a physical. I had this bruise on my arm that I got while working out with weights at the gym. The doctor asked me if I had been abused by a husband or boyfriend."

"That would be Doctor Helen Badden?"

Allie nodded. "The question kind of surprised me, but the plan just fell into place right there. Up to that point, I had everything worked out. My false identity, the bank account in Belize, everything except how I was going to get away from Moses. The best plan I had was to just leave one day and try to get as far away as fast as possible before he found out what I'd done. Then, sitting in the doctor's office, there it was, my way out. I told Badden that I was being abused, that I was terrified of my boyfriend and didn't know how to get away from him. I was as convincing as she was sympathetic. At one point, she suggested I get a restraining order, but I convinced her that Moses would never obey any kind of order from the court. I told her it would only make things worse.

"One thing led to another and we came up with this plan. It was really Helen's idea. I know that's hard to believe, but it's true. I just kept asking questions and looking unsure about the whole thing. The more reluctant I was, the more determined Helen became. At the end, she was practically begging me to do it."

"So she suckered Annette Traylor into the whole thing then you added me as a way of making the whole plan legitimate," Standard said. "Is that it?"

She pulled more threads of the palm frond, adding the fiber to the string to gradually make it longer. "Pretty much."

"But Badden figured it out, didn't she? At some point she found out about the money."

"She knew I was here in the Cook Islands. I had to tell someone, and I needed her help. Telling mother was out of the question. You met her. A sweet woman, but mom is not someone who does well with secrets. Helen seemed the safest person. She converted all my medical records to the name of Karen Vincent then sent them to me in case I got sick. She also agreed to keep an eye on mom for me. I guess she even visited her a few times."

"She came down here in June, didn't she?"

Anger walked across Allie's face. She nodded. "When I moved the money to New Zealand, I set up a brokerage account using a post office box here in the Cook Islands as an address. Like a fool, I'd left one of the statements lying around. Helen saw it when she was here and put things together pretty quickly. It was a stupid, careless thing to do."

The string had grown to about three feet. Deftly, she tied one end into a neat hangman's noose and held it up to twist slowly in the breeze.

"How much did she want?" Standard said.

"A million, which is about half of what is in the New Zealand account. She didn't know about the money in Belize, and I didn't tell her. When I said no, she threatened to tell Moses where I was. I thought she was bluffing. If word got out that she'd helped fake my death, she'd lose her license to practice medicine, her and Traylor both. Probably her life as well, if I know Moses. I thought that keeping her medical license was more important than ratting me out."

"But you left the island anyway?"

"That was just a precaution. I'd met this man from Australia—Marsh. He had a charter boat in Avarua. We hung out together at Trader Jack's a lot. Sometimes he came down to Muri Beach. When he sold the boat, he invited me to this ranch he has in Western Australia. I was there from the end of June until a few days ago."

"Did you know about the picture?"

"No, not until last night when Tommy told me that you'd shown it to him. Helen was the only person who could've taken it. Sounds like she gave up on getting any money from me and called my bluff." She tossed the noose into the bushes and turned to look out at the ocean. "I didn't think she'd do it. I was wrong about that." She turned back to look at him. "I'm sorry. If I had given her some money, you wouldn't have been dragged into this."

"Thanks, but it's too late to worry about that. So, you had no way of knowing she'd been calling Piri at Sokala Villas every week looking for you?"

"No, but it didn't matter. Poor Piri doesn't know anything. I purposely didn't tell him where I was going."

Allie looked at her watch. The breeze off the ocean turned into an afternoon gale. Angry whitecaps popped up on the water between the island and the barrier reef. "It's time to go," Allie said.

"One more thing."

She looked at him like she knew what was coming. "The death certificate, right?" Standard nodded. "It was the one flaw in the plan. Helen knew she could fake everything except that. It was like she was willing to violate all kinds of oaths and commit all sorts of fraud on my behalf, but drew that line at falsifying official paperwork."

"And you didn't see the danger in that?"

"To tell you the truth, I didn't even think about it. It wasn't until after I contacted you, and you agreed to write about my death, that the question of the death certificate came up. After that, it was too late."

"You hoped that I'd take your death at face value and not check to make sure you were really dead." She looked away. "And that's exactly what I did."

Allie didn't need to answer. Standard knew his status as journalistic chump needed no further explanation.

"That was quite a load of bullshit you fed me," he said.

She gave him a pleading look. "Can you forgive me?"

Standard shrugged. "Let's see how things turn out. At this point they don't look good."

Rather than follow the shoreline back to the boat, they cut across the middle of the island. It was less than a hundred yards or so. The wind died away to nothing. Tipi sat on the bow of the boat, alertly watching the beach and the lagoon. The waters on the leeward side of the island resembled a turquoise swimming pool. When they stepped onto the beach, Tipi pointed toward the lagoon. The large flat-bottomed boat that had been tied up at the hotel was about a quarter mile off shore. It plowed slowly in toward them like a square-bowed tug moving upstream. Guitar music and singing drifted on the wind, smoke from the on-board barbecue billowing off the stern. Some of the tourists from the ride around the island earlier in the day moved back and forth on the huge deck carrying plates of food.

"We go," Tipi said.

When Allie and Standard climbed on board, Tipi maneuvered the boat out into the channel. Once in deeper water, he pushed the throttle forward and pointed the boat back up the lagoon.

There was nothing to say on the return trip to the hotel. Standard sat facing the stern, watching One Foot Island get smaller until all he could see were the tops of the coconut palms. Allie sat with her eyes closed, face turned up into the sun. She looked so innocent for someone so devious. Tipi beached the boat back near Allie's bungalow.

"Let's get something to eat," she said.

At the restaurant in the hotel, Standard ordered a hamburger, washing it down with a can of Lion Red. Allie sat across the table, poking at a fruit plate while feeding breadcrumbs to the small, black mynah birds that boldly moved around the floor. She finally coaxed one up on the table. It warily eyed her while pecking at crumbs on the white tablecloth.

It was late afternoon. The staff scurried around in an unorganized effort to get ready for another island night scheduled to start in a few hours. When the waitress came by, Standard ordered another beer. Allie asked for a glass of white wine.

They made idle conversation. He brought her up to date on events back in Oregon then told her about Benny Orlando and Valerie Michaels. Allie's ears picked up at the mention of Valerie. She started to say something, but seemed to decide against prying into his private life the way he'd pried into hers. Maybe it was because his was true.

"Did you know Helen Badden was gay?" Standard said.

Allie laughed out loud. "How could I not know? As soon as she showed up down here, she was on me like sand on the beach. It was when I told her to back off that things started to go sour. I don't know what she had in mind when she got here, but it didn't take long after I said that I wasn't interested in her that she found the statement from the brokerage and started demanding money. A woman scorned. Hell hath no fury. All of that." Allie spread a crumbled-up oyster cracker across the tablecloth for the bird. "I made a mistake trusting Helen Badden. I should have paid attention to that old saying that two can keep a secret if one of them is dead."

"One of them is dead. It was just too late to do you any good."

Allie froze, a fork full of papaya inches from her mouth. Standard told her about the exploding house, the flying green door, and his night in the hospital.

"Accident?"

"Suicide, at least that's what the police think."

"But you have doubts."

He hesitated, preferring to keep suspicions to himself. "Not really. Traylor seems to think Badden killed herself because she couldn't cope with being gay. Traylor should know. They were lovers."

Allie pushed her plate of fruit away and reached for the wine. "Jesus."

They were still eating when the flat-bottomed boat returned from its day on the lagoon. It chugged around the point of the island, looking like some tricked out tropical version of a Mississippi stern wheeler. It moved slowly up the channel then slid softly onto the sandy beach in front of the restaurant. The passengers walked down the gangway and headed toward the parking lot on the other side of the footbridge and the truck ride back to the airport. The day trip was coming to an end.

"You're not leaving, are you?" Allie said. She looked scared and worried.

Standard knew he could leave, go back to Portland, and tell Moses

Blue that Allie was in the Cook Islands. He also knew that as soon as he got on the plane, she would be gone, her and her money off to some other remote location to renew her hot-wired life. That would only piss Blue off that much more.

He also couldn't prove she was dead.

He was stuck.

"No," he told Allie. "I'm not leaving. Not yet."

Chapter 36

They picked up where they left off. This time, though, there was no learning, only remembering.

Allie held nothing back. She made love as if exorcising demons, passion mixed with the determination to get something out of sex that no one had ever experienced before. Standard found little to do but hang on as she pumped, bounced, and moaned her way into some deep recess in her mind where no one could reach her. He felt like little more than an amusement park ride, with Allie as the patron who paid for the right to scream.

At first, he thought it was her way of trying to erase some image, perhaps how she'd had her father killed or what she'd done to Moses Blue or the death of Helen Badden. But it was something much deeper than that, something primordial that she could only escape by getting lost in sex. Maybe it was what her father told her twenty years earlier: "Allie, you're just like me."

She said nothing to him other than the words of encouragement and pleasure that any man would pay good money to hear. All he could hear, though, were the words of a woman who wanted more than anyone had to give.

When it was over, she came back playful and friendly, eager to call room service for a bottle of champagne. When it arrived, she let the cork fly into the rafters of the bungalow and poured the champagne into the plastic cups from the bathroom. She slipped out of her robe, picked up the two glasses, and climbed back into bed.

Standard stared up at the ceiling, doing his best to keep thoughts of Valerie Michaels out his head.

"What did you do after I . . . died?" Allie said. "How did you feel?"

They were under a single, cool sheet, her head against his chest, smelling of suntan lotion and sex. The room had no air conditioning, just a single ceiling fan silently shuffling the humid air around like dough in a mixer.

"It was tough. But I got over it and wrote the articles and did the interviews that you wanted me to do."

"I saw you on CNN."

"That must have been weird."

"Very. And when you thought I was alive?"

"I didn't believe it."

She moved closer, draping one leg over his. He felt like she wanted to hear more. Instead, he watched the ceiling fan kick lint around the room.

"Remember the dining room table?" she said.

"Who could forget it? Do you remember what you said that night?"

"No."

"You said, 'Tell me this isn't happening.' What did you mean?"

She waited a long time to answer. "Finding you. I so wanted to get out of there without complications, to just disappear. I'd worked so hard, waited so long, and put up with so much from Moses. I was so close. I had the money. Thanks to Helen Badden, I had the plan. But I found that I had no self-control around you. I know it was only one night, but something happened. You felt it the same as I did, didn't you?" She rolled over on her back. A thin film of sweat made her tan chest and shoulders glisten in the light that filtered in through the windows. "You have no idea how close I came to forgetting the whole thing and telling you how I felt. Especially when I saw you on TV. I was on Rarotonga, in a little hotel I stayed at for a few weeks before moving over to the Sokala Villas. Watching you being interviewed made me want to come back and get you."

He traced the tan line on her breasts. "Why did you come to me in the first place? You could have done everything you wanted without involving me."

"It sounds like you wish I had." When he didn't answer, she rolled over to face him. "You're angry, aren't you?"

"Who wouldn't be?" The sharp edge to his voice made Allie move a few inches away. "You sold me a bill of goods about killing yourself, disappeared while I peddled your phony story to anyone with a checkbook and ended up as an errand boy for a drug dealer."

"I'm sorry."

"Sorry doesn't cut it." He was trying not to sound angry and doing a bad job of it. "My ass is in a sling and you're the only one who can get it out. The problem is that you're dead and we're on an island in the middle of the ocean. There was no reason to come to me in the first place. You didn't need to make this public. You'd won. You were free and clear."

"I came to you for two reasons. Your stories would be more proof that I was really dead. Proof that Moses needed."

"And the second?"

"Moses is a very private person. In his business, you have to be. He hates publicity. No, he fears it. It's the one thing that can kill him. With some public aspect to my death, such as a story in a local newspaper, then I knew he'd be more inclined to cut his losses and move on."

"But he didn't. He came to me."

"It never dawned on me that he would do that."

"But he did."

"Yes, and I'm sure he told you that if you write one word about all of this you're a dead man. Am I right?" He answered with silence. She was right and he knew it. "See, he knew that you could find me, but he had to protect himself against word getting out of what I'd done. He went to you after he found out the money was gone. That had to have been Helen Badden's fault. The plan was working exactly the way I wanted up to that point. If she hadn't sent him that photo, he never would have gotten suspicious. It could have been another year or more before he knew the money was missing. Believe me, seven million dollars is not a lot of money to Moses. It's his pride that's hurt and his reputation with his so-called business associates. This has nothing to do with his bank account."

"What if it's not all his money? What if someone else, someone bigger, is involved?"

A sly smile walked slowly across her face. "Then he's a dead man and we're both safe."

Allie sat up, sitting cross-legged with the sheet draped across her lap. Her eyes bright, her face full of excitement, her breasts firm and tan. "But forget Moses. Don't you see? Helen Badden made things more complicated, but she doesn't have to ruin everything. In fact, maybe she made things better. It brought you here. It made you find me. You can stay. You don't have to go back."

Standard got up, found his shorts in the pile of clothes on the floor, put them on, and paced the room.

"We have a second chance," she said, watching him from the bed. "I have all this money. We'll have nothing to worry about. The police aren't after me. I'm not a criminal that they're going to hunt down using computer records or something. The only things I lost by creating Karen Vincent were my Social Security benefits and some frequent flyer miles. Besides, I've covered my tracks."

"I found you."

"Moses isn't you."

"If I don't go back, Moses will know something is wrong. He'll figure it out. He'll know we're together. Someone else will come after you. This time he'll hire someone who knows what to do, a professional with no conscience. Then there are my friends. They know where I am. God knows what Blue would do to them."

252

"We don't have to stay here. We have the whole world to hide in. We can leave tomorrow. Paris, Rio, Morocco. You pick. I'll take you there."

Standard paced the floor a few more times. "Did you meet Skinny Hale?"

The question startled her. "Just once. Moses told me everything. Skinny being his father, losing his eye, all of it. It all sounded pretty pathetic to me. Why?"

"Skinny thinks I made a deal with the devil when I agreed to try to find you for Moses. Do you think he was right?"

She pulled the sheet up to cover her breasts, as if more talk of Moses Blue made her cold.

"Moses isn't the devil."

"But he's close."

Standard grabbed a cigarette from the table next to the door and went outside to the bungalow's small porch for a smoke. Lights from the other bungalows glistened across the lagoon. From the restaurant, the drums of another island night beat an erotic rhythm that fit perfectly with what he and Allie had just shared.

Thirty yards across the sand, Tipi's boat sat with its bow pushed up on the beach. Inside the small cabin, Tipi's shadow stood out against the dim light of a propane lantern. He was using a screwdriver to work on what looked like the boat's radio. Tipi looked up. He either sensed he was being watched or he was doing his duty keeping an eye on Allie. Standard gave him a casual wave. Tipi gave a half-hearted wave in return then went back to working on the radio.

Standard checked the time. Valerie would be just getting home, pouring a glass of wine, turning on the evening news. He suddenly wanted to call just to hear her voice. It was part guilt, but also a need to know the real world was still out there with all its flaws.

Standing there, he knew he would do everything possible to protect Allie Shafer. He couldn't just walk away, not after what they shared. Allie made things that way. She'd done it to Tommy and Tipi. She'd done it to him.

But the idea of staying here or anyplace else with her had little appeal. They were like matches in dry timber. All they would do was burn each other up, their legacy nothing more than a scorched path across whatever land she'd drag him to. If he left, he would always remember her. If he stayed, he would end up hating her. Living on the run with another man's money and woman was not his style. If he explained it to anyone, they'd think he was crazy. They'd probably be right. Most men would give anything to have a beautiful, rich woman like Allie ask them to spend their lives in paradise.

For the only time in his life, Standard wished he were more like other men.

Thoughts of Valerie came back. Her love was a tattoo—permanent and deep. Allie's was a bruise that would gradually turn a sickly yellow before disappearing.

Allie was suddenly behind him, using his body to hide her nakedness from Tipi and anyone else who might happen by.

"Well?" she said.

"Can we talk about this in the morning? I can't make decisions at times like this."

She laughed. Her arms snaked tightly around his waist. "With you and me, there will always be times like this."

That's the problem, Standard said to himself.

They made love again, but more slowly. Sadness replaced passion. Standard knew this would be their last time together. If Allie felt the same thing, she didn't show it. She didn't have to. She knew. Women always know when men aren't committed. He didn't have to tell her. She knew he wouldn't stay. The only unanswered questions were what to do about Moses Blue, about Allie, and, more important, how to protect Valerie and Benny.

Standing under the shower, holding Allie in his arms, he tried to think of how to get out of the deal with Blue. Skinny Hale was right. Getting out of it was going to take a good plan and a lot of luck. So far, Standard didn't feel like he had either one.

After the shower, they sat on the bed drinking the last of the champagne. Allie talked about Australia and more about the history and culture of the Cook Islands, most of it learned from Tommy and Tipi. Standard acted interested, but his mind was miles away, searching for a way out. Her voice became elevator music as he drew blanks the size of theater screens. They fell asleep around midnight. The drums of island night were silent, the other guests back in their bungalows.

Chapter 37

Standard woke up alone.

The room felt empty. Allie wasn't there. He felt both fear and relief then found her note on the pillow. It said she'd gotten up early to take a walk down the beach and not to worry. Tipi was with her.

Standard called room service, ordered a breakfast of poached eggs, fresh papaya, and toast, and headed for the bathroom. When he got out of the shower, breakfast was on the small table on the bungalow's porch. He was on a third cup of coffee when Allie came back.

She kissed him on the cheek. "Finish up," she said, grabbing a piece of toast and popping it in her mouth. "Tipi's taking us snorkeling."

Ten minutes later, they were back on the boat, heading south again. This time they went past One Foot Island toward the far end of the lagoon and one of the smaller motus. The trip took the better part of an hour. The speed of the boat once again left the humidity behind and gave the air a fresh, salty taste. Standard spent the time trying on the mask and swim fins stored beneath one of the seats. Allie faced into the wind, her eyes focused beyond the boat's bow.

"There's a wrecked ship over there on the other side of the reef." Allie pointed off the starboard side. She was yelling over the roar of the boat motor. "It's the *Alexandria*. There's not much of it left now. It crashed into the reef in the 1930s. It was headed for New Zealand with a load of Model T Fords. Over there is Maina." She pointed ahead toward an island that looked exactly like One Foot. "It means 'Little Girl.' That's where we're going. It has great snorkeling."

Tipi slowed the boat as it neared the island. Fifty feet offshore, he cut the motor and jumped onto the front deck to drop the anchor into about fifteen feet of water.

Allie and Standard had their masks and fins on before the anchor hit bottom. Allie went over the side. He was seconds behind her.

The water was bathtub warm. Brightly colored fish moved easily on the invisible currents. Standard took a deep breath and dove. The water turned cooler just a few feet beneath the surface. He moved quickly around one of the huge rocks that dotted the sandy bottom. Poking around a small pile of coral, he disturbed a little octopus that jetted away in a cloud of ink.

With his lungs aching, Standard headed toward the surface. Looking up, Allie floated just beneath the surface. With the sunlight directly overhead and silhouetting her body, he realized that, from this angle, she was the most perfect woman he'd ever seen. Of course, she was a shadow. She would always be a shadow.

With a kick of her feet, she moved away and the glare of the sun hit him square in the face. Allie had disappeared. All he could see was water-diffused sunlight. One second she was there. The next she was gone.

When he hit the surface, she was ten feet away, treading water and smiling. They paddled around for another hour. Allie hopelessly chased the tropical fish along the rocky bottom while Standard pursued the octopus two or three more times until it disappeared under a giant head of coral.

At midday, Tipi motioned them back on board. They dried off with towels brought from the bungalow while Tipi slowly edged the boat toward the shore and up onto the sandy beach. Standard carried a Styrofoam cooler to a spot deep in the cool shade of the coconut palms then sat on the sand to catch his breath before having a cigarette he didn't want or need.

Tipi put on the mask and fins Standard had been using and pulled

257

a spear gun from inside the boat's cramped cabin. After taking a half dozen deep breaths, he dove off the stern and disappeared under the water.

Allie opened the cooler and pulled out a small bag of charcoal briquettes. She poured them into a rusting, three-legged barbecue that was there for anyone who came along to use. Standard grabbed a can of Lion Red before retreating to a spot in the shade. He watched while Allie lit the briquettes.

"Tipi will be back in a few minutes with lunch," she said.

Allie moved with the ease and confidence that comes with experience. She and Tipi were like an old pair of shoes, each knowing exactly what the other was doing without having to say anything. She got things ready, confident he would return with something to cook.

Thirty minutes later, the coals were perfect. As if on cue, Tipi waded up out of the lagoon with a string of brightly colored fish, each no bigger than a paperback book. He quickly cleaned them and put them on the grill, carefully arranging each one while drinking a beer that Allie delivered without having to be asked.

They ate using banana leaves for plates. In addition to the fish, there was fresh fruit, rice, and some kind of root vegetable known only to Cook Islanders. It all went nicely with more cans of cold Lion Red. Tipi told stories of growing up on the island and about having no desire to live anywhere else. Standard had a hard time imagining what that must be like.

Finished eating, Tipi offered to clean up while Allie and Standard walked down the beach and out onto a narrow sand spit that stuck out into the lagoon. A cool breeze off the water made the incessant sun easier to bear.

"Tell me about Blue, Carp, and your father," Standard said.

Allie tried to look shocked. "What do mean?"

"Come on, Allie. You used Blue to kill your father because he raped you when you were ten years old. Carp was the weapon."

"My mother?" she said. Standard nodded. "Moses offered to do it as soon as I told him about it. I didn't say yes or no, but Moses did it anyway. That's the way things work in his world. Silence equals affirmation. I can't say I'm sorry that he took matters into his own hands, just shocked that he would kill someone like that without seeming to really think about it, to just take my story on faith and then act on it. It was the first time I realized just how dangerous Moses is."

"How did you find out?

"I overheard Carp talking to Rico. I never mentioned it to Moses and he didn't offer."

There are no heroes in this story, Standard thought. Everyone involved had too many secrets to come out unscathed.

The silence signaled what was next.

"You're not going to stay, are you?" Allie said.

"No." The answer came easier than he thought it would.

"Is it because of the money, my father, or something else?"

"It's all of that and more."

"Is it okay if I'm disappointed?" They stood at the end of the spit, each poking at the sand with their toes like two, shy teenagers. "It's Moses, isn't it? You have to go back because of Moses."

"I can't explain. It would be a lot easier if you didn't make me."

"Your friends, right? You're afraid something might happen to them. That Moses will do something to them."

"That's a lot of it."

"I'll go back with you, then." Her voice was filled with a false determination.

"That won't work either, at least not for me. I can't stop you if that's what you want to do, but do it for your own reasons and not because of me." The hurt registered on her face just long enough to make Standard wish he were something less than what he was. "Anyway, you know you can't go back. Moses would kill you. Even if you gave the money back, he'd still kill you. He'd have to. You disrespected him. He has to save face."

"So, I stay here alone."

"That was always your plan."

By the time they got back to the boat, Tipi had everything loaded and ready to go. The wind had picked up and turned cold. Dark clouds moved out of the west and chased them up the lagoon. Allie huddled on the floor of the boat, a towel wrapped around her shoulders.

The boat and the rain hit the beach in front of Allie's bungalow at the same time. The drops came like gunfire as they ran inside while Tipi took refuge in the boat's small cabin. Allie got a robe from the hook behind the bathroom door, put it on, and sat on the bed staring at him.

"You told me once that you had a fearless heart," she said, shivering under the robe. Goosebumps rippled across her legs.

"I do."

"Then why won't you stay?"

Reasons cascaded through his head: Never get involved with a woman who has more problems than you do. Never get involved with a woman who stands by while her boyfriend kills her father. Never get involved with a woman who embezzles seven million dollars from a dangerous gangster. Never get involved with a woman who fakes her own death and sets you up as an alibi. Never get involved with a woman who tempts you with a life of leisure living on stolen money, traveling to exotic places, and unbridled sex. Well, maybe not that last one.

Still, the minuses outweighed the pluses. Then there was the really important one.

"Because," Standard said, "that would be the easiest thing to do."

Chapter 38

Standard sensed someone else in the dark room even before his eyes opened.

The air seemed to vibrate as he tried to remember how the room was arranged. Allie was next to him. He could feel her breath damp on his shoulder, her leg clammy against his under the thin sheet. The only things on the nightstand were the lamp, the digital clock, and an empty bottle of beer he'd drunk earlier while Allie was in the shower. A couch, end tables, and a coffee table occupied the wall on his side of the bed. A small dinette with a table and two chairs occupied the other side next to Allie. Across from the foot of the bed was the front door. Next to that another table, a chair, and a floor lamp.

Based on all of that, Standard knew whoever was in the room had to be standing between the door and the foot of the bed.

The rain had stopped sometime during the night. Water dripping off the bungalow's thatched roof onto the soft ground beneath the windows was the only sound. The air felt heavy and humid.

But none of that mattered. Something was there, or someone.

Standard slowly opened an eye just enough to make out the time on the digital clock. It was a few minutes after two in the morning. There was enough light to see the beer bottle. It was less than a foot away. He wondered how long it would take to grab it and hurl it into the space between the foot of the bed and the door. Or, he could smash it barroom style and use the jagged neck as a weapon. Would it take a second? Two seconds? A half second? What good would it do? It wasn't like he was an expert at stabbing people in the dark with a broken beer bottle.

But who was it? Tipi maybe? The last time they'd seen him was just before midnight. He was in his boat. He had one eye on the dismantled radio and the other on their bungalow. But why would the islander sneak into the room in the middle of the night? Maybe he just wanted to check on Allie. He was, after all, fiercely loyal to her. Maybe it was the guy from room service coming to collect the empty bottle and deliver fresh towels. At two a.m.?

Then again, this could all be nothing but paranoia.

With a deep breath, Standard rolled over and sat up.

The figure at the end of the bed blocked the faint light seeping in through the open door. Standard squinted in an effort to bring things into focus, get the sleep out of his eyes. Still, he couldn't tune the face in, but when the figure spoke, he didn't have to. He knew who it was.

"Do you have any idea what I'm going to do to you?" Carp said.

Standard jerked up. Things came into focus quickly. It wasn't good. Seeing the gun in Carp's hand, he pushed himself back against the headboard as if a few inches farther away would somehow make him safer.

"Carp! How did you—"

"Shut up," Carp said, moving the gun back and forth between Standard and Allie.

Carp had covered his head pirate-style in what looked like a linen napkin from one of the breadbaskets in the hotel restaurant. His sweat-stained T-shirt, a size too small, stretched tight across his chest, distorting the lobster on the Trader Jack's logo. His camouflage pants rippled in the breeze that followed him in the door. The large bandage that had covered his mangled eyebrow the night in Seaside was gone. In its place, a small scab that looked lost on the side of his huge head. He looked like a tourist who'd lost his luggage in a bar fight.

It was the handgun, though, that got Standard's attention. It was three feet away and pointed at the middle of his chest. The barrel looked like a sewer pipe. Standard wondered how he'd gotten a gun to a place accessible only by airplane. It was an odd thought, because at this point, it really didn't matter. What did was being milliseconds away from being dead.

Allie stirred. Her eyes opened, squinted sleepy and confused.

"What's wrong?" she said, turning her head toward the foot of the bed. Seeing Carp, the scream that started somewhere deep in her stomach came out as a squeak. Standard put a hand on her shoulder in a lame gesture that did little more than confirm to her that they were in deep trouble.

Carp's eyes moved toward Allie, but the gun stayed pointed at Standard's chest. "Where's the money, bitch?"

Allie's mouth opened but nothing came out. Instead, she pulled the sheet up around her neck. Carp grabbed it and flung it across the room. He stared at her nakedness. Allie pulled her knees up and wrapped her arms around them.

Carp sneered at her. "I'll do whatever it takes to get the money. Do you know what that means? It means we're going to have a lot of fun, or at least I will. You, probably not so much."

"Blue?" Standard said.

"Fuck Blue. Give me the god damn money and I'll disappear just like she did."

Allie shivered. Even in the dim light he could see goosebumps dance across her tan skin. Her hands trembled at her mouth. She couldn't have told Carp what time it was, let alone where she'd stashed seven million dollars.

Carp let his eyes scan Allie's body again then turned his attention back to Standard. "You led me right to her, you dumb shit."

Allie gasped. A look of disappointment and betrayal joined the fear already on her face. "You?" she said, looking right at him.

Suddenly it all made sense. Carp had gone native, and not just in the last couple of days. He'd learned about the money while hanging around The Blue Café, listening to Blue and his accountant. What he didn't pick up from them, he'd learned from Rico, probably while blowing holes in the little man's knees. Carp's plan all along was to betray Blue for the money. That was why Carp was in Seaside. That was why he was at the airport. That was why he followed Standard to the Cook Islands. It was the money—Blue's money—that Allie had.

Standard felt like a fool. Again. Only someone Allie trusted could find her, someone she wouldn't run from. Who better than him? Blue had turned Standard loose with a pocketful of money, and he had performed like a hunting dog. But for Carp, not Blue.

"I hope you feel as stupid as you look," Carp said. He leered at Allie again then looked back at Standard. "How does that make you feel? Like the same smartass you were back in Seaside? I'll take care of you later. Right now, this is about the money. The only way anyone walks away from this alive is to give me the money. Don't fuck with me. Just tell me where it is." Carp turned his attention back to Allie. "I couldn't care less about this fucker. It's you that knows the answers. When I'm through with you, we won't have any secrets, will we, honey?"

Allie pulled her knees tighter to her chest. She pushed her head back hard against the headboard. She squeezed her eyes shut. Her lips started trembling, then her whole body.

Carp reached out and grabbed one of her ankles, pulling her toward him and leering down between her open legs. When she was close enough, he reached out and grabbed her by the throat. Allie's eyes popped open. She started to cough, her face inches from Carp's. With one eye on Standard, Carp kissed her, forcing his tongue deep into her mouth. He pushed the muzzle of the gun hard against her breast then began sliding it down her stomach.

Allie flailed her arms before finally digging her nails into Carp's cheeks. Red welts appeared like lines on an Etch-A-Sketch. Carp smiled and looked at Standard. "I love it when they do that, don't you?"

Then he hit her with his fist. The cobra-like blow knocked Allie back against the headboard. She looked stunned, her eyes half open. The entire left side of her face started turning a bright red.

Standard sat frozen between concern for Allie and for his own life. Jesus, he thought, it never dawned on him that Carp would find them. This wasn't Seaside. They were in the middle of the South Pacific. He'd underestimated the big man.

Allie cringed against the headboard. Carp moved the gun back and forth between them, as if trying to decide who to shoot first. Maybe there was time to figure something out.

Charging a gun-wielding man-beast wasn't Standard's style, so he looked around for alternatives to a suicide mission. The beer bottle was still beside the bed, but it might as well be a mile away. Words were the only weapon he had, the only weapon he had ever had. Now they had to save his life and Allie's.

"You better think about this," Standard said. "We both know what she means to Moses."

"He cares about the money, not about the bitch. He owes people, big people. People that will kill him if they don't get their money. Besides, Moses would have to find me first. I can do a hell of lot of hiding with seven million dollars in the bank."

"He'd hunt you down. You know it."

"Fuck you. All I have to do is tell Moses' business partners that he let this bitch get away with their money and he'd be road kill. He knows I'd do it. He'll never touch me. Hell, he may be dead already. Those guys he owes the money to don't dance."

Standard's brain went into overdrive. There had to be a way out of this. Maybe, just maybe, there was.

"It sounds like you got things all figured out," Standard said. "Let's say you win. Let's say all we want is to get out of this alive. You don't have to do anything to anybody. You win. Our lives are more important. The money is yours, pure and simple. I know where it is. I'll

265

tell you, but you have to leave her alone."

Allie's head snapped in Standard's direction. A trickle of blood ran from corner of her mouth.

Carp snorted his disdain. "What do I need you for? I could kill you right now and fuck the truth out of her between now and dawn. Look at her. I'd have the money before my pants were off."

"You don't understand. It isn't like there's seven million dollars in that suitcase over there." Standard pointed toward the closet. "Or buried in a coffee can out back. Besides, she doesn't know where it is," Standard looked at Allie hoping that she'd read some silent message that would tell her to go along with him. "She expected something like this would happen, so she gave the money to me. I'll take you to it, but touch her and you'll never see a dime."

The confused look that wandered across Carp's face gave Standard hope that at least Allie could get out of this alive. He was less optimistic about his own chances.

"No way," Carp said. "You only found her yesterday. There was no time to move the money that fast."

"Think about it, Carp. Blue was right. Allie and I were in this together from the start. It was always our plan for me to join her. All that running around Oregon looking for her was a snipe hunt. I was just waiting until the time was right. Blue hiring me to find her was never part of the plan. It just worked out that way."

If Carp was buying the story, his face didn't show it.

"I don't give a shit. I want the money. I want it now."

"Then let's go get it. It only takes a phone call." Standard was adlibbing as fast as possible and hoping that Carp would believe half of it. "I moved the money from one account to another. It isn't that hard, even from a place like this. All it takes is a transfer from my account to yours. It will only take a few minutes. She's an accountant. She helped me set it up. I know how it works."

Carp moved the gun to his left until it was pointed at Allie. One shot would rip through her legs and into her chest.

"You better not be lying to me," Carp said.

Standard sensed a change in Carp's tone. Maybe he was getting through to him. If he was, Allie wasn't picking up on it. She could do little more than whimper.

"Listen, Carp," Standard said. "I'll get dressed and we'll get out of here. There's a plane first thing this morning. We'll be on it. You'll have your money by the time the banks open on Rarotonga. No one has to die."

"Screw that. You said all it takes is a simple transfer."

"It does," Standard was thinking as quickly as he could. "But seven million is a lot of cash. We need a bank and there isn't one on the island."

Carp's face got that confused look again. The offer squirmed around inside his huge head. The room grew hotter and smaller. The ceiling fan labored uselessly overhead. Sweat beaded up on Carp's face.

Standard glanced at the clock. "The plane leaves in four hours. We'll go to the airport. It's not that far. We'll walk. Don't blow this."

Standard was trying his best to sound convincing, even though he had no idea if a plane left in four hours or, if there was, what to do when he and Carp got to a bank in Rarotonga. He'd have to figure that out later. All he wanted now was to get Carp away from Allie, away from the hotel where it would just be the two of them. He'd take his chances after that. All he could do for now was keep talking.

"I'm telling you right now, anything happens to her and I'll never tell you where the money is. I'll be dead, but you'll be empty-handed. You didn't come all this way for nothing. You can't go back to Blue, and you won't have the money you need to hide from him. If you did, you wouldn't have followed me. Think about it! The money is yours. All you have to do is play it smart."

Standard looked over at Allie. She was still pressed against the headboard. Carp's eyes were moving back and forth between the two of them. They were doll eyes, blank and stupid in the dim light.

Slowly, Standard stood up. Being naked made him feel vulnerable and defenseless. "I'm getting dressed. You and I are getting out of here. In a few hours, you'll have all of Moses' money. What do you say?"

Carp leered at Allie again. The bruise on the side of her face grew darker by the second. Blood dripped from her lip on to her chest. "I could take a knife to this bitch and find out in ten seconds where the money is." He grabbed Allie by the ankle again, pulling her closer. She struggled, reaching to cover herself with a pillow.

"Jesus, Carp! How stupid can one man be?" Standard was nearly yelling. "Even if she told you where the money is, which she can't, you couldn't get to it. It's in a goddamn bank account in Belize! You can't get it out without my help. I'll get it for you. All you have to do is leave her alone. Think about it. These are not hard choices, Carp!"

Carp's head began to nod like a boulder balanced on the edge of a cliff. "Get your clothes on. You too, bitch. We're all going together."

When Standard reached for his clothes, Allie didn't move. She lay frozen in fear, staring over Carp's shoulder. Her face turned white, her mouth open as if to scream. Again, nothing came out.

Standard followed her gaze. When he saw what she was looking at, his body tensed. He fought to keep the surprise off his face. Carp didn't notice, his eyes still buried somewhere between Allie's legs, probably lost in thoughts of the bad clothes and great sex he could buy with Blue's money.

The figure that came silently through the open door behind Carp moved barefoot across the room. Three steps and the figure was behind Carp. A glint of light flashed off the steel of the machete as it came around Carp's' shoulder, up under his chin, and against his throat. Standard wanted to relax, but couldn't. This wasn't over. Not yet.

Standard didn't recognize Tommy at first. The bartender with the friendly smile was dressed only in a pareau wrapped tight around his waist and thighs like a pair of briefs. Intricate tattoos covered most of his upper body. Jagged streaks of black paint covered his face. Sweat gave the lightning-shaped designs a sheen that glowed in the faint light. White teeth flashed in a half grimace, half smile.

Tommy the bartender had become Taomia, the ancient Polynesian warrior.

Chapter 39

Blood drained from Carp's face when the machete's steel edge hit his throat. Instinctively, his hands went up. The gun that had been pointed at Allie now had the drop on the ceiling fan.

Allie could only mouth Tommy's name. Fear stayed painted on her face. Standard said nothing. Things were out of his hands. He'd said enough. Tommy was in charge. Standard could only wait to see what came next.

"Who the fuck are you?" Carp said

"Cruise director," Tommy said. "Time for a lagoon trip."

Tommy was shorter than Carp, but broader across the back and chest. His arms were the size of Carp's neck. Tommy whispered in Carp's ear. "Don't move." He pressed the machete harder into the big man's neck, breaking the skin. A stream of blood collected on the blade then dripped down inside the front of Carp's T-shirt. Tommy raised his other hand. In it was a heavy metal hook attached to a rope that ran out the door and across the porch toward the beach.

Carp hissed. He still had the gun pointed harmlessly at the ceiling.

The gun, Standard thought, make him drop the gun. His mouth tried to form the words. Nothing came out.

Keeping the machete hard against Carp's neck, Tommy used his other hand to clip the hook to the back of Carp's belt. Then, with a quick motion, he looped the rope twice around the big man's neck. With two hard jerks on the end of the rope that ran out the door, Tommy stepped to one side.

Outside, the powerful engines of Tipi's boat came to life then grew louder. Carp's eyes got bigger. He turned his head from side to side before using his free hand to grab the bed's footboard. The slack in the rope coiled on the floor began to snake out the door.

Carp knew what was coming, knew the loop around his neck was becoming a noose. He gripped the footboard tighter as his face turned a deep red on its way toward purple. He started to yell. It was cut short by the tightening rope.

Then his other hand came down.

Standard watched as Carp tightened his grip even more on the footboard, but all he could see was the gun in the other hand. As if in slow motion, he stared open mouthed and helpless as Carp's gun came down from pointing at the ceiling to pointing at the bed.

Pointing at Allie.

Standard looked at Tommy. Their eyes locked as both realized what was about to happen. Terror crossed the islander's face. His mouth formed the word, "No." At the same time, he raised the machete and swung at Carp's gun hand. Standard fought the urge to hit the floor. Instead, he watched the scene play out in front of him. The race between Carp's trigger finger and Tommy's machete looked like a dead heat.

It wasn't.

Carp strained against the rope, the loop around his neck ready to snap his spine at any moment. In another second he'd be out the door. As the gun came down, Allie's hands went up in front of her face. Her body turned sideways. She had no place to go. If she screamed, Standard didn't hear it.

The room exploded three times, one for each gunshot fired at Allie. Carp didn't watch the gun or where the bullets went. His eyes were on the machete as it came down on his wrist, severing it like the blunt end of a carrot. The hand that clutched the gun plopped on to the foot of the bed at Allie's feet. Carp screamed something from deep inside. Black blood spurted from the end of his arm, spraying Allie's chest, arms and face.

At that moment, the last inch of slack went out of the rope. It tightened, quivering like a guitar string. The screaming Carp let go of the bed and flew backward out the door. In an instant, he crashed through the bamboo porch, dropped five feet to the sand, and plowed ass first across the beach.

Standard ran to the door, getting to the porch just in time to see Tipi's boat disappear into the offshore darkness. Carp slid backward into the water. As the boat picked up speed, he skipped across the lagoon a hundred feet behind. Within seconds, the only thing visible was the bloody stump of Carp's arm held high out of the water, still spurting blood as it waved back and forth above the boat's wake. Ahab beckoning to the crew of the Pequod. The night swallowed the boat first then, seconds later, Carp.

Standard turned and glanced around for Tommy. The bartender hadn't watched Carp's exit. Instead, he was still at the foot of the bed staring at Allie. The gentle islander turned warrior was on his knees, elbows resting on the footboard, crying. He dropped the machete to the floor. The sound of metal against wood filled the room.

With one hand on Tommy's shoulder, Standard stared at Allie and the blood-soaked bed. "Jesus." It came out as a whisper. Tommy could only bow his head to stare at the floor.

Standard pulled Tommy to his feet. "Listen to me. We need to move fast. Sergeant Taere, the police officer on Rarotonga, said you have relatives here. One of them is with the police. I think you better get him over here right away.""

Tommy nodded dumbly, refusing to take his eyes off Allie. "Doctor?" he said.

Standard shook his head. "No need."

Chapter 40

Standard didn't see the Portland International Airport runway until the Alaska Airlines jet was a few hundred feet above it.

Looking out the window, it was easy to see that Oregon had begun its inevitable slide into the darkness of another gray, damp fall that would be like living inside a wet sleeping bag. The blue skies that he'd left ten days earlier had turned the color of old sheets. The Willamette River, which split the city in half, looked high, brown, and angry. Marine Drive, along the north edge of the airport, came into view. The headlights on cars and trucks glistened off the asphalt and lit up the raindrops.

All Standard wanted was to get off the plane and talk to Valerie. Since leaving Aitutaki twenty hours earlier, hers was the only voice he wanted to hear. The only face he wanted to see and touch. He'd called from the Los Angeles airport as soon as the Air New Zealand flight from Rarotonga landed, and again an hour later before boarding the flight to Portland. There was no answer either time. He tried again as soon as the plane's wheels hit the tarmac.

The only thing good about the flight from LA was that it was direct. He'd even paid extra for first class just so he could get off the flight quicker when it reached Portland.

He called her apartment again as he walked through the airport. Damn. Where was she? It was late afternoon. Maybe she was still at work. When the receptionist said Valerie hadn't been to work for two days, it was all he could do to not to toss the phone through a window.

It felt like he'd swallowed a live rat. Didn't she understand? Seeing her was the only thing that would keep him from going over the edge, from being overwhelmed by the events in Aitutaki. Blaming the panic on too many hours crammed against the bulkhead on a full flight from Rarotonga, or the stress of getting off the island was too easy. The same was true of the frustration of those extra days on Aitutaki, tying up loose ends before leaving. Maybe it was the fear of missing the Air New Zealand flight to Los Angeles only to find out it wouldn't arrive for another two days.

If those excuses didn't work, he could relive the sight of Carp with a bloody stump where his hand had been, disappearing out the door of Allie's bungalow, crashing through the railing, and into the lagoon. Then there was Allie. It would take a while–a long while–to forget that scene.

Standard dialed again. When Benny answered, he cut short the little man's questions about what happened in the Cook Islands to ask about Valerie.

"I talked to her yesterday morning before she went to work," Benny said. "I told her about your e-mails and asked if she'd heard from you. That was about it. She sounded fine. Still a little pissed about being left behind while you jetted off to the South Seas. Why?" Standard told him about not being able to get hold of her. "Maybe she took some time off."

"I don't know. It's just not like her. She wouldn't go anywhere until I got back."

"She didn't know when you'd be back. Neither one of us did."

"That's not it. Something's wrong. I can feel it."

"I'm sure everything is fine. Valerie's not the type to do anything stupid."

Standard gave a half-hearted agreement and hung up. Despite Benny's reassurances, questions about Valerie still lingered as Standard walked through the terminal, down the escalator, and out to the sidewalk in front of baggage claim. With no checked luggage, he could avoid the slow parade of bags on the carousel. There was only the bag he'd left with, plus a manila envelope of papers for Moses Blue.

The rain made the cab ride into town twice as long as usual. When it dropped Standard in front of his apartment building, he ran upstairs rather than take the decrepit elevator. The smell of sour milk filled the apartment. He threw open the windows to let the rain in and the smell out. The message of an approaching winter came on a steel cold breeze that stung his face. He checked the time again then reached for the phone. He dialed her number. Still nothing.

It took a minute to remember where the Jeep was parked. It was two blocks away near The Old Church on SW 11th. He sprinted down the back stairs, out into the alley behind the apartment building, and up SW Clay.

After sitting idle for two weeks, the Jeep was slow to start. It caught on the fourth try. He jammed the transmission into drive and pulled into the street. Traffic moved through the city like molasses. The trip that normally took ten minutes took thirty. Standard spent the last five blocks screaming out the window at drivers who couldn't grasp the enormity of the situation. Valerie was missing.

He parked at a fire hydrant in front of her apartment building and ran up the stairs. Using the key she'd given him, he opened the door without knocking. All he wanted was to see her sitting at the table and wondering why he looked so scared. Instead, the apartment was empty. Worse. It felt like it had been that way for a while.

Maybe she'd quit the insurance agency. Think, goddamn it, he muttered. Maybe she'd grown tired of the short money and gone back to dancing at one of the clubs where she used to work. Maybe the club's owner found her a gig in Bend, Eugene, or Salem. Maybe she found a new job all together and took a few days off.

The possibilities were still rambling through his head when the answer came, impaled to the kitchen cupboard with a steak knife. It was a book of matches from The Blue Café. When he pulled the knife out, something white and bloody fell out from inside the matchbook, landing silently on the counter top. It took a few seconds to realize what it was.

A finger.

Chapter 41

Standard stared at the bloody finger then at the matchbook before sitting down and putting his head between hands. The finger had to be Valerie's. No doubt about it. He couldn't imagine what she went through. What she was going through. He kicked himself for underestimating Blue, for not calling him to keep him up to date. Standard knew that both Valerie and Benny were at risk as long as he was on Blue's payroll. He also knew that Blue wasn't one to sit around waiting to find things out. Taking Valerie was his way of making things happen and guaranteeing that Standard would show up with some kind of explanation.

But the finger.

Damn. Goddamn!

Think things through, he told himself. Charging into The Blue Café with guns blazing—tempting as it sounded—was not the way to go. Getting himself killed, and probably Valerie as well, wasn't going to solve anything either. She'd lost a finger, but he had to believe she was alive. The manila envelope he brought back from Aitutaki had what Blue wanted, what he paid Standard to find. Giving it to Blue would save Valerie—minus a little finger.

Standard sat there for ten more minutes thinking about Valerie. That would be his Valerie, who'd spend the rest of her life with one less finger because some sick fuck had let his girlfriend steal seven million dollars right out from under his nose. That he had spent two nights with that girlfriend on an idyllic South Pacific island didn't make him feel any better, but it didn't change anything. Blue was going to pay. Standard didn't know how or when, but he would pay.

Standard forced himself to not panic, to run through all the options again. Now was not the time to make a mistake. All he knew was that if he found Blue he would find Valerie.

Finally, he picked up the matchbook and called The Blue Café. A woman answered.

"This is John Standard. Tell Moses Blue I'm on my way. He has something of mine and I want it back."

"Mr. Blue is—"

"Just tell him."

Moses Blue's Jaguar was parked in the alley behind The Blue Café. Sitting next to it, looking like a poor relative come for Sunday dinner, was Skinny Hale's ragtop Oldsmobile.

Standard drove by, then out the other end of the alley and back out onto NW Hoyt. Cars filled the street in front of the nightclub. It took fifteen minutes to find a space two blocks away that offered a view of the front door. It was ten o'clock. The mist falling since Standard's plane landed had persisted through the afternoon and into the night.

People moving along the narrow sidewalks and rain-slick streets had the hoods up on their parkas and raincoats. They looked like Druids marching off to a secret sacrifice. Each time a parking space closer to The Blue Café came open, he moved the Jeep into it. By midnight, impatience and anger still lingered, but at least he was close enough to see both the front of the building and one end of the alley.

The manila envelope he'd brought from Rarotonga lay on the passenger seat. Next to that was the Beretta. If one didn't work in getting Valerie away from Blue then the other might.

Standard went over the plan in his head for the thousandth time. It could work, he thought. Be smart. That was the only way to get Valerie back. It was just hard to be smart and angry at the same time.

He kicked himself again. This was supposed to be so easy. Just give Blue the information in the manila envelope, collect his fifteen thousand, and be done with it. He should have known better. When it came to Moses Blue and Allie Shafer, nothing was going to be easy.

If the Jaguar was parked in the rear of the club, then Blue had to be inside. That meant he'd gotten the message. Maybe that meant that Valerie was there as well. No, not maybe. She *had* to be there. She *had* to be all right. Standard refused to believe anything else.

It was a weeknight. So, by half past twelve, the streets were nearly empty. Fewer and fewer cars drove by. More and more parking spots came open. Three couples emerged from The Blue Café. The nightclub had to be getting ready to close.

Standard started the car, drove around the corner into the alley, and parked in the driveway across from the dumpsters, the back door into the kitchen in plain sight. He waited. Ten minutes later, Skinny Hale came out carrying plastic garbage sacks in each hand. The old bluesman wore a food-stained apron and a white paper hat.

Standard got out of the Jeep, slipping the Beretta in the small of his back and covering it with his coat. He reached back inside the car for the envelope on the passenger seat and tucked it under his arm. He had the two weapons he needed.

Skinny Hale had just finished tossing one of the sacks into the garbage when Standard walked up behind him. "Is he here?"

If Hale was surprised, he didn't show it. He lowered the dumpster lid before turning around. The old man's face appeared to have sagged even more under the weight of his life as his son's dishwasher. The blues that had been Skinny Hale's music had become part of his body. Man and music melded together for what little time he had left.

"He got your message. He's been waiting." Hale spoke slowly, his voice sad and resigned to the fact that something bad was going to happen.

"Is she all right?"

"She will be if you stay smart."

"Fuck smart." When Standard headed toward the kitchen door, Hale grabbed his arm.

"Wait here a minute. Let me tell him you're here."

"No. He knows I'm coming. That's why he took her, to get me here. Well, here I am, goddamn it. I even called ahead to let him know."

"I know about these things. Let me go in first."

"You know what he did to her?" Hale nodded, started to say something then stopped. "Telling him I'm here won't change anything."

"So what's the harm?"

Hale walked off. Standard leaned against the fender of the Olds and fumbled a cigarette out of his coat. He struck a match and stared at the flame. His hand wasn't shaking. It should be, but it wasn't. Halfway through a second cigarette, Hale came back.

"You sure you want to do this?" the old man said.

"What choice is there? He has what I want. I have what he wants. It's just best to get it over with."

Hale sucked in his cheeks until his lips turned into a keyhole. "Before you go in there, you best be giving me that gun." Standard tried acting like he didn't know what Hale was talking about. "I know you got one, son, and so does he. Guys like you don't show up at times like this without a gun. Like I said, I know something about these things. I ain't washed dishes all my life."

"If I give it up, will I get Valerie out of there alive?"

"There's a lot better chance of that without the gun than with it. Now, give."

Reluctantly, Standard pulled out the gun and handed it over. "What am I walking into?"

"It'll be pretty obvious once you get in there," Hale said, slipping the Beretta into the front of his pants and pulling his shirt over it. "Play things right and no one will get hurt."

"That's it?"

"He's wounded. Not so you can see it, but it's there. Men like him are dangerous when they're wounded. Just remember, he's got all the cards."

Standard waved the envelope at him. "We'll see about that."

"Just remember. You made a deal with the devil. Now the devil wants his due."

"And if things go wrong?"

"It's been known to happen," the old man said. He went back to throwing another sack into the dumpster. "It's been known to happen."

Chapter 41

The inside of the club was completely dark. No music. No rattling of dishes. No clinking of ice cubes in glasses. The only sounds were an occasional car hissing by on the wet street outside and the distant whine of a train whistle.

Standard moved slowly in the dark, reaching out with his hand until bumping into the end of the bar, knocking over a chair. A step to the right and his knee banged hard against a table. The sound echoed in the empty room, announcing his arrival. He suddenly felt naked without the gun, thinking he might have given it up too easily.

"Welcome home, Mr. Standard." Blue's voice, smooth and controlled, came out of the speakers in the walls. "I hope you have something for me."

"Where is she?"

"Patience, Mr. Standard. First things first. You work for me, remember. Not the other way around. Now, do you have something for me or not?"

"The hell with patience. Tell me she's alive. After that we can move on to what you care about."

"She's alive and she's here with me." Blue's voice carried a hint of impatience. "Now, what do you have?"

Blue could be lying, but Standard didn't care. He held the manila envelope in both hands like a peace offering. "Here's what you hired me to find out, but you can't read it in the dark."

On cue, the lights slowly came on, stopping at dim. The tables, chairs, and couches seemed to float in the faint light, looking more like bodies than furniture. Standard squinted, searching for Blue among the shadows. When he took two steps forward, a burst of light hit him directly in the eyes. The room disappeared, replaced by a giant white spot.

"You'll find a chair a few feet to your right," Blue said. The announcement was followed by the distinctive feedback of a speaker system. He could be anywhere in the club. "Please be seated."

The white spot began to fade, but Standard still stumbled into the chair before seeing it. "Save the melodrama, Blue. Where is she?"

"I could ask you the same question," said the voice in the walls.

"I've held up my end of the deal. I found Allie, and I came back with what you asked for. You can keep the rest of what you owe me. Just let Valerie go."

"You would take love over money? How noble. I'm not sure I would do the same thing in your place. Fifteen thousand dollars is a lot of money to someone like you. How about I double it or triple it and I keep the girl? Are you still noble?"

Standard's eyes were adjusting. The spotlight was still in his face, but the giant white spot had faded from a hot sun to a bright yellow moon. He could make out the outline of the stage, now, and of a man. The whole scene was backwards. The lights were on Standard, but the show was on the dark stage.

"Forget the money, goddamn it!" Standard said. "Just let her go. She's never had anything to do with this."

"What do you have for me?"

Standard took a deep breath. Now was the time. "Everything is right here." He held up the manila envelope again, using it this time to shade his eyes. On the stage behind the spotlight were two pairs of legs. The perfectly creased gray slacks belonged to Blue. The other pair, trembling a few feet to Blue's left, belonged to Valerie. He recognized the frayed knees of her favorite jeans. Her legs moved. He heard her whimper.

She was alive. Thank God. But was she all right?

"Let her go. There's no reason to hurt her any more than you already have. This isn't about her. It's about Allie Shafer."

"Unless you believe in insurance." The spotlight went out. The club plunged back into darkness for a few moments until the house lights slowly worked their way back to dim. Standard's eyes adjusted again.

Blue was sitting on a stool behind a microphone. In his right hand was a remote that ran the lighting system. In the other was a gun held at arm's length and pressed hard against Valerie's temple.

Valerie sobbed through the duct tape around her mouth. More tape tied her hands behind her back. The gun at her head pinned her against one of the giant speakers, like a bug against a wall. The confused terror in her eyes was of someone about to be dragged down a dark hole. Blue pressed the gun harder against her head.

"You have fifteen seconds to tell me everything you know," Blue said. "You better pray that I believe you."

"I don't need fifteen seconds." He tossed the manila envelope on the floor. It slid toward Blue, stopping when it hit the front of the stage. "Allie Shafer is dead. All the proof you need is right there."

Chapter 42

Blue's features were hidden in the shadows. Dark glasses covered his blind eye. Even with that, the hatred was there. Standard had said the last thing in the world Blue wanted to hear. What more was there to expect?

"I've been told before that she was dead," Blue said. "Forgive me if I'm a little skeptical."

"Look for yourself." Standard nodded toward the envelope on the floor. "The death certificate signed by the only doctor on the island where she died. The report by the investigating officer tells how she died. There's even a police photo. It's not pretty."

Blue took the gun from Valerie's head. She slid down the wall into a heap, her back against the speaker, sobs coming in short hard breaths. The silvery tape sucked in and out of her mouth. Standard could see her hands now. One was wrapped in heavy white bandages the size of a boxing glove.

Blue ignored her and bent down to retrieve the envelope. It rested in the palm of his hand as if he were trying to guess its weight. He slid the gun into the waistband of his slacks, undid the clasp on the envelope, and slowly pulled out the contents.

No one made a noise for the next ten minutes. Blue read each page carefully. He glanced at Standard twice and at Valerie once. Valerie, her sobs muffled by the tape, was little more than a shadow against the wall. Standard wanted to tell her everything would be fine, but didn't because he wasn't sure how the next few minutes would play out.

Blue took off his glasses and pulled the photo from the envelope.

Looking at it, he sucked in air and closed his eyes. Standard knew what he was looking at. Allie on the bed covered in blood, her body slumped to one side. Bullet holes in the wall behind her. The scene captured in vivid color under the harsh flash of a police camera.

"I told you it wasn't pretty," Standard said, "but you wanted proof. There it is. End of story."

"Allie and this Karen Vincent woman are the same person?"

"Were. Past tense."

"Who killed her?"

"You read the police report. The description of the man hanging around her bungalow sounds a lot like Carp, doesn't it?"

Blue looked confused. The photo dangled from his hand. "Why would Carp kill her?" He seemed to ask the question of himself.

"I don't know. He got to her before I did. I didn't even know he'd followed me. By the time I found her, she was dead and the killer gone. The police were there, along with a couple of dozen guests from the hotel standing around gawking. It's all right there in the report."

"And the money?"

It was the one question Standard expected. He had practiced his answer hundreds of time on the plane coming home and in the car outside the nightclub. He knew it had to be perfect.

He forced himself to look confused, then said: "Money? What money?"

Blue pulled the gun from his waistband and pointed it down at the cowering Valerie. She squeezed her eyes shut and crawled a few feet away, dragging her bandaged hand behind her.

"Don't fuck with me!" Blue shouted. "Allie stole money from me. I need that money back."

Standing up, Standard stepped toward the stage, as if being two feet closer would somehow provide Valerie with some kind of protection. "I don't know what you're talking about. You wanted me to find out if Allie was dead or alive. You didn't say anything about money. You didn't say anything about sending Carp after me."

"I didn't send Carp after you."

"Fine, but did Carp know about this money?"

"Yes." Blue said it slowly.

"Well, there you go."

Lights were coming on in Blue's head. The dimmer switch on Carp's betrayal was being turned up.

"Maybe he has this money you're talking about," Standard said. "Maybe he got the money from her before he killed her and took off. How in the hell would I know? I got there too late."

"The money." Blue once again sounded like he was talking to himself.

"How much are we talking about here?"

Blue had become a statue, a piece of art with a gun pointed at a cowering woman. "A lot."

"Jesus, Blue. You should have told me. I thought I was looking for your girlfriend. If this was all about money, then my guess is that Carp has it and he's disappeared. Then again, maybe not. All I know is right there in that envelope."

"How did Carp know where she was?" Blue said.

Standard expected that question as well. He had another rehearsed answer: "He must have followed me to the Cook Islands, figured out where she was, and got there before me. Nothing else makes sense."

The gun was still pointed at Valerie. Blue held up the photo and shook it. "I gave you fifteen thousand dollars to make sure something like this didn't happen. Now someone has to pay. I'm out some serious cash, but fuck that. Money comes and goes. The problem is that my woman is dead. I'm thinking that maybe yours should be dead too."

Valerie's scream sounded like a muted trumpet. Standard wanted to believe that she was screaming his name. Her head came up, her eyes darting around the room, first at Blue then at Standard.

"You can't blame me for this," Standard said. "If you didn't send Carp after me then he must have gone solo on you. He must've wanted the money for himself and he killed Allie to get it. Carp was your man. If it wasn't for him, Allie would either be here right now or you'd at least know where she was. And you'd have your money. Don't put this on me. You fucked up." The last words hit Blue like body blows. "Sounds to me like she used you, Moses. You may think this is about love and money, but it sounds to me like Allie didn't. She got you. She took you for I don't know how much money and made a fool out of you. To make matters worse, Carp did the same thing. Face it. It's over."

"But someone has to pay." Blue's voice was a pleading whimper. The gun moved closer to Valerie's head.

"No!" The voice came from nowhere, deep and resonant. Standard thought God had intervened. Instead, it was Skinny Hale. At that moment, they were one and the same.

The old man stood behind the bar, still dressed in the stained apron and paper hat, Standard's Beretta in his hand pointed at Blue's chest. The gun looked like a toy in his huge paw. Without taking his eyes off Blue, Hale moved closer to the stage, the gun held in front of him at arm's length.

"It's over, son. Don't make it any worse."

Blue laughed. The schoolyard bully confronted by the class wimp. "Get out of here, you old fool, before you get hurt. This is man's business."

Hale narrowed his eyes. "I guess I've deserved everything I've had to take from you." Hale's voice was an octave deeper, the tone stern. "I made my apologies a long time ago about what I did to you. Blinding your own son in one eye ain't something a man should be proud of. No one should have to live with that. But don't talk to me about a man's business. You been busting my hump for thirty years over what I done. You paid me back by making me wash your dishes and tote your garbage. No *man* would do something like that."

Hale looked at Standard then over at Valerie. "What I did was wrong," he said. "But what you're doing is worse. Sounds to me like you fucked up letting Carp go after your woman without you knowing about it. Seems like you should have kept a better eye on him than on me. Don't fuck up twice. Now, let the girl go."

Blue put the dark glasses back on, hiding whatever he was thinking behind the black lenses. A muffled moan from Valerie made him look down at her, like he'd just discovered she was there.

"Be a man," Hale said. "I heard what he said. This fellow is right. Your woman is dead because of what Carp done. That's all there is to it. Now let it go."

"Allie is dead." Blue sounded like a child who'd lost his favorite toy. "Someone has to pay for that."

"No. They. Don't." Hale's voice was even more harsh and firm. He nodded toward the cowering Valerie. "Killing her ain't paying nobody back. She don't even know what this is all about. She don't know nothing about no Allie Shafer. What's the point of killing her?" Hale moved the gun to his left and fired into the one of the speakers at the back of the stage. Blue ducked, out of instinct. Valerie pushed herself tighter against the wall. In the closeness of the room, the gunshot sounded like a bomb going off.

"You ain't given me much to live for, so I got nothing to lose," Hale said, the gun pointed at his son again. "End this. Be a man."

"And if I don't?"

"Don't force me to make that choice."

The tables had turned on the devil. Blue looked at Standard then down at Valerie. Seconds ticked by, like dog years, until Blue finally turned away from Valerie and lowered the gun. Standard exhaled, suddenly realizing that he'd been holding his breath ever since Hale walked in the room.

Without a word, Blue let the gun slip out of his hand. It hit the floor with a benign thud. "You're right, old man. For once in your life, you're right."

Chapter 43

Valerie Michaels didn't say a word for nearly a week. She didn't talk when he took her to the hospital for her hand. She didn't bat an eye when he told the doctor she was coming home with him rather than spend the night there. Once back at his apartment, she stayed in bed, either sleeping, crying, or in a stupor from the painkillers the doctor insisted she take. Food was a few sips of soup or a couple of bites of a sandwich. Her eyes were dead coals in a forgotten fire.

Standard never left her. He sat in a straight-back chair, watching her sleep, curled into a ball on his bed the same way she had cowered against the wall at The Blue Café. In her mind, Moses Blue's gun was still inches from her head.

When the food ran out, Standard called downstairs and asked Benny Orlando to run to the store. When he showed up with more soup and a couple of sandwiches from the deli across the street, he offered to watch her for an hour so Standard could smoke a cigarette and walk around town for a while. He said no.

On the eighth day, the fear drained from her eyes. She stopped jumping out of her skin when the telephone rang or a car squealed its tires on the street below. Her first words were, "He was going to kill me."

"I know," Standard said, "but he didn't. You made it. We made it."

She looked at her bandaged hand. "Well, most of me made it." Her laugh was the best sound he'd ever heard.

"But why?" she said. "Why did he do it? Why did he take me? Why did he do this to me?"

"He just wanted insurance, honey. He wanted to make sure I came back and told him what happened to Allie Shafer."

"You mean there was a chance you weren't coming back?"

He kissed her. "Never, but Blue didn't know that. He freaked. That's why he did what he did."

Valerie looked like she wanted to know more about what took place in the Cook Islands then seemed to quickly change her mind. Someday she would ask. When she did, he would tell her everything. For the time being, though, she looked like someone who just wanted more than anything for her life to get back to what it was before Allie Shafer, Carp, Moses Blue, or Skinny Hale.

Two days later, and with Valerie's reluctant agreement, Standard felt confident enough to leave her with Benny and walk down SW Columbia toward the river. It was four in the afternoon, rush-hour traffic just beginning to clog the streets leading to the bridges across the Willamette or west toward the suburbs. The rain had stopped. The march into fall darkness temporarily halted to provide one last stretch of days with clear skies and temperatures in the sixties. Standard turned north on SW Second and walked the two blocks to the Portland Police Bureau.

Al Vlasic was on the telephone in his cubicle on the second floor of the Justice Center. He motioned Standard to sit in the Steelcase chair next to the door. Vlasic rolled his eyes, pretending to patiently listen to the caller.

"You know we don't comment on pending investigations and no, I won't go off the record." He listened for a few more seconds. "We'll have a statement when we have something to announce. Now, I need to go. Good luck."

He hung up. "I've been here twelve hours and this is eating into my drinking time."

"That sounds like an invitation."

"Damn straight."

They walked three blocks up the street to a brew pub that was just starting to fill up with the after-work crowd. Finding an empty booth near the bar, Vlasic ordered Scotch neat with a beer back. Standard settled for a Corona.

"I've been out of town on a story," he said. "I wanted to catch up and see if you came up with anything in the death of Helen Badden."

"You mean the autopsy? There was nothing out of the ordinary. The medical examiner said the blood work turned up traces of a barbiturate, but that wouldn't be unusual in a suicide victim. There were no needle marks that we could find, so she probably took the drugs orally. My guess is she was depressed and dealt with it by self-medicating. Drugs are not hard to get when you're a doctor. Eventually she stuck her head in the oven."

"Case closed then, huh?"

"Yeah. The fire marshal ruled the explosion an accident caused by the gas build-up in the house. We released the body a week or so ago to a doctor friend of hers, Traylor, I think her name was. Annette Traylor."

Vlasic downed the whiskey and followed it with a sip of beer. "So, what's this all about?"

"Nothing. I just find it odd that someone like Helen Badden would kill herself."

"Get over it. It was probably nothing more than a guilt-ridden lesbian thing. Who knows what goes on inside their heads?"

"Yeah." Standard knew better but had no intention of telling Vlasic. "You're probably right."

They ordered two more drinks then decided to have an early dinner. Vlasic got a New York steak, Standard a chicken Caesar. When the food came, he took a few bites then pushed the lettuce around on the plate before giving up on it altogether.

"Did you get anywhere with Rico's murder?" They'd finished

eating. The waitress had hauled off the plates.

"You mean Dunston, that guy out at the race track? No, he was just some low-life wise guy that worked for Moses Blue. Some other guy that worked for him disappeared about the same time. We talked to Blue. No surprise, he said he didn't know who killed Rico or what happened to the other guy. Victor Carp, I think his name was. We traced to him L.A., where he got on a flight to New Zealand. He never arrived. The plane stopped in some place called the Cook Islands. We contacted authorities there, but never heard back. Probably never will, and it's not worth the time or money to send someone there. So, case closed. Why? You know something about that as well?"

Standard pleaded innocent. Rico's killer was beyond Vlasic's jurisdiction, far beyond.

Vlasic picked up the tab and they parted with a handshake in front of the pub after promising to get together more often. Standard walked back to the apartment to check on Valerie. Benny was with her, reading a book while she slept. He kissed her on the forehead then left again. The Jeep was in a lot two blocks away.

It was time to take care of some unfinished business. Time to close the book on Allie Shafer.

Chapter 44

Standard squeezed the Jeep into a metered parking spot near the sky bridge into the Oregon Health & Science University. Finding Doctor Annette Traylor would be easier this time. He knew which nurses' stations to check and which floors to search. Traylor didn't look surprised when he found her in a small office, typing notes into a computer, reading glasses perched on the end of her nose.

The sterile, cramped room smelled of disinfectant. The only other place to sit was a metal folding chair in front of shelves that were a jumble of magazines, medical journals, and softbound books. Standard didn't feel like sitting, so he leaned back against the closed door.

Traylor stopped typing and turned to look at him over the top of her glasses. Something in her face said she knew why he was there. The first move was his, but he let her stare for a few more seconds.

"I know you killed Helen Badden. I just want you to know that your secret is safe with me."

Traylor took off her glasses. Her hair was shorter and more butch than the first time they'd met. Still no makeup. The dress she'd worn before had been replaced with slacks. She seemed to be ridding herself of all things feminine.

"I don't know what you're talking about."

"Save it. I'm too tired to play games with this."

Traylor took off her glasses and set them on the desk. Her shoulders slumped. She rubbed her eyes. "When did you figure it out?"

"Suicide didn't make sense. Why would anyone with a new

computer, a bag of groceries, and kitten stick their head in an oven? It wasn't until I got to Rarotonga that things started falling into place. Helen Badden cooked up the idea to fake Allie Shafer's death. Maybe she told you about it ahead of time. Maybe she didn't. It really doesn't matter. Either way, you figured it out. What's important is that Badden didn't care if she lost her license over it. You told me that Badden was more interested in being a good lesbian than a good doctor."

Traylor's eyes turned feral, telling him all there was to know.

"You, on the other hand, like being a doctor," he said. "It's what defines you. Losing your license over your role in a fake physician-assisted suicide would be the end of your career. If anyone found out, you'd be lucky to get a job changing diapers in a rest home. So what happened?"

"You tell me."

"My guess is that Badden told you about Allie and about the photo she'd sent to Moses Blue. That didn't leave you with many choices, did it? Badden knew she wasn't going to get any money from Allie. It pissed her off. She was ready to tell Blue everything. You couldn't let her do that, could you? You couldn't take the risk that Blue would hold both you and Badden responsible."

Traylor waited a long time to answer. She fiddled with the computer's mouse then fell back into the chair. "Helen was in love with your Miss Shafer. I agreed to go along with the fake suicide because I thought it would make Helen happy, and I believed the story about Miss Shafer being abused by her boyfriend, at least at first. It was a stupid thing to do, but Helen and I had been . . . close once. We still were, but not like before. I knew at the time it was not the right thing to do, but I did it anyway. I should have heeded my instincts and stayed away from the whole thing."

"And then?"

"Helen followed her to the Cook Islands. I even took her to the

296

airport. When she got out of the car, I told her it was a bad idea, but she had this thing for Allie. Helen was gone for a couple of weeks. She called me when she got back. Helen was in tears. Allie had rejected her. Helen didn't deal well with rejection, but you've probably figured that out by now. She was distraught, devastated, and very angry. She was determined to do something that would hurt Allie."

"But you couldn't let that happen?"

"There was no reasoning with her. She didn't care about anything other than getting even with Allie. She told me what she'd done, sending the picture to Allie's boyfriend and how she was eventually going to tell him where Allie was. You're right, I couldn't let that happen. If too many people found out, I was the only one who had anything to lose. Helen had already thrown in her career. She never stopped to think that I didn't want to throw mine in as well."

"That's why you drugged Badden, stuck her head in the oven, and turned on the gas. The explosion was an accident. I was just in the wrong place at the wrong time."

"You have no proof of that." Traylor's voice was little more than whisper.

"You're right, but I don't want any." Traylor looked confused. "The more convinced the police are that Helen Badden killed herself, the longer the story of Allie Shafer remains a secret."

"And that's what you want?"

"More than anything in the world."

"Then why are you here?"

"Allie Shafer is dead. As far as you're concerned, she committed suicide eight months ago with the pills you and Helen Badden prescribed for her. Let the dead stay dead. If you tell anyone anything different than that, then I tell the police and the Board of Medical Examiners the whole story. The best that can happen is that you lose your license. The worst is that you get charged with murder and there's an ugly and messy trial. Regardless of the outcome, you're

297

tainted for life. Goodbye hospital. Hello nursing home."

"And you'll be the lead witness against me."

"You can bet on it. The fake suicide, the phony diagnosis, how Allie Shafer really died."

"How did she die?"

"You don't need to know that."

"But you have the proof?"

"Absolutely."

Traylor picked up a pen. She snapped the cap on and off enough times that Standard wanted to grab it out of her hand and throw it against the wall. "What guarantee do I have that you won't tell somebody the truth?"

"None. Murderers don't get guarantees. All I want is for Allie Shafer to be forgotten. She died last winter. She used a perfectly legal means to take her own life rather than endure the indignities of uncertain cancer treatments. Her ashes were dumped out of a plane over the Pacific. End of story."

Annette Traylor nodded in agreement. "You know I can't afford to tell anybody the truth about this. So, why did you come here?"

"I just wanted you to know that there's someone in the world who knows what you did and why. You committed murder. Murder! For whatever reasons, and regardless of who it was or what kind of person they were, you shouldn't be able to go through life thinking you got away with that. Always remember that I know."

When Traylor started to say something, Standard stopped her. "Don't think you can do to me what you did to Helen Badden. Everything I know is in writing and will go to Eldon Mock, publisher of *Inside Oregon*, if anything happens to me."

Traylor's mouth closed.

It was a good bluff, Standard thought, one Annette Traylor would never call.

Chapter 45

Standard left the hospital a little after seven o'clock. The bridges across the Willamette River were starting to empty out following the afternoon commute. Still, it took nearly thirty minutes to get over the Ross Island Bridge and down SE Powell to the offices of *Inside Oregon*.

It was deadline day. Eldon Mock was pumped up, his face red, spittle on his lips. He was yelling at a new copy editor, a twenty-something with multi-colored hair and a goatee.

"Don't you know the difference between a burro and burrow?" he asked, slamming an Associated Press Stylebook down on the desk. "One's an ass and one's a hole in the ground. Now, don't ever make that mistake again."

Standard watched from the waist-high counter that separated the newsroom from the small waiting area. Mock's cluttered desk was ten feet away.

"And where in the hell have you been?" Mock asked. "Where's my story about that dead doctor?"

"We need to talk."

"I've got no time to talk."

"You do about this."

They left the office and walked down the street to a coffee shop and found a narrow booth with torn vinyl seats. Standard waited until the waitress poured the coffee and left.

"Okay, what's so goddamn important?" Mock was shouting, his face red, spit in the corners of his mouth.

"Helen Badden was gay. She killed herself because she couldn't reconcile her sexual feelings with her Midwest upbringing. Sadly, it happens, but it's not the kind of story I want to write and it's not the kind you want to publish."

Mock looked angry at first, then stunned. Telling Eldon Mock not to write something was like telling a diabetic not to eat candy. "Lesbian, huh? That's good copy."

"Stop it."

"All right. All right. Calm down. So your advice is to drop the whole thing. There's no story here." When Standard nodded, Mock looked skeptical. "There's something you're not telling me."

"It's a dry hole, Eldon. Badden's death had nothing to do with Allie Shafer, physician-assisted suicide, or anything else. The autopsy shows there were barbiturates in her blood. She took the drugs and turned on the gas."

"And the house just happened to explode while you were there?"

"That's what the fire marshal believes, and the police have no problem with that. I talked to Vlasic this afternoon. Case closed."

Mock poured three packets of sugar into his coffee. He motioned to the waitress and ordered two cinnamon rolls. When they arrived, he wolfed both of them down in a matter of seconds. "Let's say I believe you and a week from now I read something about this in that rag where you used to work. What then?"

"You know that won't happen. It's not their style to write features about suicidal lesbians."

The waitress refilled the coffee and took away the plate. Mock laced his with another trio of sugar packets. "So, there's no Allie Shafer angle to this?"

"None." Standard kept one eye on Mock to check his reaction. "Other than the obvious coincidence."

"I don't like coincidences."

"Neither do I, but they happen."

"So, there's nothing that we can tie into a neat little bundle with a headline that reads 'Physician Kill Thyself' or something like that?"

"Nice try, but what's the point? She was a tormented woman who stuck her head in an oven. Leave it alone."

Mock looked suspicious. "Okay. I'll trust your judgment on this, but I still think there's something you're not telling me. If I get burned on this story, then I think you owe me."

"Fair enough."

Chapter 46

Two weeks later, Valerie went back to work half days, but her heart wasn't in it. The severed finger, and the thirty-six hours she'd spent as Moses Blue's guest, had left a wound slow to heal. With good reason, Standard figured, but that didn't make it any easier when he caught her sneaking drinks from a bottle of Glenlivet she kept in a cupboard for special occasions. When that was gone, she started in on tranquilizers slipped to her by one of the dancers she used to work with. When Standard mentioned it to her, she laughed it off, a sure sign that she was getting in over her head.

Still, he decided to be patient and opted to take her on weekend trips to the mountains or the coast where they spent the last of the Blue Money. They went back to Seaside, but stayed in a different beachfront motel than the one where Carp had found them. A place that was more secluded, away from the promenade, with a fireplace, ocean view, and a king-size bed.

It worked. Gradually, almost imperceptibly, Valerie Michaels came back. The final step happened on a Saturday night in a cabin on the Metolius River in the Cascade Mountains, southeast of Portland. He looked at her over a dinner of pasta and salad whipped up in the cabin's tiny kitchen with its two-burner stove. The fear that had burned in the back of her eyes like a pilot light dimmed and disappeared.

When Valerie went back to work full-time the following week, Standard spent a day cleaning and organizing his office. It was time to find freelance work again. Get back to making money again, a regular routine that offered a renewed sense of rhythm and purpose. Projects trickled in during the next few weeks. A golf magazine wanted a piece on the new family-friendly atmosphere at country clubs. A small software company that had gone public, and survived the latest economic downturn, needed someone to write its annual report. An advertising company wanted help ghostwriting an opinion piece for a large corporation that shipped tainted meat patties to Guatemala.

Standard buried himself in the work, letting it fill the days. The nights were more difficult. He spent more and more time with Valerie or sipping Coronas while watching Benny create websites for amusement parks and casinos. He'd all but forgotten about Moses Blue until UPS delivered a package. It was the second payment of fifteen thousand dollars. In cash. There was no note. There was no need for one. Standard had fulfilled his end of the bargain. Now Blue, true to the code of the streets, had fulfilled his.

Staring at the stack of hundreds, Standard suddenly felt sorry for Blue. Whatever price he'd paid the first time Allie disappeared probably hadn't been any easier the second time around. Too bad the nightclub owner would never know the truth about what happened that night on Aitutaki. The gunshots, the blood, Carp.

Then again, Blue didn't deserve to know the truth, not after what he'd done to Valerie.

Two weeks later, there was a headline in *Inside Oregon*: "Night Club Owner Missing." The story said that Moses Blue had disappeared three days earlier and that his accountant had filed a missing person report with the Portland Police. The rest of the story was a laundry list of Blue's suspected criminal connections. The implications were obvious. More obvious to Standard, however, than anyone else.

Staring at the page, Standard remembered what Carp had said about Blue owing people money, big money. All he could figure was they came to collect and Blue's life was collateral. Now he could finally breathe a sigh of relief and close the book on Moses Blue, his money, and Allie Shafer.

Mid-December turned cold and wet. One night a storm moved in off the Pacific, packing sixty mile-per-hour winds. Gusts up to a hundred miles per hour tore down streetlights and business signs along the coast then moved inland to knock power out in the suburbs west of the city. A couple of rivers flooded. A few homes were lost. Some cows died.

Hating storms, Valerie demanded to spend the night at his apartment. With the wind clawing at the windows, she fell asleep in the fetal position that was the only surviving remnant of her time with Moses Blue. He watched her. Sure she was asleep, he slipped out of bed and down to Benny's apartment.

"I need to send an e-mail." Benny was watching a video of *Trapeze*, indulging his life-long fascination with Gina Lollobrigida in tights.

"Can't you send it from your computer?"

"It's not that simple."

"Nothing with you is." Benny never took his eyes off the screen. "You know where everything is."

In Benny's computer room, Standard sat down at one of the terminals. The message was one line. In a matter of a few minutes, maybe less, it would appear as a beep on another computer halfway around the world. The girl in the flowered dress who worked the counter at the perfume store on Rarotonga would see it. She'd call the bar at the Edgewater Hotel to let Tommy know he had a message.

Standard rejoined Benny in the front room. The movie was over and Benny had turned off the television when Standard sat down on the couch.

Benny looked at him over the top of his reading glasses. "Now that everything is back to as normal as it gets around here, are you ever going to tell me what happened on that island?"

Standard wanted to tell Benny everything. He wanted him to know about how Tommy had spotted Carp hanging around the hotel, and about how others on the island had told Tommy about one strange American following another. He wanted to tell him about finding Allie, about the money, about why he didn't want to stay with her, and how Tommy had followed Carp to Aitutaki. More than anything, he wanted to tell him about the night Carp showed up and see Benny's reaction to how Carp died.

But not enough time had passed. The wounds were still raw and sore. Benny would ask too many questions. Too many regrets still bled from too many wounds.

"Someday, Benny, when we're old and sitting on a beach in Mexico, drinking beer, and watching the sun set, I'll tell you the whole thing beginning to end."

"But not now?"

Standard leaned back against the couch, hating himself for doing this, especially to Benny. "There are different kinds of death, Benny. Allie's was a better death. Let's just leave it at that for now."

Chapter 47

The envelope that arrived in the mail a week later was covered in exotic stamps and postmarked Perth, Australia. There was no return address. It didn't need one. Standard knew who sent it, so he set it on the desk and stared at it for a long time before cutting it open with a pair of scissors. The note inside was handwritten on blank paper.

> John,
> It worked. Thank you. Someday, my
> love. Some day.
> Always yours,
> Allie

The note was wrapped around a cashier's check for a quarter million dollars.

Standard stared at the check for a long time, thinking he could be insulted, but also knowing that money was Allie's most precious possession. The only gift she had to give. The only way she knew to say thanks for what happened after Carp's shots went harmlessly into the wall all around her, for the spurting blood from Carp's severed hand that covered the bed, for the way Tommy and Standard had staged her death with the help of Tommy's relatives. And for the way they all assembled the photos and police reports that went into the manila folder he'd given Moses Blue.

Standard slipped the check into the desk drawer then called Valerie. "I think we need a vacation."

"Great, but what about my job?"

"Don't worry about it."

"Are we going to the South Pacific?"

Standard didn't hesitate to answer. "I don't think so."

THE END

Made in the USA
Las Vegas, NV
24 January 2021

16489059R00174